BOOKS BY JAMES ATLAS

The Great Pretender   1986

Delmore Schwartz: The Life of an American Poet   1977

THE
GREAT
PRETENDER

THE
GREAT
PRETENDER

JAMES ATLAS

ATHENEUM

NEW YORK   1986

Portions of this work have appeared, in very different form,
in *The Atlantic* and *Triquarterly*.

The five lines from "The Hollow Men" quoted on page thirty-one are
from *Collected Poems 1909–1962* by T. S. Eliot, copyright 1936 by
Harcourt Brace Jovanovich, Inc.; copyright © 1963, 1964 by T. S.
Eliot. Reprinted by permission of the publishers, Harcourt Brace
Jovanovich, Inc., in America and Faber and Faber in Canada.

Library of Congress Cataloging-in-Publication Data

Atlas, James.
   The great pretender.

   I. Title.
PS3551.T65G7   1986   813'.54   85–48127
ISBN 0–689–11800–7

I

THE services for Grandma Sophie, I learned from a placard on a wooden easel, would be held in Parlor One. Sun poured through the double glass doors of the Piser Memorial Chapel, but the air-conditioned lobby chilled my skin as I came in out of the heat of a Chicago June. It was the summer of 1968, the end of my junior year at Harvard. I'd flown in from Boston the night before, skipping my last exam.

Mourners pushed through the doors. Agnes, my surviving grandmother's maid, inconceivably old behind her walker, clutched its bars with tremulous spotted hands like a tottering baby in its crib. She waited patiently outside the chapel, unable to drag open the heavy doors herself, until a Piser attendant in sunglasses saw her predicament and helped her inside. After Agnes came my mother's cousin Minna, dough-faced and heavy, a spinster librarian at the Belmont Avenue branch. And there was Sylvia Glasser, my grandmother's niece, who lived in a Western suburb and enclosed a mimeographed letter about her children with every Christmas card. Since both my parents were only children, I could never figure out where all these relatives came from. They showed up at weddings and funerals. "You remember Grisha," my mother would say: "Your father's uncle. His wife is Grandma Sophie's sister." But despite her prompting, I couldn't hide the bafflement on my face.

We filed into a pine-paneled auditorium with movie-theater seats and recessed lights. David Sills, his gold cuff links sparkling, strode up to the podium and adjusted the microphone. He cleared his throat. "We are gathered here today to mourn the passing of Sophie Janis, beloved mother of William, grandmother of Ben," he began. "To mourn the death in old age of a woman I knew in my own childhood is a mysterious thing. Sophie was a young woman in those days. She was practically a girl herself. I remember her standing at the sink preparing lunch for William and me in the kitchen above the family drugstore on Peterson Avenue one summer afternoon." He sipped from a glass of water and mopped his nut-brown face. Where did he get a tan so early in the summer? "The whole apartment was filled with books. You knew the minute you walked in these were people of culture. Morris"—my grandfather, long since dead—"was a man of profound learning. When he was a young engineering student in Warsaw, he graduated first in his class, and he could read five languages besides. And Sophie . . ." David faltered. His eyes were wet. "Sophie loved opera, literature, art. She loved the finer things in life. When William played in the high school orchestra, she never missed a performance. She even came to rehearsals, and sat in the back row."

My father wept. His old friend David Sills was giving a beautiful eulogy. I'd heard them talking on the phone that morning; David, stalled in rush-hour traffic, had called from his Mercedes to verify a few details. My father couldn't remember how old Sophie was, or the name of the town where she was born. "Just make it up!" he'd shouted over the blare of horns on Michigan Avenue. "It doesn't matter. Whatever there is to know, you know."

David and my father had grown up in the same neighborhood on the West Side of Chicago; David's father was a grocer. They'd gone to Carl Schurz High School together. They'd played stickball in Humboldt Park. Now David was a figure in Chicago. He'd made millions in real estate. He was on the board of Northwestern University, a patron of the Chicago Symphony. He visited Chagall in Vence. Larry Rivers did his portrait. His name was on foundation letterheads. When I hear the word Culture, I reach for my wallet.

"It has been a long journey for Sophie Janis," David said. "From a village in the Ukraine to the shores of New York, and finally to the community our people made here in Chicago. That world is disappearing now, in the march of generations, but we remember it in our hearts. I think it was T. S. Eliot who said: 'They have all gone into a world of light.' " Donne, I silently corrected him. (It was Vaughan.) Still, it was a good line. And I liked that business about Sophie in the kitchen. You could make forty million dollars and still get off a vivid image now and then. Like Wallace Stevens said, money is a kind of poetry. Too bad it wasn't the reverse.

"William," David addressed my father. "You're my dearest friend in the world, and I grieve for you on this sad occasion. I've shared your joy over the years, and now I share your loss." He said a few words in Hebrew, dabbed his eyes with a handkerchief, and strode away from the podium.

An attendant hurried up and led us to a private room with Kleenex dispensers on the end tables. My father sank down on a Naugahyde couch, pulled a fistful of Kleenex from a dispenser at his elbow, and held it to his face as if it were an oxygen mask. My mother, dry-eyed, held his hand. "That was fantastic," he murmured. "How could he remember so much?" Sweltering in a brown wool suit, he seemed uncomfortable, a child dressed up in his Sunday best. He blotted his face, and we made our way through the crowd of relatives to the limousine that waited out front for the immediate family: my parents, Grandma Rose, and me.

It was a long drive to Woodlawn in the blazing summer heat. The limo's hood flashed like foil in the sun as we coasted through red lights, past drive-ins and filling stations, shopping centers and condominiums. SATURDAY NIGHT IS LADY'S NIGHT: LADY'S BOWL FREE. HAPPY HOUR 4–7 TWO DRINKS FOR THE PRICE OF ONE. Grandma Rose was excited; the nearness of death made her talkative. She told me how the Cossacks had lunged on their horses through the snow when she was a girl in Yekaterinoslav, bursting into the kitchen and dragging her brother out into the yard, where they beat him in sight of the family huddled by the window. "He knew so much," she sighed. "And died so young." Pneumonia. He was twenty-three, a student. "He wore himself out. Was night and day politics, politics, politics. Kropotkin, Marx: every other word was revolution." My mother stared out the window; she'd heard it all before.

The cemetery was vast—acre upon acre as landscaped as the big industrialists' mansions on the North Shore: hedges, arbors, lawns cropped like a putting green. Gardeners crawled around in the flower beds. We wound our way among the monuments until we came to a plot where men in denim overalls leaned on their shovels. An employee from the funeral home distributed gray gloves to the pallbearers—David, my mother's cousin Harold, two gravediggers, my father and me —and we dragged the casket from the hearse. Grandma Sophie was inside.

I thought of the last time I had seen her, in the nursing home on Devon Avenue. I was home for spring vacation. She'd had a stroke and sat oblivious in a wheelchair, her eyes cloudy marbles, hair sprouting from her chin. "Here's the boy,

Mother," my father announced in a cheerful voice, straightening a vase of flowers. "You want the television on?" There was a sour smell in the room. Tears started from my eyes. I ran out the door and down the corridor, past old women sitting with their hands in their laps. It was a warm April morning, cleansed with rain. I pounded down the sidewalk toward the lake, a block away. There was no one on the beach. The sand was damp and fishy, still hard-packed from the winter. A sailboat rode against the horizon. So people die, I thought. They grow old, and then they die.

When we reached the plot, the gravediggers lifted the casket off our shoulders and loaded it onto a cradle of ropes and pulleys above the grave. My father had wanted no text. He flung his gloves into the trough, murmured "Goodbye, Mama," and walked away, sobbing, to the limousine. A small engine started up, whirring in the dead heat of the day, and the casket disappeared into the ground.

We retrieved our rented Pinto and drove through the empty weekday streets to Ashkenaz's delicatessen on Morse, beneath the elevated tracks. I recognized the cashier, a middle-aged woman with rusty hair swept up in a hive and crescents of blue mascara beneath her eyes. When she counted out change, she laid her cigarette in a tin ashtray next to the rubber-bristled pad. I wondered if she would still be here when I was an old man. Behind the counter were bins heaped with corned beef and slabs of tongue in white enameled trays. It was the middle of the afternoon, and we were the only customers.

My father looked tired. He picked at his smoked fish and studied the menu while the two women argued in their mother-daughter way. "Will you stop cracking chicken bones with your teeth?" my mother said. "And don't lean over your soup like that. Bring the soup to your mouth." Grandma Rose glanced up slyly from her plate. She was in the midst of a story about my grandfather, who had traveled around the Midwest in his youth hawking postcards out of a suitcase—" 'Pos'l cards,' he called them"—when my mother signaled for the check. "Mother, we know from 'pos'l cards' already. You've told the boy about it a hundred times."

But I liked these stories. They gave us a tradition, a history, a past. The *Social Register* families in Lake Forest weren't the only ones who dated back. Anyway, three of my grandparents were dead; my cousins lived in Queens or Florida; that spring my father had given up his medical practice, sold our house in Evanston and moved to California, whisking my mother off to the West in their big Oldsmobile like a new bride. I felt like an anthropologist among the Nambikwara; if I didn't study these people now, it would be too late. The old generation was virtually gone; whenever I showed up at my grandmother's apartment in downtown Evanston, she would cradle my chin in her spotted hands and scrutinize my face with the ecstatic zeal of an archaeologist happening on a find—only the artifact was new, its discoverer old.

Out on Morse, the heat was Saharan. The mica-speckled sidewalk shone like a riverbed. We turned up Sheridan Road and headed for Winnetka, where my mother's cousin Edna was having people in. There was nowhere else to receive. Sophie's apartment in Rogers Park was too small; and besides, it was in chaos. I had arrived the night before to find my parents sorting through her stuff. They had arranged to auction off the mahogany sideboard, the bristly sofa, the dining room table where we'd gathered for a thousand Sunday dinners. There were packets of letters and photographs strewn everywhere. In the guest room where I slept were Pelican editions of Nietzsche and Schopenhauer and stacks of old 78s—boxed and ready to go.

Harold and Edna had moved out to the suburbs from Rogers Park the year before, to be closer to Harold's restaurant in the

Old Orchard Shopping Plaza. The driveway of their new ranch house was full of cars when we arrived. Harold answered the door. He had changed from a dark suit to chinos and a parrot-colored Hawaiian shirt. "Come eat something," he said as he moved off down the hall. "We were getting worried."

In the dining room, guests surged around a table laden with platters of roast chicken, breadboards heaped with cheese, trays of celery and coal-black olives packed in ice, bowls of fruit and bottles of champagne spread out on a tablecloth of fringed white linen. On the sideboard, rows of rope-stemmed glasses sparkled in the late afternoon sun.

I watched my father help himself to a piece of herring. He was small and dapper, with manicured hands and French cuffs on his shirt. In the old days, he used to get a haircut and a manicure once a week in the basement of the Palmolive Building. For as long as I could remember, he'd had a busy correspondence with a Chinese tailor. Blue aerograms from Hong Kong were always arriving in the mail. Watching him get dressed to go out when I was a child, I'd been impressed by the intricacies of his wardrobe: the tie pin, the monogrammed handkerchief, the plastic spears for stiffening shirt collars, the shoeshine machine with its furry buffer. As a boy growing up in Valparaiso, Indiana—his parents had a pharmacy there before they moved to Chicago—he'd gone hunting for toads on hot summer afternoons dressed in spotless white shorts and a long-sleeved shirt buttoned up to the neck, crouching over the fetid swamps with a jar and a colander.

He came over and laid a hand on my neck. "Well, Sonny, I guess I'm next." He fingered the gold watch chain draped across his vest—his father's, and his father's father's before him. I was in no hurry to inherit it.

"Come on, Dad. You've got decades left." It was true. My father trotted off the court after an hour of singles with a dry brow, his Lacoste shirt unstained beneath the arms, while I collapsed, sopping wet, on a bench. "I hate it when you talk like that."

"It's something we all have to face," he said. "I'm not going to be around forever."

My father's old friend Ned Levis appeared at his elbow. Ned was a music teacher at Niles High School with a mournful, kindly face. His eyes, magnified by thick black-rimmed glasses, were of the type that looked deep into your soul—and forgave what they saw. Listening year after year to the terrible sounds produced by reluctant violinists in cinder-block practice rooms had made him willing to tolerate any extremity of failure. Studying in my room, I used to hear him conducting the chamber music group that met in our living room once a week. "No, no, no," he'd murmur in a weary voice, imploring the librarians and high school teachers perched behind their music stands to pay attention. "*Presto*, it says. *Presto*, not *andante*." It pained Ned to point this out. Who was he to criticize? Before he got the job at Niles, he'd been a shoe salesman, bending on the carpet at Florsheim Shoes on Wabash, the open boxes strewn about. He was lucky to be doing what he loved. But it had to be done right.

"So, William, the older generation's going fast," he said genially. "And you, *boychik*?" He gave my hand a powerful squeeze. "What are you writing these days?" Ned loved to shoot the breeze about literature; I could see him warming up, his morose jaw working as he chewed a cocktail hot dog. "That poem about your grandparents in *Poetry*," he said. "I liked it. You make the reader see how really foreign they still are. How does that line go? 'The odor of old Russia in the kitchen . . .'" He massaged my shoulder absently and stared across the room. Remembering his own parents? He'd brought them to the house once, a dignified old couple dressed up for *shul*. They asked for hot tea in a glass. His father was a jeweler on State Street. When they left the house, they walked arm in arm, helping each other to the car. They were both dead now. "The trick is to get in the feel of ordinary life," Ned resumed. "Know what I mean? Trust in what you know. Look what Joyce did with Leopold Bloom. He even shows him in the can."

More guests were arriving. My father fought off tears as they came forward to offer their condolences. "William!" cried Jack Rossner. He threw his arms around my father. Jack didn't show his age; his gray hair was thick and ample, and his linen suit had a *New Yorker* ad look. He was large and prosperous, with the rosy tinge of the rich. A confident man: his parents were American-born. While my grandfather was lugging his suitcase crammed with pos'l cards all over the Midwest, Jack's father was starting up a pharmaceutical supply house in Chicago. Jack had inherited the firm and moved the whole operation to new headquarters in Des Plaines, complete with an indoor tennis court for management and a workout room for the employees.

He came toward me like a wrestler looking for a hold and slipped his arm around my neck. "*Nu?*" he cried joyfully. "When are you gonna come work for the company? We could use some new blood in our PR office." He steered me toward a trap of canapés while he filled me in about his son, an SDS type at the University of Michigan. "Tod's coming aboard after graduation to start a recruitment program in Woodlawn. We want to bring some blacks into the firm." He glanced at my wan father and sighed. "These funerals are tough. When the parents go, kid . . ." He let the thought complete itself. "And what's it all mean? What's it all about?" Jack had been hit hard by Judaism lately. He was active in his temple; he bought Israel bonds; he had joined the Jewish Book Club. He was reading Buber, pondering the mysteries. *Tales of the*

Hasidim had moved him greatly. He peered down into my face as if he were searching for a sign. "You're the writer. You tell me."

"I don't know, Jack. I'm struggling myself." I'm also twenty years old.

My mother spotted me and motioned me over. She was talking to Janice Glabman, a friend from her Northwestern sorority days. Wasp-waisted and small-boned, she wore her raven hair in bangs, bought her clothes on Michigan Avenue, and put a lot of effort into her makeup. Sometimes I'd look at my parents' friends and get a sudden glimpse of how they must have looked when they were young. Wrinkles fanned out from the corners of Janice's pale blue eyes, but I could see in her the college girl of thirty years ago—flirtatious, smart, aware of her good looks. "Hello, dear," she said, offering me a dry hand. "How's school? How did your Wordsworth paper turn out?"

Janice taught English literature at Roosevelt, and had published a book on Freud and the Romantic poets. I'd sent her a paper on *The Prelude* that came back with many penciled "goods" and some corrections: "Not known as *Prelude* this early; original title *The Recluse*."

"I got a B+."

"That's respectable. I tend not to give out A's, and I'm sure your man doesn't either. Perkins? I use his anthology. Though why he left out *Youth and Age* I can't imagine."

"*Youth and Age?*"

"Coleridge, dear," Janice said patiently. "It's a beautiful poem." This was a funeral? I felt like I was sitting for my orals.

The noise in the room had increased. The mourners nibbled pound cake and sipped their coffee—no drinkers in this crowd. I was glad to be home. One thing about Harvard that bothered me was the way you had to apply for everything: classes, clubs, residential houses, even tickets to the football game. Here I had only to show my face—one that bore a distinct resemblance to several others in the room—to gain admittance.

I headed for the bedroom to call Lizzie Sherman. Through the sliding glass doors, the floodlit lawn had a tropical sheen. The princess phone's illuminated dial glowed in the dark. Lizzie. Would I ever get over her? A dark, Sephardic-looking girl with crow-black hair, she'd swept through the halls of Evanston High in serapes, Mexican shawls, high boots, as exotic at sixteen as a flamenco dancer. She didn't care about school—an attitude that put her right up there with Stavrogin as far as I was concerned. While her parents organized peace marches and collated petitions for Democratic congressmen in the kitchen of their fourteen-room Tudor home, Lizzie sat on her bed listening to Cannonball Adderley and getting stoned. "That girl goes out of her way to defy her parents," remarked my mother, a shrewd judge of my friends.

Only she couldn't seem to leave home. She hung around Evanston year after year, studying ceramics at the Art Center or waitressing at the Hut. She'd go off and study Spanish in Cuernavaca for a few months, or sublet an apartment in New York and audit some courses at the New School, but she always came back to her teenager's bedroom with the striped wallpaper and the stuffed animals. "My parents don't love me enough," she had complained to me once. "They're not into being parents. If they loved me, I could move away. I'm enslaved by their indifference."

Lizzie's father answered the phone. He wasn't happy to hear from me. A lawyer for good causes, he tried to be tolerant of his daughter's long-haired boyfriends, but it wasn't easy; he had a cloud of liberal white hair himself. "I'll go see if I can find her," he said without enthusiasm.

I leafed through the North suburban phone book while I waited. Our name wasn't in it anymore. Pretty soon there would be no trace of us, no evidence that the Janis clan had ever lived in the Chicago area. Gone, just like the generation of immigrants that came before us, those broad blank Swedish faces you saw in old photographs of the city, clustered around the bar of some turn-of-the-century tavern with sawdust on the floor. The city was black now. Jewel advertised specials on pigs' feet.

Lizzie came on the line. "Where are you?"

"I'm at my cousins' in Winnetka. My grandma died."

"Oh, God, I'm sorry."

"It's been pretty strange. Can I see you?"

"Now?" she said doubtfully.

"Well, like in an hour or so. I should stick around here for a while."

"Um . . ." It was embarrassing to be found at home. "Oh, come," she blurted. "I'm sick of watching the *Late Show* by myself."

I lingered at the party until after nine. Grandma Rose held court from the couch, her cane by her side, one foot propped on a hassock. Her rouged cheeks and brocaded shawl gave her a fortune-teller's look. In the kitchen, my cousins' maid Eula was doing the dishes. I was sorry to leave this familiar scene. Harold and Edna's house was new, but inside it looked just like their Rogers Park apartment. In their own way, my mother's cousins had taste. Harold was an amateur photographer; the walls were hung with blow-ups of Lincoln Park, Lake Michigan, Marina City. The hardwood floors were covered with colorful scatter rugs Grandma Rose wove on her loom. The lamps on the end tables were made out of Japanese vases. The teak cabinet in the dining room was filled with Harold's collection of antique surgical implements.

I sat down next to my father and asked for the car keys. Didn't anything ever change? It could have been one of those Friday nights in high school when I'd splash Old Spice on my face after dinner, grab the keys to the black-finned Chevy that had belonged to Sophie until she was too old to drive, and head out to the cold garage. There was always that feeling of guilty joy as I turned on the radio full blast, revved up the engine and backed out the driveway at insane speed, nearly running over my neighbor Wally Pinsker's dog.

"How are we going to get back to the city?" my father asked.

"Mother said the Glabmans can take you."

There was no reproach in his face, only a bewildered look. "Be careful," he said.

"I will." He patted my wrist. The back of his hand was knotty with veins and walnut-tan from the California sun. I saw that he was about to cry, and hurried out to the car. In the warm June night with the stars out and the sound of crickets all around, I breathed in the summer air with a sense of incredible relief, and burst into tears.

In downtown Winnetka, I pulled into a gas station and got out of the car. It was something I'd seen my father do when I was a child, and for some reason the gesture had impressed me. Driving around in high school, I would stay in my seat and roll down the window whenever I had to fill the tank, but lately I'd found myself pulling up to gas pumps and leaping from the car. Thus did heredity assert itself.

The attendant came over, a boy about sixteen with a head of blond bedraggled curls. The stitched red signature on his shirt pocket identified him as Eddie. He pulled the hose over to the tank and cranked up the pump. The numbers whirred by in a blur. I could feel the warm air against my skin and sensed the lake a mile away, its bland fishy odor mingled with gas fumes. I left Eddie counting a roll of bills in his grease-blackened hand, drove over the clanging rubber hose, and headed toward Evanston.

On the radio, Ray Norstrand—or was it Norman Pellegrini? —was talking in his somber voice over WFMT, Chicago's fine arts station. I could never tell those two apart; they even managed to read ad copy as if they were lecturing on the Quattrocento. "The Gregorian Brothers have been in business since 1948," intoned the lucid commentator. "They have traveled the world, from the deserts of Baluchistan to the markets of Kabul, in search of fine rugs. Why not stop in and examine these lovely wares for yourself? The showroom is open from noon until eight every day of the week." Bertolli's Wine Shop; Kroch's and Brentano's; the Scandinavian Furniture Mart; Toad Hall, for the finest in stereo equipment: a civilized litany more moving to me than the Mozart piano concerto that followed it.

Idling at a light, I heard a click inside the aluminum post on the curb. The summer air, perfumed with newly mown grass, came in the window, and leaf shadows rippled in the dark like the shadows at the bottom of a swimming pool. The old streetlamps made the leaves canopied over the road a bright emerald green. I sped around a bend and the Baha'i temple rose out of the dark, its dome the shape of a gigantic orange juice squeezer. My sense of the neighborhood was primitive, territorial, innate. I knew every house, every turn in the road: the mansions behind their wrought-iron gates, the boats in Wilmette Harbor, the ice-cream shop with the flavors chalked up on a blackboard and the screened windows that looked out on the beach. On the other side of the road, away from the lake, were newer houses: plantation-style with white pillars, Mediterranean with terra-cotta roofs, imitation Tudor with ivy-covered walls, Italianate ochre villas, colonial, neo-Gothic, contemporary glass. The suburban international style.

Just past the temple was Laurel Avenue, where my mother grew up. Grandma Rose had lived there until she couldn't manage the stairs and had to move to a residential hotel in Evanston. I turned off Sheridan Road and pulled up in front of the house; it was the last one on the street, next to the community golf course. I was stunned; it was so small. I had remembered a big old burgundy-brick house with French doors, a spacious lawn, a garden with a latticed gate, a long gravel driveway where my grandfather parked his Lincoln— not this 1920s bungalow, with its cracked sandstone urns and weed-seamed walk.

The house was out of another time. Upstairs, in a sun-warmed attic, Rose had worked at a giant loom, weaving rugs and wall hangings. In the garage, her bachelor brother, Igor, made ornate bronze clocks. In the living room hung a portrait of my mother by Nikolai Remisov, a White Russian who had been a satirical artist for *Krokodil*; he'd known Diaghilev, collaborated with the famous set designer Leon Bakst. He was an old man now, sitting by a pool in Palm Springs with a transistor radio in his lap—a gift from Frank Sinatra for his work as a set designer on *Ocean's Eleven*.

I leaned against the car and breathed in the damp, loamy scent of the fairway. Rose used to give lawn parties for the Russian society of Chicago. The men wore three-piece suits and smoked their cigarettes underhanded, the ash pointed toward the palm. Their accents were full of soft consonants. *"Bozhe moy!"* they'd cry, squatting down beside me. *"Sheynuh punim."* Their skin smelled of talc and shaving cream. Beneath the Japanese lanterns strung in the trees, maids in crisp white uniforms made their way through the crowd with trays of champagne and *piroshki*. On the porch the men played pinochle. I could hear the slap of cards through the screen.

On the Fourth of July, I'd go sit by the canal on the other side of the fairway and watch the fireworks from the North-western football stadium. Arcs of light burst in the cloudy sky, flaring traceries that looped and corkscrewed and cascaded down. Voices floated over the fairway from the party in

Grandma Rose's yard. Half those people were dead now. I could imagine people dying one by one, but a whole generation? There was a photograph of this crowd in our family album: my parents' parents in their youth. Seven or eight young people in front of a bay window somewhere in the city: my handsome grandfather, with tiny round glasses like Trotsky and bushy hair brushed back; a dreamy-eyed man with a hand tucked Napoleonlike inside his jacket; a brooding woman with a string of pearls around her neck and a cigarette in a holder dangling from her heavily ringed fingers. Grandma Rose, plump and sensuous in a long embroidered gown, clutched my grandfather's hand in her fist. They were lovers. I couldn't believe it. No one ever did.

I got back in the car and headed toward Evanston, where the suburbs became the city. On Chicago Avenue, the used-car lots were festooned with strings of lights. An elevated train clattered overhead, the single empty car bound for Chicago. I turned up Main Street, the cobra-headed parking meters glinting in the Pinto's headlights. Two blocks down, on Forest, was the house where I grew up. Nothing had changed in this neighborhood since my father's undergraduate days. There were the same turreted Victorian homes, the same elm-lined boulevards. The globed lamps shone in the dark like giant pearls.

The house was dark. I wondered who lived there now. An insurance executive, my father had told me. I parked the car and sat at the wheel, peering through the bamboo gate. The house, a split-level under a sloping pebbled roof, was hidden behind a high brick wall. Where the front yard should have been, my parents had installed a Japanese garden: bonsai, a ceramic Oriental lamp, big boulders strewn about. The interior was neutral, barren, spare: beige nubbly couches, teakwood coffee tables, a Herman Miller chair beside the slate fireplace.

There were skylights in the stippled ceiling. The windows had louvers on either side. They didn't open. In the summer, the air conditioning blasted away in that icy tomb; in the winter, it was as warm as a greenhouse.

The walls were museum-white, and covered with collages of rubble-strewn cities done by my father's cousin Eli, who had escaped from Auschwitz during World War II. In the hall was an abstract sculpture, a Henry Moore–type sphere mounted on a pedestal—the work of a local sculptor who had a studio on Main Street. The marble coffee table was piled high with copies of *Encounter, Commentary, Partisan Review.* The built-in shelves were loaded with books: Mann, Joyce, Nabokov, Pasternak, the Random House two-volume Proust.

Our house was like a Bennington dorm. In the dining room, my mother sat with a French primer open on the table, muttering, *"Dis donc, Paul, où est la bibliothèque?"* In the laundry room behind the garage, my father crouched over a Formica counter among the sheets and towels hung out to dry, a pair of magnifying glasses strapped to his head, making oboe reeds. Knives and thread, minute cylinders of cork, strips of fish skin were scattered about among the socks and underwear. He pared away at wedges of bamboo for hours. Upstairs in my room at the end of the house, I could hear a high, shrill whine as he put a reed to his lips and tested it.

He'd lost interest in medicine by then. He was annoyed when patients phoned, as if he'd been called away from his real work: reading Thomas Mann or listening to Berlioz. Whole days were spent accompanying his *Music Minus One* albums—recordings by an orchestra lacking one instrument. I would come home from school to find him planted before a music stand in the living room, his face scarlet, earphones on his head, swaying like a snake charmer as he struggled to keep up with some Telemann concerto. "What is it about this music?" he would cry, pulling the earphones off his head. "It lifts up the soul. It has the power to intoxicate."

My father counted himself among Stendhal's Happy Few, that tribe of independent types who lived and felt on a more exalted plane than ordinary people. Not that they were actually *happy*. Prominent among their number were Dostoyevsky, Proust, and Kafka. Especially Kafka. My father found his own experience "kafkaesque"—his favorite adjective until he came across it in *Time*. Mysterious forces thwarted him. He marveled over Kafka's *Letter to His Father*. "This is me," he would gloat nervously, reading aloud the passage where Kafka complains that his father controlled him by means of "abuse, threats, irony, spiteful laughter, and self-pity."

What had his father done to him? When I knew him, Grandpa Morris was a frail old man who sat by the cash register of his drugstore all day reading pharmaceutical journals or cleaning his gold-rimmed spectacles with a handkerchief. The store had a deserted look: dusty placards advertising Sealtest and Squibb in the window, grime-coated beach balls in wire bins, out-of-date magazines in the rack. He'd started out as an industrial engineer, working on the Chicago Bridge. "He was a genius," my father maintained. "A physics wizard. He had a diploma from the Czar." But he got laid off during the Depression. Grandma Sophie had made him buy the store so they'd have "a business of our own." It didn't work out that way. She failed the pharmaceutical exam year after year, was incompetent at keeping the books, annoyed the customers with her talk. The store lost money. Morris didn't care. He read Schopenhauer, *The World as Will and Representation*, an old edition he'd picked up at Staver's in Hyde Park. When I was nine, he gave me a Classic Comics edition of *Crime and Punishment*; it made no mention of Sonya the whore.

According to my father, though, Morris had been an intellectual bully. Doing his homework at the dining room table, he was reprimanded for using a slide rule. "You should be able to do it in your head," snapped Morris.

"But he *wants* us to use a slide rule."

"What does he know? If he had any brains, he wouldn't be teaching physics in a school."

Brains were a very important commodity in our household. Philistinism was rampant in the land. My father deplored Howard Johnson's and the House of Pancakes, Jack Paar and Arthur Godfrey, Leon Uris and Herman Wouk. When Dwight Macdonald's famous essay "Masscult and Midcult" was published in *Partisan Review*, he was ecstatic, chuckling over Macdonald's assault on the pretensions of those contemptible middlebrows Thornton Wilder and Archibald MacLeish. He was furious when Arthur Miller married Marilyn Monroe. "The man has a responsibility to the intellectuals in this country," my father stormed. "We'll lose credibility." (That wasn't the way I saw it, beating off with the notorious *Playboy* spread of Marilyn open on my knee.)

One night, after a drive in the country, we stopped off for dinner at a restaurant in Kenosha called the Homestead. It was one of those pseudocolonial country inns with a brick-cobbled sidewalk and a cannon on the lawn. The waitresses had on Sturbridge Village outfits: long-sleeved black dresses with frilly collars, little bonnets, buckled shoes.

"*Ersatz!*" my father muttered as we sat down.

"What's *ersatz*, Dad?"

"Fake, inauthentic. That maître d' in knee socks: you'd think he just crossed the Potomac with George Washington." Suddenly he rose out of his chair, a look of panic on his face. "Muzak!" he gasped in a strangled voice, as if he'd just detected mustard gas seeping through the ventilators. "I'm going to make them turn it off." He hurried off to find the manager, threading his way through the crowded tables.

My mother and I awaited his return in silence: the head of

the household had gone off to war. A few minutes later he was back. He sank down in his chair and picked at his roast beef.

"What happened?" I prompted. "What'd he say?"

My father stared morosely at his plate. "The other patrons like it."

The music that blared from my room night and day—Bobby Vinton, Neil Sedaka, Leslie Gore—was a betrayal. "How can you listen to that junk?" my father would say whenever he turned on the radio after I'd had the car out the night before and heard the voice of Wolfman Jack instead of Norman Pellegrini. Listening to WLS, Chicago's Top Forty station, I was as furtive as a citizen behind the Iron Curtain tuning in the Voice of America. Only it wasn't barbed wire that cut me off from freedom; it was culture.

Still, I was my father's disciple, and I spread the word with the fervor of a Jehovah's Witness. When my civics teacher, Mr. Bein, asked us to subscribe to *Reader's Digest*, I raised my hand. "But Mr. Bein, isn't *Reader's Digest* for ignorant people?" I enumerated its failings: the trite, optimistic "Life in These United States" feature; the inane "Toward More Picturesque Speech" column; the pathetic vocabulary lists. "Why don't we subscribe to something more stimulating?" I proposed. "Like *The Nation* or *The Christian Science Monitor*?"

My room was a museum of self-improvement. Above my bed was the "honor board"—a bulletin board covered with memorabilia of my accomplishments: a blue ribbon commemorating the occasion when I came in fourth in the hundred-yard dash at the Ravinia School Field Day in 1958; a yellowing photograph from the *Evanston Review* that showed me doing push-ups at a tennis clinic when I was twelve; a medal from Camp Shewahmegon in Drummond, Wisconsin, for second place in Arts & Crafts; a letter from Senator Everett Dirksen congratulating me for an editorial on school spirit that had appeared in the *Nichols School Newsletter*; and a photostat of my scores on the high school aptitude tests. On the far wall was a framed copy of the Constitution on crisp imitation parchment, brought back from a field trip to the nation's capital in seventh grade, and a reproduction of Picasso's *The Old Guitarist*. On the shelves were my paperbacks: *The Sun Also Rises, Tortilla Flat, Of Mice and Men, A Portrait of the Artist as a Young Man, Rhinoceros.*

Our dinner table conversation was as high-minded as *The David Susskind Show*. I never knew what the moderator had in store. "What's wrong with this?" my father said one night, waving a form letter from some politician in front of my nose.

"William, let the boy eat," my mother objected.

"This is important." I studied the letter. "Well?" my father said. I speared a lima bean and scanned the cheerful sales pitch again, hunting for the error.

"It's near the top," my father hinted.

"I give up," I said at last, hungry for the brownies my mother had warming in the oven.

My father snatched away the letter. " 'No one concerned about the future of this country can remain disinterested in the coming election . . .' *Disinterested* means impartial, objective; the word they want here is *uninterested*." He wiped his plate with a slice of rye bread. "That's known as a *catachresis*, or *solecism*—a grammatical lapse."

"Why do you need two words for the same thing?" I asked.

"Well, they're not exactly the same," my father said. "Let's look 'em up." He pushed aside his chair and beckoned me to follow.

"William!" my mother protested. There was an edge of anger in her voice. "Why can't you finish dinner before rushing off to the dictionary?"

But he was already out of his seat and heading for the

living room, where the one-volume *OED* stood open on a metal
stand, exhibited as proudly as if it were the *Book of Kells*. I
fled my mother's reproachful gaze and hurried off to join my
father. We stood side by side, feeding at the trough of
knowledge. "Let's see," he muttered, running his finger down
the page. "Ca-ta-*chre*-sis. Here." He read the definition aloud:
" 'Improper use of words; application of a term to a thing
which it does not properly denote; abuse of a trope or meta-
phor.' And a so-le-cism," he said, drawing out the word while
he searched for it, "is . . . 'impropriety or irregularity in
speech or diction.' " He slammed the volume shut. "So there
is a subtle difference," he pronounced with satisfaction. We
trotted back to the kitchen, where my mother was furiously
clearing the table.

"Do you have to leap up in the middle of dinner like that?"
she said tearfully, scraping dishes into the disposal. "You're
just showing off for the boy." She hurried from the room,
shoes clicking on the parquet floor.

"Mom's not an intellectual like us," I volunteered.

My father blew on his coffee, wrinkling the surface. "Being
an intellectual isn't everything," he said.

No, but my mother's failure to measure up to our scholarly
standards troubled me all the same. For a woman who had a
degree from the Medill School of Journalism, she was sur-
prisingly unlettered; she'd never read *Heart of Darkness*, she
hadn't finished *Ulysses*, she failed to identify lines from *The
Waste Land* that I recited at the dinner table. " 'Datta.
Dayadhvam. Damyata,' " I chanted while she hurried back
and forth with steaming plates of food. "Come on, Mom.
What's it from?"

"I really haven't the faintest idea, dear." She dipped down
to straighten my knife and spoon. "Take your elbows off the
table."

My elbows! I was quoting T. S. Eliot—in Sanskrit yet!

"Just guess, Mom," I wheedled. "I'll give you a hint. It's twentieth-century."

"I told you, dear," she said, a note of impatience in her voice. "I really don't know."

My father knew. He gave me a sly smile. "It's Eliot, Mom," I announced. *"The Waste Land."*

" 'I grow old, I grow old,' my father intoned in a sonorous voice. " 'I shall wear the bottoms of my trousers rolled.' "

"Easy." I supplied the title: *"The Love Song of J. Alfred Prufrock."* My father knew the whole poem by heart.

Why couldn't my mother quote Eliot? I fumed. It never occurred to me to imagine what my life would have been like if she *had* been an intellectual. What if I'd come home from school every afternoon to find her, in faded jeans and a flannel work shirt, a Gauloise smoldering beside her, reading *Being and Nothingness* at the kitchen table? Who would have driven me to the Varsity Shop and helped pick out my back-to-school wardrobe? Who would have sorted out my laundry and left it in tidy stacks on the bed, the socks piled up like cannonballs on a New England green? But I was oblivious of the impeccable service—the meals on the table, the "after-school snack," a glass of milk, already poured, that stood in the refrigerator beside a plate of Oreo cream cookies. I was oppressed by my mother's trivial demands. "What do you mean, my nails are dirty? Come on, Mom. Did Verlaine's mother complain about his personal hygiene?"

"Who?"

"Verlaine, Mom, Verlaine. The great French *symboliste*." (I gave it the French pronunciation: *sambo-least*.)

One day, after a big argument that started when I refused to tuck in my shirt, I yelled at her, "You're just a housewife, Mom!"

She fled to her bedroom in tears and slammed the door. I sat at my desk reading *The Outline of History*, by H. G. Wells, but my chest was tight with some primal fear. Had I gone too far? I ran down the hall to her room. "Mom?" I called, pressing my ear against the door. "Mom, I'm sorry about what I said." Silence. The house was so still I could hear the refrigerator hum in the kitchen below. "Mom, please talk to me. Forget about what I said."

On the other side of the door, she blew her nose.

"Forgive me, Mom," I pleaded. "I know you go to French class and everything. And you liked *The Stranger*, right?" There was no reply. How could I have said that? I felt as if an evil spirit had spoken through me: the debbil made me do it! Oh, Momma, please come out. Say something, please.

"It's all right," she said through the door in a shaky voice. "It doesn't matter."

"Mom, please come out." A sob rose in my throat.

"I'm not angry. Now go away."

In my room, I could hardly read for the tears that streamed down my face.

I tried to keep up. I took flute lessons, going on the train to the North Shore Music School in Winnetka. Every night after dinner, I practiced in my parents' soundproof bedroom, standing before the full-length mirror on the bathroom door to perfect my embouchure. Finally the teacher, Mrs. Edvig, told them it was hopeless. "Deeb down," she said in her Viennese accent, "he doesn't *vant* to learn."

I painted. For my fourteenth birthday, I was given a set of expensive oil paints, fine brushes, an easel, and enough canvas for *Guernica*. I set up shop in the basement, and within a week had completed my first work, a gaudy web of blotted shapes entitled *Composition #1*. By the time it came back from the framers, I'd stowed the easel in a closet. The brushes, soaking in a can, were thrown out by the maid.

Never mind. It was literature that absorbed me now. After

school I would bicycle over to the Out-of-Town Newsstand on the corner of Main and Chicago, a low brick building with a scalloped awning out front and racks of paperbacks inside. I must have spent a million hours browsing in those aisles. Leafing through a book about the Beats, I studied a photograph of Kerouac declaiming *On the Road* from the stage of a smoky club, his rugged Canuck face exhausted in the spotlight. To think that he was still alive! He probably lived in Greenwich Village. (Little did I know he was in Florida with his mother.) Then there was that book by Malcolm Cowley, *Exile's Return*, where everyone was always boarding ships and going off to Paris. And *The Great Gatsby*! I could never go past it on the shelf without reading over the end. When I got to the scene where Nick stares out at the green light across the bay, I nearly wept in front of the hawk-faced clerk stacking newspapers by the door.

My favorite, though, was Salinger. I was amazed by the Glass family. They lived in a world I knew from *New Yorker* covers: rows of brownstones and car-clogged streets; Washington Square in the rain; the Plaza Hotel at dusk. There was one story—I think it was in *Nine Stories*—where these girls are sitting around after their tennis lesson on a Saturday morning and talking to one of the girls' brothers . . . I can't remember what they were talking about, but the brother was some kind of writer. I think he was working on a screenplay or something. No one I knew was working on a screenplay.

The only writer I'd ever seen was Auden, when he gave a reading at Northwestern. It was a Saturday night; I remember, because *Leave It to Beaver* was on, and I couldn't decide whether to go or not. How could I confess to my father that I'd rather spend the evening with Beaver and Wally ("Hey, Beav!") and Eddie Haskell than sitting in a drafty auditorium listening to some old poet? Besides, it was freezing out. But I could see my father wanted me to go; he had that expectant

look he got in his eye when he was about to ask me to play
chess.

I trudged upstairs, put on my ski jacket with all the lift tags
on the zipper from Boyne Mountain, Gander, and Wilmot; snow
boots; a woolen ski cap; and a boa-length muffler. In the bathroom, I glanced at myself in the mirror; I looked like a Sherpa
guide.

In the car, we barely spoke. My father hunched over the
wheel, peering through the windshield with the intent gaze of a
sea captain at the helm in a bad storm as he negotiated the icy
streets. I tried to think of something to say about Auden, but
I didn't know much about him except that he was a famous
poet. Other topics came to mind: the Chicago Black Hawks'
progress in the National Hockey League; the latest adventures
of Wally and Beav; the stupidity of my locker mate, Gary
Dybka, who had forgotten our combination and gone home
without a coat when it was twelve degrees below zero. But I
knew it was futile. My father would have nodded uncomfort-
ably—*I have an idiot for a son*—and kept on driving. It was
Auden or nothing.

We found seats in the back of the auditorium. Auden
shuffled onstage in bedroom slippers and mumbled his poems
into the microphone. His seamed face was as white as flour.
I could hardly hear a word he said. My father was moved.
"Awesome," he murmured as we headed back out into the
Siberian night. "Now you can say to your children that you
heard Auden read."

It *was* awesome. Not what he read, but that he existed. I
wished I'd had the nerve to join the crowd that clustered
around him afterward. There were things I needed to know.
Like, how did he become a poet? My father had no answers.
Contemporary writers were men of unreal eminence to him, as
remote from our world as Joyce or Kafka. He couldn't get over
the stuff he read in magazines. It amazed him that critics were

so opinionated. They said whatever they pleased—in print! He
read the polemics in *Commentary* with nervous incredulity,
chortling over bad reviews. Meanwhile I was up in my room
typing letters to the editor. "Sirs: How Irving Howe can dis-
miss the profound truths uttered by J. D. Salinger's exhilarat-
ing creation, the Glass family, as 'chic erudition' is beyond
me . . ."

I pored over the Manhattan phone book in the Chicago
Public Library, searching for the names of famous writers. It
was eerie to see Lionel Trilling (35 Claremont Avenue) and
Auden (77 St. Mark's Place) listed in the fat directory. Didn't
their phones ring off the hook? There weren't many writers in
Chicago. Nelson Algren was around, and Saul Bellow lived on
the South Side. (They were both unlisted.) That was about it.
When I read in Henry James's *The American Scene* that he'd
been introduced to a literary salon in Chicago, I couldn't
believe it; the only salon I'd ever heard of was the beauty
parlor in the Orrington Hotel where my mother got her hair
done once a week.

The literary life in Evanston centered around Great Expectations, a bookstore under the Foster Street elevated tracks, between a pizzeria and a vacant lot. No sign announced its
presence, and the display windows on either side of the door
were smudged with dust.

It was scary to enter that Dickensian gloom. Truman Metzel,
the proprietor, would glance up from his desk with a bored
look on his face and return to his invoices without a word.
Stout, bearded, owl-eyed, he wore the same oyster-gray pullover in every season. I rarely saw him out of his chair. Whenever someone asked for a book, he would gaze around at the
shelves, hoping to spot it without having to get up. On those
rare occasions when he failed to find what he was looking for,
he would ease himself up and trundle over to the shelves with
the ponderous lethargy of a bear prodded from its winter

sleep, so reluctant, so pained, so resentful that he made you
feel the simplest request for help was a tremendous imposition.
There were times when I was convinced he would rather lose a
sale than stand. But the bibliographic lore in his head was
uncanny. Metzel required only the most fragmentary—even
erroneous—data to identify a book. I once heard him construe
from a reference to "this sculptor who knew Joyce in Trieste"
the memoir by Frank Budgen, a British painter who was Joyce's
drinking companion in Zurich; and I myself managed to get
out of him the author and title of a book "by a librarian whose
father believed in God and he didn't"—Edmund Gosse, *Father
and Son.*

For a long time I had my eye on a set of volumes with
somber black dust jackets: René Wellek's *History of Modern
Criticism.* They were high up on a shelf in the back room, and
I had to ask Metzel to fetch them down—which he did with
ostentatious effort, dragging over the ladder and hoisting himself up step by step. It wasn't for him to question why a seventeen-year-old boy in a leather jacket coveted these four heavy
volumes with their funereal covers: *The Later Eighteenth Century, The Romantic Age, The Age of Transition, The Later
Nineteenth Century.* (A fifth volume, *The Twentieth Century,*
was said to be forthcoming.) Wellek's classifications were so
orderly. The Russian radical critics, the Russian conservative
critics, the minor French critics, the English aesthetes: he had
it all worked out. His erudition was beyond imagining. Every
page was dense with names: Chernyshevsky, Dilthey, Vico,
Taine. The more obscure they were, the more they fascinated
me. To know these names would give my life a new gravity, a
high purpose; it would open up another world. Some boys
memorized the Torah and had *bar mitzvahs*; when I knew who
Dobrolyubov was I would become a man.

One Christmas, or Hanukkah, or whatever it was we celebrated, I opened a hefty package and there it was: the whole

four-volume set. I read the card: "That my boy, who knows so much, should know still more." It was signed, "Your loving father." I hurried upstairs and put *A History of Modern Criticism* on my shelf; I wanted to see how it looked. Over Christmas vacation, I kept the fourth volume on the table beside my bed; it had more names I recognized than the earlier volumes. Only I hadn't read a lot of the authors these critics were writing about, so it was kind of hard to follow. When school started, I had so much other stuff to read that I put Wellek back on the shelf. I never looked at it again.

Another gift I got that Christmas was a Caedmon album of T. S. Eliot reading from his work. I sat in my room and listened to *The Hollow Men*:

> *Between the idea*
> *And the reality*
> *Between the motion*
> *And the act*
> *Falls the Shadow.*

Suddenly I was at my desk, writing a poem. It was about the concert my father's chamber music group had given for homeless people on Christmas Eve. In the drafty basement of a Catholic church on the West Side, we set up folding chairs for the old men in overcoats who loitered shyly in the corridor. They seemed appreciative, and applauded after every movement, not knowing when a piece was over. When the concert ended, church volunteers served coffee and cake. Afterwards we drove around looking for somewhere to have dinner. Grandma Sophie was in Miami, and the dining room of Grandma Rose's residential hotel in downtown Evanston was closed. There was nowhere to go. We ended up at some Italian restaurant on North Wells.

My parents didn't mind. More secular than the Janises you

couldn't get. No Christmas tree dropped its needles on our parquet floor; no menorah flickered on the sideboard. During
the High Holidays we played indoor tennis in Skokie. We
never had any trouble getting a court on Christmas Day, when
the heat was turned way down and the rhythm of our volleys
echoed in the empty shed. They say holidays are the loneliest
time of the year for the old, the widowed, the unmarried. Also
for the assimilated.

The poem was about that Christmas.

CHRISTMAS CONCERT IN THE MEN'S SHELTER ON WEST MONROE

In the lonely basement
Where the old men lurk,
The sad tootle of a bassoon
Reverberates among damp walls.

The musicians tune up
Beneath flickering fluorescent lights.
My father sits with sweaty brow
Before his music stand.

Through the grimy window
I watch the snow swirl down.
A bus grinds through the deserted street,
Empty.

Christ is born.

I was dissatisfied. The poem needed something. I got out
my pastels and colored in the spaces around the poem.

My father made copies on the photocopying machine in his
office. The colors didn't reproduce, but the poem was ac-
claimed by Rose and Sophie, by Harold and Edna, even by our
maid, Sabina. Maybe I should send it around. I subscribed to
Writer's Digest and studied the poetry markets. *Lucifer's*

Lamp, a journal published out of Davenport, Iowa, advertised a "national poetry contest," so I sent off "Christmas Concert." Two weeks later it was accepted. "Momma! Momma!" I cried downstairs. "I'm published, Mom! I'm gonna be in *Lucifer's Lamp*."

"That's nice, dear," my mother answered. "What's *Lucifer's Lamp*?"

Count on her. "A *maga*zine, Mom."

The only catch was no free copies; I'd have to order them, at $12.95 apiece. I ordered three: one for my parents and one each for my grandmothers.

A month later, I arrived home from school to find a parcel from *Lucifer's Lamp*. I rushed upstairs and tore it open—my first appearance in print! The magazine had a curious format, though; instead of a compact, book-size periodical like *Partisan Review*, I held in my hands an assemblage as thick as a telephone book, loosely bound by plastic rings. The cover consisted of a sheet of blue paper with the legend LUCIFER'S LAMP: A MAGAZINE OF VERSE typed across it. There was no index, but the poems were arranged alphabetically by author. I quickly found mine—just after the work of B. Jabarwarhal of Bombay and next to poems by Hobart B. Jenkins of Baltimore and R. W. Joad of Eureka, California. There were nine poems on the page. The type was blue and smudged—a bad mimeograph job. I stashed my copies of *Lucifer's Lamp* on a shelf in the closet, beside my baseball glove.

But I didn't give up. I kept sending out my poems, and when *The New Yorker* returned them with printed rejection slips, I wondered what was wrong. One day I came across an advertisement in *Writer's Digest* from a "poetry consultant" in Nacogdoches, Texas, and wrote soliciting his services. A few weeks later, I received a manifesto for *Cyclops*, "Songs of the Last Frontier." "Commercialism, propaganda, and ignorance roil the waters of literature," it began. "Only gradually are

men being enjoined away from provincial pride—Abaddon—
The Destroyer. Will they depart the Abyss in time?" Hunched
over my desk, a Tensor lamp trained on the page, I pursed my
lips. This manifesto was heavy going. Who was Abaddon? He
wasn't listed in my *Dictionary of Mythology*. My eye drifted
up to the built-in bookshelf above my desk—a row of *Freddy
the Pig* books; *Stuart Little*; *Charlotte's Web*. I tried again to
focus on what Raymond Winkley, the publisher of *Cyclops*,
had to say: "Poetry can find hope in an age that seems hopeless, can begin the reconstruction before the ruin is visited.
Today, especially, those monolithic axioms that have been
thought to be Truth Absolute are scaling and crumbling to
reveal the shape of a more enduring core."

It was that enduring core I was after, and I was glad to find
enclosed a "checklist of common errors." "Check your poems
for these errors," read the directions, "and if you want us to
aid you, submit one poem for a detailed criticism, plus $1.00
for consultant's time and years of training, writing, publishing,
and personal interest in all sincere poets." I submitted one
poem and a dollar.

Within a week, I had a reply:

> SIR: Your poem will be held 10 days pending the
> arrival of a SASE for its return. The ethic of sending re-
> turn postage with a manuscript is so well established
> that it would seem unnecessary to remind anyone of this.

I sent Mr. Winkley a self-addressed, stamped envelope and
waited.

The response was again prompt: of the twenty-one failings
listed under the category *Avoid*, only one had been checked
off, but there was a terse comment in the margin: "A good
start in 'Summer in Maine' ends up in landscape rambling.
Poetry asks 'So What, So Why, So Whither.' " This Winkley
was pretty strict. I submitted another poem—too soon, it

turned out. Under the category "How to Submit a Manuscript,"
Mr. Winkley had checked off "Wait sixty days after a poem is
rejected or published to resubmit." In the margin of my second
evaluation sheet he scrawled: "Sir, we are busy." The size
of the envelope (approximately four by ten inches) was another problem area: "Note how *stuffed* your small one is,"
scolded the consultant. Under *Avoid*, two errors were noted:
"Ideas not fresh or original, far removed from our own age";
and "Literalism, not imagery, the soul of poetry." But there
was a hopeful message from Mr. Winkley: "Although she
would be more critical of craftsmanship in a sonnet, I would
like to have Miss Lorraine see 'A Painting.' Try to give the
title more force—like 'Captured Awareness,' 'The Senses
Bound,' or other."

I never heard from Miss Lorraine—apparently she was un-
impressed with "A Painting"—but I had a new mentor by
then: Edna Laver, the creative writing teacher at Evanston
High. A gaunt, hectic woman with a big blade of a nose, she
spent whole periods reading aloud from *The Oxford Book of
English Verse*. "*That* is poetry!" she would announce, slamming the book down on the table and fixing us with a defiant
stare. "These were the ones who had it. They knew the joy of
words."

Mrs. Laver expected a lot of her students. She thought we
were all going to become great poets. "Your greatest enemy
is intellectualization," she advised me during one of our weekly
conferences. "You need to work to your own internal music
and word-joy." She sat up straight at her desk, staring across
the room and drumming her bony fingers on my manuscript.
"Find that spontaneous well of emotion, and *use* it."

One afternoon Mrs. Laver turned off the fluorescent lights,
flicked on a projector, and showed us a documentary about
Theodore Roethke. A fat, sweating man with a sorrowful face,
he muttered his poems with tense, incantatory fervor, standing

awkwardly before the camera in a rumpled suit. He was shy,
morose, inaudible; his mouth worked nervously, his eyes were
full of pain. When he recited the poem that begins "I knew a
woman, lovely in her bones," he seemed on the verge of tears.
I was puzzled: how could anyone capable of writing a poem
that beautiful be so unhappy?

Mrs. Laver nominated me to represent Evanston High in
the state poetry contest, and one wintry Saturday she drove
me to the Chicago campus of the University of Illinois, in a
decaying Greek neighborhood on the West Side, for the
regional competition. "Now remember, if they ask for a
Petrarchan sonnet, it's ABBAABBA, then a six-line coda," Mrs.
Laver coached me as we walked across the empty, windswept
campus beneath an iron sky. "And you know what a sestina
is."

In the classroom, a nun scrawled our assignment on the
blackboard: "A sonnet on the theme of seasons." We had one
hour.

The other contestants—seventeen girls and a bush-haired
boy with a scarf around his neck—opened their notebooks
and started to write. I sat there without a thought in my head.
I could see Mrs. Laver through the door, pacing up and down
in her shiny fur coat. Finally a line occurred to me, and
then another:

> *As a November day, desolate calm,*
> *My own irretrievable, missing loves*
> *Are preserved, impenetrable, embalmed—*
> *Eternal as rhythms of flying doves,*
> *That remain immortal in memory,*
> *Enhanced by the fact that they ne'er shall be.*

When the hour was up, I glanced over my lines. I'd gotten the
rhyme scheme wrong! I rushed from the room and buried my
face in Mrs. Laver's musky lapel. "You *are* a poet," she re-

assured me when I had blurted out my tale, "but art demands work and work and more work. No one said it would be easy." And we walked back to the car in silence, wrapped up in our separate perceptions of my destiny.

Hunched over my portable Olivetti one night, I was working on a poem about what it felt like to ride my bicycle through the deserted streets of Evanston after dinner. There was this other kid in Mrs. Laver's class, Oliver Bram, who didn't write in forms, and I was trying to get some of Bram's colloquial style into my own work. A tall, stoop-shouldered boy who came to school in an olive-khaki army jacket, he had no patience for my stiff rhetoric ("O to return to lofty, stiffened pines/That populate the undulating hills . . ."). His knapsack was full of William Carlos Williams, Ginsberg, Pound; his own poems were unfettered by rhyme or meter:

> *we stopped loving—*
> *the other*
> > *night*

> *when power mowers of reason*
> *stripped the green fields*
> > *of our minds . . .*

Why couldn't I do that? Working late, I listened to the hush of cars on Sheridan Road, the clack of the Chicago Avenue elevated three blocks away. "The forlorn twinkle of the distant stars," I wrote, "reminds me of my own mortality." Somehow, though, that wasn't the whole story. I was stirred by the warm fragrant air, the dense foliage, the halo of light around the old streetlamps . . . How it excited me to unzip my shorts as I rode, pull out my cock and expose it to the summer air.

I got up from my desk and looked out the window at the dark apartments across the way. I wondered if July Clark was home. A stocky blonde who lived with her divorced mother,

Judy wore platinum-colored lipstick and hung around with
guys from auto workshop. The roar and splutter of their
souped-up Chevies reverberated through the night. Judy liked
me "as a friend." She didn't want to mess up our relationship with sex, she would explain, kissing me on the lips.
Sometimes she let me sit on her bed while she got ready,
applying lip gloss and putting on eye shadow with a stubby
pencil. Perched on a stool in front of her dressing table, she
would lean forward to study herself in the mirror, and the
sight of her pear-shaped ass bulging against her cut-off blue
jeans made me want to curl up on the shag rug beside her
bed and howl.

I reached up and got down *Sexus* off the shelf. Flipping
past the pages of windy rumination, the cosmic thoughts on
life and death, I searched for the scene where Miller is walking
Mara home from the subway and they do it under a tree.
" 'Don't ever take it out again,' she begged, 'it drives me
crazy. Fuck me! Fuck me!' " My eye raced on, wildly scanning
now. " 'Do it, do it,' she begged, 'or I'll go mad!' " All I ever
heard was *No, Stop, You can't do that*: a litany of prohibitions.
And what was this "sopping cunt" Miller kept raving on about,
a "thirsty flower," "hot as a Bessemer steel furnace," "juice
pouring down her thighs"? The only cunt I had ever touched,
Sharon Kolb's one night when I went over to her house on a
study date and ended up wrestling on her bed, was a damp
downy crease beneath cotton underpants. It was hardly wet
enough to get my finger in.

I read on. "The great joy of the artist is to become aware of
a higher order of things. . . ." Yeah, yeah. Where was that scene
where Miller is doing it with *two* girls? Ah, here we are.
"Maude was stretched out on her back, Elsie squatting over
her on bent knees, her head facing Maude's feet and her mouth
glued to Maude's crack. I was on my knees, giving it to Elsie
from behind." Phew.

It was a warm spring night. I had on a pair of tennis shorts and nothing else; no shirt, no shoes, no underpants. Writing got me so worked up I was tempted to roam the neighborhood in the nude, a thong around my waist like some Kalahari bushman. Poetry was supposed to have a shamanistic power; maybe it could lure Judy down to the pier at the end of our block. Sometimes she came to look for me when she got home from a date. I glanced up at her window: she was probably getting finger-fucked in a parking lot somewhere.

My parents had gone to a party. The second they walked out the door I went insane, staring at myself nude in the mirror, trying on my mother's bras, smearing cold cream on my cock to simulate the feel of a wet pussy. . . . I gulped down Scotch from the cut-glass decanter in the liquor cabinet, beat off like a maniac, turned up the Stones so loud it made the ivory figurines on top of the stereo vibrate. I tried to write ("Choked by the loneliness of the swings in the park,/I pump back and forth in the dark"), scribbling by the light of a scented candle from Edith's Boutique. But all I could think about was Judy Clark with her underpants down around her ankles in the back of some hood's car. "You think you'll ever write about us?" she had said one night when we were hanging out on the pier. "You'll probably forget all about me." Her silvery lipstick shone in the dark, the mouth a puckered oval as she dragged on her Parliament. Forget you, Judy? Never. Art is an act of remembrance—on the artist's own terms: "I took her hand and led her 'neath the pier . . ."

So why was it, I used to wonder as I lay on my bed, "Satisfaction" pounding on the stereo, that all this striving, this culture, this rage for self-expression, made me sad? Taken by my parents to see Morris Carnovsky in *King Lear*, I shifted in my seat, bored by the old man's long-winded speeches; with his flailing arms and histrionic shouts, he seemed like a vaudeville actor. *Crime and Punishment* bewildered me; this

Raskolnikov was a hysteric. And Milton J. Cross, whose dire voice boomed through our living room every Saturday afternoon, bringing us the Metropolitan Opera from New York: something about that somber baritone of his oppressed my heart. "Violetta tries to rise from her bed," he would announce before the last act of *La Traviata*, his voice dropping to a low murmurous dirge, "but it is too late." My father, in his Herman Miller chair, stared vaguely out the window. "Comforted by the presence of Alfredo, she sings, '*Ah, io ritorno a vivere!* I shall live after all,' only to fall back lifeless on her couch." There was an ominous pause: "A moment later, she is dead." Applause crackled through the speaker like static as the curtain descended and Cross renewed his grim narrative: "And now Renata Tebaldi emerges for a second curtain call while the orchestra stands to applaud. She beckons to the conductor, Fausto Cleva, who bows; and summons the whole supporting cast from the wings." My father switched off the radio and I trudged up to my room. Slouched in my wicker basket chair, I gazed around at the shelves of paperbacks, the reproduction of *The Old Guitarist*, the chess set on its inlaid-mahogany board, the mandolin in the corner, the pastel-colored poem on the bulletin board. Through the wall I heard a shrill piercing squawk—my father testing oboe reeds.

I hated art.

II

I TURNED up the circular gravel driveway of Lizzie's house and parked beneath the portico. I hadn't seen her since Christmas. I rang the bell and waited in the dark vestibule. Lizzie came up behind the screen. "Is that you?"

"It's me." She flung open the door and embraced me. Almond skin, black Latin eyebrows, strong perfume—the same old Lizzie. She dressed like a courtesan: tonight she had a red saronglike thing wrapped around her body in a way that mystified and excited me. She led me through the foyer into the living room, a clutter of hassocks and low leather chairs, braided wall hangings and Navajo rugs, lacquered masks and African spears. The walls were hung with giant canvases by Lizzie's mother, pale distended figures floating above an arid desert landscape. In one, a troubled-looking infant sprang from the forehead of a wizened old woman; another showed a nude bony man floating through the sky.

"I'm sorry about your grandmother," Lizzie said. She curled up in a high-backed wicker chair.

"I know, it's sad. But it wasn't sudden, and she was old."

"It's always sad," Lizzie said. "My grandfather's eighty-seven, and I worry about him all the time." She lit a cigarette and put her feet up on the table. "When did you get here?"

"I flew in last night. We're staying in Sophie's apartment on Lunt. It's weird to be here and not be living in our house."

"It's a whole lot weirder to be living at home," Lizzie said fervently. "I should have stayed in Mexico. I had a good setup: a room in these people's house, a shop that carried my batiks, a psychiatrist who cared about me. I mean, what else is there, right?"

"So why didn't you?"

"I don't *know*! I'm all fucked up. Even my mother's pissed that I'm back again. She left me a note the other day telling me to clear my brushes out of her studio. She needed a room of her own."

"Her and Virginia Woolf." I draped my arm over the back of the couch, luxuriating in Lizzie's presence. "I love Evanston."

"You'd be real happy here." She leaned forward and picked at one of her toenails. They were painted red. "You could get a nice apartment in the neighborhood and work in the Whole Earth Bookstore. We could even get married and have kids."

"You don't have to be sarcastic about it." There was some new Lizzie here I couldn't grasp. A pursed, angry look around the mouth. Don't tell me she wanted a life, too. Evanston was supposed to be like those dioramas of cavemen sitting around campfires in the Field Museum, year after year the same grim-jawed Neanderthals with their deep-set eyes crouched over a glowing pyre. Lizzie wouldn't stay put. Already she looked older; her face had filled out, and she'd lopped off her long black hair at the neck. Her makeup had been carefully applied: instead of the flagrant red lipstick I remembered, she wore a dab of lip gloss. The next thing I knew she'd be driving to the supermarket with a station wagon full of kids.

"Well, don't give me this bullshit about the past," she said.

"You have this whole romantic thing about Evanston, but I don't see *you* hanging around."

"What are you so mad about?" I said, patting the couch. "Come on over."

"There's not going to be any fooling around tonight," Lizzie said firmly. "My parents are home." I could hear them moving around upstairs.

"Well, what do you want to do?" I mean, we couldn't just sit around talking all night. I needed to clear my head of the day's events: Grandma Sophie being lowered into the ground in the blaze of the noon sun, my father's anguished face, the women weeping behind dotted veils . . .

"Why don't we go to a motel?" Lizzie said.

"A motel! What for?" I knelt on the carpet and buried my face in her lap.

"I mean it." She pushed me away. "Nothing's going to happen here."

"Okay, okay." I slumped in a low-slung chair made out of some animal's skin. Why couldn't we just go down to the basement where that sofa with the canvas cushions was? Why couldn't we be seventeen? "So where's this motel?"

"There's one on Touhy that I forget the name of, but I know where it is."

Lizzie got a bottle of Dewar's from her parents' liquor cabinet and we headed out west on Dempster. Warehouses and bottling factories lined the access roads. Giant floodlit billboards advertised the nearest Hertz location and the number of daily Piedmont flights to Baltimore. To the west, out by O'Hare, planes dropped down through the cloud-shrouded sky, their taillights winking in the dark. The air was gritty, furnace-like.

At a light, I turned and studied Lizzie. She was fiddling with the radio dial. The silver bracelets on her wrist clinked and swayed with the motion of the car. The radio on, the bottle between us on the seat, the scent of Lizzie's perfume in the air: another familiar scene. "We've had a lot of adventures," I said.

"We have," she agreed. She arched her neck and stretched. "Remember the time we found that cart?"

We had just seen the last showing of *8½* at the Coronet and were walking back to Lizzie's house. It was snowing hard when we came out, and the streets were nearly empty. The lights on the marquee flicked off as we headed into the night. A few cars crawled by, making tracks that were instantly covered up. As we passed one of the big Victorian houses on Judson, Lizzie noticed a red cart in the yard. "I want a ride!" she cried. She romped through the snow and clambered in. "Pull me," she commanded. I harnessed myself to the handles and set off down the snowy street like a coolie, the cart's high wooden wheels creaking in the clear cold air. When I glanced back, Lizzie flung open her long fur coat. She was nude.

"I've always wondered how you got your clothes off so fast," I said.

"What makes you think I was wearing any? You were so involved in the movie you forgot to feel me up."

On the radio, Dick Biondi, the WLS d.j., said hello to about fifty people, and "My Boyfriend's Back" came on. "The Angels," I announced. "Nineteen sixty-four. The year *Herzog* was published." And I finally got laid.

It happened that summer. The summer of Blithedale Farm. Browsing in the classified pages of *The Saturday Review* during the spring of my junior year at Evanston high, I had come across an advertisement for a "liberal arts workshop" with "excellent recreational facilities and an emphasis on self-directed study." It was located in "the scenic Berkshires." I sent away for the brochure and showed it to my parents. "I never heard of a summer camp that required transcripts," my father grumbled, but when I pointed out the "cultural amenities within driving distance"—Tanglewood, Jacob's Pillow, the Lenox String Quartet—they let me go.

Owned by a couple of ex–Putney teachers who went around in baggy sweatshirts and believed that exposure to the elements builds character, Blithedale Farm consisted of a weathered farmhouse on a hill, a barn out back where the girls slept, and a big tent with bunk beds for the boys. On cold nights I lay in my narrow bunk and listened to the scratch of pine needles against the canvas as the wind whipped up the hill. For tuition of two thousand dollars a summer, we did all the chores ourselves: scything the field, washing dishes, swabbing out the latrine with ammonia. The only "free time" was an hour in the late afternoon, after Music and Drama; dinner was followed by compulsory Study Hall, held in all weather at two picnic tables on the porch. Lights out was at nine.

Blithedale was a small camp, and I mean small; there were only twelve of us. In the morning we gathered around a pot-bellied stove in the front room of the farmhouse for Creative Writing and a grueling seminar in The History of Western Ideas taught by a gaunt, ascetic-looking Yale divinity student named Lester Wayland. Every Monday he passed out copies of the text for the week, thin blue paperback editions of *The Communist Manifesto, On Liberty, Areopagitica*—hard going for a high school student who had trouble with the plot of *Silas Marner*. Night after night I crouched beneath the covers with a flashlight, struggling to make sense of the tiny print while rain dripped from the pine boughs above my head.

I couldn't figure out these books. For instance, Bentham. Utilitarianism was hard to grasp. It seemed obvious, but when Lester called on me, I'd get it all mixed up. If the end of society was to promote the greatest happiness of the greatest

number, what about the people who *weren't* happy? Did they
just put up with it? Sorry, guys. You lose. Hunched over the
little blue books on the porch after dinner, moths batting
against the screen, I could feel the wind through my Beethoven
sweatshirt. It was cold out there at night.

That Blithedale was coed had been one of its attractions,
but I couldn't get too excited about the girls. They were too
studious, too good. Like Jane Elliott, a fine-boned girl from
Greenwich, Connecticut, who sat on the front steps after dinner
with her guitar and sang "Michael Row the Boat Ashore." She
reminded me of the girls in my honors English class at Evanston, who donated blood to the Red Cross and waved their
hands as if they were shipwrecked on a desert island when
old Mrs. Gund asked what the gold mosaic stood for in "Sailing
to Byzantium." The only camper who interested me was Rhoda
Baumann, who chewed gum and doodled obliviously in class.
I could see that Chekhov left her cold, but her indifference
titillated me. Rhoda didn't worship in the church of literature.

I courted her with tireless intensity, walking her back to
the girls' dorm every night after study hall and reciting poems
that I thought would get her hot. " 'Come, my Celia, let us
prove,/While we may, the sports of love,' " I'd intone as we
made our slow way through the summer dark toward the bug-
smeared yellow lamp over the double doors of the barn. " 'The
grave's a fine and private place,/But none, I think, do there
embrace . . .' " Once, when she was going on about what a shit
her mother was, I tried Donne's " 'For Godsake hold your
tongue and let me love.' " Nothing doing. We necked until we
were red in the face, and one night, at a performance of *Who's
Afraid of Virginia Woolf?* at the Williamstown Theater, I even
got her to put her hand in my lap while George and Martha
were bickering onstage. But Rhoda hadn't come to Blithedale
to "fool around," she explained. She was there to learn. She

had flunked algebra twice at Great Neck High, and was de-
pending on a good recommendation from Mr. and Mrs. Hag-
erty, who ran the place.

These grappling sessions under the elm left me in a very
overheated state as I headed up the hill to the boys' tent, my
cock still hard, my flashlight bobbing in the dark. Out on the
road, Lester Wayland would be strolling in the moonlight with
the music teacher, Miss Tupelo, a sweet-voiced, high-collared
schoolteacher from Savannah who taught us hymns. My favorite was

> *In a harbour grene aslepe whereas I lay,*
> *The birds sang swete in the middes of the day,*
> *I dreamed fast of mirth and play:*
> *In youth is pleasure, in youth is pleasure.*

But was it? Sometimes when we sat in the parlor singing, Miss
Tupelo at the piano, hymnbooks open on our laps, I was so
homesick I could hardly stand it. I craved the beach down the
street from our house, going to 31 Flavors with my parents
after dinner, hanging around the pier with Judy Clark . . .
Anything but this intellectual boot camp.

One morning I got a letter from my friend Aaron Temkin.
He had gone out to San Francisco and found a room in the
Mission District through a notice on the bulletin board of the
City Lights bookstore. He was sharing "a big old Victorian
house" with a carpenter, a bluegrass musician, a waitress and
her three-year-old son; and he had made it with a girl on a
yacht moored in the Sausalito harbor:

> It was really strange. We met in this Mexican restaurant
> on Telegraph Avenue, and it was just so easy. She asked
> if she could sit down (this happens all the time out here)
> and we started talking and she invited me to come see her

boat. It's not hers really, she's just watching it for some people.

We went down in the hold and got undressed. It was amazing—the boat rocking under us, the stars out on the bay. I couldn't believe it was happening.

Lying on my bunk, I stared at Aaron's letter. He was getting laid in California while I was freezing my ass off on the Hagertys' porch composing villanelles. A change was happening in the land: that was the message of the new Dylan album on the radio. *The Freewheelin' Bob Dylan*. The one with Dylan on the cover walking down a snowy New York street, a laughing blond girl on his arm. In the background were tenements latticed with fire escapes. Dylan had on a chamois jacket and boots; his hands were stuck in the pockets of his blue jeans. ("What, no gloves?" my mother commented.) His real name was Bob Zimmerman, and he was from Hibbing, Minnesota. Now he lived in Greenwich Village, and had a last name that was the first name of a famous poet. He probably had lots of girl friends, and stayed up until all hours of the night jamming in nightclubs with old Negro bluesmen from Mississippi. What he didn't have was a mother who sniffed his head when he came home to see if he'd been smoking.

I was glad to get back to Evanston at the end of that summer. Slipping out to the pier to watch the sun come up, I sensed the approach of autumn. A chill rose off the dewy grass, the air was crisp, the waves out on the lake were subtly darker. *The New Yorker* was full of back-to-school ads: fresh-faced boys in pullovers and corduroys, Viyella shirts and shiny loafers. Soon it would be time to visit the Varsity Shop with my mother and pick out my fall wardrobe, then on to Chandler's for school supplies: gym shoes, an "athletic supporter," blue satin trunks and an orange Evanston T-shirt, a smock, a combination lock, a three-ring notebook with dividers, new textbooks with unbroken spines. I'd had enough of summer. I felt about school the way that guy Joseph in Bellow's *Dangling Man* feels when he gets drafted: "Long live regimentation!"

Sometimes when I went down to the pier at dawn, Ted Stansky would be there, smoking a cigarette. Ted was a year older than me, and lived in the building across the street. He had a talent for the saxophone. I had gone to hear him once at the Teutonia, a dance hall above a cocktail lounge on North Clark where you could buy wax cups of beer for a quarter without showing ID. Stooped over his horn beneath a spotlight, a black drummer flailing away behind him in the shadows, Ted was in another world. His eyes were shut, his wavy greaser's hair swept back in a pompadour. He stayed up all night; when I ran into him down at the pier at five o'clock in the morning, he'd be on his way home from some gig, and looking pretty wrecked.

Ted didn't give "a flying fuck" (as he put it) about school. The night before a big exam, he'd go down to Howard Street and shoot pool. He cut classes, and participated in no extracurricular activities. He had two punches on his driver's license for moving violations. He kept Trojans in his wallet, and showed up for biology once with a miniature bottle of Seagram's in his pocket; I could smell it on his breath.

Ted's girl friend, Debbie Podowsky, was as bad as he was. They fucked in movie theaters, in school washrooms, while she was sitting on his lap in the back of the Chicago Avenue bus. "So I show up at Debbie's," he reported one night, "and —you ready for this?" I wasn't sure. "She opens the door in her bathrobe and says she isn't finished dressing. So she goes upstairs and a few minutes later she calls down in this wheedly voice, 'I'm re-e-ady.' Only she doesn't come down. So I go out in the hall to see what's happening and she's standing at the top of the stairs in—get this—high heels, a garter belt, and these incredible black underpants open at the crotch. I mean, there it was." His eyes widened, conjuring the scene. "A twat." I stared out at the lake; there was a band of light on the horizon. My mouth was dry. An hour later I was on the phone to Rhoda Baumann in Great Neck, beating off while she told me how her dog died. "And then I heard the squeal of brakes, and this United Parcel truck . . ." *I'm re-e-ady.*

Late one night I was working at my desk when a pebble thudded against the window. I cranked open the louver and Aaron Temkin called up: "Come on out. We're going down to the pier." Sandals in hand, I crept past my parents' bedroom and slipped out the back door. It was after three; Forest Street was as shadowy and deserted as a country lane. Even the crickets had quieted down. Aaron and a girl were standing at the end of the driveway. She had on dirty tennis shorts and a billowy white blouse. Her hair was long and Indian-black. "Aaron!" I was glad to see him. "When did you get back?"

"Last night. But I almost didn't come back at all." His eyes shone with a kind of ecstatic intensity; Aaron was an excitable person, very passionate and easily moved. Our reunion was a momentous thing. "You should have been there. It was unbelievable." Tell me about it. All I had to show for the summer was a notebook full of haiku.

"This is Lizzie," Aaron said as we headed for the pier. "Did you get my letter?"

"Yes, I got your letter." Do I have to hear again about the girl in the boat? In front of this other girl? I suppose you're doing it with her, too. "You can't imagine what's happening out there! There were millions of kids from all over the country. You could sleep in the park, or people let you crash in their living rooms. Oh, and the best thing!" He grabbed my arm. "Like, every Sunday they had these free concerts in Golden Gate Park, and free dope, and these families with kids and dogs would show up, everyone just lying around on blankets in the sun and sharing everything they had, passing around big jugs of wine." Far out, Aaron.

Lizzie turned to me. "Aaron says you went to camp?"

"It wasn't a camp, really. It was this sort of school." Poets don't go to camp.

"Okay, school," said Lizzie, tossing her raven-colored hair. "So what kind of school?"

It was hard to explain, I said. We wrote poetry and studied the British philosophers and swabbed out the latrines, and then at the end of the summer we put on a production of *Oedipus Rex*.

"You do that in the summer?" Lizzie said incredulously. "I mean, like what do you do for fun?"

Fun? Who said anything about fun? "It was pretty interesting," I said. "I learned a lot." That Milton was against censorship; that Bentham believed in the greatest happiness of the greatest number; that Oedipus was unlucky.

On the pier, Aaron pulled out a small plastic bag filled with tiny twigs and olive-colored seeds. "A treat from Telegraph Avenue," he said, sprinkling a pinch of grass over a funnel of ZigZag paper. He ran his tongue along the gummed edge and rolled it up, twisting the fat cigarette at both ends.

"Yummy," Lizzie commented. I was looking around for the cops. They drove by often at this hour, shining a spotlight on the pier.

Aaron took a long pull that made the flame race over the paper and handed it to me. "What do I do?" I said nervously. "Smoke it like a cigarette?"

"You have to keep it in," he gasped, swallowing his syllables. I gulped the harsh smoke down until it burned my lungs. I could probably still get into that junior college in Wilmette when I was paroled. What was the name of it? My mother could bring me chicken soup in a thermos.

Lizzie sucked on the joint and handed it to me. "Want another toke?"

"A what?"

She gave me a curious look. "Haven't you ever done this before?"

I shook my head. "What's supposed to happen?"

"A beautiful experience," she said dreamily. "I've been stoned practically all summer. I love swimming in the moonlight stoned, and walking on the beach. Sometimes I even go to my analyst stoned."

"You should try fucking when you're stoned," Aaron said. Is that so. Who do you think you are? Henry Miller? He was a real bon vivant, this Aaron. He didn't make a big deal about being sensitive, though he clearly belonged among Stendhal's Happy Few. Slight and Semitic-eyed, with shiny black curls and a sensuous mouth, he was a great fan of Isaac Rosenfeld's novel about a bookish adolescent growing up in Chicago, *Passage from Home*. His mother, Francine, had actually known Rosenfeld; she was supposed to have dinner with him the night he dropped dead of a heart attack in a dank basement apartment on the Near North Side. He was only thirty-eight. Saul Bellow had come to see her once about Isaac, his closest friend since their Tuley High School days. He was writing a memoir and Francine had some of Isaac's letters. They spent the afternoon sorting through them, Francine in her old kimono, Bellow in hundred-dollar loafers and a gray plaid suit from Savile Row. He was sitting at the kitchen table when Aaron got home from school, a small man with soulful eyes and a head of silky white hair. His fedora was beside him on the table. Bellow's hat.

Once Francine discovered that I had read *Passage from*

Home, she would answer the door whenever I came over and talk to me about Isaac. "He was such a remarkable man," she rasped in her two-pack-a-day voice. "Did Aaron tell you? I was supposed to see him on the night he died."

Aaron's father, Herb, was impatient with these reminiscences. An accountant for one of the big law firms on Wacker Drive, he didn't see what all the fuss was about. "Not Isaac again," he said in a weary voice, looking up from the *Sun-Times*. "If he was so great, how come nobody's ever heard of him?"

"Oh, Herb!" Francine protested. "How can you say that?" She looked as if she was about to cry. "He *was* a great man! Saul Bellow's writing a whole book about him."

Aaron hurried me past his mother and closed the door. "I have Isaac's letters here, if you want to see them," she called plaintively up the stairs.

Aaron wasn't obsessed with culture the way I was. He didn't write poetry, he didn't paint, he didn't play a musical instrument. But he had an artistic temperament—what my Grandma Rose called "soul." When we listened to records in his room, especially an album of Peruvian folk songs that enchanted him with their mournful piping of wooden flutes, he would pace up and down with a rapturous look on his face. One January night when we were driving to Chicago in a snowstorm, he gazed out at the whitening blur on Lake Shore Drive and cried, "I love being alive!"

Aaron admired *A Portrait of the Artist* as much as I did, but he was more the D. H. Lawrence type. While I sat hunched over my notebook, *Roget's Thesaurus* beside me on the desk, he and Lizzie were out cruising around, a joint in the glove compartment and Aretha Franklin on the radio, turned up loud. It was summer and they were seventeen.

The pier gave off a clammy scent of cold concrete. The boulders piled up in a seawall had a chalky whiteness like bone. Across the water, the cast-iron lamps on Sheridan Road glimmered in the hazy night. I studied Lizzie as she sat on the end of the pier kicking her legs. She was smoking a cigarette, her head thrown back, her eyes half-closed. Her skin in the moonlight had a mulatto sheen that looked even darker against her creamy peasant blouse. The top two buttons were undone, and I could see her breasts beneath the gauzy cloth; she wasn't wearing a bra. Her kohl eyebrows, swirling hair, tea-colored skin gave evidence of ancient origins, some early Mediterranean race. Where did Aaron find these girls?

"Feel anything?" he said.

"I'm not sure. How do you know when you're stoned?"

"You'll know," Aaron said, but I had no idea whether the exaltation I felt was from grass or from sitting next to Lizzie. "It's like an orgasm of the head," he explained. "We were listening to 'Good Vibrations' on the way over? And it just went on and on, and every time you think it's over some incredible new thing happens. Like that eerie wail that comes at the end?" He gave a falsetto Beach Boys whoop.

"Only dogs can hear it," Lizzie said.

"Dogs 'n Suds," Aaron giggled.

"My favorite drive-in," Lizzie said. "I like the way they bring your order on a tray and hook it on the window." She looked over at me. "Well?"

"You are getting sto-oned," Aaron chanted, waving his fingers like a hypnotist. "When I snap my fingers you will be stoned."

Was I or wasn't I? Even turning on was a production. The moonlight on the water was a shimmering silver trail that rose and dipped in the waves; but did it look any different than usual? It was hard to get stoned when you were worrying about whether your poetry was any good and why you hadn't gone to California and gotten laid and whether your parents would wake up and find out you weren't home in bed.

The sky was lightening over the lake and birds were beginning to chirp in the park as we walked back to Aaron's car. "Write well," said Lizzie, and they drove off in the dawn. I stood in the driveway inhaling the moist odor of roses and soil. I loved this hour, before the traffic started and exhaust hung over Sheridan Road; the air had a balmy freshness that reminded me of what it was like to step off a plane in Miami in the middle of winter. Too bad you couldn't get that kind of happiness into poetry.

A few days later, Lizzie called and invited me up to Circle Pines, a camp in Michigan where "progressive" Jewish families rented cabins, played volleyball, and rowed on the lake. She was there by herself, and needed company.

"But aren't you and Aaron . . . ?"

"We're just friends. Come. It'll be fun."

Hurrying through the Greyhound bus station on Randolph, a canvas backpack slung over my shoulder, I was in a state of high excitement. On the Indiana Turnpike, I gazed through the tinted glass with an exalted eye, as responsive to the flaring furnaces of Gary, the silvery tanks and twisting pipes of gasworks, the flames wavering palely above blackened smokestacks like gigantic Bunsen burners, the junkyards and truck stops, as a landscape painter contemplating some bucolic valley. I lit a foul Gauloise and opened my book—Sartre's autobiography, *The Words*—but I was too elated to read.

I got off in Grand Rapids, its wide main street deserted in the middle of the afternoon. Sweating in the heat, I walked out to the highway and waited for a ride. There was a new curb where the road had been widened, and a shoulder of tar-coated pebbles that glistened in the sun. A pickup truck whipped by, deepening the silence, then a big-finned Chevrolet, chrome flashing in the sun. A few hundred yards ahead, it slowed to a stop, its red taillights glowing like embers, and backed up in a hurried swerve. There were three girls in the front seat. I flung my pack in the back and slipped in beside it, inhaling a musky scent. The girl by the window turned around and looked me over. "Where ya going?" she said in a bored voice.

"Circle Pines?"

"I know where it is," said the driver, a fat girl in a mesh visored cap. She reached for a pack of Camels on the dashboard. "Just beyond the dairy farm. We're going right past it."

I studied the neck of the girl in the middle; her cornsilk hair was clamped in a blue barrette. She was staring at me in the rearview mirror. The driver leaned her elbow out the window, cradling the wheel one-handed. On the radio, the Chiffons sang "He's So Fine" in those little-girl voices of theirs. A maddening odor of perfume and sweat, warm vinyl and cigarette smoke filled the car. It was all I could do not to reach over and put my arms around the row of girls up front, burying my face in the middle one's sunburned neck. Maybe they would invite me home with them to some trailer on a back road, the yard littered with old refrigerators and rusted cars, and let me fuck them one at a time—or even all at once, crouching over the fat one while she sucked off the one with the barrette and the other one watched. If Henry Miller could have two girls, why couldn't I have three?

The car slowed down by a sign that said CIRCLE PINES in birch-bark letters, and I ducked out the door with my pack. "By-y," the girls called in a mocking chorus. The Chevy's wheels spun on the shoulder, spewing gravel, and a warm blast from the exhaust pipe brushed against my legs. The driver waved a fluttering farewell as they sped off down the road.

Walking up a dirt lane through the trees, I came to a clearing where a volleyball game was in progress. The players, bearded men with wire-rimmed glasses and pale-looking women with their hair wrapped in bandannas, seemed out of place up here in the woods; they were the kind of people who showed up at peace rallies in Lincoln Park. Lizzie was standing on the sidelines, dressed for the city in baggy hussar's trousers and a Mexican blouse with puffy sleeves. She hurried across the lawn and flung her arms around me. "I didn't think you'd come!" Incredible: she was as needy as I was, even if she did have screaming arguments with her parents and get thrown out of school for smoking in the washroom.

"I wanted to see you."

"I'm glad," she said, taking me by the hand. "You're just in time for dinner." We strolled across the playing field toward a low-screened building. Through an open door I could see white-uniformed cooks moving about the kitchen amid the clatter of dishes. Within were two rows of refectory tables crowded with chattering families—a Camp Shewahmegon for grownups. We got our trays and moved through the line, helping ourselves to fish sticks and salad, wedges of pie on paper plates and iced tea from a dispenser. "I feel like I'm eleven years old again," I said, gathering up a handful of silverware. "Only at the summer camp I went to you had to finish everything on your tray. I gagged on a bowl of cottage cheese and called my mom in tears. She told them to lay off."

"You don't have to clean your plate here, but if you do, you might get a prize."

"Oh, yeah? What? As much bug juice as I can drink?"

"You'll see." Lizzie smiled. "How did you remember about bug juice? I've never met a seventeen-year-old who lived so much in the past. What did you do before you had any memories?"

"I lived in the world of Babar the Elephant."

We sat down at a table by the window. It was getting dark, and the lamps on the porch had come on, filling the night with a soft yellow glow. There was a chill in the air—the end of summer, when the grass turned shiny and the night sky shone clear. Lizzie pushed aside her tray and lit a cigarette, snuffing the match out with a flick of her wrist. "How long are you staying?" she said.

"Actually, I should probably go back tomorow. I'm in the middle of this poem . . ."

She gave me a queer, appraising look. "Where'd you get this idea of being a writer? I mean, you're really fanatical about it."

What makes Sammy type? "I don't know. I guess when you feel really intensely about something you just want to write it down. You know, like, capture the experience."

"But why do you have to capture it? Why can't you just live it?" Lizzie said. "Like, when I'm throwing a pot or doing batik, I never think about what other people will think of it. I'm just doing it for myself, because I feel like it."

"You think writing a poem is like making ashtrays?" I protested.

"Oh, so what I do isn't art?"

"I didn't say that." Or did I? There was no pottery column in *Partisan Review*. "But I mean, admit they're not the same. There's art, and then there's arts and crafts."

"Where do you *get* these ideas?" She reached over and ran her fingernails up and down my arm. "You are one weird boy."

"If your father read aloud to you from *Ulysses* every night you'd be a little weird yourself."

Lizzie gazed at me with her olive eyes. "He really did that?"

"He still does. He's only up to 'Oxen of the Sun.' " *Agenbite of inwit, epiphany, ineluctable modalities of the visible*: these Joycean phrases were as familiar around our house as *Winston tastes good like a cigarette should* was to the Stanskys sitting in front of their TV across the street. "Listen to this!" my father would cry from his Herman Miller chair, the heavy novel open on his lap.

My mother's head shot up from her elementary French textbook. "I'm trying to concentrate, William."

"One paragraph," my father pleaded. "He's at Paddy Dignam's funeral." Who could argue? It gave him such pleasure to recite that lovely prose. My mother closed her textbook with a sigh and took up her knitting. Sprawled on the couch with an Eskimo Pie, I listened to Leopold Bloom ruminate about burial rites:

> Only a mother and deadborn child ever buried in the one coffin. I see what it means. I see. To protect him as long as possible even in the earth. The Irishman's house is his coffin. Embalming in catacombs, mummies, the same idea.

I could see why Bloom appealed to my father. For one thing, they both liked music; and they were both lonely men, very inward and ruminative and without a lot of friends. Men in search of a son—though my father's was right across the hall. Sometimes he would knock and come in while I was at my desk reading, and I could sense that he wanted something—I wish I'd known what. He would sit on the bed and gaze at me with a look of wonder in his eye, an artist contemplating one of his own half-finished works. But is it art? Or maybe he was just looking for company. Once, we were driving up to Wisconsin somewhere on vacation and stopped for gas, and as we stood side by side at the urinal, my mother waiting in the car, I thought of that scene where Bloom and Stephen step out into the garden of Bloom's house beneath the stars for a companionable whiz. The damp ammonia scent of the men's room, my father and I staring at the cinderblock wall, not talking but somehow, in that moment, happy . . .

"I thought he was a doctor," Lizzie said.

"He is, but he's hung up on books. The first thing he does

when he gets home from work is sit down with the latest issue
of *Encounter* and go wild over some interview with C. P.
Snow."

"Listen, my father doesn't even read. All he cares about is
raising money for SANE."

These liberal households were tough on kids. How could
you rebel against parents who were so good? They had cornered the market in decency. "My parents are big liberals,
too," I commiserated. "They won't even let me watch *Amos 'n
Andy*."

"At least they care what you do. Mine don't give a shit."

You mean they don't buy up your first oil painting for
twenty dollars and rush it off to the framer's? They don't
complain to your English teacher on Parents' Night that you
were "devastated" by your semester grade? ("B+? He gave
you a B+ for that beautiful paper on *The Old Man and the
Sea*?") They don't drive fifty miles to watch you lose in the
first round of the Hinsdale Junior Open, then take you out to
dinner at Hackney's, your favorite restaurant in the world,
famous for its giant hamburgers on pumpernickel, as a "con-
solation prize"? Families like Lizzie's I'd read about in
Dickens. Her parents didn't give a shit: she might as well have
told me they kept her chained in the cellar.

"God, mine are like a pair of private eyes. They trail me
everywhere. I get out of the shower and my mother hands me
a fresh towel."

Lizzie grabbed my wrist to silence me. "Let's go," she said.

My heart was leaping furiously as I followed her out of
the dining room. We groped down a dark trail, tripping over
roots, until we came to a cabin deep in the woods. I could
make out four bunk-beds in the moonlight. "A whole house
just for us," said Lizzie. She reached beneath her arms as if
embracing herself and pulled off her blouse. "What are you
standing around for? Don't you want to play doctor?"

I undid my shoes, unbuckled my belt, and stepped out of my pants. Just like gym class. Lizzie flung back the sheet and climbed into one of the lower berths. "Come on in, my baby."

I hesitated. Should I go get the condom in my pack?

"You don't need anything," Lizzie said firmly. "Just get in."

I lay down beside her on the narrow cot. It was a shock, after so much fanatical conjecture, to finally see it: the rounded breasts, the wine-dark nipples, the shadowy thatch below. I put my hand between her legs and worked a finger in. It was wet! Maybe not "sopping," not as hot as a Bessemer steel furnace, but definitely wet.

"God, you're sweaty," Lizzie said. It was a cool night, but I was perspiring as if I had a fever. She got on top of me, reached behind her as if she was unfastening the catch on a skirt, and slipped my cock inside. The heat was enveloping, intense. Lizzie moved slowly up and down, pushing against my chest. Beyond the screen, crickets filled the air with their one repetitive note. A squirrel scampered over the roof, scrabbling for a hold. Lizzie peered intently down at me, her long black hair lightly brushing my face. I put my hands on her breasts, surprised by the sudden pinchy rush in my groin. "Not yet," she muttered, but it was too late. Pinned beneath her, I could feel myself beginning to go limp. Lizzie sighed and collapsed on my chest. "You have to learn to wait," she said.

Up ahead, a sign bordered with pulsing lights announced: PARADISE MOTEL TV IN EV RY ROOM. In the parking lot I noticed a pickup truck, a dusty Buick with Iowa plates, and lots of cars from Illinois.

"This is it," said Lizzie.

"Why would so many people who live in Illinois be staying here?"

She stared at me. "Think about it."

I hesitated at the office door, but Lizzie motioned me inside. A girl in a Cubs T-shirt was leaning against the check-in counter leafing through a magazine. "Do you have any rooms available?" I said, looking her in the eye. "It's for my wife and me."

The girl shoved a registration form at me. "What's your license number?"

My license number? Uh-oh. They'd trace the car to my father. Reported stolen. Hertz phones up in the middle of the night. My father stands there in his robe, old Sophie still warm in the earth. Cupping the phone, he asks my mother: "Could Ben have gone to a motel?" "He said he was going to visit a friend." "What would he be doing in a motel at a time like this?" Then, to the Hertz clerk: "No, he couldn't be there. It must be stolen. You see, his grandmother died this morning . . ."

"It's for the maid," the girl at the counter said.

"The maid?"

"The license number. So they'll know when it's okay to clean the room."

"Oh." I finished filling out the registration form: Mr. and Mrs. Thomas Eliot of Batavia, Illinois.

"That's twenty-six dollars," the girl said. She handed me a key and I hurried out to the car.

Our room had a queen-size bed and an olive motif: olive bedspreads, olive carpeting, two olive-upholstered chairs. There was a television on the bureau and a framed drawing of an old Model T Ford on the wall. Lizzie went into the bathroom and I turned on the TV. A gaunt figure was perched on a parapet, his cape flapping in the wind, while a crowd dressed in togas milled around in the plaza below, shouting, "Fly, Simon, fly!" Simon hesitated, then leaped through the air and plunged to the ground.

Through a gap in the curtains I could see the cars outside,

bathed in yellow light from the globed lamps over the doors. Suddenly I remembered a time when I was nine years old and had stayed home from school with the flu, and how whenever I got up to go to the bathroom I would put on a pair of Norwegian sealskin slippers with curling toes that my mother had ordered from some kids' store in Yarmouth, Maine, through a *New Yorker* ad, and how I huddled feverish and shivering beneath the afghan my Grandma Sophie had crocheted, a glass of apple juice on top of the clock-radio, a pile of *Highlights* magazines on the llama-skin rug. Every hour or so my mother would tiptoe in and lay a cool hand on my sweaty brow to see how my temperature was. That achy, tremulous feeling you got with a fever, drifting in and out of sleep while night began to fall and I waited for my father to come home . . . It made me sad to think about it.

It was still dark when we pulled out of the parking lot and headed toward Evanston. Touhy was nearly empty of traffic. The few cars out on the road had an ominous look about them—old beat-up Fords and Buicks with noisy mufflers trailing acrid fumes. What kind of person would be out driving around at four o'clock in the morning?

The air on Touhy was stale from truck exhaust, but on the side streets of Evanston it was mild and summery, and blew in the windows with a rhythmic swish as we drove past orderly rows of elms. I glanced over at Lizzie; she looked so . . . normal. She had changed to a summery white dress with straps; I still had on the suit I'd worn to the funeral. It was a little the worse for wear by now, but it made me feel grownup. We looked like a couple on the way home from a country club dance.

"I wish I'd taken you to the prom," I said. "Instead of Sharon Kolb." It would have been nice to do all that ordinary high school stuff: going to football games and dances and Halloween parties instead of hanging out at the Hut scoring dope off spades with names like Pop and Shaky.

"That wasn't your style. You liked to pretend you were a regular guy, going to sock hops at the Y, then skulking over for a quick fuck. Good Ben and Bad Ben."

"Now I'm just Bad Ben," I said glumly. "Going to the Mayfair Motel on the night of my grandmother's funeral."

"You're not so bad," Lizzie said, patting me on the arm. "You're celebrating life in the face of death."

Right. I'm celebrating life. Twelve hours after I watched them put old Sophie in her grave, the black casket lying in the wet, crumbly earth like buried treasure, I was in a motel room on Touhy Avenue, crouched over Lizzie Sherman like a dog. What was that line in *The Trial*? *"Like a dog,"* Joseph K. thinks as the guard slits his throat. *"It was as if the shame of it would outlive him."*

I dropped Lizzie off and turned up Sheridan Road toward Sophie's. It was just beginning to get light. The stars were still out, but the sky was turning blue, and the streetlights shone palely in the dawn. In the stillness, I could hear the buzz of wires overhead. Waiting at a light, I inhaled the bland, cleansing air off the lake, glad to be home—even if it wasn't home anymore. It was where I used to live.

Sheridan Road was empty. I sped past the cemetery that divided Evanston and Chicago—more dead!—and whipped around the turn by the Standard station. I glanced at the speedometer: it was wavering at forty-five. A whooping siren split the air. Fuck. Just what I needed. I slowed down as a white-and-blue squad car pulled up behind me, its flasher whirling. Too late, I noticed the bottle of Dewar's on the seat beside me. I reached down to stash it beneath the seat, but the cop was at the window, peering in. He had a swollen nose seamed with tiny red veins like a shrimp, and dull papery skin. His knuckles were cracked and raw.

"Whatcha got there?" he said, beckoning with a thick finger.

"What do you mean?"

He grabbed my wrist. "On the floor, asshole. Don't fuck around."

I retrieved the bottle and handed it to him.

"Looks like you been havin' a good time." He leaned down and rested his hands on the window, like a neighbor chatting over a fence. "License?"

I fumbled for my wallet with trembling hands.

The cop studied it. "Why the rented car, Ben? This is a local address." I could feel his meaty breath on my face.

"Well, I don't actually live around here anymore. I mean, I was here for my grandmother's funeral and . . ."

"Get out of the car, Ben, and put your hands on the roof."

I leaned against the Pinto. The air was fresh and damp. The cop was frisking me when suddenly a pain shot through my groin; he was squeezing my balls. I jerked my arm reflexively, and elbowed him in the stomach. Before I knew what was happening, he'd locked his hands around my head and smashed it down on the hood of the car. I heard my glasses crunch, and then—oh god—my bowels gave way. I'd shit my pants.

"Did anybody tell you to move, Ben?" the cop said in my ear. His voice was calm and reasonable—my geometry teacher, Mr. Wachter, correcting a proof. He pinned my arms behind my back, snapped handcuffs on, and pushed me toward the squad car.

It was light now. Up ahead the huge Standard Oil sign blinked in the dawn, without my glasses a blur of red, white, and blue. The cop shoved me in the back seat and got in on the passenger side. His partner, behind the wheel, turned around and studied me through the metal grille. "You smell somp'un?" he said.

The other cop sniffed. "You know what, Ben?" he said. "You need a bath. Ain't you got no respeck for your grandma?" He turned to the driver. "His grandma died," he explained.

The driver shook his head. "Gus," he addressed his partner, "that is one sad story. Hey, Chuck," he called back to me. "Sorry about your grandma."

"My name is Ben," I corrected him.

"Your name is doodle-squat," Gus said.

Who could argue? As we drove through the quiet morning streets, I nearly gagged on the sour smell of diarrhea. The handcuffs chafed my wrists. My glasses were on Sheridan Road. Now I'd done it. Here was authentic *tsouris*. My good-boy neighbor Wally Pinsker would never land himself in a mess like this. He was a junior Phi Bete. When *his* grandmother died, he probably went home with his parents and sat around in his blue *bar mitzvah* suit drinking ginger ale. "Making nice," grandma Sophie called it. And when everyone went home, and Wally's parents were in bed, he'd clean up the dishes, empty the nut bowls—anything but go fuck a girl in a motel, get busted by the cops, and call up from the Jarvis Avenue lock-up with a load of shit in his pants, rousing his grief-stricken father from bed to make bail. How about that, Dad? But listen, don't get mad at me, okay? I'm a poet. Anyway, this is nothing. Verlaine shot Rimbaud. In the stomach. He nearly died.

The squad car pulled into a parking lot behind the station. Gus got out, pulled open my door, and yanked me out of the back seat. He didn't have a light touch. Marching me up the stairs, he gripped me by the armpit and nearly lifted me off my feet.

The sergeant, a bald man with heavy-lidded eyes, gazed down from a table on a raised platform.

"Drunken driving and resisting arrest," said Gus. "He was speeding on Sheridan Road. We found a bottle in the car."

"Resisting arrest?" inquired the sergeant, looking me up

and down. Gus must have been over six feet tall, and twice my weight.

"He tried to break away while I was frisking him."

"That's ridiculous," I protested. "You molested me."

"Shut up, fuck. You'll get your day in court."

The sergeant made some notes on a pad, and pushed a buzzer on his desk. An old black man in a janitor's uniform came up. His stiff Brillo hair was cottony white. He led me into a room with cinderblock walls and told me to empty my pockets. I laid my watch, my wallet, my keys and change on a table. He pushed the change back, put the rest in a plastic bag, and motioned me to follow. Keys clanking, he shuffled down the hall with rheumy eyes, clutching my elbow tenderly like a father leading his bride up the aisle. At the end of the corridor was a steel door with a tiny barred window. He sorted through his keys with maddening deliberation, humming "Swing Low, Sweet Chariot" under his breath as he tried one wrong key after another. "Wheah dat key?" he muttered. Finally he found what he was looking for, and the heavy door swung open.

"You get one call," he said, pointing to a pay phone on the wall. I fished out a dime and dialled Sophie's number.

"Ben!" my father cried. "Where the hell have you been?"

At the Paradise Motel, Dad, eating Lizzie Sherman's cunt. "Oh, Dad," I sobbed. "I messed up. I did a terrible thing."

"What is it?" he said in alarm.

"Something terrible." When he found out I hadn't murdered eight nurses like Richard Speck he'd be relieved. "I'm in jail." I blurted out my story between sobs.

"I'll be right down."

The guard ushered me into a cell and slammed the door. I had nothing to read. My father never went anywhere without a book. He disdained people who stood in line at banks "staring at the walls." Waiting at the checkout counter of Whitney's

Market, he'd whip out a paperback of *Either/Or*. His son was empty-handed. Nothing to do but sit in his own shit. I took off my pants and tossed my soiled underwear in a corner. Not even a handkerchief to clean myself off. My father had a drawerful of monogrammed hankies: WJ.

The cell stank of urine, and of something worse. Decay? Vomit? Death? But who was I to complain? My Jockey briefs made their own contribution to the fetid air. The toilet stood like an ancient cistern in the corner. It didn't flush; there was no handle, no tank, just a discolored porcelain bowl. The bed was a metal plank chained to the wall. The only light came from a caged bulb in the corridor.

"What chu in for?" I peered across the hall. A young black stared back at me, his eyes white in the gloom.

"A traffic violation," I said. "Speeding."

"They put chu in the slam for dat?"

"Sort of. What about you?"

"I didn' do nuffin!" he answered vehemently. "I was in the *wrong* place at the *wrong* time. Get in my buddy's car, he pulls up to the curb, and goes inna liquor store. How'd I know he was gonna stick it up?" He raised his hand. "Swear to god, man."

I heard the door creak open down the hall, and a minute later the old guard appeared. "Hey, man, gimme twenny dollahs, huh," the boy pleaded. "I on'y need twenny more dollars to get sprung." His eyes were tearful, pleading.

"I really wish I could help you," I said. "But I just don't have it."

"Oh, man," he moaned. "My papa's gonna whup my ass." Yeah? Mine's going to suggest that my arrest was kafkaesque.

The heavy metal door swung open, and there was my father in his brown wool suit. He looked exhausted. He came up to me and laid a hand on my brow as if I were a fevered child. "Are you all right, Sonny?"

"I'm okay. Now what?" I looked for a sign of anger in his eyes, but saw only deep anxiety.

"They're dropping charges. I talked to the sergeant. A fine man, by the way. When I told him you were a poet, he was very impressed."

Maybe I should show *him* my Wordsworth paper.

"Where are your glasses?" my father said.

"They got lost in the scuffle." Suddenly I remembered the boy in the cell. "Dad, there's this kid who got locked up, and he only needs twenty more dollars to get out. Could we loan it to him?"

My father sighed and reached for his wallet. It was thick with bills. I wondered if my wallet would ever be so thick. I was always short of cash. I went up to the sergeant and gave him the twenty, explaining who it was for. "You're throwing it away," he said. I scrawled my name and address on a piece of paper. "That boy ain't goin' nowhere."

It was mid-morning when we came out of the station. Birds chirped in the trees, and the sun beat down on the asphalt parking lot. A cab was waiting at the bottom of the steps. We got in the back. My father wrinkled his nose and sniffed. "I threw up," I explained. "That cop was really rough on me."

"What did you do to him?"

"I didn't do anything," I said angrily. "He grabbed my crotch, and before I knew it he was bashing my head against the car."

"That's horrible." He looked concerned. "It reminds me of that scene in *Crime and Punishment* when Raskolnikov gets arrested . . ."

"I read it, Dad." It's a little early in the day for a seminar on the nineteenth-century Russian novel.

"Your mother and I were worried," he said as we settled back in the cab.

You were, huh? That was the whole idea. But can't you come

up with anything better than *worried*? I mean, you're not gonna get mad? Not even a little? What do I have to do before you notice that I'm, uh, having a hard time? Shoot heroin? You could go to Harvard and still fuck up. I read the alumni magazine: there were guys in every class reported lost. I even knew one, a guy I'd gotten in a conversation with at Cronin's one night. He was tossing back boilermakers. A desk clerk at the Sheraton Commander. Class of '31. His father had been a classics professor at Boston College. He never even graduated. A drinker. It happened. Even to people who grew up in houses with Aristotle's *Poetics* on the shelf.

I stared out the window at the apartment houses of Rogers Park, clay- and burgundy-brick, with concrete courtyards. Without my glasses, I could hardly make out where we were. "Is Mom upset?" I said.

"She was until you called. I told her it was a misunderstanding." He paused. "*The Misunderstanding.* Isn't that the name of a book by Camus?"

The cab dropped us off on Sheridan, where the Pinto sat by the curb. We drove back to Sophie's in silence. I hadn't read Camus.

My mother was asleep when we came in. There were crates and boxes piled up everywhere. Paintings were stacked against the piano bench. You could see where they'd hung on the walls by the squares of lighter paint.

III

Two days after Sophie's funeral, my parents had an open house and sold her things. Strangers tromped through the apartment inspecting the table where we'd sat at Sunday dinner, the glass cupboard with the ivory collection, the plump old sofa. The woman who'd arranged the sale, a chain-smoking, harried antique dealer in the neighborhood, kept a vigilant eye on the crowd, but some people tried to make off with stuff anyway, hurrying past the card table she'd set up by the door. I saw one furtive-looking guy slip an enameled cigarette case in the pocket of his windbreaker, but I didn't have the heart to say anything. It was too depressing. Even the beds were carried off.

We stayed with Harold and Edna that night, but my parents were eager to get back to California. I had a summer job as a manuscript reader for *Poetry* magazine, and after I saw them off I moved down to the North Side, where one of my Evanston friends, Herbert Lowy, had an apartment. A composer who was studying at Roosevelt University down in the Loop, Herbert lived in a ground-floor apartment on Sheffield, west of the elevated tracks, a neighborhood of wooden houses layered over with aluminum siding or brick-patterned tarpaper, the scruffy yards enclosed by waist-high cyclone fences. The kitchen looked out on a dense fretwork of laundry lines and creosote-stained telephone poles.

Herbert's apartment was willfully minimal; the walls were hospital green, the linoleum floors high school brown, the windows spotted with grime. The only furniture was a card table littered with Herbert's scores and monographs, an upright piano, two mattresses, a few folding chairs, and bookshelves constructed from raw planks propped up on cinderblocks. The kitchen was never used; the paint-specked sink had a bone-dry look about it. Swollen clots of ice bulged from the freezer compartment of the refrigerator. Just visible beneath the crust was a package of Green Giant peas. There was nothing on the shelves but a box of Domino sugar and a jar of freeze-dried coffee. Herbert took all his meals at the Victoria Restaurant, a coffee shop beneath the Belmont elevated tracks. "It gives me an excuse to go out," he explained.

The son of a dentist in Evanston, Herbert reminded me of the urban poor I'd read about in *The Other America*: he didn't have a phone (until I arrived on the scene), never got any mail, and slept late to avoid a meal. Dr. Lowy lived in one of those stolid old buildings on Sheridan Road with a marble foyer and a sun porch overlooking Lake Michigan, but Herbert was a Marxist. Money was "shit." (When I told him I was reading Michel Foucault's *The Order of Things* he scoffed, "You mean *The Ordure of Things*.") In his cheap brown slacks and ivory short-sleeved shirts from a discount men's wear outlet on Belmont, Herbert looked more like a storefront insurance salesman than a composer. He was an "internal émigré," as he put it, an heir of Isaac Babel, Walter Benjamin, E. M. Cioran—victims in one way or another of our totalitarian century. Cesare Pavese, a suicide; Osip Mandelstam, dead in a Soviet labor camp; Guillaume Apollinaire, fatally wounded in the trenches during World War I: these were Herbert's representative men. Hunched over the card table in the front parlor, fists clenched, a cigarette burning in a tin ashtray by his side, he read "in order to survive." North Sheffield was exile. "Chicago is meteorologically and topographically identical with certain regions of Central Siberia," he had written me the previous winter, offering me what he called my "poet's daily dose of transfiguration." "The city really becomes itself in winter. Only then does the inner torture of its inhabitants find confirmation in the weather." Shivering in his overcoat beside a porcelain-glazed gas stove, Herbert was as far from his father's cheerful office in the Old Orchard Shopping Plaza, with its piped-in Muzak and tinsel-decorated waiting room, as a dissident hauling wood in a Siberian penal colony.

Herbert was always trying to draw me into discussions of "the means and the mode of production," the "early" and the "late" Marx. "Read this, so we can discuss it," he would say, handing me Trotsky's *Literature and Revolution* or some essay by T. W. Adorno in *New Left Review.* I shut my ears to the tinny Latin music blaring from the juke box in the El Lago Club across the street, the landlady's television rumbling overhead, the kids yelling in the alley—"Louie! Hey, Louie! Where the fuck's my bike?" "On the back porch where it always is, asshole!"—and applied myself to dialectics as if I were cramming for an exam.

By the time I'd gotten through one of these assignments, Herbert invariably had some new enthusiasm. "I'm beginning to see how wrong Lukács was about so many things," he announced after I'd struggled through four hundred pages of *History and Class-Consciousness.* "You really have to read Gadamer to know what's up." The year before he'd sent me an album called *The Real Bahamas in Music & Song.* "This ought to get you through the Cambridge winter." For months the vibrations of steel drums and exuberant voices singing "Yellow Bird" filled my room in Dunster House. But when I arrived home for Christmas babbling about how great Calypso was, he gave me a peculiar look and put on his latest find: Bulgarian folk music.

Why did Herbert subject me to this rigorous course of study? To root out my reactionary impulses. "Saw your poem in *Poetry*," he acknowledged at the bottom of a nine-page letter devoted to the problems of composing twelve-tone music in "our late-capitalist moment." "If you are a poet, I hope you can use language not just as it is, an oily lubricant for the frictionless working of the system." He had no patience for my nostalgic family poems ("My heart simmered with angry love/Like chicken soup on grandma's stove"). "Why don't you write about North Vietnamese peasantry?" he suggested. "How they live and work the fields, the satisfaction they must experience in such a unified and just effort. Or the joy of a group of villagers who've just shot down an American plane."

Herbert was right. My poems didn't have a whole lot to do with the class struggle shaping up right outside my window, where sirens shrieked and warbled in the humid night and the blue flashers of squad cars accelerating up Sheffield flitted past our open door. This was Amerika, 1968.

"Listen to this," Herbert said one sweltering night when the Puerto Ricans were drag-racing up and down the street, their tuned-up engines splintering the air like a chain saw. Seated across from him at the wobbly table, I was working on a new poem, "The song of a lover who loves his death/And sees the few years as the long." "*Señor Ministre de Salud,*" he recited in a stern dictatorial voice. "*¿Qué hacer? Ah, muchisimo que hacer.*"

"What's it mean?"

He squinted at me through the smoke of his cigarette. "They don't teach you things like that at Harvard? 'Too much. There's too much to do.' It's a poem by Vallejo that I set to music: 'Manifesto for Woodwinds and Voices.' " He went over to the piano and played a few notes that sounded as if a cat were scampering over the keyboard. "That's the oboe," Herbert explained, "and then a bassoon comes in . . ." He pounded out a thunderous chord. "Defiant, bitter, furious. Followed by a chorus of a hundred mournful women." He sang in a piping voice, " 'Too much to do.' They're supposed to sound imploring: 'What can you do for the revolution?' "

"You really think you could get a hundred mournful women?"

"Sure. Mahler scored his Tenth Symphony for a thousand voices. A hundred's nothing."

A lot of the books Herbert gave me to read were on permanent loan from one library or another, the embossed frontispiece sliced out with a razor and the call numbers on the spine effaced. ("I'm just protecting a genius from the barbarians in my analysis class," he said of some Schoenberg scores he had appropriated.) The pages were heavily underlined, the margins crammed with annotations: "In other words, the form is ideally an index (i.e., the existential bond) of the content." "Today's aural time is a humming interrupted by noise. It is alien. Time as we know it, historically and biographically, has been destroyed."

This dense theoretical atmosphere, invigorating as it was, had a dampening effect on my love life. "Who *is* that person?" Lizzie said the first time she came over. We were lying on the mattress in my bedroom, an alcove separated from the parlor by a burlap curtain. "I mean, does he just sit there reading all the time?"

"He goes out," I said in Herbert's defense. His black-rimmed glasses and oxford shoes belied a romantic intensity that appealed to the flutists and English majors he picked up at the library. Smallish and dark-bearded, he had the old-fashioned manners of a Weimar intellectual; his line with girls was to ask them out for "coffee and talk." On the rare occasions when he brought one home, he would read aloud from Kafka's

Journals or put on some bewildering piece by Stockhausen, a storm of electronic noise that made the windows vibrate. They didn't stay long.

Maureen, the waitress on the day shift at the Victoria Restaurant, was a real city girl. Hefty and double-chinned, she leaned against the counter smoking. Her white uniform was spotted, her skin pearly and coarse-pored. She had grown up on the South Side in an Italian neighborhood of bungalows with scalloped curtains and concrete stoops and flamingos in the yard. Her father worked in a Gary steel mill. Maureen had dropped out of college after a semester at Chicago Circle because she was pregnant by a masseur at the Standard Club, but she had no intention of getting married. "My kid's gonna have a masseur for a father?" she said indignantly. "Forget it. If I can't do better than that, I'll bring it up myself."

Arriving with our morning coffee, she would perch on the edge of the booth—"jus' for a second; I can't sit around all morning like you guys"—and tap a cigarette from her pack. Her stomach was beginning to fill out beneath her soiled apron. A pregnant girl: I found the whole thing deeply mysterious. In the bright fluorescent light, I studied her grubby nail-bitten hands, her straw dry hair, her gray cat's eyes: couldn't I stop thinking about girls for *ten seconds*? Not that it ever turned out like it did in *Sexus*. " 'Jesus, Henry, I never thought it could be like this. Can you fuck like this every night?' " I should have been reading *The Sun Also Rises*.

The truth is, I was happiest on those nights when I didn't have a date. I would come home from the office, get a beer out of the fridge, and sit on the front steps in the cottony heat watching the sky become a deep lavender as the sodium-vapor streetlamps flicked on and the windows were kindled by the last sunlight. Popping open my can of Budweiser, I savored its metallic chilly taste and talked to the landlady's five-year-old daughter, Melody, who came down after supper to dig in the yard with a plastic shovel, filling her pail with dirt, then emptying it out again. Squatting on the scrubby grass, her smudged yellow shorts tight against her thighs, she worked with purposeful absorption, distractedly pushing aside a wisp of damp blond hair that had come loose from her barrette. My heart quickened when she came up and put her little arms around my neck, grabbing for my can of beer. Her skin smelled of calamine lotion. "Want a Pez?" she said, whipping out her Goofy dispenser.

"No, thanks, Melody. Beer and Pez don't mix."

"Can I have a sip of your beer?"

"That's probably not a very good idea. Your mother would get mad." When I held the can away, she climbed up on my lap to reach it.

"Well, pull me in my wagon then."

She got in and sat down hugging her knees, an expectant look on her face. I grabbed the handle and headed off down the sidewalk, pulling her back and forth in front of the house until Mrs. Underwood leaned out the window and called "Mel-o-dy"—a melancholy three-noted song in the dusk. I lifted her out and she tromped poutily upstairs, dragging her pail behind her. Another girl betrayed.

Across the street the glad syncopated beat of Latin music came through the open door of the El Lago Club. A phone rang two doors down. Go in and work, I ordered myself. Go write a poem about the sunset. But after Melody had gone upstairs I was overcome by a familiar desolation, that ache of solitude I used to feel wandering through our empty house in my underpants when I was seventeen, "Satisfaction" blasting on the stereo while I stared at myself in the full-length mirror and wondered if I would ever grow up. "I can't get no-o sa-tis-fac-shu-un . . ." You're not the only one, Mick. I strolled over to World Drug in the twilight and leafed through magazines, inhaling the medicinal air. The white octagonal tiles, the propellerlike fan suspended from the stamped-tin ceiling, the combs in a cardboard easel beside the cash register and the grimy beachballs in a bin reminded me of my grandparents' drugstore on Peterson Avenue.

Maureen. She was working nights now. Maybe I'd stroll by the Victoria . . . I peered through the dusty plate-glass window and saw her wiping the counter. "Hi," she said when I came in. "We're just closing up." She undid her apron, and I could see the faint swell of her stomach. Maureen's baby.

"You want to go for a walk or something?" I said.

"Sure."

Loose change clinked in her pocket as we walked down Belmont toward the lake. The storefronts were dark, and we glimpsed ourselves in the window of a surgical supply store, two shadowy faces superimposed on a display of walkers and prosthetic limbs. "Are you scared about having a baby?" I said.

"Nah. I could use the company. It'll be fun to go to the zoo and stuff, pushing around a pram. I'll be a good mother."

She was so confident. A woman at nineteen. "But, like, don't you think it will make you feel old?"

"If you're old enough to get knocked up, you're old enough to be a mother," Maureen said. "I mean, it wasn't anything I planned on, but what the hell? Things don't always work out the way you thought they would."

Lying beside her on the grass, I felt like a boy with his mother. A vague sadness crept over me as I remembered how my mother used to drive me to local tennis tournaments in the summer. There was a secret between us, some furtive understanding; I couldn't look her in the eye. Out on the court, I watched her through the chain-link fence, reading or knitting, as patient as a chauffeur. Once when I was fifteen, she had driven me and Sharon Kolb to an open-air performance of *As*

You Like It in the Grant Park band shell, and I'd made her go
sit by herself. All through the first act I kept glancing over at
her, alone beneath a tree. But when I went to keep her company
between acts, she made me go back to Sharon: "She's your
date. I'm fine." But Momma, I want to sit with you.

In the harbor, yachts knocked against the pier. Children
pounded up and down the esplanade in the dark while their
parents sat on the grass in canvas lawn chairs and talked. The
smelt were running now; on the beach below, men armed with
nets and lanterns waded in the shallows. Maureen guided my
hand over her stomach. "Feel the baby?"

I leaned down and laid my ear against her blouse, pretending I could hear it. "Are you in there?" I said. Her uniform
gave off a clean, laundered scent. "What are you going to call
it?"

"Raymond if it's a boy, Deirdre if it's a girl," she said
promptly. "Aren't those pretty names?"

"They are. They're really pretty. You'll have a beautiful
child, Maureen."

She would. In the glow of the old-fashioned cast-iron lamps
on the esplanade, her pale skin had a porcelain tint. It had lost
the pallor that made her look so washed out in the Victoria. I
brushed my lips against her neck. "You want to go back?"

Within a block, the fresh lake air gave way to the city's
heat, a stifling blend of asphalt and gasoline. Maureen lived
down the street from me, in a storefront that had been con-
verted into an apartment; an old velvet curtain hung in the
plate-glass window. There was a wooden staircase at the back,
and we climbed to the roof, where it was cool. The tarred gravel
still gave off a faint warmth from the day. Just across the alley
was the trestle of the elevated tracks, and every few minutes a
train hurtled by. Electric sparks crackled between the rails as
the metal wheels shrieked around the turn and the earth-brown

tenement walls lit up like a cave illuminated by torchlight. Faces flashed past in the yellow windows and vanished in the dark. Maureen's skin gave off the fragrance of girls in summer, a bouquet of dried sweat and perfume. I stroked her bare white arm. Miles to the south, the towers of downtown office buildings shimmered in the heat.

"Are you staying?" Maureen said.

"If you want me to."

"I do." Like in the marriage ceremony. Only the vow we made bound us only for a night. Our commitment was to gratification. No eternal promises would be exchanged.

Back in her room, Maureen pulled the curtain shut, lit a scented candle in a saucer on the floor, and stood before the mirror caressing her stomach. I watched her in the flickering light as she reached behind her and started to pull her uniform up over her head.

"No, don't." Its starchy whiteness excited me. Maureen as a nurse. She stepped out of her cotton underpants and hiked up her dress, then turned away and dipped her legs, hands on knees like a referee. I undid my pants and stood behind her, studying our bodies in the mirror; eyes closed, lips pursed, she looked as if she were thinking hard. I crouched like a quarterback waiting for the hike, in the same deep trance that came over me when I leafed through porn magazines in the sex shops on South Wabash, gazing with stunned eyes at the cum-smeared faces and outsized cocks, the toiling threesomes giving it to each other every which way. Did people really do that stuff? Dimly I heard a car swish past, its headlights flashing through the curtain. Maureen looked at me in the mirror and began to move up and down while I spread my trembling knees. Suddenly she shuddered, her shoulders quaking as if she had a chill. I clasped my hands around her swelling stomach and came in a spasm so fierce that I cried out with a bereaved sob more like a mourner's lament than a moan of pleasure.

"Jesus, Maureen," I murmured as we collapsed on the bed. "What was that all about?"

"There's something about sex when you're pregnant," she admitted. "I never used to come like that. It's like my body's all keyed up for the big event."

"I just had my big event," I said, reaching for a cigarette. My hand shook so much I could hardly get it lit. Maureen got up to go to the bathroom, and I had an impulse to grab my clothes and get out. Emission accomplished. Only that kind of left out Maureen, didn't it? What did *she* want? She padded back to bed, her doggy face illuminated by the guttering candle in its saucer. Could it be that she was as lonely as I was and just wanted company? There was no need for remorse. I'd done no wrong. She liked me. "Why, to get laid is actually socially constructive and useful, an act of citizenship"—thus Herzog. I was striking a blow against the repressive sexuality that deformed human relationships under capitalism. No one ever said the revolution would be fun.

When I woke up, the transom was filled with gray light, floating above the door like a Rothko. Maureen's body gave off a warm sleepy odor. There was a chalky taste in my mouth from cigarettes and beer. I slipped out of bed, pulled on my clothes, and walked up Sheffield. It was early, but a haze rose off the empty street and the trees had the parched dusty look they got in midsummer, wilting in littered patches of dirt. The rows of two-family houses with scrubby yards and sagging porches gave this part of Chicago a strangely rural look; except for the elevated tracks, it might have been some dying Georgia town. Hardly the kind of neighborhood to nourish fantasies of literary fame, but its shabbiness didn't trouble me. Byron and Teresa Guiccioli floated in a gondola through the Venice canals; Maureen Duffy and I hung out at the Victoria Restaurant. Did that make the nervous exaltation I felt in her presence any less momentous? Hours later, lighting a cigarette at work, I could still detect the musky odor of cunt on my hands. I glanced over at Eloise, the spinster secretary whose office I shared, held my fingers under my nose, and inhaled.

Cunt. It was like the blood on Lady Macbeth's hands. No matter how often I washed them, I'd pick up the phone or lift a spoon to my mouth and get a whiff of it. If it wasn't Maureen, it was Lizzie. We couldn't seem to keep our clothes on for ten minutes. Lying on the mattress in my alcove after work, I'd hear footsteps on the front porch and know I'd get no further in *Remembrance of Things Past* that night.

The more we did it, the more outrageous Lizzie got. She made up lewd scenarios with the zeal of a football coach diagramming plays. "Lean on your elbow," she instructed me, "I want to watch it going in." She squatted over my face like an Indian hunkered down around a fire and had me lick her anus. She brought a hand mirror so she could watch me fuck her from behind.

"Why are we doing this?" I asked one night after I'd put on her black bra and panties and watched her masturbate.

"We're playing," Lizzie said. "It's a game."

On the other side of the curtain, Herbert was listening to Stravinsky's *Sacre du Printemps*. I should have been out there with him, seated at the card table underlining passages in the new edition of Walter Benjamin's essays that I'd ordered from Great Expectations. It was one thing to sit in my room leafing through *Sexus* or trying to figure out just what was going on in *Lady Chatterley's Lover* when Connie and Mellors "burn out the shames, the deepest, oldest shames, in the most secret places." (Does he fuck her up the ass, or what? And what are "loins," anyway?) When it came right down to it, my text was *A Portrait of the Artist*. I could hear that priest's harangue every time I fumbled for a condom in my wallet.

Lizzie worked from different sources: Fritz Perls, Paul Goodman, Wilhelm Reich. The message of these books, as far as I could tell, was that repression was bad for you. Society was fucked up because people ignored their instincts and then felt resentful. It was therapeutic to do your own thing. It made you a whole person. Only my thing was browsing in the basement of Kroch's and Brentano's.

I undid Lizzie's bra and turned off the light. Lying beside her in the dark, I remembered how when we were seniors in high school, she would creep up beneath my window and toss pebbles at the glass. Reading Flaubert's *Trois Contes* with a fat blue Larousse by my side, I was easily distracted. I would cast a reluctant glance at my tidy room—the chessboard, the shelves of paperbacks, the llama-skin rug, the Picasso print on the wall —grab my windbreaker from the closet and sneak out the back door.

Lizzie waited across the street in her father's Cadillac. "Did you finish your homework?" she would tease, brushing her lips against my neck.

"You're destroying me," I complained. "I'm going to end up at Northern Illinois University."

"So what's wrong with Northern Illinois University? People do go there, you know."

Yeah, but not people whose fathers gave them a complete set of Gibbon's *Decline and Fall of the Roman Empire* for their twelfth birthday. Make good, Sonny. Make good or else. No wonder I begged my father to come up and look at my dinosaur collection the minute he got home from work, before he had time to get a beer out of the fridge or take off his tie; boasted about the progress I'd made on my forehand, banging a tennis ball against the garage door all afternoon ("Watch me, Dad, watch me!"); phoned him at the office to report my grades, pleading with the receptionist to put him on the line even though he had a half-nude lady on the examining table: "Three A's and a B, Dad! Twenty-seventh in the class." See, Dad?

I'm doing it. I'm making good. Now can I go fuck Lizzie Sherman?

The problem that year was where to go. By October, it was too cold for the beach. One night when Lizzie's parents weren't home, we had a candlelight dinner in the nude. "Aren't you glad we didn't eat out?" I said after we'd finished off a carton of Stouffer's egg rolls and a bottle of chablis.

"Not yet we didn't," Lizzie said, inviting me to crawl under the table and suck her off.

How come she never felt guilty? I wondered, slipping into the house long after midnight. Too wound up to sleep, I turned on the radio beside my bed and caught the last inning of a twi-night doubleheader with Kansas City. I nearly wept for my lost innocence as I listened to Jack Brickhouse, that voice out of my childhood, announcing the play-by-play. "Two on, two out here in the top of the ninth," he reported. In the background, the crowd chanted and clapped while Brickhouse rummaged through his catalogue of pointless lore: RBIs, attendance, records for the most errors in one inning, the longest game, the most consecutive walks. "I will *never* forget the night Ryne Duren loaded the bases on walks," he recalled, filling time while a relief pitcher trudged to the mound. "He was so wild the guys in the on-deck circle were running for cover."

I'd been listening to Jack Brickhouse since I was nine years old, and suddenly instead of oiling my mitt every night, massaging the creased palm with greasy fingers while Brickhouse pattered on, I was fretting about my supply of Trojans. "What if you get pregnant?" I said to Lizzie one night. "I'll have to drop out and get a job at the Texaco station on South Boulevard." Like Eddie. My by-line would be sewn on the pocket of a grimy denim shirt.

"Where do you get these fantasies?" Lizzie said. "Can't you ever do something just because you feel like it?"

No.

So why did I take up with Lizzie's best friend, Elaine Schachter, a snarly-haired girl with a hostile, psychiatrist's-daughter look in her eye? "God, you are sick!" she would scream when I described my study habits—how I came home after school, drank a glass of milk with two Oreo cookies, and went upstairs to memorize the chronology of the Russian Revolution.

For Elaine, sex was a way of getting back at her parents: she liked to do it in her father's office, and if a trace of semen found its way onto his black Naugahyde couch, so much the better. (I often imagined some patient stammering out a confession of sexual miscreancy—only to have his eye fall on a suspicious milky smear that stopped him cold.) I listened for her parents' arrival home with the guilty suspense of that character in the Poe story who fancies he hears his murdered victim's heart beating beneath the floor. "They're in Miami, for god's sake!" Elaine protested one night when I rose off the couch in alarm, insisting I'd heard a car pull up.

"I know, but they could have decided to come back early. My parents hated Miami."

"Oh, knock it off. They only left last night."

Such a fearful boy. People used to believe you could only come so many times in your life before it was all used up; with me, every ejaculation represented another point off my SATs.

The thing with Elaine started one night when Lizzie brought her down to the pier. They were having a big discussion about boys who turned them on. "What do you think of Sam?" Lizzie said as we twirled on the swings in the park down by the pier. Sam Wieghart. A brooding hulk who played his guitar in the No Exit Cafe under the Dempster elevated tracks on weekends and rode a motorcycle. He was rumored to deal dope. Sam was heavy.

"I fucked him once, but it wasn't too great," Elaine volunteered. "We were wrecked on acid." Lautrec should see these girls; in their leather jackets and tight jeans, they made his *Absinthe Drinker* look like a librarian. "What about him?" Elaine said, nodding her chin at me. My heart speeded up as I gazed out over the water in the dark. Now what?

"Find out for yourself," Lizzie said. "My parents are at some fund-raising thing in the Loop."

Elaine turned to me. "You want to?"

"Uh . . ." I scuffed my sneakers in the dirt path beneath the swing. I'm sorry, I have a paper due on the War of 1812. But it was a Saturday night; and besides, I couldn't resist a new adventure. I could think of it as experience, research— like Flaubert in Egypt. If that mama's boy could satisfy himself with whores and belly dancers, why couldn't I do it with Elaine Schachter? "Only if Lizzie doesn't mind," I said.

"Why should I?" Lizzie said. "Anyway, *La Dolce Vita* is on *The Late Night Movie.*"

We were in Lizzie's bedroom getting undressed when headlights flashed across the ceiling and I heard the crunch of gravel in the driveway. "Oh, shit!" Lizzie cried up the stairs. "They're home." We fumbled for our clothes in the dark and rushed downstairs just as Lizzie's parents walked in, her father in a stiff brown hat and mohair coat, her mother in a swirl of fur. They made no comment on our hasty descent; I'd noticed before how embarrassed parents got when they walked in on their children's illicit doings. They didn't want to know about it.

On our way out the door, Lizzie whispered, "Come over to Sam's later. I want to make it with you."

Sam's parents were away a lot on weekends. His father, a violinist with the Chicago Symphony, was usually on the road, and his mother had a studio with a cot down on Clark Street; she was a sculptress. I envied the Wiegharts' chaotic household. (Our house was so orderly I half-expected my mother to put up velvet ropes around the furniture.) Their front porch was littered with tricycles and broken furniture. The walls of their living room were hung with posters: BAN THE BOMB, SUPPORT OPEN HOUSING, END THE WAR IN VIETNAM. Mr. Wieghart went around in blue jeans, his wife in a paint-stained sweater that might have belonged to de Kooning. Evanston was like Kafka's Great Nature Theater of Oklahoma: Everyone is welcome! If you want to be an artist, join our company!

I dropped Elaine off and headed up Chicago Avenue, pounding the wheel during the long waits at enpty intersections. On the radio, the woman d.j. on the FM jazz station was talking about Miles Davis in a husky, late-night voice, introducing "Kinda Blue." *I want to make it with you*: what a mouth that girl had.

I should be so liberated. If it feels good, do it: the credo of our time. Only the week before, Aaron's little sister had propositioned me while he was out getting a pizza. "Consider it a favor," she'd said. "I'm so hung up on my virginity my psychiatrist says I should get it over with so we can work on other areas."

"But you're just a kid!" I protested. "I mean, it doesn't work that way. Besides, Aaron's coming back in fifteen minutes."

Yet somehow it happened, right there in Aaron's living room. Never mind that Sally Temkin was a *zoftig* sixteen-year-old with earrings the size of handcuffs, a junior Marcuse who informed me that "big questions" were on her mind while I was struggling with the straps and buckles on her olive-khaki aviator suit; who screamed so loud when I broke her hymen that I half-expected cops to show up at the door; and who, when I pulled out, squirting an arc of semen over her plump stomach (I didn't have any Trojans on me), complained that I should have come inside her because Norman Mailer said that sex lost its edge unless there was a chance of getting

knocked up. Everyone did it. No-fault sex. Only somehow I was
paying up. I wondered if my mother could see the ravages of
sexual excess in my eyes. When I looked in the mirror, they
seemed haunted and sunken—the visible evidence of my
debility.

Turning down Sam's street, I could pick out his house at the
end of the block; there were lights in every window. I rang the
bell and Sam came to the door in a terrycloth robe. "Lizzie's
upstairs," he said. "I'm watching Jack Paar. He's got some
incredible magician on."

Lizzie was sitting Indian-fashion on Sam's bed in a maroon
caftan, smoking a cigarette. Her black hair shone in the light
of a Chinese lantern with a pleated shade. She had a moody
look on her face, but she brightened when she saw me. "Come
here, baby," she said. She shrugged back the wide sleeves of
her gown and held out her arms. "I'm stoned."

I sat down on the bed and buried my face in her neck. "Let's
fuck," she said in a sultry voice, unzipping my pants. "I want
to feel your big hard cock inside me." Had she been reading
Henry Miller, too?

"Let's not."

She stared at me. "What's the matter?"

"I don't know." I looked down at my feet.

"You really think getting laid will fuck up your life, don't
you?" Lizzie said.

I nodded glumly. "I guess so."

"You want to control everything." She reached for a cigarette. "But you can't. Look at my parents: they gave us music
lessons, enrolled us in dance class, taught us to write thank-you
notes—and one of their daughters is a drug addict . . ."

I looked at her in amazement. "Who?"

"Susan. They don't know it, but she is. She's been doing
smack for over a year. She even got arrested for dealing in
Haight-Ashbury." Incredible. Susan Sherman. Lizzie's older

sister. A National Merit scholar. A member of the girls' volley-ball team. An actress: I'd seen her in *The Zoo Story*. Now she was peddling dope on the streets of San Francisco. Some people must be even madder at their parents than I was. "Another is in Evanston Hospital, zonked out on Thorazine," Lizzie resumed her chronicle of madness and disorder in the Sherman household, "and the third"—she pointed to herself—"is flunking two subjects and isn't even *going* to college."

"You're not?" I would have found it easier to believe if she'd announced that she was about to hurl herself out the window.

"I doubt it." Her eyes were sad. Suddenly she reminded me of the little girl whose face I'd seen in the yearbook of Nichols Junior High School, a solemn twelve-year-old with dark hair parted down the middle—early Lizzie, before the onset of adolescence.

"Why not?"

"My psychiatrist says it's because my parents want me to, but I don't know," she said meditatively. "I think they really didn't want us to be like them. You know, brought up by these strict Jewish parents. That's why they let us stay out all night, screw in our rooms, get stoned. It's supposed to be a privilege. And anyway, who wants to discipline their kid? They just get mad at you. It's easier to let 'em do as they please. You want to stumble home strung out on mescaline at five o'clock in the morning? Fine. See if I care. The only thing is, it makes you feel they *don't*. No wonder we're so fucked up." She stroked my thigh. "So what do you want to do?"

"I don't know." Go back to my room with the books and the prints and the Joan Baez records—that shrine to self-improvement. Cultivate your own garden: I yearned to get down on my hands and knees and work in the soil of my sensibility, plant something that would grow.

"You're weird," Lizzie sighed. She turned over on her

stomach. The house was silent. Sam had probably gone to bed. I stole a glance at the illuminated clock on the table next to the bed. It was ten after two. I had to get home, I thought drowsily. My parents would be frantic.

When I woke up, the room was filled with milky light. Lizzie lay sprawled beside me on the crumpled sheet. I grabbed my jacket, crept downstairs, and slipped out the front door. There were no cars on the street. It was seven o'clock on a Sunday morning.

My parents were sitting at the kitchen table when I came in. They stared at me with grim, exhausted eyes. For a brief instant, I wondered if they even recognized me. Was I their son, or some mysterious phantom? Their own Dr. Jekyll and Mr. Hyde. My face burned with shame as I hurried past them to my room.

That afternoon, hungover and half-asleep, I was at my desk reading *The Tempest* when I heard the doorbell chime. A minute later there was a knock at the door. "You have visitors," my father said coldly. Elaine and Lizzie walked in.

"You won't believe what happened!" Elaine cried as they closed the door behind them.

"What?" I was embarrassed to have them in the house; it was Sunday, and I had a paper due.

"Look at your pants," Elaine said. I glanced down, and knew why they seemed tight. "Yours fit perfectly." The girls were in hysterics as she pulled them off, knocking over my chess set and spilling my penny jar. I hurried out of Elaine's jeans and reached for mine, but she dodged away and pranced across the room in her black underpants.

"Come on, Elaine. Give me my pants." I could hear my parents moving about below.

"Do it to me, big boy," she whispered in a sultry voice. "Do it or I'll tell your father what a lousy fuck you are."

"Will you come on?" I pleaded, but she waved my blue

jeans in the air like a bullfighter's cape, and wouldn't hand them over until she saw that I was on the verge of tears.

When they were gone, I picked up my pennies and chess pieces and sat down to finish *The Tempest*. My hands were trembling so hard I could scarcely turn the page.

I studied and studied. Every night after dinner I closed the door and struggled through another lesson in my French grammar or boned up on the Constitution. On weekends I ran wild. By Friday afternoon I was incredibly hopped up, staring out the high windows in study hall as it got dark. On the playing field beyond the parking lot, the football team raced up and down, a football spiraling through the twilight. The fluorescent lights flicked on. The clock above the proctor's desk ticked off another minute.

At the dinner table I couldn't wait to excuse myself, splash Old Spice on my face, and ask for the keys. I put on my army jacket, combed my hair for about an hour, and slid behind the wheel of Sophie's beat-up Chevy. On the radio, Dick Biondi was talking up Clearasil. I lurched out of the driveway and swerved around the corner just as Wilson Pickett came on. "We're gonna wait for the midnight hour . . ." The Song of the Open Road.

My usual destination that winter was a drab neighborhood of taverns and package stores just within the city limits of Chicago, where Sam Wieghart had moved in the wake of some tremendous quarrel with his parents. His building, a five-story apartment house of clay-colored brick, surrounded a concrete courtyard veined with cracks. The floors in the entry were chipped and seamed with grime; an empty light socket gaped overhead. Beneath the tarnished copper mailboxes was a speaker in the shape of a Victrola gramophone. I had a key to the apartment, and when Sam wasn't home I brought over Lizzie or Elaine, stopping off on North Paulina to buy a pint

of gin from the local drunk. (I had given up trying to persuade
him to get me Pimm's Cup No. 1 after a suspicious clerk
showed him the door.)

Sam's apartment consisted of a single room with a bed, a
swamp-green carpet, and a refrigerator. Between this room
and the bathroom was a large closet with a mattress on the
floor and a blue light bulb overhead. The walls were covered
with poster-sized photographs of famous novelists that I had
bought in the basement of Kroch's. The dapper Joyce with his
wire-rimmed glasses and tidy moustache; the gaunt, tubercular
Lawrence; the frail Proust with his tired raccoon eyes: they
gazed down with mute reproach as I grappled with Lizzie on
the sour mattress.

Sometimes I'd drive over to Sam's after dinner and write at
the scarred oak table by the window. The carpet was musty,
and curlicues of paint hung from the ceiling. The muslin
curtains were stained. The radiator clanked and shuddered;
the silvery pipes gave off a dry, stifling heat. But I preferred
it to my Formica desk, the Tensor lamp and swivel chair, the
Honor Board cluttered with documents attesting to my dili-
gence. Sam's had a more authentic feel. It was the kind of
room writers lived in—like Roquentin in *Nausea*. It made me
feel *in life*. A few blocks away, my father's chamber group
would be tuning up in the living room while my mother made
coffee in the kitchen. Just over the border, in Chicago, their
son sat hunched over a notebook, pencil in hand, working
on a poem about a derelict with a bandaged head I'd seen
in a Demar's restaurant beneath the Wilson Street elevated
tracks:

> *The shabby day is leaving.*
> *Oh, Mister, are you grieving*
> *For a life you never had?*
> *Old guy, speak to me! My nerves are bad.*

If not that old guy, someone. I gazed longingly at the woman in the window across the way. Her gray hair was pulled up in a bun. She was making herself a cup of tea. She looked nice. It was lonely in Sam's apartment, but loneliness came with the territory. What poet had a mother who came in after dinner and offered him a plate of homemade cookies?

One night I was at the little table reading Eliot's *Collected Poems* when there was a knock at the door and Elaine and Lizzie burst in. "Trick or treat," Lizzie said, flinging her fur coat on the bed. It was a freezing winter's eve. The window-panes were laced with frost, and you could feel the wind beneath the door. Down in the courtyard, dirty clumps of snow were piled against the walls. "Wow, it's cold out there," Lizzie said. She shivered and embraced herself. She had on leotards and a tight black sweater. "What's there to drink?"

I looked in the cupboard. "Just a bottle of Kahlúa."

"Yum." She filled two water glasses to the brim and handed one to Elaine. "So what are you doing here? Where's Sam?"

"He went to a double feature at the Clark. Some Paul Muni films."

Elaine sat on the bed with her coat still on, leafing through a book of photographs: *The Family of Man*. "Take off your coat and stay awhile," I said.

"I'm cold." She didn't look up.

Lizzie glanced over my shoulder. "What are you reading?" I showed her the book. "Not him again! Why don't you read Cummings or Dylan Thomas? Somebody with a little life. Eliot's a down." She pirouetted across the room. "I'm going to take a hot bath," she announced, disappearing into the bath-room. "Yuck!" she called out a minute later. "This tub is filthy. Come here and look."

The porcelain was bruised and discolored, the faucet edged with rust. The bottom of the tub was coated with mildew. "Doesn't Sam ever take a bath?" Lizzie said.

"I guess not."

She got down on her knees and swabbed the tub out with a moldy washcloth. "There!" She turned on the water. It was strange to hear it drumming against the drain—a sound out of childhood. It reminded me of how my mother used to draw the water for my bath.

Lizzie peeled off her leotards, tossed her sweater on the floor, and lowered herself down in the tub. In the steamy heat, her mocha skin had a moist film over it. The cracked tiles were damp, the mirror fogged up. The cracked plaster on the ceiling sweated. Above us, the upstairs neighbor was watching *Gunsmoke.* "Come on in," Lizzie said.

"What about Elaine?"

"She can come, too. Elaine!" she called. "Come and join us."

"Unh-unh. No," I said nervously, halfway out of my pants. "I can't deal with that."

"What do you mean, 'deal' with it? We're just taking a bath." Elaine appeared at the door. "Get in," Lizzie directed her.

I stood watching, khakis in hand, as Elaine stepped out of her boots, undid her skirt, and pulled her sweater up over her head. Her breasts were bigger than Lizzie's; in the glare of the bathroom, they had a pearly sheen. She put her hand on the sink for balance, crooked her leg, and stripped off a stocking. A little plump, but as lovely as that Degas ballet dancer in the Art Institute. God, girls' bodies were beautiful. I had a tremendous hard-on. Elaine came toward me and sank on her knees to the cold tile floor. I glanced down: she had my cock in her mouth. Lizzie leaned over the side of the tub and nuzzled Elaine, lapping me with her tongue. "M-m-m-m," she murmured. "Just like a lollipop."

It was too strange. "Look," I stammered. "Cut it out. I just can't handle this." I looked in the mirror: a bank robber looking for the hidden camera. Where would it all end? Remanded to the Peoria Boys' Reformatory for accepting a blow job?

Lizzie glowered up at me. "Oh, Ben! What's the matter with you? It's *fun.*"

Elaine wasn't having fun. Her brown hair trailed damply down her neck. There was a fearful look in her eyes—the kind of look I associated with visits to the dentist. So I wasn't the only one. "It's not just fun," I said. "It's . . . dangerous."

"You're hung up," Lizzie pronounced.

"I'm seventeen years old!" I shouted. "I live in a roomful of tennis trophies. I'm not ready for *la boue.*"

"*La* what?"

"*La boue!* You know: decadence, debauchery. I can't even buy a six-pack and I've done more than Baudelaire."

"Fuck it," Elaine said. "I'm getting out of here." She grabbed her clothes and hurried from the room. In the silence, the radiator knocked and hissed.

Lizzie stared through the water at her lap. She had the look of a child who's just been told to go to bed. The twelve-year-old again, pouty and sorrowful. Give me the love I never had. "You're so uptight," she said. "What are you worried about?"

I'll get syphilis and my nose will fall off.

Lizzie hoisted herself out of the bathtub, dripping like a mermaid. Why *did* I give up this opportunity? It would have been pretty hard to explain to Henry Miller. *So then I got nervous and told them to go home.*

You WHAT!?

Elaine was standing at the door, ready to go. In her muffler and thick stockings, clutching a book against her chest, she looked as if she'd just been to the library. Lizzie pulled on her leotards, dabbed on makeup, laced up her furry boots. Bundled up in their winter clothes, they were safe to touch; they embraced me like sisters on a train platform seeing their brother off to war, and closed the door behind them.

When they were gone, I sat for a long time looking out the window. It was starting to snow, delicate white flakes that swirled down out of the dark like the snow in a paperweight. What made me resist the very scenarios I dreamed up? The desire to be a good boy? The fear of getting what I wanted? Or was it a way of getting what I wanted while pretending I wasn't getting it? Let Lizzie Sherman suck my cock? Why, Mom, I'd never do a thing like that! You think I'm a wild kid like that underachiever Sam? Who smokes dope and doesn't do any homework and isn't even on the Honors track? *That's* the kind of person who lets girls suck his cock!

Nights like these left me stunned; I arrived home tremulous from liquor and fatigue. At two in the morning, the rumble of the automatic garage door sounded like an earthquake. I coasted in and turned off the ignition. A dense silence surrounded me as I stood in the driveway beneath the stars, ecstatic to have made it home.

In the kitchen, I opened the refrigerator and reached in for a carton of orange juice, gulping convulsively from the spout, then climbed up to my room and switched on the Swedish teakwood lamp above my bed. There was the bulletin board, and my facsimile Constitution. In the corner, my tennis racket leaned against the wall. I collapsed on the bed and gazed at *The Old Guitarist.* "Be regular and orderly in your life, like a bourgeois," Flaubert advised Louis Bouilhet, "so that you may be violent and original in your work." Forget that. Live like a bourgeois and you'd write like one. The depraved Verlaine, the syphilitic Maupassant: I was their unhappy heir. Look at the record: Joyce wrote pornographic letters to his wife, Baudelaire lived with a whore, Gide was a pederast. What was I supposed to do? Put on a Boy Scout uniform and go learn how to build a fire?

The traces of my fallen state lingered everywhere. The medicinal odor of semen clung to my underpants; my shirt reeked of perfume. There were times when I wondered if I had ruined my life, succumbed to an irreversible corruption. Why couldn't I be like my cousin Paulie, only sixteen and already a freshman at M.I.T. majoring in physics? He'd never even had a date. Or my neighbor Wally Pinsker, who worked in his father's sporting goods store on Saturdays and was always calling up to see if I wanted to "toss the old pea around." But no, I had to sit in Sam Wieghart's dreary apartment choking on Gauloises and reading *The Waste Land*. I was a poet.

IV

WORKING at *Poetry* was fun. I'd get in around ten, read manuscripts for a couple hours, then shoot pool at the hall upstairs from Walgreen's or go for a walk in Lincoln Park on my lunch hour. In the afternoon I'd look through galleys, write rejection letters, talk on the phone. It was my first real job. (I had been a ballboy at the Birchwood Club one summer, chasing down housewives' wayward forehands while the pro yelled, "Put a little hustle in it, Mrs. Sugarman.") A hundred and twenty-five dollars a week. Lounging like a city-room reporter with my feet up on the desk, the phone by my side, a cigarette dangling out of the corner of my mouth, a styrofoam cup of coffee on the desk, and a stack of bad poems within easy reach, I was happy. I had a good life.

Once a week I had lunch with my old friend Bob Wolin. We went way back. Our parents had known each other since before we were born, when they were neighbors on the North Side. The Wolins lived in Glencoe now, and Bob drove in to his summer job at *Playboy*, where he edited the magazine's Party Jokes page. I could see his office, on the twenty-ninth floor of the Palmolive Building, from my ground-floor window at *Poetry*.

Tall, rangy, powerful, Bob hurried through the midday gloom of Eli's Stage Delicatessen on Oak with a tense, purposeful stride, giving off the nervous energy that was a Wolin trait. The whole family had it: Bob's Amazonian little sister Lisa; his fullback-sized brother Don; his youthful mother, who roamed the Birchwood tennis courts with a muscular stride; his sturdy father, a tax lawyer with nightclub-singer hair and a golf pro's tan. On the piano in the Wolins' Glencoe house was a photograph of the family lined up at the foot of a slope in Aspen, earbands around their foreheads, their faces ruddy from the winter sun. They towered over us; no one on either side of my family exceeded five foot six.

"Got some great jokes for you," Bob would announce, sliding in across from me and grabbing a roll. "Dear Joke Editors," began a typical submission, scrawled in pencil on a torn sheet of yellow legal paper:

> Why did the elephant cross the road?
> To fuck the chick on the other side.

> Please send my $25 to BOB BRUSKI, 3477 Champlain Street, Terre Haute, Indiana. (P.S. Don't use my name. My wife would have a cow.)

"How can you read this junk?" I said.

"I'd like to see some of the stuff you have to plow through."

It was true: the sack of manuscripts the mailman dragged into the office every morning contained some pretty dismal efforts. How did these people keep their spirits up? I wondered, glancing through the day's submissions, fifty or sixty fat envelopes crammed with a dolorous assortment of rhymed and free verse from all over the world. Most required only a glance at the first few lines ("Eagle and lambs, together, share/Of the sweets of the wilderness"), and there were repeaters whose manuscripts I didn't have to read at all after a while: a nun from St. Paul, Minnesota, who specialized in Jesus poems ("Christ came to me in bed one night/His head with a crown of thorns bedight"); the inmate of a mental institution in upstate New York who covered yellow legal sheets with an illegible scrawl; a librarian from Kenosha who submitted multiple versions of a poem on the death of Keats ("Oh, poet! Slain by bad reviews . . .") in the hope of "getting it right." If these people had only known that their submissions were doomed to languish in a file cabinet for six weeks before they were sent back—a policy designed to discourage eager poets from inundating us with manuscripts.

I usually came across two or three poems in each mail that required further attention, because they either were by contributors to the magazine or had possibilities; the rest got a rejection slip. Stuffing the manuscripts back in their stamped, self-addressed envelopes, I felt sorry for the authors and couldn't resist scrawling a few words of encouragement on their slips: "Try us again" or "You have a feel for words." But these consoling messages only provoked more thick envelopes. "I don't know who you are," wrote a court stenographer from Cincinnati, "but yours are the first personal words I've received from an editor in twenty-seven years. I wonder if you would mind reading my novel, *O Bloody Land*." Enclosed was a three-hundred-page manuscript, the pages faded to parchment yellow. I read the first two sentences: "Abe Lincoln leaned forward in his chair and buried his face in his hands. 'By God, Mary,' he cried, 'I'll see the slaves freed if it's the last thing I do.' " After that I gave up writing on the rejection slips.

One day Bob came into Eli's and handed me a new poem: "One of the few sonnets ever written in the bleachers at Comiskey Park." I pushed aside a plate of borscht and laid it on the table.

NIGHT GAME

I sit in the bleachers among a chanting crowd,
My eyes stunned by the emerald lawn.
High above the upper deck, night lights

Blaze down through the steamy dark. A cloud
Scuds past the pearly moon.
The players trot out in their dazzling whites.
The stadium is a luminous bowl
As Lollar chops one through the hole.

Loitering among the hopped-up fans,
I watch a pop-up arc through the tropical night
And think of those exotic ancient clans
—Egyptian, Sumerian, Coptic, Hittite—
Who scanned the skies for omens and prayed to strange gods.
On the mound, the pitcher looks in for the sign and nods.

"I don't like 'hopped-up' and 'pop-up,' " I said.

"Hey, thanks a lot. I can always count on you for a generous response."

"Sorry." What was it Yeats said at a crowded meeting of the Rhymers' Club? *The only certain thing about us is that we are too many.* As far as I was concerned, two was too many. "It has some good things," I conceded, scanning the poem. "I like 'pearly moon,' and that line about 'exotic clans.' But the metre's off, and I don't get the last couplet. Are you saying the pitcher is a primitive god, like the kind these old clans worshipped?"

"No, I'm saying that Sherm Lollar is the reincarnation of King Tut."

Five minutes into the meal and we were ready to step outside. What was it about Bob? His seersucker jacket had a crisp summery look, and his short haircut gave him a boyish air. Just right for *Playboy*, where the editors lounged around in big offices with television sets and Abstract Expressionist prints in gallery frames. The secretaries were probably former Playmates of the Month. They looked as if they'd just gotten up off a bearskin rug and slipped into those tight-fitting jump suits with necklines down to their *pupiks* that were the standard uniform over there. I shared an office with Eloise, who buttoned her long-sleeved blouses up to the chin. "But what's this poem really saying?" I pursued. "I mean, what's it about? Baseball is one of our sacred rituals?"

"You just don't think a poem can be written about baseball," Bob said hotly. "Jewish family life isn't the only subject on earth, you know."

"I'm not saying it is. It's just this is somehow so . . . obvious."

"Fuck it." He snatched the poem away from me. "There's no point in showing you my work." His blue eyes were furious. But goading him had mollified me—a tidy transfer of resentment.

"Come on, Bob," I said, spearing a knish. "Lemme see it." I studied the poem again with a professional eye. "It's really good. The rhyme scheme's very taut." Magnanimity was a pleasant emotion. It was satisfying to dole out praise once you'd made your real feelings known.

"You think it's good enough for *Poetry?*"

In the dim booth, I weighed my response. It wasn't easy having all this power. You wanted to be encouraging, but not create false hope. Besides, did Bob really need to get published in *Poetry?* I mean, he was six feet tall, with a face right out of a back-to-school ad; he had won the Illinois High School Poetry Contest two years in a row. Enough was enough.

Still, it wasn't a bad poem. "It might get in," I said, having hesitated long enough to convey my doubts. "I'll send it on." And be credited with a good deed.

"Thanks, Bobo." Bob signaled for the check. "This one's on me." On the sidewalk in front of Eli's, he lit a Tiparillo. It was time for our ritual summing up. "So here we are," he said. "Two North Shore boys in the big city."

"It's amazing," I agreed. With us everything was amazing. We marveled over ourselves the way we had marveled over the gigantic walk-in heart at the Museum of Science and Industry on a field trip in fifth grade. I had been moved by the rustle of blood in the huge plastic auricles and ventricles, the rhythmic thump of the pumping muscle. On the bus home, Bob and I nearly came to blows over what the aorta did. And now we were standing on a hot sidewalk in Chicago with ties around our necks. Life! Was it possible that everyone grew up, left home, got jobs, had lunch in "the city" and headed back to the office with their jackets slung over their shoulders on a thumb? It couldn't be; it was too momentous. We would have read about it by now.

"Well, Bob," I declared, "I wish you luck in your endeavor to find jokes that will leap off the page, stun readers with their savage wit, and earn you a permanent niche in the pantheon of Playboy Party Jokes editors."

"And you, Kippy," Bob solemnly replied. "May you go forth and discover a poem beside which *The Waste Land* will seem the mere puling babble of a madman, a poem that will illuminate what you call 'our predicament' and transform the landscape of modern literature."

Back at the office, I settled down with the afternoon's batch of manuscripts. The air conditioner rattled and hummed in the window, and bars of sunlight filtered through the dusty Venetian blinds. Eloise's ancient black Underwood clacked in the drowsy silence. I studied my name on the masthead of the June issue: Editorial Assistant. Well, well, well. I should send a copy to Mr. Bein.

Toward the end of the afternoon Derek Holmes, the editor of *Poetry*, phoned from down the hall, summoning me for our daily conference. A bachelor near retirement, he came to work in sandals and Bermuda shorts, smoked Gitanes and kept a bottle of Cinzano in his office; he had once done a year of graduate work at the Sorbonne. "What is it now, dear boy?"

he would say in his coquettish voice whenever I came in un-
announced, the phone tucked under his chin like a viola—
then, to one of the friends he gossiped with all day: "Could
you hold on for *one* minute, Richard? The boy has just walked
in."

Derek had published a couple of my poems, but he was
capricious about it. One day he would deliver a crushing
remark—"These are rather silly, I'm afraid," or "These are
third-rate Lowell"—then turn around and accept one of the
nuclear war poems I was working on that summer ("Death
Ode: A Final Meditation"), or some long-winded monologue
I had put in the mouth of a dead Bulgarian poet. One afternoon
he shuffled down the hall with a fat biography of Hart Crane
in hand and asked if I was "at all interested" in reviewing it.
"Shall we say a thousand words?" I leafed through the glossy
new book with joy, admiring the illustrations, the author's
photograph, the printed slip listing the price and publication
date. They gave it authority: whoever owned this book hadn't
just gone out and bought it, but had a special purpose, a man-
date to "review" it. For weeks afterward I left the Crane biography lying on the card table with the reviewer's slip sticking
out so Herbert could see it.

"Any new *finds* today?" Derek said when I came in for our
daily conference. He put his bony feet up on the desk. "I'm
afraid we'll have to pass on these." He handed me a sheaf of
poems—among them one of my dramatic monologues, "Kafka's
Prayer."

How could he not like it? I brooded on my way back down
the hall. Spoken by Kafka as he lay dying in a Swiss sana-
torium, it engaged the big themes: the collapse of Europe, the
Holocaust, the pathos of the writer's life. The last stanza, where
Kafka atones for the vitriolic "Letter to His Father," was
especially good:

What I needed, father, you could never give.
You made me the invalid I became.
But now we both need to forgive,
Or endure the memory of our shame.

What was the matter with Derek, anyway? I slumped down in my wooden swivel chair and noticed Bob's poem on the desk. "Night Game." I looked out the window for a while, listening to the bleat of traffic on Rush Street. Then I slipped the poem in an envelope, tucked in a rejection slip, and dropped it in Eloise's OUT box. Why make him wait six weeks?

I loved living in the city, but there were times when I longed for the comforts of suburbia. Now that my parents were gone, I missed the Evanston beaches, the Northwestern tennis courts, the leisurely mornings on the patio with a tall glass of iced coffee and the *Sun-Times*. Summers in Chicago were long and hot.

One Saturday morning I was sitting on the front steps after my regular breakfast at the Victoria. Maureen and I had gone to John Barleycorn, where they didn't card you, the night before, and had about nine drinks apiece, so I didn't feel too great. Herbert was inside, reading an essay on Marxism and psychoanalysis in *New Left Review*. It was only nine o'clock, and already the day was heating up; the sun beat down on the hoods of cars parked out front and made the tarry street shimmer like the air over a grill. Maybe I'd go out to Bob's.

I rode the El to Howard and got on a Northwestern train. It was air-conditioned, and the salmon-colored seats were cool—a relief after the baking, sweltering El that clacked and swayed above the tar-paper rooftops with a tremendous racket, exposed to the hot sun. There was no one else in the car.

"Main Street, Evanston," cried the conductor. My old stop.

Home of the Janis Inn. I had stayed there for sixteen years. A superb residential hotel: I was sorry it had gone out of business. The service was beyond reproach, the proprietors—"Mom" and "Dad"—as friendly as any folks you'd ever want to meet. Mom had been in the family for years, serving up three delicious meals a day from her spotless kitchen. Breakfast was my favorite. It started off with choice of juice: grapefruit, Mott's apple, or, best of all, fresh orange juice squeezed by Mom, mightily pressing orange halves down on the automatic squeezer while her good-natured husband stood beside her slicing them in two with assembly-line precision. You were in good hands with Dad. "Don't forget to use the strainer," he would remind his wife. "The boy doesn't like pulp in his juice."

Then you could have either waffles (and not out of any frozen package, either; these were made with real homemade batter and poured over a heavy waffle iron painted with butter) or Swedish pancakes. The ones that came out right were given to the guest; the ones that got wrinkled or torn as Mom chiseled away at the edges of the skillet were given to Dad. You could also have, if you requested it the night before, an apple popover the size of a chef's hat and a side order of bacon or sausage (but no eggs; they had been taken off the menu after those cholesterol studies came out).

Guests were encouraged to loll about on the patio, weather pemitting, with the morning paper; or you could head straight for the "breakfast nook," where Dad, who had eaten earlier so he would be "out of the way," was ready for a good discussion. (Once in a while there were clashes, as when Mom made the guest wash his hands or Dad objected to his NLF button, but the staff was generally tolerant.) No sooner had Dad cleared away the breakfast dishes and handed them on to Mom at the sink than orders were being solicited for lunch.

"I have some leftover chicken . . ."

"Nah, I don't feel like leftovers."

"Well, I could make you a hamburger or defrost those blintzes in the freezer."

"Don't we have any cold cuts?"

"I'll pick some up at the deli," Dad volunteered. "I have an errand downtown anyway."

"Make it lean, Dad," I called out as he headed for the garage. "I don't like that fatty stuff they fob off on you unless you ask for it special. And get a couple of knishes while you're at it."

When I sat down to lunch, there were two knishes on my plate.

We pulled our chairs up to the table, everyone talking at once. My normally mild-mannered father got "overstimulated" and started doing imitations of his patients, like the man with Parkinson's disease who persisted in shaving himself despite his trembling hands. "He gets in one quick stroke," my father demonstrated, "and his hand flies off again." Then there was the senile woman who kept a hand pressed against her cheek to keep her head from turning. "But when you pry it loose, she turns it in the wrong direction!"

His favorite routine was Nathan Berg, a psychiatrist afflicted with a terrible nervous twitch. Twisting his mouth in a grimace, teeth clenched, my father yelped and moaned until my mother called out: "That's enough, William! The boy's going to pick that up and start doing it some day when a patient of poor Nathan's is in the room." But my father, whining, groaning, writhing in his chair, could no more be called off than a German shepherd that's been ordered to attack. "Huh-huh-huh-hello, William," he stammered, gulping air and grimacing like Nathan Berg. "S-s-s-so nu?" Reaching out a palsied hand, he knocked over a glass.

"See?" my mother cried, rushing off in search of a towel. "You get overstimulated when the boy's home, William. Now that's enough about Nathan Berg."

Besides, it was her turn. "I can't get a word in edgewise," she complained, launching some elaborate tale. Sylvia Glasser's son Joey was threatening to drop out of high school and join the marines; my grandma's nephew Sidney, a math professor at the University of Illinois, had quarreled with the chairman of his department; Ruth Eisen had finally put her mother in a nursing home. My mother's narratives were like the ballads of those Albanian shepherds I'd read about in Albert Lord's *The Singer of Tales*: endlessly digressive, Homeric in length, capable of improvising whole myths out of a single incident. What Sylvia had once said about Joey over lunch at the Indian Trail restaurant ("Whoever heard of a Jewish boy on the wrestling team?"); the number of businesses Sidney's brother Marvin had failed in (a shoe store, a delicatessen, a maternity shop); what Marvin's crotchety father, a furrier on West Madison, used to say when Marvin brought home a poor report card ("nobody home upstairs")—somehow these other stories became prologues to the main narrative, were woven into the sequence of events that led inexorably from Joey Glasser to Ruth Eisen. My mother was the one on whom nothing was lost.

"Yeah, so then what?" I glanced at my watch. I had better things to do than sit around listening to the long-winded lady, as we called her (after *The New Yorker*'s voluble Talk-of-the-Town correspondent), babble on about Ruth Eisen's problems with her aged mother . . . "So then Ruthie's mother decided she couldn't live in the Rogers Park Hotel a minute longer," Mom rattled on. "And do you know what she said? 'I'm surrounded by old people.' As if the woman wasn't eighty-three years old herself. But Ruthie wouldn't let her move in with them . . ."

Why was I listening to this? Did I even *know* Ruth Eisen's mother? Not, as Grandma Sophie used to say, "from Adam." Yet there I was, still at the table an hour later, the plates uncleared, the ice cream melted in its wax carton, hanging on the

long-winded lady's every word. "So did her mother end up in a
hotel, or what?"

My father was bored. He wanted to discuss an article by
George Steiner that he'd just read in the *TLS*. But I was curious
about Ruth and her mother. There was a quote from Henry
James I liked: "Art *makes* life, makes interest, makes impor-
tance." In a way, that's what my mother did.

Bob was on the platform when I got off the train in Glencoe.
He had on a Cubs T-shirt, and was brandishing a baseball bat.
"Let's go, Babe!" he shouted. "Game time. It's a beautiful day
for baseball."

"I came out here to relax, Bob."

"So what's more relaxing than a nice game stickball?" he
said in an old-Jewish-man's voice. "You're 0 and 47: this is
your chance to win that first big one. 'Buy me some peanuts
and Crackerjacks,'" he sang in a high wobbly soprano, "'I
don't care if I *never* come back!'"

There was something to be said for the suburbs, I thought
as we drove through the fragrant, sun-warmed streets. The top
was down, and the giant oaks formed a leafy bower. Sprinklers
flung lazy parabolas of droplets over the well-kept lawns. A man
in Bermuda shorts hosing down his MG waved as we went by.
"Larry Benesch," Bob explained. "He owns the Mercedes
dealership out on County Line Road." It would be nice to be
greeted by your neighbor like that. My neighbor on Sheffield
was a hillbilly from Kentucky who'd been laid off his job as a
subway token clerk and sat on his front stoop all day oiling
his shotgun.

We turned up the gravel drive. Mr. Bruno, the Wolins' Italian
gardener, was mowing the front lawn with a power mower the
size of a tractor. On the sun porch around by the side of the
house Bob's mother, in a tennis dress, was watering the plants.

Through the kitchen window I could see their maid, Serena, washing dishes at the sink. The house, a white-pillared neo-colonial with a swimming pool out back, had the cluttered look of a family resort in the Catskills. Everywhere there was evidence of activity: a basketball hoop in the driveway, skis and tennis rackets in the hall, bicycles in the garage. What I liked about the Wolin household was the amount of traffic it sustained. People were always making arrangements to pick up other people at the station or the supermarket or the Y. They even had a "children's phone."

Our house felt like a hotel out of season. I don't know, maybe three people wasn't enough to constitute a "family." When we sat down to dinner, we never quite filled up the table; for one thing, there was always that empty fourth side. I used to go to the Wolins' for Seder, and between the parents, the three brothers and sisters, and the grandparents, there were so many they had to put extra leaves on the big dining room table. Bob's grandpa Hymie would hide the matzoh, and we'd all run around the house looking for it. Whoever found it got a dollar, but then Hymie slipped the rest of us dollar bills anyway. The number of places you could hide a matzoh in that house! Every room was crammed with furniture, athletic equipment, drawers and closets, bins and cabinets, hampers and trunks, a chaotic archive of Wolin memorabilia. Nothing was ever tidied up. In the middle of July you'd find a hockey jersey draped over a chair, where it had been since last winter. Our house was so immaculate I couldn't think of anywhere you could even put the matzoh where somebody wouldn't find it in five seconds. You'd have to bury it in the yard—except there wasn't any yard, just a stony Japanese garden.

I leaned on a bat while Bob warmed up, lashing a tennis ball at the batter's box outlined with masking tape on the garage door. "Awright, boy," he called, firing off a curveball that nicked the inside corner low. "Who you gonna be today?" I had to face him as a specific team so that he could announce the game. "How 'bout the Braves? There's Del Crandall behind the plate, Spahn or Burdette on the mound, Wes Covington in left field, Aaron in right . . ."

"Okay, the Braves." I knocked some dirt off my Keds and stepped into the batter's box. In the driveway, Bob pawed the mound and looked in for the sign, shaking the invisible catcher off twice before he nodded. Sideways to the garage door, he cradled the ball in his hands, reared back, and uncorked a fastball that crossed the plate two inches from my head.

"Strike one!" Bob bawled, pumping a clenched fist high in the air. Three feet outside the box, I waited for the second pitch. "You're never gonna hit anything standing out there," Bob commented. He wound up and whipped the ball in low, eluding my feeble swipe. "Stee-rike two!" The sun beat down on the asphalt and bees hummed in the bushes. Twenty years old, a poet, an editor, a "Harvard"—as my Grandma Rose referred to me—I waited for the pitch. It was "low and away," Bob decided, but he recovered with a fastball that slammed against the door before I even saw it. "He's out of there!" Bob yelled. "Who's up?"

"Uh, Covington?"

"Nah, he bats clean-up. Adcock." Bob retired Adcock in four pitches, got Covington on a weak grounder, and trotted in to face the Braves' hurler, Lew Burdette.

Burdette was off today. He threw six pitches before he caught the strike zone, walking the Cubs' catcher, Randy Hundley, and getting behind the count on Billy Williams. The seventh pitch hit Bob on the arm, and there were men on first and second. He swung hard on the first offering to Ernie Banks and the ball soared high, dropping down in a hedge across the street. "A ground-rule double for Banks," Bob announced, hooting and clapping as I trudged after the ball. "That brings in Hundley. Banks on second, Williams on third, and no one out in the bottom of the first. It's a beautiful day for baseball out here at the friendly confines of Wrigley Field, the home since 1907 of our own Chicago Cubs." Branches lashed my face as I crawled in the shrubbery, groping blindly with one hand while I tried to protect my glasses with the other. Finally I spotted it, nestled against the wall. I pushed aside a prickly bramble, slashing a scratch on my arm, and picked it out of the dirt. "Way to go!" Bob called as I emerged from the underbrush. "Batter up!" My glasses were fogged over, my shirt torn, my hands as black as a coal miner's. And it was only the bottom of the first.

Four innings later, with the score eight to nothing, I got a walk, then connected with a change-up, knocking it over the left-field hedge. "Williams is drifting back," Bob chattered. "He's on the warning track but he can't get a glove on it." He drifted back and nearly collided with a milk van coming down the street. "Bruton is rounding third," he babbled, darting onto the neighbor's lawn. He stormed up the driveway and hurled the ball in the direction of home plate, where I had flung aside my bat and crouched waiting for the throw. (Team affiliations didn't matter to Bob in the middle of a play, only how it looked.) It came in right on target. "He's out!" Bob cried. "Hundley got 'im as he dove for the bag."

"Hey, wait a minute! That was my first hit. You can't just call him out."

Bob held up a placatory hand. "Sorry. It was a beautiful play, that's all. Forget it. Aaron's on second."

An hour later, I "fanned" (as Bob gloatingly put it), ending the game. The final score was twelve to one. "My fastball was really humming today," Bob apologized, patting me on the shoulder. "Let's go get us some chili dogs."

The parking lot of Big Herm's was empty. It was the middle of the afternoon, that dead time in the suburbs when no cars are on the street and the only sound is the buzz of a lawnmower

in someone's yard. Bob leaned down to the window and gave
our order to the girl at the counter, a ghostly shadow behind
the screen. Flies hovered around the garbage can. I studied the
posters for ice-cream cones: medium, large, and jumbo (how
come there was no small?), chocolate and cherry dip, pineapple
sundaes and banana floats. Stale griddle fumes poured through
a tin ventilator out back.

I leaned against Bob's car, feeling the hot metal against my
shorts. "Life," Bob said, handing me a root beer and a hot dog
wrapped in a napkin.

"Yeah, I know what you mean." I did, too. We'd kicked the
subject around a lot.

"Can you believe how old we are?"

I shook my head. I couldn't believe it. How time flies. That
was my role in these metaphysical discussions—Lear's fool.

"It's incredible. A decade ago we were eleven. A decade,
guy: you know what that means?"

I shook my head again. What does it mean, Bob?

"A decade's nothing." He tossed his crumpled napkin in the
garbage can. "And four or five more is all we get—if we're
lucky."

"I know. It *is* incredible." I tossed my napkin toward the
garbage can, but the wind caught it and I had to go chasing
after it across the parking lot. These discussions unnerved me.
For all my worrying about the bomb, I secretly subscribed to
that line in *Paradise Lost*: "The world was all before them,
where to choose." I may have bored Lizzie with my apocalyptic
theories, ranting on about how we were going to be blown up
any minute now ("All the more reason to fuck and get high
while we can," she retorted), but before the world became a
cinder hurtling through space I'd have a poem in *The New
Yorker*. It was Bob, the strapping, fresh-faced boy from Glencoe, who brooded on the mystery of death. Sitting around on
his patio, he made his way through Freud and Jung, Kierke-

gaard and Unamuno, glancing up at a portable TV every few pages to see how the Cubs were doing.

"My Grandpa Hymie's in the hospital," Bob said. "He slipped in the bathroom and broke his hip. My grandparents are really getting old. I can see it now. Pretty soon my parents will get old, and then I'll get old." Mortality was a special insult to the Wolin clan. I could imagine getting old; it was a tradition in our family. But the Wolins were so big, so vital; they were always off skiing in Aspen or working on their backhands at some tennis clinic in Palm Springs. Somehow they should have been exempt from the biological condition that turned children into parents, parents into grandparents, and grandparents into dust.

"I feel old right now," I said.

Bob studied my wan face. "Out with Lizzie?"

"No, someone else." How could I explain to Bob about Maureen? That I was fucking a pregnant waitress while he sat out here in Glencoe drinking Hawaiian Punch and watching the Cubs lose to Philadelphia.

"So what happened?" Bob prodded.

"I don't know. Girls mess up my head."

"You'll get over it. How does that line go? 'Men have died and worms have eaten them, but not for love.' "

" 'Worms have died and men have eaten them, but not with any particular relish.' "

"Oh, yes, with one particular relish," Bob said, holding up a finger. "Mambo Sauce," he declared in the voice of Purvis Spann, our favorite d.j. on WVON, Chicago's Station with a Soul. "When it's bahbecue time, on'y one sauce'll do, and thass Mambo Sauce. Say it again, Mambo Sauce. You add a little, it add a lot."

That cracked us up. Bob: what a guy. "Well, Kippy, here we are again," he said, draining his cup of root beer. "It's like we've never been away. I was in Woolworth's yesterday buying some cleats and Janey Glick comes up to me. Remember her?"

"Barely." She was from Glencoe—beyond the boundaries of my nostalgia.

"She used to go out with Ronnie Rubinstein. Anyway, she comes up to me and says, 'Guess what? I'm getting married.' "

"To who?"

"I don't know. Some guy she met at the University of Wisconsin. The next thing you know she'll be living in Glencoe and sitting around the Birchwood pool with her two kids." He stared moodily out the window, depressed by the image he had conjured up. But I was comforted by it. If everyone moved away, there would be nothing distinctive about our escape.

"What do you want her to do?" I said. "Go to New York and get a job as a receptionist at *The New York Review of Books?* I mean, not everybody has big plans. Some people just want to lead regular lives."

"But that's just it," Bob said hotly. "*I* want to lead a regular life. Writing's weird. Who wants to sit alone in a room all day hunched over a typewriter?" He reached in and turned on the radio. Smokey Robinson and the Miracles doing "The Tracks of My Tears." "Now *that* is music!" Bob stated in his Purvis Spann voice. " 'So take a go-od look at mah face,' " he howled in Smokey's falsetto. " 'You'll see mah smi-ile looks out of place . . .' " He whirled around, snapped his fingers, and laid a hand out, palm up, for me to slap. "You know what?" he said, Bob Wolin again. "I don't even *like* poetry."

"You think anyone else does? They're just in it for the fame. And you can't even get that anymore. Nobody reads poetry these days." Except my relatives. Some of the little magazines I published in had suspiciously healthy circulations on the North Shore.

"So why do we do it?" A rust-eaten black Ford with dirty

whitewall tires pulled up beside us. There were two girls in the front seat—a blonde in a sleeveless nylon T-shirt and a red-head with frizzy hair tied up in a bandanna.

"To get girls," I said. But I doubted poetry would work on these two the way it did on Lizzie, who had once rolled up a copy of *Word Mosaic* that included some of my new work and rubbed it between her legs. The girls in the black Ford were hard-looking. Their mouths had a sullen, pouty smirk—the kind of mouth that swallowed cum. There were girls you could just look at and know they did everything. The way they chewed gum and held their cigarettes, the cruel indifference in their eyes . . . These girls could care less that I'd been published in *Poetry* magazine; they didn't give a fuck. I was about as likely to end up with one of them as with Marilyn Monroe. How did Arthur Miller do it? Maybe I should write plays.

"You write because you want the world to love you as much as your parents did," Bob said. "You're just looking for that old unqualified love. You want to suck your mother's tit."

"You are gross, Wolin." All this poring over Freud between innings had really gotten to him. "I have a lot to say."

"Like what? That line about 'The dream where hands rise up out of the dark and embrace me' "?

" 'I discover that these hands are mine.' "

"They're not yours. They're your mother's."

"Okay, they're my mother's. So what?" I didn't need these therapeutic sessions. Poets relied on feeling, instinct, not analysis.

"The point is that you keep thinking poetry, literary fame, or whatever it is you're after, is going to make you special—but it's not. And even if it does, you'll still have to live with your-self. The National Book Award's not going to give you a new identity."

"I can live with myself," I muttered. It's you I can't live with, Bob. What did he know about the sacrifices I made for art?

It was the same argument we'd been having ever since we were kids. We used to sit around the Wolins' kitchen with a Campbell's soup can in front of us for a microphone and conduct roundtable discussions like the ones on *Kup's Show*. "I think what you just said about the role of the artist in society is very interesting," Bob would respond to my persistent claim that poets were the unacknowledged legislators of the world. "But what makes you so sure they're more sensitive than other people?"

"Well, Bob, I just don't see how poets *could be* like other people. I mean, it's their business to know and feel and suffer more than anyone else." Especially to suffer.

"Uh-huh," said Bob, reaching for the can. "That's very interesting. Well, it's time for a word from our sponsor."

After a plate of Oreo cream cookies and a glass of milk, we were back on the air. "Welcome again to *Roundtable*," Bob intoned in his Kupcinet voice. "Our guest tonight is Benjamin Janis, a Chicago-area poet who just this year won an honorable mention in the Illinois Poetry Contest. Could you tell us, Ben, who some of your poetic models are? Like, who should a young poet read?"

"That's a tough question, Bob," I said, grabbing the soup can. "I think it really depends on what kind of poet you want to be. I mean, there are very rebellious poets like Allen Ginsberg, who wrote a long poem called *Howl* that was really a howl against the whole establishment. Or a poet like Theodore Roethke, who's very sensitive to stuff like animals and plants and nature. But my own feeling is that poetry has to deal with our modern predicament, our drift toward nuclear war, or else it's just not doing its job."

There was a scratching sound at the door. "We'll be right back," said Bob, getting up to let in Sparky, the Wolins' old cocker spaniel. "Anyway . . ." Sparky stretched out on the floor and let loose a sour doggy fart. ". . . I've noticed that you have a way of talking a lot about this modern predicament without really defining it."

Fuck you, Bob. "Well, I think it's pretty obvious, Bob. Look, the atom bomb is hanging over our heads and we could be wiped out any minute now, so it's kind of pointless to go on writing about birds and flowers and stuff as if life was just going to go on no matter what."

"Yeah, but life does go on," the host said heatedly. "Does the Bomb change the fact that the Cubs dropped a double-header to St. Louis yesterday? That loss mattered to a lot of people. The big question yesterday wasn't what the Russians were up to, but can Ernie Banks connect with his twenty-seventh home run of the season and pull the Cubs out of the cellar?"

Bob wasn't deep. Sensitive, sure; but not marked out by that awareness of one's difference from others, that secret knowledge I shared with Aaron Temkin when we sat in the cafeteria and gazed with haughty contempt at the herd, pitying them their ignorance, their blind instinctual lives. They would die without ever once knowing what it was like to stand on the pier beneath the stars and feel swallowed up in eternity—"two souls," Aaron had said one night, "poised on the verge of nothingness."

It was living in Glencoe that made Bob innocent. He didn't understand my Evanston friends. I may have been one of the Happy Few, but Bob was, well, *happy.* "You're too wholesome," I complained. "You don't drink, you don't get stoned. You probably still oil your mitt before you go to bed." There was no angst in Bob's poems, no awareness of our predicament; they were all about cars and girls, department stores and Chinese food:

> *Luckily, then, I hear that a few miles*
> *From death there's a Cantonese restaurant*

Where we can have some barbecued pork
And talk.

That stanza had us screaming over the phone for hours. "What's this Cantonese restaurant shit?" I demanded. "Is that what you think of when you think of death? Little cartons of take-out food? I mean, if you think life consists of phoning up Kim Toy Lunch for barbecued pork, you are very out of it, buddy—and that's what's wrong with your poem. It's suburban. There's no experience in it. You haven't lived."

What kind of poet is this? I used to wonder when Bob showed up on Saturday mornings with a new sonnet in the glove compartment and enough gear to fill a Little League coach's station wagon. For him, poetry was just another sport, another skill to master. For me it was a matter of life and death—mostly the latter.

In the parking lot of Big Herm's, I lit a cigarette and stared pointedly at the girls in the black Ford. They didn't notice me. "So what are you doing tonight?" Bob said.

"I don't know. Work, I guess. Go back to the city and confront *le vide papier que la blancheur défend.*"

"Hey, that's a good line. Why don't you try it out on those girls over there?"

Mallarmé was wasted on Bob. "What are you gonna do?"

"It's Family Doubles Night at Birchwood and I'm teamed up with my mom."

"Talk about wanting your mother's love."

"Poets can play tennis, too, you know. Pound did."

Not me. I had to work on my new poem: "Loitering Toward the Apocalypse."

It was a bad summer. Martin Luther King had been shot in April, Bobby Kennedy in June. Sitting in Harold and Edna's house the day after Sophie's funeral, we'd watched Kennedy's

cortège creep up the East Coast. Thousands of mourners lined
the tracks. No one could stop crying. It was just like when his
brother was killed and the riderless horse pranced before his
coffin. Outside, the sun shone, robins hopped on the lawn,
cherry blossoms carpeted the driveway. We sat behind drawn
curtains with the TV on.

Things were out of control. I'd sensed it when I moved in
with Herbert. Jeeps crammed with National Guardsmen
patrolled the glass-strewn streets of the South Side. The whole
city felt as if it was about to go up in flames. You could see
burned-out tenements from the Edens Expressway; gangs of
black kids on the overpass hurled concrete down on the
cars below until the city installed chain-link fences topped
with barbed wire. All summer, smudges of billowing smoke
floated over the South Side. Fire trucks roared up Belmont
toward the West Side ghettos. Fluting sirens pierced the
night.

During the last weeks of August, the *Sun-Times* was full of
speculation about the Democratic Convention in Chicago and
the Yippies converging to disrupt it. While Herbert sat at the
card table making notes in the margin of *New Left Review*, I
lounged on the steps reading about Jerry Rubin's plot to release
a bunch of pigs in the streets of Chicago. Mayor Daley had
refused the demonstrators a permit to sleep in Lincoln Park,
and it looked as if there might be trouble.

One night I decided to walk over and see what was happening. "You're wasting your time," Herbert said, looking up
from his book. "They're just a bunch of kids playing at
revolution."

"Come on, Herbert," I protested. "Things are really heating
up out there. I'm sick of Marx. I want some action." I laced
up my Keds and stuffed a paperback copy of *The Liberal
Imagination* in my hip pocket. "It'll be an experience."

"You know what Kafka says about experience?"

1e. "No, what?"

dry land." But he was putting on
ry short-sleeved shirt, brown poly-
ords he looked like a 1930s Com-
union organizers who stood shiver-
ries in the dawn with a fistful of

ot to the park. The sky over the lake
of demonstrators were camped out on
round in faded army jackets, T-shirts,
nds, cowboy hats, motorcycle helmets,
, blue jeans, sandals, boots, vampire
d contingent than the troops routed at
ered in trash cans and columns of sparks
s. The faces of the demonstrators shone
with a Goyalike intensity. The damp air
dope.

, the curfew stipulated by the police, and
n Park had begun to mill about uncertainly.
ad priests near the speakers' platform raised
All around them people were busy making a
age cans and picnic benches. I spotted Allen
enet, and William Burroughs huddled beneath
Ginsberg's patriarchal beard flowed down his
nearly bald, but he had the brainy, goggle-eyed
chool math wizard. Genet wore khaki slacks and
forehead was wrinkled like a rotting fruit.
a gaunt, papery face, and his gray suit needed

who had been talking to the trio of writers walked
vas my chance. "Mr. Ginsberg?"
poet glanced my way. "Yeah?"
ust wanted to tell you how much I admired *Howl*.
great poem."

"I suppose you're a poet?" His voice was angry, basso rasp.

"Well, I don't know about that. But I do write poetr

"*Qu'est-ce qu-il dit?*" said Genet. He gazed at me wi eyes full of tenderness.

"*Un poète*," Ginsberg said shortly.

"*Il est beau*," Genet murmured. He gave me an ador and reached up to stroke my hair.

Just then a boy with a bandanna wrapped around h raced up and shouted, "They're coming, man! The p coming!" A herd of demonstrators pounded by. "I do like getting my ass whipped," Ginsberg said. "Let's get here." The writers trotted off beneath the trees, and I beside them for a few yards, but they didn't notice me— Genet, who waved a tiny hand as they disappeared in the

Spotlights swept through the fog of tear gas and marshy glare over the scene. I could hear glass shatterir Lincoln Avenue and, close by, the pop of tear-gas caniste squad car's beacon flashed through the trees and a wedg cops charged over the knoll. My heart skipped with fear. "D run! Don't run!" someone chanted, but the crowd was ma a fast retreat. All around me people sprinted by. Suddenly tear gas hit me. My eyes winced shut, my throat burned, face stung as if it had been swabbed with ammonia. I stumb forward, lost sight of Herbert, and slipped on the wet gra There were cries and groans in the darkness, and the holl thud of nightsticks. My lungs were on fire as I raced the l few hundred yards to the edge of the park.

Herbert was leaning against the hood of my mothe Oldsmobile, holding a handkerchief over his face. "I thoug I'd never find you!" I shouted over the whoop of sirens an the crunch of tires kicking up gravel as cars skidded out of th parking lot. I fumbled for the key, flung open the passenge door, and we lurched through the swarm of cars heading awa from the park. Wooden barricades had been set up at the intersections. The streets were strewn with broken glass. Wisps of tear gas hung in the air.

"This isn't a good neighborhood to be in," Herbert said. "You want to stop at Miyako's?"

"Excellent. I could use an order of tempura."

I drove past the taverns on Division, their neon Pabst and Schlitz signs pulsing over the doors, and parked in front of a restaurant with a beaded curtain in the window. It had the look of an ordinary luncheonette, with a counter and three booths; only a paper lantern overhead and the old Oriental men who hung around reading tissue-thin newspapers dense with columns of spidery characters distinguished it from a neighborhood coffee shop.

The restaurant was nearly empty. A Japanese family sat at one table, and there was a man in a rumpled business suit at the counter. "History!" I exulted. "Blood in the streets." My heart was storming in my chest.

"This is child's play, hippie pranks," Herbert corrected me. "It has nothing to do with politics."

"I don't know," I said doubtfully. "I thought we made a point."

Herbert squinted through smeared glasses. "What point?" There was impatience in his voice; he would explain it to me again. "Without the proletariat there is no such thing as revolution. Until the proletariat is enlisted in the struggle it's just a game."

"But how do you do that? I mean, how are you supposed to go about enlisting them?"

"Study." He pulled out a cigarette and tapped it on the table. "First you have to grasp dialectics, which I think you don't. The difference between the means and the mode of production, the labor theory of surplus value, dialectical materialism. Forget Yeats. Forget about running around in the street dodging cops. What's important is to master the objective truth."

The waitress arrived with our dinner, a clear soup in a red enameled bowl and shrimp in a lacy glaze of batter. I drew my chopsticks from their paper sheath and raised the bowl of soup to my lips; the steam was like a warm washcloth. My eyes still ached from the tear gas, and adrenaline was pouring through me. But the bright restaurant, the bowl of soup, the cooks' urgent cries in the kitchen had calmed me down. I popped a shrimp in my mouth, hoping Herbert would notice how adept I was with my chopsticks, but he was eating with a knife and fork. "Look, why not see yourself as the petty bourgeois producer you are," he said. "Your product—poetry —is determined just like a shopkeeper's product. The idea that he can decide what to stock on his shelves is an illusion. He supplies demand. You identify your own feelings with those of society because you must; it's part of the writer's trade."

"But what about you?" I protested. "What are you doing for the revolution? I mean, you just sit around by yourself like I do."

"Not so," Herbert said in that definite voice of his. "My music is an allegory of revolutionary development. The order and arrangement of the notes is necessary, like the revolution. And I mean a revolution of the working class, not this anarchist bullshit." He drained his tea while I paid the check. Whoever had money paid. To each according to his needs, property is theft, and so on. Only somehow it was always my allowance that got appropriated.

Out on Division a squad car sped past, its dispatcher crackling. The air was dense with ozone, gasoline, tear gas. Down by Lincoln Park, sirens yelped and fluttered in the night. I was tempted to go back and see what was happening, but Herbert wanted to get home. He was on the last chapter of *Capital.*

The phone was ringing as we came up the steps. "Kippy!" Bob cried when I picked it up. "I've just been down to Lincoln Park. Incredible scene! Tear gas, cops: the revolution is definitely happening."

"I was there," I said in my weariest voice. "It was just a lot of anarchist bullshit."

The night before I flew back East, I called Lizzie to say goodbye.

"She's not here," said her father.

"Do you know when she'll be back?"

"No."

Thanks a lot, Mr. Sherman. I like you, too. "I mean, will she be back tonight, or next week, or what? Is she in Mexico?"

"She went to New York."

"Well, did she leave a number?" I pursued. "There's a lot of people in New York."

"No, she didn't leave a number," Mr. Sherman said impatiently. "Goodbye, Ben."

"But . . ."

The line was dead.

V

COMING up the narrow wood-slatted escalator of the subway station in Harvard Square, I waited for that familiar view: the deep doorway of the Coop, its dirty mosaic floor littered with scuffed newspapers; the Holyoke Center plaza where hawkers had spread out necklaces, cartons of records, Mexican handbags, and African figurines beneath the dusty trees; the kiosk on its concrete island and the spiky wrought-iron roof of the MTA.

I lugged my suitcase through the hurtling traffic and started off across Harvard Yard. Bob and I had rented an apartment on a cul-de-sac behind the Law School, the top two floors of a gray clapboard house that was suitably quaint: warped linoleum floors, wainscoted walls, a fireplace in the parlor. It was my last year at Harvard, but I felt no regrets. I was tired of college life: the drunken jocks, the clamor of the dining hall, the Saturday-night ritual of setting up speakers in the windows and blasting "Purple Haze" through the Yard. Gone was the excitement of that momentous summer before freshman year that I'd spent filling our forms, ordering stuff from Harvard Student Agencies—a Harvard bedspread, a Harvard chair, even a Harvard wastebasket—and answering questionnaires with the zeal of a shut-in sending away to some radio evangelist in Waco, Texas, for a corner of Christ's handkerchief. Loung-

ing on the patio in Evanston, I'd admired the introductory
brochure with its photographs of Harvard Yard in winter, a
mufflered student on the steps of Widener, the colonial dorm
windows dusted with snow. I'd studied the course catalogue
with the wild surmise of Keats when he first looked into
Chapman's *Homer*. "Transcendentalism and the New England
Mind"; "Whitman and the Democratic Myth"; "The Romance
in America: Hawthorne, Melville, and the Optative Mood." So
there *was* an American literature. I'd have to mention this
discovery to my father. He thought we only turned out writers
like "those two Irvings"—Wallace and Stone.

Among the copious "orientation materials" Harvard had
sent me that summer was a list of entering freshmen, a docu-
ment I pored over until I'd nearly memorized it. Hearst,
Vanderbilt, Peabody, Lodge: real Mayflower names. And their
addresses! Deer Isle, Maine; Eagle Cove, Manchester, Massa-
chusetts; Fox Hill Road, McLean, Virginia. They didn't even
live on streets. To think that I'd be dining in the Freshman
Union with this crowd . . . Maybe I'd get invited to their
summer homes, play tennis, go sailing, lounge on the porch
plucking glasses of iced tea off a tray proffered by the family
servant ("Thank you, Truman"). No more hanging around
Big Herm's or going off to the public courts with my father. I
would be summering in the East.

But I never laid eyes on Peabody, Hearst, or Lodge, and
the closest I got to young Vanderbilt was a glimpse of the
original Matisse that his roommate showed me one afternoon
when he was out. The crowd I fell in with had names like
Weinberg, Feinstein, Cohen. None of them had gone to Groton.
They were graduates of Erasmus Hall in Brooklyn, the Bronx
High School of Science, Horace Mann. Their fathers were
teachers, psychiatrists, insurance salesmen. My room in Mat-
thews Hall was our club. (I had rented a small refrigerator
from Harvard Student Agencies along with my Harvard chair,

my Harvard bedspread, and my Harvard wastebasket, and kept it stocked with beer.) Weinberg, a licheny black beard sprouting from his chin, had a rabbinical manner; he'd memorized a few stories from Babel and Agnon which he told in a wheedling, singsong voice, a hand flung out palm down, the fingers splayed, reciting with studied mimicry the speeches of rabbis and peddlers, tailors and wise old men who spoke in aphorisms. A prima donna, that Weinberg, cloaking his need for attention in Old World humility. I should have thought of it myself.

And Feinstein, sixteen, acne-mottled, the valedictorian of Erasmas Hall out of a class of two thousand, 800s across the board on his SATs: he talked with a gulping eagerness, a stammering intensity, pulling at his pitted face as if to smooth it out, a flannel work shirt open at the neck, his chewed-up fingernails edged with grime. He was always on the phone to his mother, who wanted him home for the High Holidays.

"But I just got here, Mom!" he was shouting one day when I wandered into his room. "They have a *shul* on campus, at Hillel House. I'm going with Weinberg."

He held the phone away from his ear. I could hear his mother's suspicious voice. "What Weinberg?"

"My *roommate*, Mom. The bearded guy who reminded you of Uncle Nathan?"

"I don't know from any Weinberg."

"Well, I'm not coming home!" He slammed the phone down and dropped to the floor, writhing as if he'd been kicked in the groin. "Momma!" he screamed in a strangled voice. "See that?" He pointed to a parcel on the table, the brown paper spotted with grease. "You know what's in there? *Gribenes.*" Onions and chicken skin rendered in vegetable oil. Grandma Sophie used to make it. "My mother sends me *gribenes* through the U.S. mail."

He threw himself down on the bed and groaned. "I shoulda gone to Y.U."

"Y.U.?" I asked.

Feinstein turned over on his back and addressed the ceiling in a weary monotone. "Yeshiva University. My mother doesn't get Harvard. I might as well have joined the Marines, as far as she's concerned. Other mothers *kvell*, O my son, the Harvard boy. Mine sits *shiva* like I died."

Then there was my roommate, Julio Stein, a hooknosed Czechoslovakian Jew whose parents had fled to Chile in the '30s. Gaunt and swarthy, with a bush of wiry hair, he needed no makeup when he played Shylock in a Lowell House production of *The Merchant of Venice*. He whiled away his afternoons in a beat-up armchair, picking away at his banjo as he tapped a bony bare foot on the floor. He was indifferent to requirements, and signed up for Sanskrit, Eastern Religion, Maritime History (known as "Boats"). He didn't bother much with notes. One day I found his anthropology notebook open on his desk with the notation: "pigs dogs cattle."

I marveled at Julio's insouciance. How could he sit around listening to Appalachian folk songs in the midst of this "intellectual ferment" (as I had described our bull sessions to my father)? We were idea-obsessed. In our survey courses we were lectured to, four hundred at a time, on Marxism, Keynesian economics, the history of medieval Europe, Restoration drama, Utopian socialism, Puritan theology . . . more ideas than Mortimer Adler ever dreamed of. Sigmund Klipsky, the Hum 5 professor ("Western Thought"), stunned us with his eloquence. Bald at forty, his magnified eyes bulging behind gold-rimmed spectacles, he chain-smoked, stared out the window, paused for effect, working the crowd like a Yiddish actor in some Broadway melodrama. By the time we got back to the dorm everyone was talking at once. "What amazes me about

Nietzsche is this demonic sense of will," Weinberg mused one afternoon, lounging against a bookcase crammed with paperbacks. "I mean, you really feel the power of his nihilism: everything must go."

"What do you mean, everything?" said Feinstein dryly. "Can I keep my underwear?"

"Modernism," declared Weinberg, tugging at his licheny beard. "The whole modern *movement*. You have to remember that we're living at the end," he stated. "We're posthistorical."

"Like George Steiner says," I put in, " 'We are what comes after.' "

Only what came before?

"Couldn't you be more specific in your terms?" implored my section man in English 10, a pale, tight-lipped graduate student who carried a briefcase and wore J. Press suits. I had claimed that Donne's Devotional Sonnets were "drenched in *Sturm und Drang*." And when I made a reference to Caroline literature, he scrawled in the margin, "Are you sure you know what this means? Your pretense to easy familiarity with the whole of Western culture somehow fails to persuade." "I know you're feeling it all very deeply," he said when I complained about my grade—a C– for the term—"but you haven't learned how to interpret a poem. Go read Cleanth Brooks." Instead I stayed up all night reading *Notes from Underground*.

Our tradition, the tradition we read and claimed as our own, was the Modern Sensibility—the title of a course popular with undergraduates that year. Brecht, Heidegger, Sartre: they brought bad news, but that was okay. We were proud to be postmodern, posthistorical; it made us unique. Besides, since we lived after the end of history, what point was there in studying its lessons? The collapse of Western civilization was upon us.

Jane Austen and George Eliot were a chore to read. What did we know about English country houses? But the Americans excited us; they were radical, democratic, "antinomian." Hawthorne, Melville, Poe (forget Whitman, that dithering, happy-hearted old man): these were figures we could identify with. Brooding, lonely, haunted, they labored in heroic solitude; they stood apart from the common life. We read Perry Miller's *The New England Mind* and F. O. Matthiessen's *American Renaissance*, thrilled to find ourselves in "the crucible of our indigenous culture" (as I put it in a paper on the Transcendental Mind). Why, Emerson had delivered his Phi Beta Kappa address in a hall that we passed every morning on our way to breakfast. Henry James had grown up over on Irving Street. In Lamont, the undergraduate library that reminded me—with its blond wood furniture, fluorescent lights, and brown linoleum floor—of the Evanston Public Library, we sat until midnight at the long tables in the main reading room, highlighting passages with yellow Magic Markers. When the lights flicked off just before midnight, we scraped back our chairs, slung our bookbags over our shoulders and drifted out into the frigid night, our work boots crunching in the snow.

Freshmen stayed up late, and the dorms in the Yard were lit up in every window as we headed back to my room, yelling our heads off about whether the chapter on "The Whiteness of the Whale" in *Moby-Dick* was a symbol of God or Death.

"Look," Feinstein was saying as we shrugged off our ski parkas, "you remember how Ishmael says, 'The man's a human being just as I am'? It's like he's saying that even a primitive like Queequeg has a soul."

"It's like myths," I volunteered, having just read the first seven pages of *Structural Anthropology*. "What Lévi-Strauss says is that there's an innate structure to myth, that, like, basically we're all the same. I mean, you can diagram these myths like a language."

"What do you mean?" said Weinberg evenly. He didn't go in for heavy theoretical stuff.

"It's like, uh, structural linguistics, where he got the idea from. It's all laid out in Lévi-Strauss . . ."

"The guy who makes blue jeans?" Feinstein interrupted.

My father was a less skeptical audience. Home for Thanksgiving, I brought up "texts" he couldn't possibly have read ("What! You never heard of Adorno? You haven't read Musil's *Man Without Qualities?*"), talking at high speed on neoclassicism and Romanticism, the Prague school of linguistics and the Russian Formalists. It was a pity that he couldn't read de Saussure in French, I said one night at dinner; the distinction between *synchronic* and *diachronic* in his *Cours de linguistique générale* was so elusive that I hadn't really come across an adequate translation. I drew up a reading list, only to discover when I got home for Christmas that my father was dutifully making his way through it. "What do you think of that passage in *The Savage Mind* where Lévi-Strauss talks about the aesthetic appeal of miniatures?" he said on the way home from the airport.

"It's pretty interesting," I murmured, "but you really ought to read his book on totemism."

Simon Danielli, my sophomore tutor in English, brought me down to earth. The son of a tailor in Boston's North End, Simon had a dark Sicilian face and ink-black hair that looked as if it had been shellacked. He had picked up a lilting English accent from a year at Oxford, and lounged about his "rooms" —as he called his Dunster House suite—in a pinstripe suit, leaning against the fireplace as he quoted whole poems by heart, his bulging eyes set wide apart like a whale's. "I'm a great believer in memorizing," he warned at our first meeting, and assigned me Keats's Odes. On his crowded shelves were many-volumed sets of Coleridge and Ruskin, and the great Victorian lives: Lockhart's *Scott*, Morley's *Gladstone*, Froude's

Carlyle. Once, when I asked him how he'd spent his weekend, he said: "I read Mill's *Autobiography* again. There isn't a dull page in it."

In the late afternoons, we would sit side by side on a plump horsehair sofa going through Keats line by line, the page warmed by the sun that streamed in like a spotlight through a small round window high up on the wall. Simon assumed that everyone was as cultivated as he was; touring Europe, he once sent me a postcard of the Jungfrau with the message: "I know this is your mountain; I know you own it." I had never heard of the Jungfrau.

No matter. What I didn't know I'd learn. Reading Macaulay's diatribe against the Industrial Revolution, I was glad to discover that the nineteenth century was just as nerve-wracking as our own, and that "alienation," "the abyss of self," "the anxiety of being"—those twentieth-century afflictions—weren't unique to the modern world. They just had other names.

Besides, I *liked* to study. To settle in at one of those long tables in Lamont with Hobbes's *Leviathan* on a frosty winter night was to know true happiness. So what if I'd never have any use for the lore I was stuffing away about Reform Bills and Enclosure Acts? This was knowledge, pure and simple, acquired without hope of gain. Making notes appealed to my need for order. If I could just get everything down in neat outlines like I'd done with my mollusk chart in seventh grade, it would all make sense. The Wars of the Roses, the murder of Thomas à Becket, the madman reign of Robespierre: I filled whole notebooks with this heady lore. History occurs the first time as tragedy, the second time as farce—and the third time as Cliff's Notes.

But you didn't forge the uncreated conscience of your race by reading up on the Corn Laws. For that I had English C: Advanced Fiction Writing. The instructor, Edwin Richter, a bearded graduate student who bore a startling resemblance to

D. H. Lawrence, had a stern schoolmasterish look in his eye.
We were expected to produce a story a week, and we couldn't
just write what we wanted, either; we had to turn in "exercises" set by Mr. Richter.

Our first assignment was to choose a novel we admired and
imitate its style. I chose *A Portrait of the Artist as a Young
Man*. My persona, like Joyce's Dedalus, was melancholy, sensitive, defiant, a young man with a call to literature. But moody?
Oy. In a Chinese restaurant, he felt "too old to be compelling."
He was convinced he had a great destiny, but a destiny yet to
be revealed: "How little I knew! here in some hollow restaurant. I would have always to be alone, exploring somewhere
on the night's far edge."

My character—"he"—spent most of his time on trains and
buses, loitering in coffee shops at midnight or wandering
through fields at dusk; he was never known to be up and
about during the day, though he rose at dawn, when "the
sky woke pale and brilliant, and the night's thin snow was
melting on the urgent land." At one with nature, he had
problems with girls. Dining with an old flame, he suddenly
cried out: "Why did you leave me? Look, I'm miserable."
Another girl friend subjected to one of his tortured confessions ("I've made a terrible mistake. Life means more to me
than art. I have no happiness without you") fell asleep: "The
sun played warmly over her sullen face."

I had finally tried Mr. Richter's patience. "No wonder
sullen!" he wrote on the back:

Aren't you getting tired of this unintentionally comical
sensibility? This creature sees and exists in literary terms.
He is words, not flesh. One of the marks of the beast is
that he is just "he"—a gas, a vapor, a miasma. The job
for the week: get rid of him! Throw him out and with

him his whole secondhand, bogus sensitivity. He should
be buried in an unmarked grave.

My assignment for the following week was to read and study
several front-page stories in *The New York Times*, then write
up the following incident: A train hits a bus. Three people are
killed. One of them is a prominent labor lawyer.

I was stunned. Mr. Richter had—to borrow a phrase from
one of my stories—"denied the ethos of my destiny with
peculiar fervor and abandon." But he was adamant, and when
I bridled at the labor lawyer suggestion, he proposed I write a
profile of a character as unlike "him" as possible. I was to
supply the biographical facts about this character as if I were
filling out a job application—where he'd gone to school, how
old he was, what he did for a living—and make up a page of
dialogue.

MME. PEILLEIN. Haven't you anything else to do all day
besides loiter in the lobby? I cannot understand it. You
are still so young.
HENRI. I'm not so young.
MME. PEILLEIN. How old? Why aren't you married?
Where are your friends?
HENRI. I don't have any. I just like to sit downstairs. It's
cool in here.
MME. PEILLEIN. Are you unhappy?
HENRI. I'm not unhappy. I love the city in the rain. I
used to lie awake at night and watch the wet streets
becoming rivers. Everyone seems to hurry when it rains.
They crowd into the cafés during the long dreary after-
noons. The noise bothers me. When I fish by the river,
I reprimand them when the others talk. I tell them it
disturbs the fish. Denise! Come to my room. You can
see the Pantheon from there.

MME. PEILLEIN. No, no, I can't. I'm old, you know.
HENRI (*passionately*). You're not! Forty is nothing.
MME. PEILLEIN. Where are you going?
HENRI. Upstairs.

A weird character, this Henri; Madame Peillein was right to steer clear of him. On the deck of a ship bound for America —I forget now why he was going there—the young Parisian brooded: "I've never before home the Catholic school we stood about in the train lost New York is there home home I have so little aimless this is all I will ever do." I was rather pleased with this stream-of-consciousness effect. Mr. Richter dismissed it as "egregious lyricism."

Where *did* I get this character? Surely he wasn't me, even if I did loiter in museums and walk moodily along the Charles, hands deep in my pockets, the wind slicing through my cape. Even if I did stay up until dawn, my nerves in agony from Dexedrine, to watch the sun come up over the Yard. I was moved by William Barrett's account in *Irrational Man* (my father's copy, with mustard stains from the time he'd brought it to Wrigley Field) of the writer's solitary struggle:

> Out of the ravages of his experience, his desperate loneliness, the writer must put forth those works which look back into his gaze with conviction and authenticity and wear about them the gleams of interest which have fled from the vast bare blank face of the world as seen in the extreme situations of *his* truth: in sleeplessness, the nervous darkness, against death and against the inexorable and dragging vista of time which is his only being.

The writer, *c'est moi*! Talk about desperate loneliness, I thought, looking up from my book at two o'clock in the morning: I hadn't had a date since I got here. The trees in Harvard

Yard were bare, their branches sheathed in snow. No one who hadn't stared out his dorm window in the middle of the night, when the moon disappeared behind a scrim of vaporous clouds and stale cigarette smoke hung in the air—no one who hadn't known, who hadn't *experienced* such moments of desolation could really hope to comprehend what this "nervous darkness," this "inexorable and dragging vista of time," was all about. So Mr. Richter could have his fun with my prose. I was the man, I suffered, I was there.

Bob had arrived a week early and moved in our furniture. He was at the kitchen table mending a net on his box hockey game when I walked in. "Bobo!" he cried, leaping up to slap my hand. "Quick game?"

"You mind if I hang up my jacket first?" Here we were in a fine old Cambridge house with stenciled wallpaper and a working fireplace, and Bob wanted to play box hockey. "I can't believe you're still carting this around."

"Sit down," he commanded.

"One game and that's it. I have to fill out my study card." I took my place across from him and tested the knobs, pushing the metal players up and down the rink in their grooves while Bob worked away on the net, hunched over it like a jeweler. He'd never liked the plastic Sears, Roebuck ones, and had made his own from coat hangers and gauze.

"You gonna try to get into Ames's course again?" he said.

"I guess so." I flicked the puck down the ice to my left forward. "Does K. ever give up trying to get into the Castle?"

I had been applying to Morgan Ames's advanced poetry seminar ever since I spotted his name in the course catalogue the summer before freshman year. Morgan Ames: it was hard for me to comprehend that a poet whose work I'd been reading since I was fourteen, who was featured in every standard anthology, whose photograph I had up on the bulletin board in

my room, was actually teaching at Harvard. His life was mythic
to me. Born to one of those old New York families you read
about in Edith Wharton, he had grown up amid the kind of
wealth—summers in Newport, prep school at Choate, a house
on Fifth Avenue—that didn't need to display itself. Only
Morgan's branch of the Ames clan was faintly disreputable;
his father was an alcoholic, his mother had suspicious "women
friends." (I knew all this from having read *Modern Confessions*, the sequence of poems about his family that made him
famous when he was twenty-nine.) By the end of the Depression, the money was largely gone. Since then, Ames had sub-
sisted on various gentleman jobs. He taught for a while at
Andover, then at Bard, and later on at Princeton. For the last
few years he'd been at Harvard, teaching one semester. He
rarely took underclassmen: I'd been turned down twice.

I fired a slapshot at Bob's goalie. "What about you?"

"I don't know. I'm more interested in prose right now." He
transferred the puck from his left guard to his center, moved it
deftly down the ice, and flicked it in my net. "Goal! Did I tell
you I got a letter from Harper & Row about my piece in *The
Crimson*? They want me to expand it into a book."

Maybe you'll get leukemia first, or be run over by a truck
in Harvard Square.

"What piece?"

"The fast food one." Bob writes an essay on the significance
of Macdonald's in American life and gets offers from publishers while my nuclear war poems ("Oblivious to our final
fate/The missiles in their silos wait") come back from *The
New Yorker* with rejection slips. "You ready?" He got out
a stopwatch and laid it on the table.

"Ready."

Bob tossed the puck in for a face-off and slapped it away.
My center twirled futilely on its metal stem. The puck skidded
toward Bob's right forward, who caught it on his stick, held

it for a beat, then fed it across to his left forward. On the defensive, I maneuvered my goalie back and forth in its groove.

"Esposito to Maki," Bob chanted. "Maki crosses the blue line and feeds it over to Hull." Another hesitation, and the puck was in the net. "Did you see that?" Bob exulted. "The way it hung up there in the corner?" There was no gloating in his jubilation. It was an aesthetic triumph.

The late-afternoon sun lit up the kitchen window and the reddening leaves of a maple in the yard scraped against the glass. Autumn in New England, and I was playing box hockey with Bob.

When I stepped off the elevator on the tenth floor of Holyoke Center, the corridor was already crowded with aspirants to Ames's seminar. I sat down on a bench near the elevator bank, away from the others. Their eagerness put me off.

The elevator doors opened and the poet emerged amid a coterie of graduate students, like a Mafia don surrounded by his lieutenants. Winston Walker, a teaching fellow whose introductory poetry course I'd taken freshman year, was hugging Ames's side. I rose to greet him, but he hurried past with a brusque nod, clearing a path through the crowd. Ames shuffled down the corridor, an aging professor in a fullback's body, staring ahead with the prescient gaze of the blind. We pushed into the classroom after him, so many that we spilled out into the hall.

Ames glanced around in bewilderment. His eyes, magnified by black-framed glasses, flicked warily from face to face. His wrinkled suit hung from his shoulders as if it were a size too large, and a wreath of whitening curls trailed back from his broad marmoreal forehead. Flecks of spittle formed at the corners of his mouth. The class fell silent, like birds before an eclipse.

"I can only take ten or twelve of you," he began, in a faintly Southern drawl. (He'd been an undergraduate at Vanderbilt, and studied with Allen Tate.) He winced in the bright fluorescent light and smiled through taut lips. "I'm sure everyone is qualified. Why don't you leave your poems with me," he suggested hesitantly, as if the idea had just occurred to him, "and I'll post a list in Warren House before next week's meeting." That was all. He made his way toward the door.

On the crucial day, I consulted the bulletin board in Warren House every few minutes, glancing at my watch as if I had an appointment. Finally a secretary wandered in and tacked up the list. There was my name—and Bob's. *Mon semblable, mon frère!*

I rose in the Holyoke Center elevator with an elated heart that afternoon and hurried to the seminar room—only to find it as crowded as it had been the week before. There must have been forty people perched on the windowsill or sitting cross-legged on the floor among piles of coats. Tutors and graduate students, local poets, white-haired women with veiny Brahmin cheeks, a reporter from the *Crimson* with a notepad on his knee. The list, it turned out, was a formality; anyone could attend.

Ames passed around copies of a poem and asked who the author was. A girl with kohl-encrusted eyes and silver stars pasted on her cheeks raised her hand. Ames nodded and began to read the poem in a low, droning voice—the voice I had listened to on a Caedmon album in high school, lying on my bed while the TV boomed up through the floor:

> *The night when you became my lover,*
> *Goats cavorted above the star-dappled sea.*
> *I saw the whitewashed villages whiten,*
> *The moon intensify its beam of light.*

Ames's hand, the figures splayed, moved in circles over the page, as if he were conjuring it to rise off the table. "You feel this last stanza's almost a parody, it's so weird," he said. "You could almost say it's a satire on the genre." The girl gnawed a fingernail and lit a cigarette. "It reminds me of Swinburne's '*Cor Cordium*,'" Ames persisted. "It has Swinburne's florid energy." He turned a mild, inquisitive face to the girl, tucking a feathery wisp of hair behind his ear. "Isn't that what you had in mind? It's a translation of an English poem."

"I guess so," said the girl.

"How do others feel about the poem?" A few tentative hands rose up, but Ames was studying it again. "Or you could have the goats cavorting first: 'Goats cavorted when you became my lover.'" Dissatisfied with this variation, he tried another: "'The star-dappled sea cavorts . . .'" His eyes had a hectic glint. "Why doesn't someone else talk now?" he said softly.

"I wonder if that last image is really earned," ventured a boy in a motorcycle jacket. "I mean . . ."

"But then you couldn't really say Swinburne," Ames cut in, his hands circling like gears above the poem. "It doesn't have Swinburne's lushness." He stared out the window, thinking hard. "And you could queer my argument by saying that it doesn't rhyme."

Through the picture window that looked out over Harvard Yard, the needlelike spire of Memorial Church pierced the sky. A line of geese floated over the Yard. Ames studied the poem for a while, then turned again to the author. "It's as good as Edna Millay."

Eventually we got used to these sudden reversals. Ames would sit before one of our poems, seemingly transfixed by it, a cigarette cradled in his hand, another smoldering in the ashtray—then glance up and offer some bizarre advice: "Have you tried writing this in couplets?" "What if you made the speaker a priest instead of a poet? Then maybe his sins would seem more real."

Ames's interruptions were involuntary. Hunched down in his chair, smoke dribbling from between his thin moist lips, he would spin his manic fantasies, imagining how the poem would have gone if Wallace Stevens or T. S. Eliot had written it. Once, discussing a poem by the boy in the motorcycle jacket, he peered intently at the page and stated, "You've been reading Hardy."

"Not really," said the boy, in obvious confusion. Wasn't Hardy a novelist? "I mean, no more than usual."

"But you could see these stanzas in *The Dynasts*," Ames insisted. "Only with Hardy it would require eight hundred lines instead of eight." He leaned back in his chair and gazed at the ceiling. "You have Hardy's grim sense of humor—his enjoyment of misery. Fate was something he could mock at and not be called cruel." The boy stared at him like a tourist trying to make out a foreign language. "But then Hardy wrote his poetry out of genuine despair," Ames mused. "You feel he wasn't so much inspired by misery as driven mad by it." And he was off on a long account of Hardy's two marriages, his reclusiveness, his strange behavior toward his wives.

Ames had the infuriating habit of devoting hours and hours of our precious class time to older poets—and I mean old. Bored with our unmetred cries of anguish, he would turn to a well-thumbed *Oxford Book of English Verse* that he carried with him everywhere, its navy-blue cover faded with age. "This poem reminds me of Wyatt," he might announce suddenly, flipping through the thick blue volume. And he would read one of Wyatt's sonnets, his voice quaking with tension, then dropping to a nearly inaudible murmur. Once he recited from

memory Sir Walter Raleigh's "What Is Our Life?" and when
he came to the last four lines—

> *Our graves that hide us from the searching sun*
> *Are like drawn curtains when the day is done.*
> *Thus march we, playing, to our latest rest,*
> *Only we die in earnest—that's no jest.*

—his voice grew rapt with terror. Eyes wide, he stared sightlessly out at the vision summoned up by Raleigh's words, a
premonitory hallucination beyond the grasp of the fresh-faced
undergraduates seated around him at the long Formica table.

We listened dutifully to Ames's recitations of these dead
poets. Only why didn't he understand our unappeasable hunger
to discuss our own work? Week after week, we entered the
classroom tense with expectation. Whose poems would be
handed out this time? You could feel the frustration when the
unlucky ones glanced down like poker players appraising their
hands and learned they'd been dealt out someone else's work.
And you couldn't fold, either; you had to stay in for the whole
two hours.

Ames, though, was never bored. Looking up from the mimeographed sheet before him, he would ask in his mild voice
whose it was, and fix upon the author an uncertain scrutiny.
The first time a poem of mine was read out in Ames's droning
intonation, I could feel him trying to bring me into focus. It
was clear he'd never seen me before.

"It's an odd poem," he remarked, pawing the air like a
blind man groping down a corridor. "It's all sensibility. You've
written yourself back to the nineteenth century, to Baudelaire." He studied the poem, as absorbed as a scientist examining a slide, and read the line again: " 'My wracked frame
wastes on a Tangiers balcony.' You've told us that you're
suffering, but not how or why." He gave me a kindly look.

"And this pathetic fallacy: 'The stars' mad vacant stare.' It's too bizarre. The reader balks."

Was my work pathetic, then, on top of everything else? I eyed the poem in disgust. "I like its strangeness," Ames broke in on my despondent reverie. "It's as if Keats had come out and told us how much he wanted to be a great poet." He smiled. "The poem's all about you, a good subject—even if it's a you that's entirely made up."

I didn't hear another word in class that day. Like a patient cut off by his psychiatrist at the end of the hour, I was resentful, angry; I needed more. My audience had ended all too quickly. I tried to remember everything Ames had said, but the message was ambiguous. Had I been compared favorably with Baudelaire? And what did he say about "sensibility"? Was that a good thing to have? My memory, cruelly accurate for once, restored the disparaging phrase. But it was the word "pathetic" that tormented me the most; not even "I like its strangeness" could cancel out that distressing epithet.

And then one afternoon it happened. I glanced down at the day's poems and was ecstatic to find another winning hand: "Washing the Dishes, I Think About My Life," a meditation on my Ukrainian origins, my grandfather's arrival in America, and our Sunday dinners on Peterson Avenue. It was dated "Evanston 1.31.68–Cambridge 2.16.69" after Joyce's "Trieste–Zurich–Paris" dateline to *Ulysses*.

The other poem was Bob's. "These are two grandfather poems," Ames said mildly. "Portraits of Jewish family life." He circled his hands, Merlinlike, over my poem. Bob and I, on opposite sides of the table, couldn't look each other in the eye. But I knew what he was thinking. Ames didn't impress him; he was uncomfortable around the great poet, and contemptuous of his disciples. What fascinated Bob was the convergence of our lives. He couldn't wait to settle down with a beer at the Harvard Gardens and gloat over the fact that the same boys who used to pass a Campbell's soup can back and forth in his Glencoe kitchen were now sitting around a seminar table at Harvard having their poems compared by Morgan Ames. Where would it end? On *The Dick Cavett Show*, maybe —with a real microphone.

Ames looked up with a sad, wincing smile. "It's an odd poem," he said in that melancholy voice of his, a low murmur I had to lean forward to hear. "I can't tell whether you miss your grandfather or whether you're just worried about getting older yourself." ("Grandpa, the generations dwindle and die," I had written. "You were new in the Old World, old in the New"—a nice Amesian paradox.)

"But . . ."

"Now in this other poem," Ames continued, raising his voice, "you can see the narrator's quite fond of his grandfather."

Hey, wait a minute. We're not through talking about *my* poem. Bob could have box hockey. He could have stickball. But the tenth floor of Holyoke Center was my turf. I had a home team advantage.

Ames didn't know the rules. He stared at Bob's poem like a fortuneteller waiting for the tarot cards to yield their message. "This is a nice line," he mumbled, as if he were talking to himself. " 'The grandsons in their sweaters on the porch.' They're so much less resentful . . ."

Than you-know-who. Bob's poems were about "the quiet understanding of generations," the women "fussing over borscht in the steamy kitchen." Mine were a litany of ancient wrongs: ("Put on a tie! Papa shrilled at noon. / I loitered in the bathroom, pale, jejune"). I had enough grievances to keep a whole team of lawyers busy. Your Honor, the plaintiff claims that on the seventh of March, 1959, the defendant gave him "a swift kick in the pants" when he refused to wear a tie to his grandmother's house. ("Remember, Papa, that terrible

day/You kicked me and then strode away?") That on Christmas Day in 1962, he accompanied the plaintiff and the plaintiff's mother to Guido's Italian restaurant for dinner instead of
celebrating that holiday as other Americans do, and caused
him to feel an acute sense of alienation from which he still
hasn't recovered. ("The jukebox in Guido's played Frank
Sinatra./I wouldn't eat my veal piccata.") If Sylvia Plath
could turn her father into a Nazi, I could turn mine into a
brooding loner. ("Even when you mowed the lawn, / Your
haunted face looked pale and wan.")

"Which of these poems do you like more?" Ames asked the
class. Bob, his face cupped in his hands, studied the mimeographed sheets. He had grown sideburns out of deference to
the '60s, but otherwise he was the same old Bob: hair neatly
cut, a light-blue shirt from the Crimson Shop open at the
collar, a windbreaker with the New Trier logo. I had on a
serape and Frye boots, and had lately started a moustache that
looked as if I'd dabbed it over my lip with a grease pencil.

"I think Bob's poem is more beautiful," said the girl with
stars pasted on her cheeks. "I love that image of the grandfather becoming the flowers on his grave. But 'Washing the
Dishes' has a kind of rawness that works for me—like the poet
is really mad about something." Hear that, Bob?

"But he seems so old," said a boy with curly blond hair who
wrote poems about hot rods and filling stations. "I mean, that
line about the nine affairs, a death, and less than half a novel
—it's too much."

"You feel that being precocious is important to this author,"
Ames volunteered through a haze of cigarette smoke. "He
wants to sound as if he's at the end of his life instead of the
beginning."

Why did I sound so weary? "You're a sensitive boy," my
father had told me when I came home from school in tears
one day, having failed even to place that year in the Illinois

High School Poetry Contest. "You'll suffer your whole life."
Thanks, Pop. Once he showed me an article in *The New
England Journal of Medicine* on the incidence of alcoholism
among novelists who had won the Nobel Prize. "They were all
drinkers," my father marveled. "Faulkner, Steinbeck, Heming-
way, Sinclair Lewis—the whole bunch." So what was I supposed to do? Sit at my desk with a can of Dr. Pepper at my
elbow? Alcohol made me dizzy, cigarettes parched my throat,
but I had before me the image of Sartre squinting wall-eyed
through a haze of smoke. Camus, hands deep in his trench
coat, a butt dangling from his lower lip, was my Bogart. (He
even looked like Bogart.) My father made fun of these smokers,
putting a pencil stub in his mouth and narrowing his eyes
against the imaginary smoke. Meanwhile I was lighting up
before the bathroom mirror, practicing for the jacket photograph of my first book.

"That was a weird experience," Bob said as we stood waiting for the elevator after class. "The Chicago boys meet
Morgan Ames."

"You think he knows we're friends?"

Bob laughed. "I doubt he could pick us out of a police
lineup."

"Bullshit!" I was offended. "He's not as oblivious as you
think."

"What's the difference if he knows us or not? He's not your
father."

"Don't get Freudian on me, okay? You want approval for
throwing a perfect pass; I want it for a perfect image."

"Hey, I write too, remember? Anyway, there are other
things in the world besides who's the best poet." Oh, yeah?
Name 'em.

Just then Ames loomed up beside us. Wiping his brow with
a soiled handkerchief, he nodded in our direction and stared
at the winking numbers over the elevator, as absorbed in their

message (8, 9, 10) as if it were the ribbon of news flashed from the billboard in Times Square.

The doors opened and we crowded in, Bob and I squeezed in a corner behind Ames's massive back. A tense elevator silence descended over us as we contemplated the tendrils of gray hair coiling down Ames's neck. When we spilled out in the lobby, I somehow found myself walking by his side.

"That was a good poem," Ames said, gazing sadly down at me.

"Thanks."

"Yours, too," he said to Bob, who had appeared on his other side. We emerged from the passageway onto Mt. Auburn Street, Ames gingerly treading the sidewalk in floppy rubbers. It was early December, and Cambridge was already in its Arctic phase. Sooty banks of snow were piled up on the curb, and the sky had a silvery polar sheen.

Our house was in the other direction, but we found ourselves being carried along beside Ames like shipwrecked survivors clinging to a mast as he navigated uncertainly down the side-walk, forcing pedestrians to stumble into the snow. "Who do you think are the good poets in the class?" Ames murmured, veering so that I had to step off the curb and slog through the slushy street—losing another three inches into the bargain.

"Brad Marsden's pretty good," I volunteered.

Ames stared mournfully before him as if I had made some overwhelming pronouncement that required him to change his deepest beliefs about the nature of the universe. "You think so?" he said doubtfully. "I liked that poem about his trip to Afghanistan."

Tunisia, I silently corrected him. Marsden. A somber, bearded boy who smoked Sobranies and carried around a copy of Gary Snyder's poems. But I was reluctant to let myself go with Bob around, inhibiting the flow of malice. "He's not bad,"

I said grudgingly. What's your opinion, Bob? But he just trudged beside us through the slush.

"You're both Chicago boys, aren't you?" Ames said. The acknowledgment of this personal detail was electrifying. He was aware of us.

"We've known each other all our lives," I answered. Ames gave a weak smile. There was a moment's hesitation as we stood at the Quincy House gate. Was he going to invite us in for a drink? At last he raised a hand in farewell and lumbered off down the path, a giant figure bowed in the dusk.

"Chicago boys!" I exulted. "He thought our poems were good."

Bob shook his head. "God, you are hung up!"

"And you don't care what he thinks, right?" This from a guy who kept a signed photograph of Billy Pierce—"To Bob Wolin, a promising hurler"—on his bulletin board.

"I didn't say that." He scooped up a handful of dirty snow and packed it in a ball. "It's your need for his approval I don't get." Well, what of it? Some people prayed. My gods were in this world—now and in Cambridge.

We climbed the stairs and flung our coats down on the sofa. "How 'bout it?" said Bob.

"How about what?"

"You know. Don't pull that innocent routine on me."

"I don't know what you're talking about." But he was already seated at the kitchen table, flicking the puck down the ice.

I was hardly alone in my hunger for Ames's attention. Everyone clamored for a share: the Brattle Street ladies who invited him to dinner; the undergraduates who clustered around him after class to discuss a late assignment or clarify some stray remark he'd made about their work; the tutors and graduate students who accompanied him to the Faculty Club for a drink. Like cripples thronging about a healer, we longed to be anointed by the great man's recognition.

Denied direct access to Ames, I cultivated his disciples.

Winston Walker had organized a workshop of his own that met once a week in the basement of Kirkland House, and now that I was in Ames's class he invited me to join. Every Thursday night we gathered in a dreary boiler room beneath plaster-swaddled pipes to read our poems and gossip about "Chip"—short for Charles, Ames's middle name. Only the inner circle used it. "Chip read this poem the other night and thought it was one of my best." "Chip says you have to tinker with a poem until your eyes pop out of your head." The name itself was poetry.

The biographical lore these disciples had at their command! They knew the names of Ames's wives (he'd had three); the variants of celebrated lines; his itinerary ("Chip's in London," or "Chip's gone off to his summer house in Nantucket"). Some of them had even visited him in New York; he spent only two days a week in Cambridge, commuting up on the shuttle.

"I had dinner at Chip's last weekend," Winston reported one night. "He has a beautiful apartment in the Dakota. Double-height windows, floor-to-ceiling books, a balcony around the living room. It's really very grand."

"Who else was there?" I said grudgingly, knowing he wanted me to ask.

"Let's see," he said, as if he could hardly be troubled to remember. "Lillian Hellman. The Trillings. Bill Styron."

Bill.

It was Winston who introduced me to Ames's "office hours" when I happened to encounter him turning in at the gate of Quincy House one morning. He was on his way to see Ames, he admitted; why didn't I come along? I followed him down a flight of stairs, past a janitor's closet and into a tiny, window-less room with cinderblock walls and a few metal folding chairs around a seminar table scarred with cigarette burns. Ames spent three hours every Wednesday morning in this cheerless cell, discussing poems with whoever happened to show up. Anyone could attend, the only requirement being that one knew about office hours in the first place; and since no one who did was anxious to share the information, word didn't get around.

Promptly at nine, Ames would shuffle into the crowded room looking pale and hungover, his forehead damp, a watery remoteness in his eyes. "Who has a poem?" he would ask shyly, lighting a cigarette.

I could never figure out why he submitted himself to this needless torture. Maybe because so many of our poems were imitations of his own—a form of homage. The brutal candor of *Modern Confessions* was our model, Ames's madness our literary myth. Hardly a semester went by without a manic episode resulting in broken furniture, threats of violence, or hysterical phone calls in the middle of the night. I had never witnessed one of these breakdowns, but I'd heard about them in grim detail: Ames showing up at the Harvard preacher's house and declaring that he was the Virgin Mary; Ames talking for two hours straight in class, revising a student's poem in the style of Tennyson or Pope; Ames wandering around Harvard Square in the middle of January without an overcoat, shivering, wild-eyed, incoherent. In the seminar room on the top floor of Holyoke Center, we waited nervously for it to happen before our eyes, watching for references to Hitler, crazed soliloquys, outbursts of inappropriate gaiety—sure signs that the poet had "gone off" and would have to be put away again.

Encouraged by Ames's willingness to put these episodes into poetry, his disciples turned out chronicles of madness, suicide, and debauchery that made the revelations in *Modern Con-*

fessions seem as tame as a country priest's journal. "When you slit your wrists," began a poem by a genial Midwestern boy who came to class in overalls, "the blood made a crimson gully on the floor." "I could feel his heart lunging like a rabbit flushed from cover" was another memorable line, this one from a poem about a three-hundred-pound diva whose lover is seized by a fatal heart attack as she bestrides him on the couch in her dressing room. The day a thin, mild-mannered divinity student whose piping voice, disheveled beard, and wire-rimmed glasses made him a dead ringer for Lytton Strachey read out the dramatic monologue of a mass murderer of little boys—"I was happy only when I had one in the trunk" —I gazed around our cell in wonderment: just how many Loebs and Leopolds were there in this room?

My own poetry revealed no homicidal inclinations; the only violence I did was to the language. But in every other respect it was so close to Ames's as to verge on plagiarism. Once I brought in a poem that Ames read aloud, interrupting with his usual digressions, until he came to the last line. He paused as if studying an unfamiliar word, and said in his gentle, murmurous drawl, "I see you've taken a line here from one of my poems." I faced his unreproachful gaze, and suddenly remembered the line; mine diverged from it by a single word.

"Huh!" I said. "I guess it is a lot like it." I could feel myself blushing, and stared down at the poem, my head cradled in my fists.

"It's a good line," Ames said, and everyone laughed.

I was elated by the discovery of office hours. It put me a notch above the poets in Ames's undergraduate seminar. But elites are like those wooden Russian dolls with ever smaller dolls inside; you keep thinking, this *has* to be the smallest one. Twenty people knew about office hours; only a handful were invited to join Ames for lunch on Wednesdays at Iruña, a Spanish restaurant in Harvard Square. Nothing dejected me more than to emerge from the Quincy House basement at noon and watch Ames amble off toward Boylston Street, surrounded by his coterie. No matter how old I was, there always seemed to be an older crowd around to exclude me. Pushing my tray along the counter in the Dudley House dining hall, I peered disconsolately through the steamed-up glass at the metal bins heaped with carrots and lima beans, mashed potatoes and Salisbury steak. After all the seminars, the books, the late-night *conversaziones* at the Pamplona, was I any less out of it than I'd been in seventh grade, unwrapping my bologna sandwich on a bench while the big boys chose sides for the lunch-hour scrub baseball game at Nichols School?

One day, after a sparsely attended office hours, I noticed Ames glancing around and realized that no one from the inner circle had shown up. Who would join him at Iruña? I happened to be sitting beside him—rather, I had arrived twenty minutes early and claimed the seat. Ames registered my presence and murmured, "Let's have lunch." It was a command, but spoken in such a diffident voice that I wasn't even sure I'd heard it.

As we headed off down the street, I glimpsed Rupert Scawen, one of the few undergraduates who had managed to infiltrate office hours. Scawen, a burly, taciturn young man who specialized in dramatic monologues by martyred religious figures —Jan Hus, Giordano Bruno, Thomas More—seemed capable of the violence Ames's disciples only wrote about. There was a taut, furious shape to his mouth, and his blue eyes had an angry glint. He was angling toward us with a determined stride, his big shoulders thrown forward, as if he were muscling his way through a crowd.

I tried to hurry Ames on, hoping to screen him from the

intruder's view. But Scawen came right up, and Ames—the distracted, indiscriminate Ames—invited him to join us. What the fuck are you doing? I raged inwardly. I could scarcely restrain myself from seizing the intrusive poet and hurling him into the snow. But it was too late; he had fallen in beside us. Fuming, I kicked a stony lump of ice. What was so special about having lunch with Ames if this weird fanatic could push his way in?

I didn't hear another word until we were seated at Iruña and Ames was filling our glasses with sangría. Oblivious of the malevolent stares we exchanged—Scawen wasn't any happier than I was about sharing the occasion—he posed his favorite question: "Who do you read?"

Scawen named some younger poets, neo-Surrealists with a weakness for hallucinatory images and improbable metaphors. I knew Ames didn't care for their work.

"I just don't believe them," I broke in. "Their poems aren't *about* anything. I get so tired of all those speaking stones and streetlamps that turn into stars. It's become a style, the latest fashion." My voice quavered with vehemence.

Ames lit a cigarette and caressed the tablecloth, smoothing out wrinkles and brushing away crumbs. He was in his element, ranking poets, assigning them their place on the ladder —beneath him, it was understood. I had worried on the way over that I wouldn't have enough to say, but I realized that it didn't matter; all one had to do was mention a few poets and Ames was off, judging, dismissing, now and then offering a shred of praise. This exercise could entertain him for hours. "Who else?" he would prompt during a lull in the conversation; or, "What about so-and-so?" He sat up eagerly whenever a new name was introduced, his hands spread out on the table, a glad look in his eye. "He's written two good poems," he would declare in that mild but definite voice of his—then proceed to name and discuss them as if the book were right in front of him, open to the page. I was amazed by how much he kept up. I never heard him say he didn't know a poet's work.

"You really think they're as bad as all that?" My rude outburst had made Ames more charitable. Why be the first to attack? "Harold Burn is interesting in his own small way," he put in, mentioning a poet of minor reputation. "He's written some good things." Ames's eyes bulged behind his glasses. "Only you feel he has nothing to say."

I nodded and glanced at my sullen opponent, but he was busy gnawing the husk of a shrimp. Ames signaled the waiter and ordered another pitcher of sangría. He hadn't touched his lunch, an omelette in cream sauce. The ashtray was heaped with bent and broken half-smoked cigarettes. Ames wasn't one of those smokers who exhale in vigorous plumes; he smoked as if it made him ill. His skin had a mushroomlike pallor; his tie was streaked with ash. But he was talking with great energy now, recalling the time he and Burn had met. "He wanted me to come read in Milwaukee or somewhere like that against the war, but I'd already been to Washington and marched against the war, and felt I'd done my part." He gave an apologetic smile, as if asking us to absolve him. Had he done the right thing?

Ames had a way of soliciting opinions from his listeners in order to draw them out. It flattered us to know that our ideas mattered—though I couldn't imagine why they did. What difference did it make what some aborigine-haired undergraduate thought of Pound's *Cantos* or the early Yeats? But Ames was achingly well-mannered. He was working his way through Yeats's whole career now, from *The Wind Among the Reeds* to the great poems of his old-man phase.

"I guess my favorite is 'Under Ben Bulben,' " I volunteered.

"Really?" Ames said in surprise, as if I were F. R. Leavis reversing a verdict in *New Bearings in English Poetry.* "What is it that you like about it?"

What indeed? The only line I could remember was "Horseman, pass by!"

"It's so eloquent about death," I babbled, reaching for my glass. Scawen probably knew the whole poem by heart, and half the plays. But he was talked out. Ames simply couldn't understand that not everyone lived for poetry the way he did. We had been comparing Pope and Dryden, Coleridge and Wordsworth, Edward Thomas and Wilfred Owen for hours, and the two pitchers of sangría had made inroads on my attention. It seemed odd to be drunk in the middle of the afternoon, the ice-etched windows glittering in the sun. I was groggy from alcohol and talk. Besides, I was eager to get word out about the momentous event. How could any experience, even this one, compete with the joys of reporting it? To refine, elaborate, revise what happened, to polish and edit the afternoon . . . I could hardly wait to get out of there. "Guess who I had lunch with?" I heard myself saying over the phone. (No need to mention old Rupert in these accounts; from now on it was Ames and me.)

But Ames, done with English literature, had started in on the poets who came to office hours. "I find Leonard's poems too much like mine," he said benignly. "You wonder where he can go from here." Leonard Wiggins was one of Ames's most devoted disciples, and had published several essays on his work. Ames had rewarded him with a blurb on his first book. "I mean, he's very good," Ames said, turning to me with the look on his face of a child caught drawing on the bedroom wall. "But can you get away with some of what he gets away with in a poem? Or can you say anything now?" There was a slyness in his eyes that dared reproof. His disloyalty was a game, a way of diverting himself.

Of course, it was a game that required another player, someone to feed him names. "What about Winston Walker?" I said. He'd gone out to Berkeley for the semester and "been through a lot of heavy changes"—or so he reported in a letter I now quoted to Ames.

"Yes, I gather he's brimming with revolutionary zeal," Ames said, leaning forward to concentrate on my words. Here was a good subject. He delighted in news of anyone he knew. "I liked his early poems, but I can't follow what he's writing now. You wonder if there isn't too much California in it." (Ames always switched from "I" to "you," as if attributing his opinions to someone else.) I introduced another name. "His poems are too grotesque, too truthful," Ames said. And of a student whose work he had praised in class: "She has a schoolgirl's bright enthusiasm, but you feel she hasn't lived."

Everyone did this, I reflected as we left the restaurant. I disparaged my closest friends just for the sake of camaraderie, for the atmosphere of good fellowship that putting down mutual acquaintances induced. Why should Ames be any different?

Yet the deference, the bowed head, the gentle drawl, were no pose: they were the visible signs of his ordeal. His oddness made people shy away from him. One night I spotted him at the Athenaeum, where a young painter who had attended office hours on occasion was giving a slide show of his canoe trip through Alaska. Sitting in the dark among that crowd of ruddy-faced old Bostonians, I wondered what Ames made of the seals and caribou, the trout surfacing on ponds, the vistas of barren tundra that flashed on the screen; the wilderness wasn't exactly his turf. Afterwards, he made straight for me, glad to see a familiar face.

Usually he didn't even recognize me. I used to see him often, shuffling down Mass. Ave. in his crepe-soled rubber boots. One afternoon, loitering by the magazine rack in the Pangloss Bookshop, I looked up to find him staring in the window, a hand cupped against the glass. I nodded and smiled, hoping to be noticed, but he just squinted through the dusty glass and walked away.

Bob wasn't interested in Harvard literary life. Cambridge could have been Glencoe for all he cared. Coming home from classes, I would see him in the schoolyard on Oxford Street playing hockey with the little kids in the neighborhood, looming over them in the autumn twilight as he dribbled toward a tiny goalie crouched fearfully between two garbage drums. One afternoon I came downstairs to answer the doorbell and found a boy in a woolen cap, a hockey stick clutched in his mittened hand, peering through the screen. "Can Bob come out and play?" he said in a small voice.

"Bob's not home right now."

"Oh," he said unhappily. "Just tell him Stevie was here." And he trudged off toward the schoolyard, his stick draped over his shoulder like a musket.

Hunched over *The Norton Anthology of English Literature* in my study after dinner, I waited for Bob to knock on the door and cry, "Let's go, babe. Got a new pass play to show ya." He and Stevie hadn't been idle while I was working my way through *Absalom and Achitophel*.

"I've got an exam tomorrow."

"Yeah, yeah. A half hour out in the fresh air will do you good." He lofted a tennis ball into the room.

"If I identify John Donne as Hopkins again, I'll know who to blame." But I was already lacing up my Keds.

One night I was in the living room with a girl I'd picked up at the Casablanca when Bob walked in.

"Bob, this is Linda," I said, hoping he'd go up to his room. But he shrugged off his satin New Trier warm-up jacket and dropped down on the couch. "Where were you tonight?"

"Watching the Harvard hockey team whip Brown. Those

guys are good. Speaking of which . . ." He gestured toward the dining room. "Get in there."

I stared at him in amazement. "What are you talking about?"

"He's ashamed to admit he plays hockey," Bob explained to Linda. "But that's how he spends his days. Down on his knees fielding slapshots. Don't think he just sits in his room writing poetry."

Linda gave me a bewildered look. A B.U. freshman from Yonkers, she had on jeans and a faded Viyella shirt. Her fluffy hair stood out on her head like Orphan Annie's.

"Ignore him," I said. "He's just babbling." But Bob was already out of his chair and rummaging through the closet. A minute later he was back, brandishing two hockey sticks and a baseball mitt.

"Let's get those pads on," he said, pushing aside a plump easy chair.

"Hey, come on, Bob. Knock it off, will you?"

"Let's go, Babe," he chanted. He pulled off his belt and tossed it to me. "Game time." He hurried upstairs and a minute later was back with the protective cup, a plastic shield for the groin. "It's you and me against him, Laura."

"Linda," she corrected him, accepting a hockey stick. Bob dribbled the ball deftly over the carpet, swept around a lamp, and lofted it into my lap.

"One game," I warned him, grabbing a pillow and strapping it around my knee. I unfastened my belt—something I'd hoped to do under very different circumstances—secured the other pillow and slid the cup down my pants.

Bob was busy rolling up the dining room rug. Down on my knees in the doorway, I adjusted my pads. Suddenly Bob whirled and drilled a shot past my shoulder. "Goal!"

"I wasn't ready!" I protested, nine years old again. How did he do it?

Bob was patient with Linda. He shouted directives—

"Screen him! Stand in front of the net!"—and fed her the ball. But he couldn't contain himself once the game got going, and raced about the room flicking the ball from every angle. "Hull comes in, he fakes to Maki, and . . . goal!" He held his stick aloft and patted his teammate on the back. "Your turn, Laura. We'll make it easy for ya."

"Linda," Linda said.

"That's ridiculous!" I cried. This girl was going to get down on her knees and let us wing slapshots at her tits? But Linda was strapping on the pillows. My face was hot with shame as I passed the ball to Bob. He played it off the wall and popped it lightly into Linda's glove. What a good boy! I wouldn't have been surprised if he'd slammed the ball at her head just to make sure she never came over again and interfered with our bachelor lives—the hours of hockey, the nights out getting ripped at the Inman Square Men's Bar, the dinners of fried squid and *steak au poivre* Bob cooked up while we watched the Bruins on his old Sony. Who needed girls?

Linda was clearly no match for us. Time and again we screened each other and beat her at the net. Her face was flushed, her shirt stained dark beneath the armpits. I felt a surge of pity as Bob whipped a stinging slapshot against her skinny arm, but suppressed it by sprinting around the drop-leaf table pattering like Bob: "Hull controlling as he skates in over the blue line . . ." To think that only an hour ago I'd been standing at the bar of the Casablanca quoting one of my poems to the goalie.

"I've had it," Linda said, tossing her glove on the floor. "You guys are crazy." There was a musky high school locker room smell in the air. My shirt was soaked. Linda leaned on her stick and wiped her forehead with her sleeve. The top two buttons of her shirt were undone; her bony chest shone with sweat.

"Time for a refreshing draft from the Land of Sky Blue Waters," Bob declared, heading for the kitchen.

"I have to go, actually," Linda said. She unstrapped the pillows from her knees and retrieved her jacket from the living room.

"You want me to walk you back to the Square?" I offered feebly. She assured me that she knew the way. "Well, it was nice meeting you," I said.

"Yeah, it really was," Linda said wistfully. "I guess I'll see you around the Casa B."

"So long." I stood on the steps in the crisp autumn night and watched her disappear around the corner. Upstairs, I could hear Bob firing slapshots against the wall.

Living off-campus had definite advantages. The turreted, bay-windowed Victorian houses on our street reminded me of Evanston, and I could hardly be homesick with Bob around. We watched the Red Sox on TV, played hockey, sat at the kitchen table shooting the breeze . . . *Roundtable* had moved its studio to another city. On Friday nights we pushed our shopping cart through the aisles of the Star Market like an old married couple, grabbing tins of oysters off the shelves to snack on during *The Late Show*. Sure, Bob was a bully; the long hours of indoor hockey were pretty grueling. (I had a hard time explaining to Lizzie when I was home for Thanksgiving why I had carpet burns.) But—how can I put this?— he *liked* me. It didn't make any difference to him whether or not I'd actually read *The Savage Mind*.

And I was glad to be in "a real neighborhood," as I wrote my parents, "among the people" and away from—Herbert's phrase—"all that elitist Harvard bullshit." After a morning of stickball, Bob and I would share a quart of Bud from the Mayflower Spa, a corner grocery store that emanated authentic poverty. The shelves were empty except for a few boxes of Brillo and Cornflakes, blue tins of Planter's peanuts, plastic jugs of Aunt Jemima's syrup and bottles of Mazola oil covered with a greasy film. The clientele was a far cry from the Brattle Street dowagers inspecting artichokes in S. S. Pierce; one day as I was loitering outside the Mayflower with a Nutty Buddy in hand a girl who couldn't have been more than fourteen came up and asked if I was interested in a blow job. (For once the answer was no.)

Still, there were times when I missed the college scene. The crowds flowing over Weeks Bridge after football games, the crews skimming down the Charles, the freshmen tossing Frisbees in the Yard: I was no closer to that world than I'd been in Evanston, leafing through the Harvard catalogue on the patio. Coming out of Tommy's Lunch after a late-night snack, I watched the drunken preppies in black tie spilling out of the Final Clubs on Mt. Auburn Street, the windows lit up, a blazing chandelier briefly visible through an open door. No Chosen People need apply.

I spent most of my time putting out Harvard's literary magazine, *The Advocate.* After two years of service on the poetry board, I had become editor-in-chief by default; no one else wanted the aggravation of raising money, finding advertisers, dealing with the trustees, or any of the other dreary chores involved in putting out a magazine. Trotting around the campus with a sheaf of mimeographed placards announcing the weekly poetry readings tucked under my arm, I could see why; no matter how many notices I posted, only a handful of people ever showed up, mostly friends or roommates of the poet. My introductions were brief—how much was there to say about a sophomore in Eliot House who was majoring in English literature?—the readings themselves spitefully long, as if to punish the audience for its sparsity. "The last poem I'll read . . ." These words never failed to evoke in me the sort of joy a prisoner must feel on hearing of his parole. It meant that Dionysius—the person in charge of the bar—would soon be hurrying over to the refrigerator and pulling out the cold half-gallons of Almadén chablis. Is there a sound on earth more dolorous than the sound of twelve hands clapping? No wonder we filled our glasses to the brim.

The Advocate operated out of a shabby gray clapboard house on South Street, across from a gas station. The downstairs rooms had the bare, drafty look of a janitor's office, and the upstairs "Sanctum" resembled the lobby of a hotel in Butte, Montana: the carpet was a gangrenous, indeterminate hue, the walls were a pallid green, the leather couch was as cracked and seamed as an old bedroom slipper. A dank odor of ashes and spilled wine hung in the air. All it needed were spittoons and dusty potted palms.

Its seediness didn't bother me. As far as I was concerned, the Sanctum deserved its name. The long refectory table we convened around on Monday nights could have been brought over from an Irish mead hall for all I knew. The Throne, a high-backed chair with claw-shaped armrests and gargoyles carved in the dark mahogany, would have done a robber baron's mansion proud. On the wall above the fireplace were old photographs from a more formal era, turn-of-the-century *Advocate* boards in blazers and white flannel trousers, moustachioed young men who looked as if they knew how to have a good time. Doing the layout at the refectory table in the Sanctum long after midnight while the fluorescent lights buzzed overhead and the furnace in the basement clanked, I could imagine these hearty Old Boy types gathered around a cut-glass bowl brimming with champagne punch, heckling Wally Stevens as he recited a salacious limerick.

Once that spring I stayed in the Sanctum overnight to get an issue ready before graduation. Alone at the big table, I clipped and fitted the festoons of galleys, leafing through the bound volumes of back issues to see how it was done. The French doors to the upstairs balcony were thrown open, and the shouts of late revelers floated up from the street. There was no festive punch bowl, no convivial knot of editors in bow ties leaning jauntily against the fireplace (now littered with charred *Advocates* we burned through the winter to keep warm), but as I curled up on the lumpy couch at two in the morning and inhaled its cold leathery smell, I was happy. Any magazine that was good enough for T. S. Eliot (on the masthead in 1909 and 1910) was good enough for me.

The next morning, I stuffed my bundle of proofs in a knapsack, leaped on the stuttering motorcycle I'd gotten through a *Crimson* ad, and sped over the Longfellow Bridge to the print shop behind South Station. The gold dome of the State House, visible above the cluster of red brick buildings on Beacon Hill, shone in the early morning sun, and the wind off the bay whipped against my face. Born to raise hell. The staff thought it odd that I showed up at our staff meetings in a leather jacket, a sheaf of manuscripts in one hand and a helmet in the other, but times had changed since Eliot's day. Bow ties were out. Poets were the wild ones now.

Old Mr. Whittaker, the printer, got down off his high stool when I came in, wiping his hands on a smudged apron. He had on a green eyeshade, and his gold-rimmed glasses were flecked with dust. He handed me the latest bill, rolling a toothpick around in his mouth while I looked it over. "We're a business, not a charity," he shouted above the thumping presses. "I can't print this issue until you're all paid up."

"I've sold a lot of ads," I shouted back. "But how can I bill them without an issue to show?"

"Well, come look at the pages, anyway." Tapping a pica ruler in his hand, he led me over to a worktable where the printed pages were spread out. All talk of money was forgotten as we stood at the high table selecting typefaces for the headlines. I glanced over the pages tacked to the paste-board counter until I came to one of my own poems, "Aubade," a sestina that I'd gotten through the poetry board at a sparsely attended meeting. The crisp black type on the bone-white page leaped out at me with eerie force: I publish, therefore I am.

Twice a week I had lunch at the Signet Society, a dilapidated yellow-and-white clapboard house on the corner of Dunster and Mt. Auburn streets. The Signet was nominally for the aesthetic crowd—poets, playwrights, directors—but it wasn't very exclusive; you needed only one person to nominate you, and I'd never heard of anyone getting turned down. The Signet attracted a very loyal group. When you went in to lunch, there would be guys in their twenties and thirties who'd never managed to leave Cambridge; they were said to be working on their Ph.D.'s. There was an untenured medievalist who roomed in a boardinghouse over by Central Square; a bachelor professor of English who'd lived in Kirkland House for decades; an alcoholic composer who taught music at Emerson College; a director of "experimental" plays who'd been banned from the Loeb after he brought the Living Theatre there and things got out of hand.

At noon we'd gather in the parlor with glasses of sherry we'd poured ourselves from the bottles in the cupboard, and cast a wary eye over the company to see if anyone interesting had shown up. Mostly it was the usual crew, huddled by the door to the back dining room, which filled up first. The instant Archie, the ancient porter, called out, "Luncheon is served, gentlemen," there was a stampede. The unlucky stragglers were consigned to the dining room near the front door, where they sat in a disconsolate cluster at the far end of the table listening to shouts of laughter from the other room. It was known as the *salon des refusés*.

Still, the Signet had a certain seedy venerability. The leather chairs and threadbare Persian rugs were "genuine old," as Grandma Sophie used to say of her antique clock from czarist Russia. The place was badly in need of a paint job. Plaster flaked off the ceiling in the parlor; the piano in the corner was perpetually out of tune; the tablecloths were stained. The waitresses were Radcliffe girls on scholarship who served in blue jeans and turtlenecks. On the walls were framed columns of signatures in a shaky, sodden hand—the record of Signet dinners past. Perusing the lists, I found T. S. Eliot, e. e. cummings, Archibald MacLeish. On admission to the Signet, you were presented with a single long-stemmed rose, which you were supposed to return pressed between the pages of your first book. People actually did this; there was a whole shelf of books by Signet members with dead roses sticking out of them.

No women were admitted in those days, but you could bring them as dates on special occasions. One of the big annual events was a luncheon before the Harvard-Yale game. I couldn't think of anyone to ask. Radcliffe girls made me nervous. You had to cram for every date. Lugging their bookbags to the Quad, I sweated like a cottonpicker with a full sack in the noonday sun. Sarah Bynum, the girl I was going out with now, was a poet, too. Her idea of a date was to sit in the Poetry Room of Hilles Library with earphones on our heads, listening to *Under Milk Wood*. The daughter of a high school principal in Westport, Connecticut, she had camped out in Tuscany, bicycled in the Dordogne, gone hiking in the Alps. Her poems were full of allusions to Voltaire and Rousseau, Goethe's *Italian Journey* and Rilke's *Duino Elegies*. She'd followed Byron's itinerary from Pisa to Venice, made a pilgrimage to the beach where Shelley drowned. Seated knee to knee at a wobbly marble table in the Pamplona, we showed each other poems. Hers were in hexameters, alexandrines, heroic couplets. They had an orderly look on the page.

Sarah was old-fashioned in a way no Evanston girl was. High cheekbones, probing eyes, a thin Puritan nose—the kind of face you saw in grainy photographs of whaling captains' wives. All she needed was a high collar and a hoopskirt. Not that Sarah was an old maid type. Her cashmere sweaters, plaid skirts, and saddle shoes gave her a 1950s coed look that was more innocent than prim. But you never knew. Look at Sylvia Plath. Who would have guessed from the photographs of that flaxen-haired Wellesley girl that she had such a murderous heart?

Sarah was obsessed with her father. That much was clear from her poetry. Even when she was writing about Henry James in Urbino or Cardinal Newman in Sicily, she managed to work her old man in—like the poem about Keats in Rome that ended up describing her father's double-bypass operation:

> *The poet on his deathbed in the shuttered room*
> *Fixed his visitors with a grim, all-seeing gaze.*
> *I saw once in my father's eyes that look of doom*
> *When they wheeled him down the hall in a daze.*

"But it's mediated through this whole other experience," she explained when I pointed out that I wasn't the only confessional poet around. "My father's an objective correlative."

I see, said the blind man.

Anyway, Sarah wasn't interested in going to the football game; it conflicted with a lute recital at the Busch-Reisinger Museum. I didn't feel like going by myself, but I figured I might as well attend the lunch.

Couples were pushing in through the front door of the Signet when I arrived. They were dressed for the game: corduroys and V-neck sweaters, buck shoes and scarves. The girls had on turtlenecks, and knee socks beneath their skirts. The cloakroom was full of heavy winter coats. In the parlor, there was a crush at the bar.

"Ben!" cried Tom Maynard. "What are you doing here? I didn't know you were such a fan."

"I'm not. I came for lunch."

Tall and gaunt, with a hunchback's stoop, a pockmarked face, and eyes that started out of his head, Maynard was a legend around the Signet. He had graduated a few years ago, *summa cum laude*—though no one had ever seen him crack a book—and was rumored to be writing the Great American Novel. He lived in Boston, in a loft down by the docks, and gave occasional readings from his work-in-progress. I'd never been invited to these recitals, but I'd heard awed reports from people who had. It was Dickensian, they said, crammed with bizarre characters, unlikely scenes, hilarious dialogue. It was about Maynard's youth in Providence, where his father had managed a downtown hotel, and the various picaresque types who made it their home.

Maynard himself was Dickensian. He walked with a limp, dressed in Edwardian black suits that he got secondhand from Max Keezer's, and fixed you with the fierce, searching gaze of a tyrannical old schoolmaster, peering into your face until you felt like you were lying even if you weren't. "Lunch, eh?" he said. "Where's your date?"

"Uh, she couldn't come. She got the flu . . ."

Maynard stared at me with a look of consternation on his face. "Pity," he muttered. "Come sit with us."

We managed to get places in the back room, at a corner. Maynard introduced me to his date, a blonde with a scrubbed cheerleader's look. Maynard wasn't interested in intellectual girls; in fact, he wasn't really interested in girls at all. Dating was a hygienic necessity, the prologue to getting laid. He hardly seemed to know this one. "What's your novel about?" she asked him as we sat down.

"About?" Maynard boomed, pulling his chair up to the table with a violent scrape. "It's not *about* anything. It *is* something. A phenomenon. It's taken on a life of its own. It's like the weather: sudden squalls, then calm, then a blossoming of wild abundance: 'Blow, winds, and crack your cheeks! rage! blow!' " he declaimed. " 'You cataracts and hurricanoes, spout/Till you have drench'd our steeples, drown'd our cocks!' "

"Someone ought to drown your cock, Maynard," a voice called down from the end of the table.

"Funny," Maynard grumbled. I'll make the jokes around here. He rubbed his mottled neck. He had survived a bout with thyroid cancer, and the scar below his ear contributed to his doomed romantic aura; it was like a German student's dueling scar. "So, guy," he said, patting my wrist. "Still writing poetry? Give it up, man. Give it up. 'Terence, this is stupid stuff.' There's no narrative in poetry now. You want action, drama, soul-stirring events. Poetry's etiolated, man."

A waitress—they had on uniforms today, black dresses like the kind they wore in Ye Olde Taverne restaurants—dipped between us and laid down plates of roast beef and Yorkshire pudding. "Food and wine!" Maynard cried. "No 'coke or milk' on the big day?" he mimicked the usual choice of beverage. He grabbed a bottle of champagne and filled our glasses. "Drink up!" He raised his glass and drained it at a gulp, his knobby Adam's apple going up and down. I gazed around the table. Everyone but me had dates—me and the Harvard preacher, a chortling, obsequious fat man whose tight clerical collar made his tomato face look as if it were about to burst. After three glasses of champagne, the laughter, the clash of plates in the kitchen, and the clatter of cutlery began to merge into one deafening, indistinct noise. Bright sunshine poured in through the small-paned windows. Out on Mt. Auburn Street I could hear the muted roar and hoot of pre-game traffic. Beside me, Maynard was talking loudly into my ear. "What color pubic hair do you think blondes have?" he bellowed.

"Cut it out, Maynard. Your date's right next to you." His eyes had a glazed, bleary look. He must have been working on his flask before lunch.

"It's a fascinating question," he slurred. "A question few have dared to consider."

"It is, I know. But this isn't the time to address it."

"Aw, Janis," he protested in a Cockney voice. "Oi didn't know you were such a prude." He pushed his plate away and lit a cigarette. "Now Donne, there was a man who knew the joys of fuckery: 'Licence my roving hands, and let them goe/ Behind, before, above, between, below.' That just about covers the territory, doesn't it?" He leaned forward and said in a conspiratorial whisper: "I can't get Alice here to let me go behind."

"Jesus, Maynard, will you pipe down?" I recoiled in my chair. His breath was a fetid bouquet of sherry, roast beef and nicotine.

"I meant no harm," he said unctuously, folding his hands in his lap with priestly contrition. "My lewd, outrageous mouth betrays a meek lamb's heart." He turned to his date. "Doesn't it, Alice?"

"What?" Alice said vacantly. She was staring down the table, where a food fight was in progress. Someone had flung a spoonful of mashed potatoes at someone else.

"Ah, the Signet's gone downhill," sighed Maynard. He gave a loud belch and poured us more champagne. The cigarette in the corner of his mouth gave him the look of a squinty, indigent tout. "Alice, let us be off," he proposed in the per-

emptory voice of an English lord. "The rabble's acting up."
He nodded curtly in my direction, and they went to fetch
their coats.

People were getting up from the table. It was nearly game
time. I wandered into the parlor and sank down in one of
the red leather chairs by the window. Leafing through the
Crimson, I heard voices in the front hall ebb as the last
Signet associates and their dates jostled their way out the
front door. In the silence, I could hear the twitter of birds
beneath the window. What to do? I got my raincoat out of
the cloakroom; pea-green and in need of a cleaning, it was the
only coat left.

A distant muffled shout rose up on the other side of the
river as I dawdled up Dunster Street: kickoff. I didn't feel
like going home; Bob was at the game. I looked in the window
of the Thomas More Bookshop. I'd never gone in; they only
carried religious books. There were no customers inside.
This wasn't a good era for religion. No one believed. Actually,
Sarah Bynum did. She went to church on Sunday mornings,
and seemed to know a great deal about the whole business.
Once, in the Fogg, we were looking at a Fra Angelico and I
asked her what those gold plates were on their heads. She
looked at me in amazement. "You don't know what a halo is?"

There were some interesting books in the window: *Pilgrim's
Progress*, the *Confessions* of Saint Augustine, an anthology
called *Poems of Doubt and Belief*. They were plain-looking
Oxford editions, with no illustrations on the cover; what
mattered was the contents. Doubt and belief: I wondered what
it would be like to worry about stuff like that—whether you
had a soul, whether it was good or bad, whether you'd end
up in heaven or hell. It would be nice to have someone to confess to, in one of those little booths. Father, forgive me, for I
have sinned: I beat off in my room and feel depressed afterwards; I read skin mags at the Out-of-Town newsstand; I've

fucked seven girls. But Father, I've hardly ever enjoyed it once. Does that mean I can go to Heaven?

The sky was clouding over. I headed up to Harvard Square and peered in the door of the Harvard Gardens. There were a few old guys on stools, watching a TV above the bar. I went in and ordered a draft. The room was a cold shadowy grotto with beer-stained tables; the air was stale and urinous. The men at the bar sat apart from each other; they all had cigarettes in their hands. There was a Big Ten football game on: Michigan versus Purdue. I studied myself in the mirror: long hair, dark eyebrows, wire-rimmed glasses, morose brown eyes. Terence, this is stupid stuff.

I had two beers and walked down to the Charles; it was getting colder, and my raincoat didn't have a lining. The river was trout-colored and choppy. There was no one else around. I could see the stadium beyond Harvard Square. Like the Coliseum in Rome. I thought of it as a ruin hundreds of years from now, crumbling arches in a grassy field . . . They all go into the dark.

I decided to go read magazines in Widener. At least it would be warm there. The huge main reading room with the vaulted ceiling was nearly empty; I could hear the echo of my own footsteps. At a table by the window I saw Naomi Berg. She was in my eighteenth-century poets class. Elbows on the table, hands buried in her spongy dark brown hair, she was deeply absorbed in a big book. She looked up as I walked by.

"What are you doing here?" she said. "How come you're not at the game?"

"I don't know. I just didn't feel like going." I peered over her shoulder. "What are you reading?"

"Bate's life of Keats. It's incredible that he did so much and died so young." She stared up at me with mournful eyes, as if she was talking about her brother or someone.

"Yeah, I know. My tutor's always saying he's older now than Keats was when he died."

Naomi pulled her shawl tight around her shoulders. She was plump and full-faced, with pale Slavic skin. Her thick hair was wrapped in a scarf. In her long skirt and linen peasant blouse she looked like one of Grandma Rose's sisters. Definitely not my type. But suddenly I was asking her if she wanted to go out for coffee. A Herbert Lowy line. We could talk about Keats.

What I really needed was a drink. I'd been drinking since lunch, and it was close to five now. Once you got going, you just wanted more. "Actually, why don't we go to Cronin's," I suggested as we waited to cross Mass. Ave. "I wouldn't mind a beer."

Naomi wrinkled her nose, but didn't say anything. I could see she wasn't the drinking kind.

In the dim booth, I ordered a draft and lit a cigarette. Smoke and drink, smoke and drink. It wasn't easy being a poet. I wondered what it felt like to wake up in the morning without a dry mouth and a headache. "So what do you think of Grayson's course?" I said.

Naomi gazed down at her coffee cup like a gypsy reading tea leaves. "I don't know," she murmured. "It's okay. Nothing ever turns out to be as good as you think it will." Her voice was so faint I had to lean across the table to hear what she was saying. "I mean, don't you feel that way?"

Did I? "Not really. I sort of feel nothing turns out the way you think it will, but sometimes it's better and sometimes it's worse. The only thing is, you never know which it's going to be."

"I don't know," Naomi said. She wrapped her hands around her coffee cup. "Every time I think something's going to be good it isn't." She looked at me uncertainly. "Like there was this one time I kept begging my parents to take me to Florida? There's this bird sanctuary down there that's really famous, and finally I got them to go. We drove and drove, and got there in the middle of the night, and it was this motel that looked out on a parking lot, and when we got to the sanctuary there were these tour buses that drove through the swamp with guides who sat up front talking through microphones. They wouldn't let you just walk around by yourself." She looked as if she was about to cry. "You know that Wallace Stevens line, 'The world is ugly and the people are sad'?"

I nodded.

"He's right," she said.

The waiter came by and I ordered another beer. The restaurant was empty. Everyone was at the game. Whenever I got drunk, I developed a tremendous urge to call Lizzie. She was out in Boulder, working in a boutique. The Purple Unicorn. Naomi was telling me about the children's librarian in Bloomington, Indiana, where she was from: "She had these real sad eyes, like a person who lives by herself and has this little kitty that she talks to when she comes home from work. I used to wonder what she had for dinner, like if she just bought one portion or what—and did she just eat frozen food or did she ever cook anything nice for herself, like a steak or something."

"Huh. She sounds really nice," I said. Who was this we were talking about?

"She *was* nice. She died when I was in seventh grade."

Jesus Christ. What next? Naomi was an orphan. Her little brother had polio. If we didn't get out of here pretty soon I was going to end up weeping into my beer. "You wanna come back to my house for a drink?" I said.

She lowered her eyes. "I don't know."

"Why not?" I pleaded. "It's more comfortable there. This place is getting me down."

Naomi looked up. Her eyes reminded me of this dog I used

to have when I hit him on the nose with a folded newspaper. His name was Sam. "Okay," she said.

It was cold and blustery out. We walked back through the Yard and headed up Oxford Street. The air smelled of soggy leaves. A man in a lumber jacket was chopping wood in his driveway; the axe strokes made a dull rhythmic thump in the dusk. There were lights on in the old clapboard houses; you could see people moving around inside, watching TV and making dinner. The front door's frosted glass was dark; Bob wasn't home. I let us in, and we climbed the creaky stairs in silence.

In the kitchen, I popped open a beer. "What about you, Naomi?" I said, aware of the loud joviality in my voice. I'd reached the point where I had to concentrate on my pronunciation to avoid slurring words.

"Nothing for me, thanks."

"Nothing?" You mean you can get through an encounter involving the opposite sex without drinking yourself into a stupor?

"Well, I guess a glass of wine."

"Good." If I grabbed her by the neck and poured the whole bottle down her throat maybe she'd get to where I was.

"This is a nice house," Naomi commented, looking around the kitchen. There was a poster of a clenched fist on the refrigerator door, and a charcoal sketch of Bob's—the view from the bay window in the living room—above the sink. "You must be happy here."

Me? Happy? What do you think I am, a Shriner? "Quite happy," I said. "But I wonder if I didn't sort of miss out on the college experience by living off-campus."

Naomi sipped from her glass of wine, a sip like a bird at a feeder. "What do you mean, 'the college experience'?"

"I don't know. Like the football game and stuff." The game must be over by now. People would be drifting back to the

houses, gathering in the common rooms for punch. There was
a big banquet on at Dunster House, where I used to live.

"You could have gone to the game."

"Yeah, but it's not the same. It's not, like, festive." Festive.
Not a concept Naomi could easily grasp. She had a way of
looking at you with those wide, mournful eyes of hers that
made you wonder what disaster had just happened. Maybe
being overweight made her sad. Probably no one ever asked
her out. In class, she sat by herself, scribbling in her notebook.
The only other time I saw her was in the library late at night.

Naomi drifted into the living room and sank down on the
bristly old fat-cushioned couch that I'd gotten at one of the
secondhand shops up on Mass. Ave. Squatting by the stereo, I
leafed through my record collection. Not Janis Joplin. Not
Purple Haze. What about The Band? I studied the album, five
guys in old-timey clothes—bowlers, vests, bow ties. There
was a photograph of a pink house up in the Catskills where
they'd made the album. Some of the songs were credited to B.
Dylan: too fucking hip. I put on "We Can Talk About It
Now," and when that organ started pounding out the rhythm
I was ecstatic. "We could try to reason,/But you might think
it's treason!" I yelled, throwing back my head and lifting a
can of Bud to my lips. It foamed and spilled down my chin,
soaking the front of my shirt. Naomi looked up at me from the
couch, her knees tucked under her long woolen skirt. She
seemed far away. What was she doing here? I lurched over
to the couch and dropped down beside her. Now what? I
reached over and patted her springy hair. She was sort of
nice-looking in her own way, with those big lips and soulful
eyes. "I love you, Naomi," I blurted. "I really do."

"Oh, Ben." She scowled and pulled away from me. "Don't
be ridiculous. You're drunk."

"I do, Naomi. I really do. Les' go to bed."

"You don't want to, Ben," she said firmly.

"Don' want to? Wadda you talking about? Course I do." I leaned over and buried my face in her neck. Her skin gave off a faint perfume that reminded me of my mother's dressing table.

"I should go."

"Go?" I studied her in perplexity. "Wha' for, go?"

"This just isn't a good idea. You don't have your heart in it." She stood up and adjusted her shawl. "I'm going home."

"Okay." I stood up shakily, clutching the arm of the couch as if it were the railing of a ship in a bad storm. "At least let me walk you back." I went to get my coat and stumbled over the wire of a standing lamp. The shade flew off and the lamp came hurtling toward me as I fell. There was a loud crash, a burst of light, and the sharp report of a shattered light bulb. Then it was dark.

I came to briefly in the emergency room of Stillman Infirmary, where a surgeon was stitching up the gash over my eye, but the whole scene was a blur. It wasn't until the next morning, when I was back in my room on Crescent Street, that I began to remember the day before.

"I came in right after you went down," Bob said. He was sitting beside my bed. "What a disaster area. There was blood all over the place. That girl was pretty upset."

Girl? I tried to think. "Oh, god. What happened to her?"

"She helped me put you in a cab and then I told her to go home." He got up and raised the blind. "Who is she, anyway?"

"Oh, just someone I know." My head was throbbing, and there was a dull pain where the bandage was, over my right eye. "How was the game?"

"We lost."

On my way to California over Christmas vacation, I stopped off in Chicago to see Lizzie. She was back from Boulder, staying in Elaine Schachter's apartment in Hyde

Park. "I just couldn't go home this time," she explained when I called from the airport. "Why don't you come see me here?"

My cab driver, an Afro-headed black with a comb stuck in his hair, drove in silence. They didn't talk much since King's death. It was a Saturday afternoon, and traffic was light on the Edens Expressway. Banks of snow were piled up against the highway dividers. All the cars had chains on the tires. As we turned south on Lake Shore Drive, I glimpsed ice floes out on the frozen water. Herbert was right about Siberia. I half-expected to see a polar bear float by.

We passed the Field Museum, then the Museum of Science and Industry—an imposing high-pillared classical monument with wide stone steps, surrounded by grassy parks. The parking lot was filled with yellow school buses. Here at least nothing had changed. New generations of children were visiting the echo chamber, where you whispered and it could be heard a hundred yards away. They were speaking into the telephones where you got to see a picture of yourself on a screen while you talked. The pendulum that swung back and forth to illustrate the earth in motion—it must still be going.

Elaine's apartment, near the University of Chicago campus, was on the top floor of an old three-story apartment building of desert-colored brick on Harper Avenue. She was majoring in psychology, and the shelves were full of B. F. Skinner, Erich Fromm, Wilhelm Reich, Norman O. Brown. She didn't have much furniture—a pair of armchairs covered with bedspreads, a wobbly coffee table, a threadbare Navajo rug. There was a Che Guevara poster on the wall in the living room, and a print of Van Gogh's bedroom at Arles.

Lizzie was working as a waitress at the Medici Café, on the day shift; she was usually out of the apartment by eleven. After she was gone, I'd make instant coffee and sit at the kitchen table, looking out over the back lots. Through the branches of a dead oak, I could just make out the spires of the university, and beyond them the South Side slums, a sprawl of tar-paper rooftops and wide boulevards. Far to the south were the steel mills of Hammond, thickets of smokestacks shrouded in white fog. Through the closed window, I could hear the clatter of the Illinois Central on its elevated track.

Mornings I idled away in Staver's Bookstore on East 57th Street. The few customers who came in were very serious. They had that U. of C. look about them: beards, glasses, bulging bookbags, tweed jackets with frayed sleeves. Their skin had never been near the sun. The books they asked for weren't intended to refine their sensibilities: Wittgenstein's *Tractatus*, Hegel's *Phenomenology*, Schiller's *Naive and Sentimental Poetry* (in German). It was strange to think of these studious types in their walled Gothic enclave, surrounded by gutted, rotting tenements. On Blue Island Avenue, blacks clustered on the sidewalk in front of Buddy's Liquors drinking out of paper bags or cruised up and down in big-finned cars with the chrome torn off. The air smelled of damp, acrid smoke —the kind of smoke that lingers after a four-alarm blaze has been put out.

In the Medici, graduate students sat bent over their books. Pushing open the mahogany door, I'd hear the soaring music of Vivaldi on the stereo, the loud whoosh of the espresso machine. The prints of Tuscan hill towns on the wall, the marble-topped tables and wrought-iron chairs, the magazine rack with copies of *The New York Review of Books* and *The Village Voice* hung from bamboo poles . . . These oases of culture had a besieged feel about them. Through the fogged-up window, I could see the dirty cars parked by the curb, the trash in the gutters, the cold ashy sky. Sitting in the corner with a cup of espresso and a worn copy of *Seven Types of Ambiguity*, I felt like a monk hunched over an illuminated manuscript high up in some ancient, clammy tower while vassals slaughtered each other below.

I liked coming in during Lizzie's shift; her short black skirt, black turtleneck, and black mesh stockings got me very stimulated. She was a good waitress, threading her way through the tiny marble tables with a tray balanced on her palm, then dipping down to put a cup of cappuccino beside a customer's open book. They never looked up. How could they concentrate with this incredible girl standing over them, her rounded breasts six inches from their face? I couldn't get through a paragraph without glancing up for another charge of Lizzie's electrifying grace. Oh, and there was this other waitress, a fleshy, red-haired Amazon with the sensual face of an Irish barmaid. When she stood by the door to the kitchen and brushed her swirling hair back from her pale, sweaty fore-head, I felt a twinge of utter hopelessness. The infinity of girls I'd never get to fuck . . .

When I got tired of hanging around the Medici, I'd walk around Hyde Park. There was a thick elm in front of Staver's where people pinned up notices, and I studied them with a kind of archaeological fascination, deciphering in their runic mes-sages a whole busy culture: mandolin lessons, French lessons, dance classes, summer sublets in the Indiana dunes, rides to Berkeley and Boston offered and sought, a Jungian therapist, a Gestalt psychology workshop, SDS, Progressive Labor, migrant farmworkers' union, talk on The Legacy of Norman Thomas, poetry reading by Robert Bly, lecture on Abstract Expressionism by Harold Rosenberg, furniture for sale, dog lost . . . I should have gone to the University of Chicago.

It was the week before Christmas. Woodlawn Avenue was decked out with strands of Christmas lights that glowed feebly in the gray afternoon light. The shop windows were sprayed with white borders of snow. In the window of a toy store I stared at an HO train going around a track, through papier-maché mountains, over a trestle, past a town with a post office and a gabled station. At the foot of the mountains was a meadow, with little plastic sheep. It would be nice to live in a town like that, where you knew everyone and the postman said hello when you came in for your mail. Like Switzerland or somewhere. The air was very clear in the Alps. People were happy there, and led simple, honest lives.

When Lizzie got off from work I'd walk her back to Elaine's. It was dangerous to be out at night. One of the waitresses at the Medici had been raped, and someone I knew from Evanston, a boy in my chemistry class, had been gunned down in front of Walgreen's the year before. We'd heat up a frozen dinner, roll a joint, and put on a Motown album or the Stones. It felt good to be back in Chicago in the middle of winter, listening to the wind rattle the windows as it whipped off the lake, whistling like an Arctic gale. But something was going on with Lizzie. She wandered around the house a lot without her clothes, but she didn't come on to me very much about sex—not the way she usually did. "What's the matter?" I said one night. We were lying in bed watching *The Late Show*.

"What do you mean? Nothing."

"I don't know," I said after a minute. "I feel like you're not really there."

She reached over and kissed me lightly on the forehead. "I'm here," she said. "It's just that . . ." She sat up and lit a cigarette. "Do we have to talk about this?"

Dread gathered in my chest. "What?"

Lizzie was silent. Light from the TV flickered over her impassive face. "I guess what it is is that I'm looking for something different now. Something more. You're not going to be around. I love you, but you just drift in and then leave, and I'm supposed to sit around and wait for you to come back."

She pulled the sheet around her shoulder. "Only you're not coming back, and I don't like to get all worked up about us. It's not, like, a real thing. You know what I mean?"

"But I think about you all the time," I protested. "It's really important to me."

"It's important to you because it's part of your life, not because of what it is."

"How do you know?"

"I just know," she said simply, reaching over to change the channel. "I'm sick of this movie."

It was *On the Waterfront*—one of my favorite movies. Brando was on the roof, looking after his pigeons. He really cared for those birds.

"I had an abortion," Lizzie said.

I stared at her. "When?"

"At the end of the summer."

That time I'd called and her father said she was away . . .

"I went to New York," she said calmly, raising herself up on her elbow. "Elaine's father gave me the name of a doctor in Queens." She gazed at me with her frank, penetrating eyes. "So now you know."

See? There *are* consequences. It's not just a game. "Why didn't you tell me?"

"Because I knew you'd panic and run away. It was easier to just deal with it myself." She switched off the set and turned to me. "You know what? I was tempted to have it."

I could have had a baby. Like Nick Gondoli, who'd sat next to me in homeroom at Evanston High. He'd knocked up his girl friend, that washed-out-looking girl who worked behind the counter at Hoo's Drug—what was her name?—and dropped out in the middle of senior year. I'd seen him in a dirty apron, sweeping the aisles in Whitney's Market. He didn't look too happy. Still . . . a baby. I wondered if it would have looked like Lizzie. A little dark-haired girl, swarthy and Mediterranean

like a Naples street urchin. I could have shown her the pier
and the lake and the house where I used to live . . . A playmate
for Raymond or Deirdre.

"I kept thinking about what it would be like," Lizzie said.
"I liked the idea of caring for somebody. I mean really caring
—having this person depend on you and need and love you."
She paused. "No matter what you did."

I lay on my back and looked out the window. The branches
of the dead oak were inky roads on a dark map. There were
stars out, scattered about in the cold black sky like sparks
flung from a forge. I reached for Lizzie's hand, but she drew
it away and rolled over on her side.

VI

THAT spring I drifted through the last weeks before graduation, preparing half-heartedly for my final exams. Seated in my alcove study beneath the marble-eyed gaze of a stuffed peahen I'd picked up at a junk shop in Chicago, I browsed among the treasures in my "library": a signed first edition of Cyril Connolly's *Enemies of Promise*; a copy of Lawrence Ferlinghetti's *A Coney Island of the Mind* which the poet had inscribed "from an older to a younger practitioner of the mysteries" when I cornered him by the cash register of the Ciy Lights Bookstore in San Francisco; and a miscellany of books that I classified as "rare" because they were old. There was something about these worn, jacketless volumes that appealed to me. They had a history; they'd passed through many hands. The creamy, rough-edged pages, the tiny print, the publishers' addresses—Pall Mall, Temple Bar, Paternoster Row—gave off an antiquarian air; the chipped spines and faded covers testified to hard use. My Camelot Classics edition of Shelley's poems was a hundred years old. Someone named Walter Scott (*the* Walter Scott?) had published it when my great-grandfather was tending his grocery store in Yekaterinoslav. How far I'd come! The mere possession of such books was a triumph over history. But that's how the second generation made good. The library was my sweatshop. The typewriter was my sewing machine.

Shelley was a radical, but I couldn't work up much enthusiasm for the issues he'd gotten so excited about. The freedom of man, and all that stuff. I preferred bookish revolutionaries like Walter Benjamin. He never went near the barricades—proof that you could be a Marxist without hanging around Lowell Lecture Hall while hoarse flannel-shirted SDS leaders harangued the hopped-up crowds. Their passion for politics eluded me. I kept my distance from the demonstrators who poured through Harvard Square night after night, smashing windows and chanting "Ho-Ho-Ho Chi Minh/The NLF is gonna win!" Loitering behind the police barricades with my bookbag slung over my shoulder, I was the very type of the *flâneur* Benjamin described in his essay on Paris in the nineteenth century, wandering idly among the crowd. The shrill sirens, the shatter of glass, the pop of tear-gas canisters, drew me toward Mass. Ave. the way a tourist out for a stroll in some foreign city is drawn toward a cluster of people gathered around a sidewalk mime. But I had no connection with these scenes. Walking home beneath the leafy elms on Oxford Street, I was eager to get back to the Penguin Classics piled up beside my bed. Louis Lambert, Julien Sorel, Frédéric Moreau: these were protagonists I could identify with, ambitious young men who rose in society until they were undone by it. Their failure proved their nobility of soul.

Lounging on the back porch, my feet up on the rail, I was awed by the plots and intrigues, conspiracies and schemes, adulteries and love affairs Balzac and Stendhal could pack into a novel. These guys had a lot of stamina. One thing I noticed, though, was how often they told the same story: a young man journeys from the provinces to Paris and gets caught up in a corrupt world of fashionable dinner parties, political intrigue, dubious financial schemes and pliant women. It was a good theme. Like a child who demands the same fairy tale night after night ("Tell me the one about that guy in the city and the whores . . ."), I was never bored by this story. Late one night, as I lay in my narrow bed beneath the sloping eaves, I came to the end of *Sentimental Education*, where Frédéric Moreau and his sidekick Deslauriers are reminiscing about the time they visited a whorehouse one Sunday morning in their youth and Frédéric exclaims, "Those were the best years of our lives!" I put the book down with tears in my eyes. What an amazing life. Would I ever know the fierce passion that drove Emma Bovary to go trudging through the rain toward her assignation with Rodolphe? That made Julien Sorel sacrifice his life for Madame de Renal? I thought of Lizzie unzipping my shorts under the pier and dipping down to suck my cock. Did Fabrizio del Dongo wreck his life for *that*?

One afternoon I was in my study working on a poem when the phone rang. "This is Eleanor?" said a tentative voice. "From the *Advocate* party?" Eleanor Josephs. We had met at the last reading of the season, when she asked me to pour her a glass of wine. Her wide pliant mouth and swanlike neck, pale cheeks and reddish Botticelli ringlets, had been haunting me ever since. It was Eleanor I thought of as I read about all these Parisian women flirting at midnight suppers and inviting their lovers into their bedrooms while they "did their toilet" (a phrase that always perplexed me). She had just left her husband, a graduate student in American history, after he found out from her diary that she was having an affair with her tutor and beat her up. Standing by the fireplace in the Sanctum, she had pushed up the sleeve of her blouse and displayed a bluish bruise. I was impressed.

"Isn't your reading tonight?" she said over the phone. I

had been invited to participate in a poetry "read-in" against the war, an honor included in the *curriculum vitae* I'd blurted out before I even knew her name. "I called every church in town, and couldn't find it."

"It's the Cambridge Baptist—next to the Gulf station in the Square."

"Oh, good. I'll see you there." She was about to hang up, but didn't.

"You don't want to go to that. It's an open reading. There'll be more people onstage than in the audience."

"Yes, I do." She sounded pretty definite about it.

"Then at least let me pick you up."

"Okay."

She was living in Bertram Hall, on the lam from her crazy husband. When I phoned up from the lobby, she came downstairs dressed like Veronica in the Jugghead comics: saddle shoes, a knee-length tartan skirt, a salmon-colored cashmere sweater.

"I'm a writer, too," she declared as she clambered up on the high front seat of Bob's VW bus. (I had decided against the motorcycle; you didn't want to come on too heavy right away.) "I don't think I told you that the other night."

So what else is new? "Oh, yeah? Poems or stories?"

"Stories. And I've almost finished a novel." She foraged in her purse for a cigarette and pushed in the dashboard lighter. "It's about my parents," she said, puffing intently as if she'd never smoked before. "They married young, when my father was just out of the army. They got divorced when I was twelve."

And now her own marriage had broken up. Experience: what luck. She had something to write about. At a light, I looked her over, admiring her willowy neck, her long eyelashes and chinalike cheekbones. When she put out her cigarette, I noticed that her nails were bitten.

In the church hall, I found her a seat near the front and climbed up onstage. There were about twenty readers ahead of me, seated on folding chairs in front of a dusty velvet curtain. I sat down next to an older poet I'd seen around—he spent his days in the Grolier Bookshop nipping bourbon from a flask—and sorted through my poems in search of the really poignant ones.

The reading was a casual affair. Whenever a poet finished and the feeble applause died down, the moderator, a thick-bearded young man whose cowboy boots thundered on the wooden platform, would ask who wanted to read next. After an hour, I raised my hand and strode up to the podium. I had decided on a poem about the summer I fell in love with Judy Clark, the girl across the street. ("Surly, tense, I lingered in the hedge. . . .") I glanced in Eleanor's direction at the end of every line, putting in my voice Morgan Ames's sonorous drone. Her eager gaze excited me. She returned my shy glances with such open ardor that I could feel myself blush. (I was reading from an issue of *The Advocate*, in case anyone thought it was just some unpublished manuscript.)

When the reading was over, Eleanor rushed up and embraced me. "You were wonderful!" We left the church holding hands. On the way back to Crescent Street, she draped her arm around my neck.

"How come you got married?" I said as we pulled up to the house. I was still brooding over this mysterious fact.

"I guess it seemed like a grownup thing to do."

"Were you in love?"

"God, no. On my wedding night I danced with everyone but him."

"What about this other person, the one you were having an affair with?"

"I left him so he wouldn't leave me first. People are always leaving me."

I doubted it. She was vulnerable, insecure, "sensitive"—as my mother would have put it—but she had a certain reckless edge, a hardness I associated with girls in *The Beautiful and Damned*. She always had a cigarette in one hand, held limply between two fingers, and a drink in the other. Bob and I were having a graduation party that night, and by the time the guests began to arrive she had nearly finished off a whole bottle of wine.

It was all happening so fast. Within an hour, we were dancing in the darkened parlor to the new Stones album, clasped in a tight embrace. " 'Please allow me to introduce myself,' " howled Feinstein as he hurtled by, swigging from a bottle of Bud. " 'Ah'm a man of wealth and taste . . .' " I heard the music as a dull distant throb. Eleanor worked a knee between my legs and dragged me to the floor. We leaned against the wall and necked, oblivious to the prancing frenzied throng.

I had always hoped to fall in love this way, but I was nervous there on the floor; I was missing out on my own party, the last before graduation. I got up and went into the kitchen to pour myself a glass of wine. In the corner, Feinstein was arguing with a frail-looking girl about Marcuse—"*Eros and Civilization* is bullshit!" His pitted forehead was shiny, his flannel work shirt open at the neck. He motioned me over, but I just waved and hurried back to the parlor. Eleanor was waiting.

The dancers had linked arms and formed a circle. Their shadows rippled on the wall as they lunged in and out. Eleanor took me by the hand. "Let's go to your room," she said. With a backward glance, I left the joyful scene behind and followed her up the narrow stairs. In my room beneath the sloping eaves, she unbuttoned my shirt with her nimble child's hands, undid her skirt, and pulled me down beside her on the narrow bed. Her mouth tasted of wine and cigarettes. As I put my hand between her legs, working my fingers in beneath the warm damp mound of her cotton underpants, she whispered, "I think I love you."

We had our graduation lunch at Elsie's. One tunafish on rye and one Roast Beef Special. Our mortarboards lay between us on the counter. I'd managed to convince my parents that it was no big deal, and not to bother coming out. I lived off-campus, and all the good parties—the ones under tents with bowls of punch and little sisters running around in frilly dresses and parents snapping away with their Kodaks—were in the residential houses. Eleanor's parents were divorced, and she couldn't invite one of them without offending the other, so she invited neither.

It didn't matter. We were in a world of our own. Every morning we lay in bed and talked for hours. I told Eleanor about *Roundtable*, Mrs. Laver, my job at *Poetry*. Eleanor told me about her father, a building contractor in Cleveland who had left her mother for another woman when Eleanor was nine, and how her mother had gone to work as a saleswoman in a department store to supplement her alimony. "Incredible!" I said. "Weren't you upset?" How could people—Jews yet— do this to their children? Divorce was for Ann Landers' column.

"Sure I was upset. I used to go visit him on weekends, and there was this whole new family. His wife had two kids of her own. And you should see how they live: it's one of those ranch houses in the suburbs with coral on the shelves. There isn't a book in the house."

Not a book in the house! She might as well have told me there was no plumbing. "You poor dear," I murmured, contemplating her mime's wide mouth and polleny eyelashes. "So how did you get to be so literary?" Sitting cross-legged on her bed in Shaker Heights, Eleanor was deep in Jane Austen while her parents screamed at each other in the sunken living room;

they called it "the conversation pit." Somewhere out there was another world: a world of formal balls, afternoon tea, wet autumn afternoons spent reading by the fire in some ivy-covered country house. Eleanor's father played golf; Eleanor took riding lessons. You never knew when she might get invited to go fox-hunting in the Cotswolds.

"My mother reads," Eleanor explained. "She's one of these people who never went to college and is always trying to make up for it. One time I went to see her at Sandler's . . ."

"What's Sandler's?"

"The department store where she works—and she was crying behind the counter. The supervisor had just told her she couldn't read on the job. 'I'm supposed to polish the jewelry.' "

"That's horrible," I said, tucking a russet curl behind her ear. "You've had a hard time."

"But I have you now." She kissed me on each eye. "You'll never leave me, will you?"

"No."

Eleanor was determined to get a divorce. I was on the phone a lot with her husband's lawyer, Schmidgal, who made it clear that his client wouldn't consider a divorce unless Eleanor promised not to press assault and battery charges.

"How do I know this guy won't come back with a gun?" I demanded. Like that lieutenant who shot Pushkin. I'd challenge him to a duel. Schmidgal probably hadn't handled many of those. The Cambridge Common at midnight. Bob could be my second.

"He's a graduate student, for Christ's sake!" Schmidgal said wearily. "You think he wants to end up before a judge?"

It seemed like every other day I had to borrow Bob's VW and drive Eleanor down to her lawyer's office in Boston. (She thought it didn't look right to show up on the back of my BMW.) She dressed up for these occasions, putting on cotton summer skirts and blouses buttoned up to the neck. Her hair, which she usually brushed with two or three hasty strokes, was tucked in place with a barrette. Her skin had a Pre-Raphaelite pallor. She always wore sunglasses to the lawyer's; they gave her a world-weary look. Leafing through magazines in the pine-paneled waiting room, I could hear her talking on the other side of the receptionist's window. Her voice was firm. "Look, I want a no-contest settlement. He beat me up."

"I know," her lawyer said patiently. "But he could claim adultery."

"Not after a legal separation." She knew her law.

"But wasn't there someone else before? While you were cohabiting?"

"What are you talking about?" Eleanor said sharply.

"You know, the one he found out about reading your journal."

"But he shouldn't have been reading it!" she cried.

In the waiting room, I leafed through an old *Sports Illustrated*. There was an interesting profile of Gump Worsley, the goalie for the Montreal Canadians. Eleanor's voice came through the partition; it was masterful, high-strung. "I'm not going to court, and that's all there is to it. You've got to make him settle." When she came out, her eyes were wet; rage made her cry. She plucked her suede handbag off a chair and pushed open the door without even glancing at me. "Let's get out of here," she said. I rose and followed.

A week later, she decided to sell her wedding ring. We were in Cleveland visiting her mother, and Eleanor figured she could get a better price if she took it to a jeweler in her hometown, someone she knew, a friend of the family. As we drove downtown in her mother's white Pontiac, nosing through mid-morning traffic, I noticed what a good driver she was. Leaning an elbow against the open window, she cradled the wheel one-handed, fiddled with the radio, lit a cigarette. She parked in two swift motions, glancing backward to maneuver her way in, and shifted into drive so fast the car lurched against the curb. Before I could unfasten my safety belt, she was putting money in the meter.

In the jewelry store, we peered down through the glass counter at the diamond rings in their purple velvet beds. A man in a creased seersucker suit came over and asked if he could help.

"I'd like to see Mr. Nathanson," Eleanor said.

"He's on the phone right now. Is there anything I can help you with?"

"No, I have to see him personally," she said. "He's a friend of my father's."

The salesman hesitated. "I'll go see if he's available."

A minute later, a balding middle-aged man in a short-sleeved white shirt came over. "I'm Walter Josephs' daughter," Eleanor said. Mr. Nathanson looked confused. "He owns the hardware store on Euclid?" she prompted him.

"Of course," Mr. Nathanson said uncertainly. "Walter." He looked up and down the store, fidgeting with a plastic pen holder in his breast pocket. "What can I do for you?"

Eleanor unfolded the ring from a wad of tissue paper and handed it to him. Mr. Nathanson held it under a Tensor lamp on the counter and studied it through a jeweler's lens attached to his glasses. "Five hundred dollars," he pronounced.

"I want eight," Eleanor said.

Mr. Nathanson looked at her intently. "The ring is worth five."

"My father said you would give me a good deal." Eleanor ran her tongue over her lips.

"Five hundred dollars," Mr. Nathanson repeated.

Eleanor snatched the ring from his hand and strode out of the store.

* * *

As the summer wore on, we never talked about what would happen in the fall, but it was in the air. I had gotten a fellowship from the Harvard English Department to spend a year in Oxford, and was leaving in October. Eleanor didn't have any plans. Her mother sent her money when she could, and her father stapled a few dollar bills to the messages he scrawled on Josephs' Hardware invoices: "Hope your ok. Nothing new here." She hadn't gotten her literary ambitions from him.

Did I want her to come with me? I couldn't decide. I was afraid to go by myself, afraid of loneliness in a foreign land— even England. It was too unknown. I imagined myself living in a drafty college room with one of those slitted medieval windows like they had in old castles, going down to the dining hall and sitting alone at a long oak table while all around me riotous undergraduates quaffed flagons of ale and shouted bawdy drinking songs. On the other hand, was I ready to set up house with an aspiring novelist? It was hard enough *being* a writer —especially a writer who got enough rejection slips to paper the study where I sat at my table day after day revising what Morgan Ames called my "Jewish homelife poems." Did I have to live with one, too? The thought of Eleanor up in the bedroom writing her novel in that round girl's script of hers, turning out page after page of suburban drama while I sat downstairs scribbling poems about my grandparents' immigrant past, was too much. Doing the dishes after dinner, I would hear Eleanor out on the back porch telling Bob about her book ("So there's this girl from Shaker Heights . . .") and wonder why I felt like hurling her over the rail.

Still, we were happy, dawdling through the long hot nights on our porch. The windows of the house across the way were filled with hanging plants bathed in purple light. Little kids pedaled furiously up and down the sidewalk on their tricycles and Dylan's "Nashville Skyline" floated up from the apartment below. Feet propped on the wooden rail, we sipped acrid

Yugoslavian wine that sold for a dollar a bottle at the corner grocery store and read our Penguin Classics.

Eleanor had her own collection: *Don Quixote*, Manzoni's *The Betrothed*, Laclos's *Les Liaisons Dangereuses*. Stubbing her cigarette out in a shell, she would narrate with a child's intensity the goings-on in those big books. "There're these two aristocrats, see, who try to seduce this girl . . ."

"You mean, like, together?" Let me know when you're done.

"They don't *do it* together." Eleanor's mind didn't work like mine. She was more interested in passions of the heart than in the genital unions they provoked. "She schemes with him to get the girl, as a way of rebelling against, you know, society." As she told me the story of the proud Marquise de Merteuil and the craven Vicomte de Valmont, her eyes shone with excitement in the velvety summer dark. It was a story, a fiction; it brought to life the kind of world conjured up by those nineteenth-century women novelists she admired as they tramped the moors in their ankle-length skirts. Eleanor was a romantic of the old school. She had trained herself to be good in bed because that's what you did now, but desire stirred in her emotions beyond simple lust. When she gazed at me with those ardent, mournful eyes of hers, I was like the young man in the Turgenev novel when he spies the beautiful princess Zinaida in her garden and flushes with a sudden joy. *First Love*.

Eleanor's younger sister, Leona, came over for dinner a few nights a week. A sophomore at Leslie College, she was waitressing nights at the Algiers Coffeehouse on Brattle Street for the summer. She was a pale, thin-faced girl with a waifish look about her, but a great dancer. While I did the dishes, the two sisters would put on the Stones' *Brown Sugar* album and practice a routine they'd worked out: arms around each other's shoulders, they skipped to the left, threw their heads back in unison and whirled around, snapping their fingers in time to the music. They were very serious about it; they had the tense, earnest look of ballerinas as they spun away, grabbed hands, and draped their arms around each other's waists. When the side was over, they collapsed on the sofa and loosened their halters to cool themselves off. In the kitchen, I put the dishes in the rack. Insects thumped against the screen.

One stifling night we were lying in our narrow bed and couldn't sleep. The fan rattled in its wire grille like a caged animal. Pigeons fluttered in the eaves, their low throaty cries so close they seemed to be in the room with us. I buried my face in Eleanor's hair and breathed in the odor of shampoo, perfume, and dried sweat that rose off her skin. In the light from the streetlamp filtering through the papery windowshade, I watched her chest rise and fall as she breathed.

I pressed my lips against her neck. "I love you so much it hurts," she murmured.

That night I asked her to come with me.

Eleanor agreed that it made sense for me to go over first and send for her when I found "digs." Early in October, I flew to Heathrow, caught a bus to Oxford, and called my only contact, a young English poet who was living out in the country; Winston Walker had given me his name. Standing in a red phone booth on Broad Street, my suitcases piled up on the sidewalk, I heard the rapid "pip-pip-pip"—England!—and stuffed a tuppence in the slot. "*Do* come by," the poet insisted in a BBC voice when I explained who I was. "And stop as long as you like. I've a couch in the parlor that should prove quite adequate—provided you're not horribly tall."

The cab drove out of Oxford, past dun-colored row houses and muddy fields where cows stood in the rain, and turned off at Swindon. "I'm looking for The Rookery," I told the driver.

I liked the way they gave houses individual names in England, a practice unknown in Evanston. The Patio? Hibachi House?

The Rookery was a low whitewashed cottage with a thatched roof set among a cluster of bow-windowed shops. I knocked, but no one answered, so I dragged my suitcases up the narrow stairs and pushed open the door at the top. A young man with shoulder-length Elizabethan hair and an oval-faced girl in a long woolen skirt were seated before the "fire," an electric coil mounted on a plastic replica of burning logs.

"You must be Warren," I said.

"I'm not, actually. Warren's gone off to fetch our tea."

Just then our host strode in with a tray. "Ah, the American!" he cried. He set it down on a wobbly butler's table and grabbed my hand. "Good, good, good. Winston told me you might call." He pointed to my suitcases. "Now put those over there, and your coat on the bed, and plop yourself down by the fire." Pouring tea, Warren chirped away with hostessy good cheer. He introduced me to his other guests—Edmund and Beatrice—asked after Winston, and offered me "biscuits" from a tin. "So you're at Balliol," he said in his clipped English voice. "I once knew a Balliol person. Went mad and jumped out a window—fractured his thigh, I believe." A cowlick drooped down over his pasty forehead, and his cheeks had a pink veiny flush, like those boys in the British Airways ad who went to Shakespeare's school.

It was getting dark. Through the window set deep in the thick wall I could see the lights of cars flash past. "Edmund is a poet, too," Warren said, "and Beatrice has done a marvelous children's book: *Lord Willoughby and the Wicked Owl*. It's about this lord, you see, who has a peculiar love of the *mice* on his estate and tries to protect them from some awful predatory owls by constructing a sort of *mouse fortress* in his garden." Warren had given up his job as a reader for Hamish

Hamilton to start his own publishing firm. "I've already drawn up my fall list. There's Beatrice's book, and a pamphlet of poems by Edmund, and an anthology of contemporary Serbo-Croatian poets translated by a Yugoslavian chap I know."

"Huh!" I sipped my tea, longing for some cake or toast, but the only food in sight was a wedge of odorous mildewed cheese and the tin of crumbly biscuits. "How are you going to support this venture?"

"He borrows from rich old men," Edmund put in, "by promising to publish their books at some unstipulated date in the distant future."

"Well, you must admit it's worked so far," Warren said. "Just last week I lunched with Lord Snow at the Savile Club and got him to pledge a thousand pounds. I had to promise you would dedicate your book to him."

"To that horrid old toad?" Beatrice cried. She turned to me. "Have you ever seen him? His face is frightfully mottled, and he has these ghastly bulging eyes." She gave a wide-eyed stare in the manner of Lord Snow. "And he talks in this horrible gurgle, as if he's drowning in his own phlegm. 'I say, Warren,' " she spluttered in a raspy gurgling voice, " 'poetry's gotten bloody hard to read these days, don't you think? All this *confession* going about. They'll put the priests right out of business.' "

"One can't be choosy about one's benefactors," Warren said primly. "And he's promised to get us on the BBC."

"Now that I should enjoy," Edmund said. "I like my poems to be heard. The bardic oral tradition and all that, you know." In his tweed jacket and mud-encrusted boots, a scarf flung casually around his neck, Edmund was very much in the bardic tradition himself. His thin aquiline nose and high-boned cheeks had the sort of sharp-featured refinement you saw in overbred hunting dogs. In the low-ceilinged room with its bumpy walls and wooden beams, rain spattering the window, he reminded me of a character out of Hardy, one of those passionate, hard-faced landlords striding across the moor on the way to some illicit tryst. His loam-colored jacket and brown pullover gave him a gamekeeper's look, and I wasn't surprised to learn that he lived in a tiny Cotswold village called Stanton Harcourt. They were just in for the day—"to see our publisher" —and had been "on the verge of setting off" when I arrived. "But you must come and see us," Edmund insisted.

"Yes, do," Beatrice chimed in. "I must show you my collection of birds' nests." Edmund jotted down the phone number, a mere three digits, and made me promise to "ring up" once I was settled.

"An odd pair," Warren confided before they'd even gotten down the stairs. "Edmund has the most violent temper. He's always threatening to beat her to a pulp. They're forever splitting up, or else she'll storm out of the house and disappear for days. I get frantic phone calls in the middle of the night. First one goes bonkers, then the other." He stacked up their dishes on a tray and headed for the kitchen alcove. "But they're lovely people all the same." He gave a low chortling laugh full of Dickensian wickedness.

Warren couldn't have been more than a year or two older than me, but he'd already perfected the manner of an Oxford don: the murmurous expostulations; the snuffling, throat-clearing stammer; the crisp emphasis of *actually* and *quite*. He had inherited some money from his father, a prosperous lawyer in Gray's Inn, but only enough to support himself on a modest budget while he started up his publishing firm. He did all the work himself, dealing with printers, corresponding with writers, billing shops. In his bedroom, piled to the ceiling, were cartons of boxes—"unsold stock," he explained. "I store it in here because there's no heat. Otherwise I'd have to get insurance." It was so cold that he kept milk and butter on the windowsill; he had never "got round" to buying a "fridge." He used a kerosene lamp to save electricity; there was a smudge on the ceiling from the smoky wick.

I stayed with Warren for two weeks, going out all day in search of lodgings and returning discouraged at dusk to a supper of bacon and eggs. "There's a drop of Bulmer's here," he would say, unstopping a brown bottle of cider that had gone flat weeks before. "I've got some crackers for dessert." After dinner I bought him a pint at the Lamb & Flag and gobbled bowls of nuts, stuffing them in my mouth by the handful. I had never been so hungry.

Over supper we listened to Warren's favorite show, some comedy with raucous studio laughter in the background and coarse-voiced Cockney accents snickering about "French letters" and "drawers." Warren found these shows hilarious, but they paled beside his own weird notions about sex. He had a vociferous horror of homosexuals, who seemed ubiquitous. Sitting over a pint of bitter in the Lamb & Flag one night, he said of a poet whose wife had just given birth to their fourth child, "He's one. You didn't know?" Then, in a conspiratorial whisper: "He likes boys."

Women were invariably lesbians. When I mentioned a well-known novelist who taught at Lady Margaret Hall, one of the Oxford women's colleges, Warren raised his eyebrows and said in a brisk, authoritative voice, "Oh, she's a lezzie—quite a famous one, actually. She was married once, but her husband left her when he found her in bed with the maid." One day, after he'd invited me to lunch with an editor of *The New Statesman*, he announced, "Nigel's got a torture dungeon in the basement." I stared at him in the rocking train compartment. We had just been to Nigel's Hampstead house; his silent Danish wife had served us drinks on a patio in the back garden. "You mean you haven't heard about his *ménage à trois*?" Some decadent heiress had moved upstairs and introduced them to the joys of bondage and discipline; Warren had even seen the hoods and shackles hanging in the cloakroom and asked what they were for. "It was most embarrassing," he giggled.

I had been at Warren's for a week when Edmund called one evening and invited me out to Stanton Harcourt. "You're in for it now," Warren predicted. "Their rows are legendary." But I was curious, and set out the next afternoon in my Wolseley Hornet, a purple wreck with tiny wheels and straw sprouting from the bucket seats that I'd bought from a departing Rhodes Scholar. The four-lane highway out of Oxford dwindled to two lanes, then one, then a narrow unpaved road between high dirt embankments like a giant mole's burrow. When I came to the old stone church Edmund had told me to look out for, I turned off down a barren macadam road, past a wooden shed where cows huddled, a wind-wrinkled pond, and a long low stone building that I recognized as the Pest House described in one of Edmund's poems; it had been a morgue during the Plague. Beside it was their cottage, gray stucco with a steep thatched roof. Edmund's car, a wood-paneled mini–station wagon with half-saucers of fungi growing on the sides, stood in the muddy driveway. It had started to drizzle, and milky trails of mist lay over the fields where sheep grazed beneath the dripping trees. Chickens scattered as I pulled up in front of the house.

Beatrice was standing by the window, a pale Brontë-like figure in a lacy shawl. Edmund, looking more Lawrentian than ever in his knee-high boots and elbow-patched tweed jacket, came up from the barn behind the house. "I've just been trying to get an owl out of the eaves," he said. "The bloody things swoop down at night and kill our chickens." He dug a pipe out of his pocket and filled it from a leather pouch. "Let's go have a look at the church, shall we, before we have our tea. It's one of the oldest in England."

"What about Beatrice?" I said as we started off down the road. "Doesn't she want to come?"

"Oh, she's having one of her fits," Edmund said. We walked for a while in silence. "She told me this morning I was demonic," he said suddenly. " 'Fucking possessed' were her words." He pushed in the rough-hewn door of the church and pointed out a whip hung on the wall. "That was for driving away the packs of dogs and wolves that used to roam about. Perhaps I ought to try it out on Beatrice."

It was nearly dark in the church. Rain beat against the leaded stained-glass windows high up on the wall, where granite plaques listed the names of parishioners who had died over the last eleven centuries: from "Bernard the Dane married Sprote de Bourgouyne died 876" to "Lewis Viscount Harcourt P.C. married daughter of Walter H. Burns of New York died 1922." Behind the altar hung Harcourt's tattered standard, carried to the Battle of Bosworth Field in 1485. In the dusky gloom where candles wavered, I peered up at a medieval fresco depicting a banquet at oak tables laden with roast boar. "God, this place is old," I murmured. I shivered in the stony chill that rose off the cobbled, trough-worn floor. I hardly knew where my ancestors were from. I had seen a photograph of my great-great-grandfather once, in a thick woolen coat, a muffler wound about his neck, a Tolstoyan beard flowing down his tunic. The village grocer. It must be reassuring to have one's relatives lying in these crypts beneath marble replicas of themselves. My grandparents were burried at Woodlawn Cemetery in Chicago, but we had stopped going there after their unveilings. I laid a cold hand on the forehead of a dead king; his crown was pocked and chipped. He seemed so tiny; his marble hands and feet were the size of a child's. They say people were smaller then. Even this marble effigy seemed vulnerable, the chiseled face delicate in repose. Was death any different if you got to spend eternity in one of these granite tombs?

Edmund was in the nave examining an ancient wooden panel, its paint faded to a dull wash. "The rood screen," he explained.

"What's a rude screen?"

"R-o-o-d." Edmund spelled it out. "It represents the cross they nailed Christ up on. It separated the rabble from the landowners." He pulled his jacket tight around his throat. "God, it's a witch's tit in here. I'll show you Pope's Tower, then let's go back." We hesitated in the doorway, watching the rain pour down. "Pope did his *Iliad* translation there," Edmund said. He pointed to a low tower of mossy crumbling brick across the road. "The Harcourts were his patrons. You know that couplet, 'How vain is Reason, Eloquence how weak,/If Pope must tell what HARCOURT cannot speak'? It's in his 'Epistle to Augustus.' "

I nodded. Pope. A neoclassical poet, eighteenth century. He was only four foot six—about the size of those marble Harcourts carved on their tombs. He wrote *The Dunciad* and *The Rape of the Lock*—a poem that intrigued me until I discovered that it was about a woman whose curls are cut off by some cruel nobleman.

Beatrice was at the kitchen table reading when we got back to the house. "Where's our tea?" Edmund demanded.

She looked up guiltily from her book. "I forgot what time it was. I just had to finish *The Wind in the Willows*."

"Oh bloody Christ!" Edmund shouted. "You've only read it twenty times." He strode angrily into the pantry and returned with a tin of Twining's tea. "What have we got to eat?"

"There're some biscuits on the shelf," Beatrice murmured, staring down at her book.

"Biscuits!" Edmund boomed. "But you knew we were having a guest. You were to get a cake from the pastry shop."

Beatrice looked up at him beseechingly, her eyes wide with fright. "I forgot."

"You forgot!" He loomed menacingly over her. "I know. You're just so busy. Reading your bloody children's books."

"Why is that any sillier than your poems?" she cried, aroused now. "What makes your verses about dead animals crushed in the road more important than my books?" Her eyes filled with tears. "Blood and fur spattered on the road. It's just a lot of nonsense lifted from Ted Hughes."

"Shut up, bitch!" Edmund leaned down and peered intently in her face. "Who sits up half the night writing reviews so that you don't have to work? Who drives in to the Extension School twice a week and teaches Cockneys from the car works what a heroic couplet is?" he chanted, bending over the table, his lips wet, his face flushed in the harsh overhead light. "Who buys the food, goes to the post office, cleans the house? Not you. You're too *sensitive*." He sneered the word. "Too frail, too busy with your talking owls and dancing mice."

Beatrice leaped up, knocking her chair to the floor, and backed away, clutching her face like Lady Macbeth in the mad scene. "No more!" she implored in a hoarse whisper. "No more!" Peering from behind her fingers, she repeated her plea in a strangled voice and hurried out the door.

Edmund slumped in a chair and buried his face in his hands. In the silence, I could hear the buzz of an electric clock on the wall. The teakettle whistled on the stove. I was stunned. I hadn't heard so much shouting since the performance of *Who's Afraid of Virginia Woolf?* I saw at the Williamstown Theater the summer I was at Blithedale Farm. Edmund rose with a weary sigh. The windows had grown as dark as a photographic negative, and his face had a pale, drained look in the bright kitchen. "I guess I better go," I said, but he motioned me to stay. "She'll be back. Besides, I'd rather have you around. Stop me from beating her up."

We were sitting at the table sipping our tea when I heard a distant muffled chant out on the road. A minute later, Beatrice strode past the window, her white shawl streaming behind her in the moonlight. "No more! No more!" her quavering voice rang out, growing fainter as she vanished down the road.

"That was nothing," Warren said gleefully when I described the scene. "Last time I was there she had to be coaxed down off the roof."

Eventually I found two rooms in a large gabled orange-brick house on Boars Hill, a neighborhood of lodges and estates on the outskirts of Oxford. The front parlor had a drop leaf table, two beat-up easy chairs, a hot plate and a small refrigerator. The bedroom, across the hall, looked out on the "grounds," a labyrinth of cracked pools, overgrown paths, and tangled hedges. What had once been a lawn tennis court was now a network of shallow trenches churned up by moles. It was called Shireton Hall. At last—a residence with a name.

My landlady, Mrs. Keithley, was an elderly widow with a thin Plantagenet face that reminded me of Edith Sitwell's. She was a direct descendant of William Wyckham, the founder of New College, she confided to me one morning over tea (a claim that caused great hilarity when I mentioned it some months later at a Balliol dinner; Wyckham, a bishop, had no heirs). But she had fallen on hard times and lived in one room on the ground floor, letting the others.

"I'm a novelist," she announced when I mentioned that I wrote poetry. She handed me three books. "If you care to dip into these, you'll find them a good read."

I was unpacking my books from my grandfather's steamer trunk one afternoon when Mrs. Keithley called me to the phone. "It's a Mr. Teitelbaum," she announced. "Or is it Teitelberg? What curious names you people have."

"Is this our Oxford man?" my uncle Dave boomed over the wire. "We're in London and we're dying to see you. Come in I'll buy you dinner."

Dave and Selma—she was my mother's cousin, but I'd called them aunt and uncle for as long as I could remember—were schoolteachers from Queens. They came to London once a year to visit the museums and take in the shows—though Dave, a thick-browed, gravel-voiced New Yorker with a head of wiry gray hair, spent most of his time at the Kew Gardens track. "My husband goes to London and gambles like he was at Belmont Park," Selma complained to my mother. "He might as well stay home." But Dave claimed that going to the track was a different experience at Kew. "It's nice and civilized. They clap instead of yelling."

Dave and Selma usually came to Chicago for the big holidays, but once when I was in high school my parents had let me go visit them in Kew Gardens for a week. They were childless, and glad to have me. Dave showed me New York: the Bronx Zoo, the Empire State Building, the Museum of Natural History. He took me to the theater: *West Side Story, Damn Yankees, Sunrise at Campobello*. He gave me books: *Animal Farm, A Tale of Two Cities*, the stories of Guy de Maupassant. Sitting in a big overstuffed club chair after dinner, he'd read to me from Blake and Tennyson while Selma finished up the dishes. Their Tudor-style house was right next to the Long Island railroad tracks; whenever a train roared by, shaking the china in the glass cupboard and making the room vibrate, Dave would put down his book and wait until it passed. They'd lived there for thirty years. The house had a comfortable, old-fashioned look: the carpeting on the stairs was worn; the family portraits on the wall were in dark oval frames; the fluffy toilet-seat covers were matted like a dog's fur after it's been out in the rain. *The New York Post* and various betting sheets lay on the carpet beside Dave's chair. There was a stained-glass window in the dining room. The upstairs smelled of mothballs. A real home.

I met them at the Savoy. Here, maybe at this very table, Katherine Mansfield had defended D. H. Lawrence against some malicious gossips; Oscar Wilde had seduced the young Lord Douglas; Swinburne and A. E. Housman had dined. "Very nice," Dave commented, admiring the chandeliers, the scrolled-woodwork columns, the red velvet banquettes.

"What are you having?" Selma said. Decor didn't interest her.

"I'll have whatever you're having," Dave said, putting aside his menu. For him, food was food. "So tell me." He leaned across the linen tablecloth. The hair on the back of his hands was thick and black. "What's it like?"

"Oxford? Okay, I guess. Only I can't quite figure out what I'm supposed to be doing."

"Can I interject something?" Selma broke in, smearing butter on a roll. "It doesn't matter what you do. The important thing is that you're here. I have students whose lives are drab beyond relief. Their homes are without books, without music, without art. And you know what?" Selma chewed and swallowed. "They love my classes. They're so hungry for the beautiful you can see it in their eyes. I play *Rigoletto* for them —they *love* it. They eat it up. They've never heard anything like Verdi before."

I was sorry for those deprived high school students, but what about me? *I* was hungry for the beautiful. Picking at my roast beef, I thought of the clubs on Pall Mall I'd strolled by that afternoon, staring in the high Georgian windows like a famished urchin and imagining the scene within: gathered around a fireplace with a mantel of veined roseate marble stands a group of men in frock coats, sherry glasses in hand, discussing the latest issue of *The Spectator*. The fire leaps in the grate as a frock-coated servant glides up and dispenses *hors d'oeuvres*. A bell chimes and the men, talking in animated groups, drift from the oak-paneled library to the dining room, where platters heaped with Yorkshire pudding and glazed trout, roast duckling and grouse (grouse?), are arranged on a mahogany sideboard. Decanters of wine give off a ruby sheen in the flickering light of a candelabrum. Glasses raised high, the diners, flushed with drink, cry out a toast to the Queen. The reflections of the narrowing, leaping candle flames dance in the windows . . .

"You have a great opportunity," Dave interrupted my reverie. "When I was your age, I never had time to read. I had to go to night school. I worked my way through college packing vitamins in a warehouse. I did my homework in the library. The E train was my study hall." Dave read on the subway; I read in the Bodleian. The burden was on me.

"Enjoy," Selma said as we stood on the sidewalk after dinner. She stroked my cheek, her eyes shiny with tears. "Remember, we expect great things."

Dave put his big hands on my shoulders. "You know Swinburne's poem to Whitman?" (One of the books he read on the E train was Palgrave's *Golden Treasury*.) Pointing his cigar at me, he recited:

> *Send but a song oversea for us,*
> *Heart of our hearts who are free,*
> *Heart of our singer, to be for us*
> *More than our singing can be.*

His rough voice rose above the grinding roar of buses in the twilight of the London street. "You're a good boy," my aunt murmured. "Come," she said to Dave, putting her arm through his. "We'll miss our curtain." And they hurried off to the

Windmill Theatre, where Agatha Christie's *The Mousetrap* was in its twenty-second year.

I stood alone on the sidewalk and wondered where to go. Maybe I should see if there were any tickets left. But no. *The Mousetrap* was middlebrow.

Whole days went by when I didn't speak to a soul. Eleanor had put off her departure for a few weeks because her mother was sick, and I hardly ever saw Warren, who was busy with his publishing firm. Besides, he preferred to write letters, even though he only lived a mile down the road. Nearly every morning a fat envelope with the Rookery logo—a sheep reading a book—awaited me on the table in the hall. Correspondence for Warren was a way of blowing off steam; sitting in his study late at night, he would knock off several thousand words on his electric typewriter. "I've just spent fourteen hours going over the books in anticipation of the taxman's arrival," he reported in a letter dated "October 17; 3:40 A.M." "No doubt he'll be sporting an evil moustache twirled at the ends like Molly Bloom's lover Blazes what's-his-name. These government crooks really get my wick up!" And a day later:

> I was up half the night deep in Antony & Cleopatra. My GOD that *is* great stuff: Hark, the drum demurely wakes the sleepers. This is my space, Kingdoms are clay . . . But enough literature! Alarum within. I've got to finish off the proofs of *Postwar Polish Poetry*. GAWD I hate proofs. Almost as much as I hate poetry. My head aches, and a drowsy numbness pains my senses, as if I'd emptied some dull opiate down the drain and lethewards had sunk.

It was strange to have these manic letters drop through the mail slot day after day from someone I scarcely knew. Whenever I called him on the phone, Warren put me off, and he never made any reference to his voluble correspondence, as if it were some secret vice.

I idled away my mornings in the Bodleian, reading at one of the long tables by the milky light that filtered through the tall clerestory windows. After lunch at the Turl, an ancient pub in New College Lane, I would go off to Blackwell's to browse— and to hang around a tremendously fat girl who worked as a clerk in the secondhand book department. I was fascinated by her huge shapeless body, the trembling flesh of her chin, her puffy sullen face, but I could never summon up the nerve to speak to her, though I loitered for hours in the area where she worked. I knew she was lonely, since I often stationed myself at the window of a pub next door when it opened at six, just as Blackwell's was closing, in order to watch unobserved as the fat girl made her way slowly down the street; she was too big to ride a bicycle. I was tempted to rush out after her and ask her to tea. Maybe she would invite me over. I had even imagined her flat: a bed-sitter on the Cowley Road across Magdalen Bridge, where the workers from the car factories lived. I pictured her lumbering up the steps, fumbling with the key, settling heavily into a battered easy chair and reaching down with a pasty white arm thick as a pig's haunch to switch on the electric fire . . . How I longed to climb, Lilliputianlike, on that gigantic body! But I never worked up the nerve to speak to her, and one afternoon when I entered the shop she wasn't there. She was probably on vacation, I reassured myself, vowing to strike up a conversation as soon as she came back to work. But she never did.

Twice a week I ducked into the porter's lodge at the front gate of Balliol to collect my mail. I could always count on finding in the wooden cubbyhole two or three envelopes addressed in Eleanor's schoolgirl hand. My heart stormed in my chest as I hurried over to the King's Arms, ordered a pint of bitter, and sat down in the corner to read her letters.

Dearest dear,

Oh god I miss you. It hasn't been fun living at home, and I literally count the days until I see you. Every night I lie in bed and think about how much I love you and how happy we are. I remember the mornings when I'd wake up by your side last summer, and how gentle your face seemed in the sunlight, like a child's. Soon, dearest, soon I'll be with you, hugging you beneath a big down comforter and listening to the rain.

This was strong stuff. Gulping my bitter, I remembered a night the summer before when we were sitting on the porch in Cambridge and Eleanor said, "Did you ever used to think you would meet just the right person, and that all the people you were with were just people to be with while you were waiting around for it to happen?" She grabbed my hand and applied it like a compress to her cheek. "You're that person."

I tore open another letter, holding it up to the sunlight that shone feebly through the pub's mullioned windows:

If I cry even as I write this letter, it is because I miss you so much that I can hardly express it in words. There is more emotion contained in what I feel for you than I've ever known before. If only we were married! Now I understand why people weep at weddings and why we'll weep at our own. How I long for that precious day!

Our wedding? That was how we talked. Among the many names we had for each other—*lamb, bear, puppy*, a whole menagerie of endearments—were *husband* and *wife*, words we pronounced as solemnly as vows. Eleanor was still trying to get a divorce, but it was only a legal matter now; as soon as the decree came through . . . I skimmed the last letter, a detailed account of her life in Shaker Heights, and glanced ahead to the end: "I love you—as much as anyone has ever loved another. Your wife always, E."

"Last call, please!" the barmaid announced. "It's time." I drained my mug, stuck Eleanor's letters in my pocket, and headed off to Blackwell's to see if the fat girl was back.

I stood behind the opaque panels that enclosed the customs area, peering through a gap. People from Eleanor's flight were starting to come out now, pushing wire baggage carts. Then Eleanor was running toward me, weaving her cart through the crowd. Her face was pale with fatigue, and I could feel her tremble as we embraced. "I thought I'd never get out of there," she said, kissing my eyes, my cheek, my neck. Her breath smelled of cigarettes and mint.

"Me neither." I held her away from me and studied her long eyelashes and sad mouth. "I couldn't have lasted another week." In her plaid skirt and cashmere sweater, she seemed about fifteen—a girl on her way home from school, clutching her American Civ. textbook against her chest. We clung to each other in the crowded terminal, surrounded by shouting porters, tour groups, turbaned Indians pushing baggage carts through the throng. The babble of flight information crackled through the cavernous hall. Beyond the automatic doors, red double-decker buses pulled up to the curb.

"Let's never be apart again," Eleanor said. We were both in tears. It was just like that scene in *A Man and a Woman* where Anouk Aimée gets off the train and they run toward each other, steam billowing from the tracks. A moment as good as a movie.

"You can't imagine what it's been like," I said as we pulled onto the M4 and headed toward Oxford. "I might as well have signed up for the Peace Corps and gone to Uganda."

"Oh, puppy," she murmured, stroking my neck. "Haven't you met anyone?" Indeed. Some quite marvelous chaps. I've had many a glorious pub crawl with my Oxford cronies.

"Just that poet Winston Walker told me to call and a weird couple who live out in the country and collect birds' nests." I didn't mention the fat girl.

"We'll meet people. My cousin Lenny's going to be in London for a few months on some apprentice program with his bank." Lenny Paprin: a smooth-faced boy with a Business Administration degree from Colgate. Hey, that's great, Eleanor. We can all go to my eating club. The Wimpy's at Piccadilly Circus. How could I confess that I'd spent my afternoons browsing at Blackwell's, had dinner alone every night at the Cantonese Palace in Ship Street and got sodden in the King's Arms, leafing through *The New Statesman* at the bar?

Mrs. Keithley was planting flowers in a giant urn when we turned up the gravel driveway of Shireton Hall. "Be nice to her," I said. "She's a little difficult. And don't forget I told her we're married."

"So you're Mrs. Keithley," Eleanor said, striding right up to her. "I've heard so much about you."

She offered a hand, but Mrs. Keithley appeared not to notice. "Now were you cautious on the motorway?" she called out to me. "The drivers are beastly on that road."

"Of course, Mrs. Keithley. I crept along like, like a . . ." Not an old woman. "Like a curate."

"Good!" She touched a finger to a heavily rouged cheek. "I've left some porridge on the stove."

"What was that all about?" Eleanor said when we got upstairs.

"Maybe she's jealous. She had me to herself for a month, and now you've shown up."

"Well, don't let me get in the way." She stood in the middle of the parlor clutching her suitcase. There were tears in her eyes.

You *are* in the way: I suppressed the thought, but not before it had registered. When I was alone, I wanted her; when I was with her, I wanted to be alone. Like Naomi Berg said: nothing ever turns out to be as good as you think it will.

"Come on, puppy," I said, putting my arms around her. "You're tired. Let's get you to bed." So I can sit moodily in the parlor by myself.

I folded down the plump quilt, so light that it seemed to float above the bed, and Eleanor clambered up over the high frame. Her head on the pillow seemed delicate, doll-like. I laid my hand on her brow and smoothed back her silky hair. "Dearest," she murmured as I rose to leave. She reached for my hand. "I'm scared."

"Of what?"

"I don't know." She huddled deeper beneath the covers, her hair a red swirl on the pillow. "That something will go wrong with us."

"But why? What could happen?"

"I don't know. I'm just afraid."

"Nothing will happen. You're exhausted, that's all." I stood up. "Now go to sleep." I closed the door and settled down in the parlor with a cup of instant coffee and the Penguin *Lost Illusions*. Where was I? That scene where Lucien de Rubempré goes in search of his actress girl friend Coralie and finds her, penniless, in a drab walk-up flat:

> The actress was more loving and tender than ever, as if she wanted to make up for the poverty of their new ménage with the richest treasures of her heart. She was ravishingly beautiful; her hair was peeping out from a scarf wrapped round her head; she was immaculate and fresh, with laughing eyes and speech as gay as the rising sun stealing through the windows to gild this charming penury.

Where was *my* Coralie? I'd searched for her everywhere. Museums and libraries, bars and cafés . . . everywhere but across the hall.

A month had gone by and I'd done nothing about my studies, so I made an appointment with A. O. J. Cockshut, the author of *Truth to Life*, a book on nineteenth-century biography I admired, in the hope of persuading him to accept me as a reader for the B. Phil. degree, which required only a longish paper. One morning in November I climbed three flights of ancient flagstone steps in the Magdalen Tower and knocked lightly on a thick oak door. "Come in," cried a muffled voice. I entered and found myself in a vast book-lined room. Near the top of the shelves was a brass rung with a ladder attached to it. There were books everywhere: on the floor, the windowseat, even in the fireplace. A pale wash of sunlight filtered through thick velvet curtains; a silk-shaded lamp in the corner gave off a feeble glow. Behind a desk piled high with tottering heaps of books, a gaunt figure in a silk vest crouched in the shadows like a soldier peering from a trench.

"Professor Cockshut?" I called out in a tentative voice. After much deliberation, I had decided to pronounce it *caoutchouc*, like the French word for galoshes.

"The name's Cockshut," he snapped, pointedly stressing the final consonants in both syllables.

"Yes, of course. Cockshut," I repeated foolishly. "I've come to see about working under you for the B. Phil."

He raised his eyebrows like a detective listening to a thief's weak alibi, and rubbed a bony hand against his forehead. "And when do you propose to supplicate for this degree?"

"Supplicate?"

"Put in for it." He spat out the words.

"Oh, within a year, I guess."

"I'm afraid that's quite impossible." His lips quivered in annoyance. "You'd have to work up Anglo-Saxon and pass a course in English hands."

"English hands?"

"English hands," he said in a bored voice, as if he were reciting from a catalogue, "is the study of handwriting from different periods, required for the reading of original manuscripts."

"But couldn't I just write a thesis?" I said weakly.

"A *thesis*?" Professor Cockshut uttered the word with distaste, as if it were some crude expletive.

"I read in the *Bulletin* that I could qualify by writing a dissertation and defending it."

"One doesn't simply *defend* a thesis as if it were one's honor," Professor Cockshut answered from the shadows. "You must be prepared to sit for an exam on the whole of English literature." But he couldn't take on any more students in any event, he concluded in a firm voice, and vanished behind his fortress of books.

I was ready to drop the matter right there, but my stipend required a note from a tutor attesting that I was under his supervision. Eventually I persuaded a frail, ancient Balliol don who specialized in Dryden to sponsor me—though I can't imagine what he wrote to the directors of my fellowship, since he resisted my efforts to see him and returned my imploring notes with scrawled assurances that I was doing "splendidly" on my own.

I did infiltrate a college, when a friend of Warren's, a tutor at New College, invited me to give a talk on Yeats to his undergraduates. I spent the whole of one "long vac" preparing and arrived on the appointed morning to find seventeen boys in blazers, cardigans, and baggy wool trousers lounging about the junior common room. Their faces had that familiar ruddy hue, a salmon tint in the cheeks, and their hair was long, but

chain-smoking Lucky Strikes and leafing through *The Times Literary Supplement.* His face had the look of a sun-baked mud flat. He glanced in my direction once, staring past me out the window, his eyes moist in the dim empty room.

For days at a time we saw no one but Mrs. Keithley and the local publican. To slake my loneliness, I wrote endless letters to Bob.

Dear Friend (the only one I have):

I know this is my third letter in as many days, but you're the only correspondent I can trust to answer my desperate epistles. The tactics for receiving enough mail to convince me that I exist, such as writing to 47 people, have been foiled. The returns are low. A madman sending out death threats would receive more attention than I do.

The other night I was hoisting a few in the Lamb & Flag when a sad-eyed fellow stepped up to the bar—42 years old, Yale grad, a failure as a novelist ("my book was just turned down by Random House") who earns his living teaching night school at the Abingdon Polytechnic. He looks like a hunted animal, and is wary of me because I cramp his bar style of spurious boasting. But at least he's read a few books. We get drunk and play bar billiards until closing time. I get the feeling he doesn't like to go home, but he doesn't say too much about it. His name is Edgar Devon, and you've never heard of him, but so far he's the only member of the expatriate literary circle I'd hoped to establish on Boar's Hill. Sounds like fun, huh?

Reading over Yeats's account of the Phases of the Moon in *A Vision*, I discovered that I was associated with Phase 17, but out of phase:

Out of phase, seeking emotion instead of impersonal action, there is—desire being impossible—self-pity, and therefore discontent with people and with circumstance, and an overwhelming sense of loneliness, of being abandoned. All criticism is resented, and small personal rights and predilections, especially if supported by habit or position, are asserted with violence; there is great indifference to others' rights and predilections.

It didn't help matters that Harper & Row had signed up Bob to write a book about the '60s. "He hasn't suffered enough to be a writer," I complained to Eleanor. "He just skates along on the surface of life while I'm down here in the depths." Phase 17 talking.

"How can you say that about your best friend?" she scolded me. "What makes you think you're the only one with problems?"

"Look, no one who still goes to Fenway Park, drives around in a convertible listening to rock 'n' roll, and plays hockey with nine-year-olds can know what it's like to sit here day after day trying to write a novel no one will ever read."

Why would no one ever read it? Because it was about a precocious only child who graduates from the University of Chicago at the age of twelve and moves into a room above Walgreen's, his only companion a mynah bird that can recite *The Waste Land*. Despondent when *The New Yorker* turns down his memoir of growing up in Chicago, he fastens the fifty-volume Pléiade edition of Balzac around his waist and drowns himself in Lake Michigan.

In the bedroom, Eleanor sat writing *her* novel, the story of a girl from Shaker Heights and her relationship with her divorced mother. "Can't you write about anything besides yourself?" I said when she showed me the first chapter.

She snatched the manuscript away. "What about your book? Who's this twelve-year-old supposed to be? Napoleon?"

"You want me to lie?" I shouted. "Fine. It's great. You're

the next George Eliot." She fled in tears and slammed the door. Numb with rage, I stormed off to the pub, striding furiously through the dark. I'd call up Lizzie. She would understand.

I pushed a tuppence into the bleeping phone and got the long-distance operator. Lizzie's father answered, his voice faint over the thrumming wire. "She's not here," he said curtly when the operator asked if he would accept the call. "She's in Mexico."

"Where?" I implored. "What's her address?" But he had hung up.

Eleanor was sitting cross-legged on the bed reading a Trollope novel when I came in. Her face was drawn from crying. "I don't know what got into me," I said, covering her face with kisses. "Your book will be good. I know it will."

She looked up at me beseechingly, wanting to believe. Her eyelashes fluttered as she blinked back tears. "Don't ever run out on me like that," she said in a taut voice. "It's the one thing I can't stand."

I held her face in my hands and murmured reassurances. I was discouraged about my studies, worried about my book. It would never happen again.

Two days later, hearing Eleanor clack away on her old Smith-Corona across the hall, I was seized with the urge to flee. As they say in detective novels, she knew too much. Chained to my desk by the fear that she would walk in and see me lounging in the armchair with a magazine, I listened for her footsteps with a tense heart, ready to fling aside the *TLS* and hustle to the table the moment I heard the bedroom door open. What kind of life was this?

One afternoon I was walking through the university parks when I passed the tennis courts and saw the Oxford tennis team out practicing. It was a cold November afternoon, and as I watched them rallying in their warm-up jackets, I suddenly recalled those chilly autumn days in high school when I'd gone out for the Evanston tennis team—suiting up in the dank locker room and heading out to the cracked asphalt courts after school, warming up in the wintry air, leaves scudding across the court beneath a platinum sky. There was something profoundly satisfying about the heft of two rackets tucked under my arm—no serious player had only one—the crisp feel of new tennis balls, the damp, sweaty odor of the terrycloth wristlets in my canvas duffel bag, the chilly crinkle of my nylon EVANSTON jacket. I liked the rhythm of warming up: ground strikes, then serve, then lobs, then up to the net while Coach Anderson yelled, "Punch it! Punch it! You don't need a full swing up there." And then the hot shower and walking to the bus stop in the dark, your legs aching from the laps around the court that ended practice . . . So why did I quit the team? Because Coach Anderson made me put away the *Cantos* when he caught me reading on the bus before a meet. I was supposed to think about the match.

One night I drove into London to attend a reading at the British Museum by Morgan Ames. Speeding through the fog in my Wolseley Hornet, I was excited; maybe he'd invite me to have a drink with him afterwards. The professor and his former student. I had persuaded Eleanor to let me go alone. "It's really a kind of private experience," I explained.

Private it was. "The evening was a crushing disaster," I reported to Bob:

When the reading was over, I went up to Ames and said hello. He didn't remember me! I clamored around him with another insignificant and obscure student, six inches shorter even than I (Dennis Wheatley; remember him? A tiny person in Ames's seminar; he's "thumbing through" Europe). Ames was in a peculiar mood. He had a sorrowful look in his eye, and I went away after a brief exchange, feeling like a fool.

"The Ames experience boringly predictable," Bob replied in his didactic way. "I trust you learned your lesson."

What lesson? A week later I was behind the wheel of my Wolseley Hornet again, heading for London. Eleanor had gone to Cornwall for the weekend to visit an old school friend whose parents had retired there.

It was early evening when I arrived, driving up Cromwell Road in the rush-hour traffic. Trucks and busses clogged the roundabout at Hyde Park Corner. I parked on a side street near Piccadilly Circus and got out to walk around. It was a mild November evening, and the pubs had just opened. Through the open doors I could see men in business suits clustered around the bars calling out their orders. Behind curtains of plastic tape were the porn shops, but I seldom ventured in anymore; they weren't like porn shops in America. For one thing, the magazines were sealed, and the few they left open for you to look at were pretty tame; the men had limp cocks, and they never showed people doing it, just a lot of simulated poses. Nothing like the cum shots you saw back home.

The British were very odd about sex. They had all these bondage magazines where people wrote in about how they liked to be spanked, and there were notecards in the windows advertising Schoolmistresses and Strict English Nannies: YOU NEED DISCIPLINE. I ORDER YOU TO CALL THIS NUMBER. I didn't begrudge anyone their fantasies, but photographs of women having their behinds lashed with a switch didn't do much for me. Sex was confusing enough as it was; why drag in physical pain?

I had a pint and two lethal-looking sausages in a pub on Windmill Street. So cheerful, these pubs, with their frosted windows, worn carpets, mahogany woodwork, mugs hung above

the bar. One thing about the English: they really knew how to
drink. The girl behind the bar had a fishy, white-skinned look
that reminded me of Maureen back in Chicago. She was sweating as she hurried back and forth, drawing pints and pushing
them across the bar. A wisp of hair was pasted to her pale
forehead. It would be nice to fuck her from behind, kneeling
on the beer-soaked floor . . .

It was dark when I came out. The sky had a faint yellowish
tint from the sodium vapor lamps. Black cabs hurtled through
the streets with a throbbing rattle. I drifted past Indian restaurants and Chinese groceries, newsshops and betting parlors.
On the curbs were fruit and vegetable carts tended by vendors
in aprons who stood smoking in the dark. The air smelled of
urine, horse manure and diesel fumes.

In a doorway I noticed a lighted bell and above it the name
INGRID: Swedish Model. I looked around, walked on a few
steps, and returned to the doorway. INGRID. You mean you
could just go up the stairs and she was there? Was it legal? I
paced back and forth on the sidewalk. I'd go up and the cops—
the bobbies—would burst in, black-helmeted, demanding to see
my passport. Wasn't that how the Profumo scandal broke? A
life ruined by consorting with hookers.

Nervously I climbed the steps. On the second floor was a
door with Ingrid's name on it. I rang the bell. Nothing. Oh,
good. She wasn't there. I was free to go—to get in the car,
drive back to Oxford, settle down in the front parlor and finish
The Mayor of Casterbridge.

The door opened a crack, and an ancient crone stared out
at me. Hair sprouted from her chin; her teeth were black
around the edges. "Sorry," I blurted. "I've got the wrong door."

The crone motioned me inside. "If it's Ingrid you'd be
wanting, she's got someone in there now. Sit down." I was
shown into a waiting room with a Naugahyde couch and two
plastic molded chairs. Between them was a table strewn with

magazines. "It's three quid, and fifty *p* for the rubber," the crone explained. "Unless you've got one of your own." I shook my head—why on earth would a student at Oxford University be carrying around a rubber?—and sat down on the couch. The crone went off. To call Scotland Yard, no doubt. I leafed through a *National Geographic*, an article about the Fiji Islanders. Women walking around with baskets on their heads and breasts exposed to the open air. Probably it was easier when they went around like that, not wearing anything but a straw skirt. You got used to it. Anyway, you couldn't have too many hard-ons wearing those little thongs.

A burly man in a raincoat hurried past me out the door. A minute later, the crone arrived with my condom and told me Ingrid was ready now. When I went in, she was sprawled on the bed in a diaphanous nightgown. The room was dark. A bedside lamp with a red light bulb cast a faint crimson glow.

"Come here, darling," said Ingrid in a Bergman-film accent. Huh. She really *was* Swedish. I sat down on the edge of the bed and looked her over. She was thirtyish, with a broad face, and pretty hefty; her arms were plump and white, like a washerwoman's.

"What is your name?" she said.

"Uh, Walter." That would throw those Scotland Yard chaps off the trail.

"Come over here, Walter." I sat on the edge of the bed. There was a mirror on the wall. My face looked pale and ghostly. Ingrid reached up and put a hand on my cheek. "What do you do, Walter?" she said.

"I'm a . . . journalist."

"That's nice. Why don't you take off your clothes?"

I got up and undressed while Ingrid watched. A blonde. Suddenly I recalled Tom Maynard's question at the Signet about what color pubic hair blondes had. Ingrid's looked pretty dark under that gown. "Hurry, darling," she said.

I went over and stood by the bed, still in my underpants. Ingrid tugged them down with the practiced efficiency of a nurse, and cradled my limp cock in her hand. "What is it, darling? Don't be nervous." She leaned down and put it in her mouth. I studied my face in the mirror as her blond head bobbed up and down. It was cold. Like when we had swimming in high school, and you had to go down to the pool through a tiled corridor without any clothes on. I used to hate swimming. You always felt so clammy after you showered and put on your street clothes.

Ingrid's head was still. "It will not go hard," she noted.

I glanced down. My cock looked tiny. I felt bad for Ingrid. Not that she was horny or anything, but I didn't want her to think, you know, I didn't like her. She was actually very nice. "I guess I better go."

"Come back when you are more in the mood," she advised in her melodious voice. When would that be? I couldn't imagine. I pulled on my pants, buttoned my shirt with fumbling fingers, and tied my shoes. "Don't forget to leave a little something for Betty," Ingrid said. Betty? "The attendant," she explained.

I nodded. "Well, goodbye."

"Goodbye, Walter." She blew me a kiss.

Betty was slumped on a chair in the waiting room, her chin on her chest. Walter dropped a crumpled pound note in her lap and slipped out the door. Ten minutes later he was back in the Lamb & Flag, hoisting a thick, foamy pint.

Eleanor and Mrs. Keithley didn't get along. It infuriated our landlady to see me wrestling the laundry into the car and driving off to the laundromat in Abingdon. "That's woman's work," she rebuked me one afternoon as I passed her on the stairs lugging a sack of dirty clothes. "What does your wife do all day?"

"She's writing a novel."

Mrs. Keithley snorted. "We're all writing novels, my dear—only some are more eagerly awaited than others." And she pushed vigorously through the swinging door to her room, rustling a vase of tulips in the hall.

She complained that Eleanor used too much hot water. "I commend her desire to be clean," she said one night when I encountered her in the hall, "but I should think a bath a week sufficient, wouldn't you?"

I padded down the hall and knocked on the bathroom door. "Who is it?" Eleanor called out.

"It's me. Mrs. Keithley said you shouldn't use so much hot water." Behind the door, the faucet drummed and thundered. I was aware of other lodgers listening.

"I can't hear you."

I turned the knob, but it was locked. I knocked again. "What!" She opened the door and let me in. The room was dense with steam. I breathed in the fragrant vaporous air, admiring Eleanor's girlish body. Tendrils of damp hair clung to her neck, and her breasts had a moist rosy flush.

I sat down on a stool under the window. "Mrs. Keithley said you shouldn't use so much hot water."

"Fuck her! The only time I'm ever warm is in this bathtub." She turned off the tap and climbed in. Water billowed over the sides. "Care to join me?"

"I think the lodgers might find it a little odd."

"Who cares what the lodgers think?" She handed me a sponge. "Could you wash my back then? I'm sure the lodgers wouldn't mind that."

But I was worried about Mrs. Keithley. "Could I have a word with you?" she called up the stairs.

We met on the landing. Her dry cheeks were spotted with rouge. "I am not in the habit of meddling," she began, "but in this instance I simply can't stand by. You are a young man with a future, and it hurts me to see it being jeopardized by that . . ." She gestured in the direction of the bathroom. ". . . girl."

"Oh come, Mrs. Keithley." (Two months in England and I sounded like Alistair Cooke.) "What are you talking about?"

Her lips trembled with fury. "You know perfectly well what I mean," she said in a voice charged with foreboding. "But it's your life. I'll say no more."

Her sinister prediction troubled me. Weren't we happy? I'd never thought about it. Still, how I lived my life was none of Mrs. Keithley's business. From then on, when I passed her in the hall we only nodded, and I slipped our monthly rent checks under her door.

Our conflict became open war when a young American couple, the friends of friends, dropped by for a visit one afternoon with their infant daughter. They were teachers at the Rocky Mountain School, and radiated a healthy outdoor vigor in their quilted vests and hiking boots. They seemed outsized in our tiny parlor; he had a longshoreman's stocky build, and his flaxen-haired wife was Valkyrian. They frightened our fragile landlady. I spotted her peering anxiously from behind the curtains while we strolled in the garden, the baby strapped to its mother's back like a papoose.

We were finishing off a jug of wine when there was a knock at the door. It was Mrs. Keithley. Silently she took in the scene: the empty wine jug, the baby feeding at its mother's breast, the knapsacks and sleeping bags strewn all over the floor. I read the message in her eyes: Shireton Hall had fallen on hard times.

"Who are these people?" she demanded, pursing her lips as if she'd tasted something sour. The baby began to scream. Mrs. Keithley's voice rose higher. "My home is *not* a youth hostel," she declared. She stared with loathing at our guests, then turned abruptly and strode from the room, slamming the door behind her.

I jumped up and rushed out into the hall, just in time to see her disappearing down the stairs. "Don't think you can bully me, Mrs. Keithley!" I shouted, leaning over the bannister. "It's not my fault you have to let out rooms."

She halted on the stairs and started back up. "Let me tell you something, young man," she said in a controlled, even tone, advancing toward me. "You are quite intelligent, and when you first came here, I was convinced that you had promise. But I was *wrong*. Oh very wrong indeed. You will come to *nothing*." She glared at me and turned to go.

"You're pitiful, Mrs. Keithley, pitiful," I yelled after her. Suddenly I was at a loss. "Your novels are no good," I said in the voice of a child whose sand castle has just been smashed by a vicious playmate.

That bothered her. Once again she began to mount the stairs. "And what about *your* novel?" she taunted. "You haven't even got a publisher."

"Just wait," I assured her. "It'll get published." And you'll be in it.

Eleanor got there first. "Listen to this," she said one day, brandishing her pad of yellow legal paper. "I started a new story."

Lydia Witherington was kneeling in the driveway beside a giant urn when they drove up. "Be nice to her," Roger had warned Susan as they headed up Boars Hill toward the house on the outskirts of Oxford where they would be living that year. "The landlady's rather eccentric. She claims to be a novelist."

"What's so eccentric about that?" Susan replied. "What do you think *I* am?"

Roger shot her a dubious look. "All I meant . . ."

I'd heard enough. "You make Roger sound like an Englishman," I broke in. "What is this 'rather eccentric' business?"

"How do you know he's not?" she answered hotly. "Just because you only write about yourself. You don't even know what the story's about yet and you're jumping all over it."

"I'm not jumping all over it," I said in a weary voice. See how patient I am? "I was just registering an objection to the language."

"That's all you ever do!" she cried, on the verge of tears. "Why can't you encourage me?"

"I encourage you," I said stonily, "but you have to learn to accept criticism."

My words were addressed to Eleanor's departing back. With a grimace of disgust, I turned to the poem on my desk:

> *In the purple dusk, our landlady kneels*
> *Like a penitent over her blossoming flower bed . . .*

*   *   *

"The kind of love you're asking the world to give you, the world can't give," Bob pointed out when I complained that he didn't pay enough attention to my poems. "Every poem reiterates the same cry—to be more, to matter. The poem itself becomes a cry for immortality, a way of writing yourself into lastingness." Guru Bob. I flung his letter on the table. He should try living in this drafty house, huddled beneath four blankets when the heat went off at night, warming up Cornish pasties for dinner in a miniature oven . . . It wasn't lastingness I was after. It was lasting out the year.

We had gotten a little Christmas tree for the parlor and decorated it with tinsel, popcorn, and a string of tiny white lights that winked on and off as we sat reading after dinner.

On Christmas Day we drove around looking for a restaurant, but everything was closed, even the pubs. Just like that other terrible Christmas when my father drove us around the North Side looking for an open restaurant and we ended up at Guido's . . . ("The lurid Santa Claus above the bar/Reminds us what we're not and what we are"). When we got home, I opened the small refrigerator beneath the sink and studied its contents: a withered head of lettuce; half a bread sausage wrapped in foil; a bottle of ginger beer. As I crouched down and peered at the empty shelves, the cold air rushing against my face, there was a knock at the door. It was Mrs. Keithley, clutching what looked like a giant clod of earth. Roots trailed from the bottom as if it had just been yanked out of the ground. "I brought you a parsnip from the garden," she said shyly, holding the clod to her bosom like a bridesmaid clutching a bouquet.

"Why, thank you, Mrs. Keithley. That's awfully kind of you." I reached for the tuberous plant, barely visible beneath a layer of dirt. A Yuletide peace offering. "Now, um, how does one go about preparing this?"

"Just slice it up," she said cheerfully, "and fry it in a little butter."

I scrubbed the parsnip in the sink, fried the pale, translucent slices, and set them on the table. An hour later we finished off a tin of biscuits. "We either have to go to bed or go find something to eat," I said. "I'm so hungry I feel dizzy."

We got in the car and drove to Abingdon; maybe someplace would be open there. It was drizzling when we reached the outskirts. The empty streets shone wetly in the yellow sodium lights. The town was shut down tight—the pubs dark, the shops shuttered, the shades in the brick row houses drawn. It felt as if the town had been evacuated. We drove around in the rain until we saw a lighted window across the street from the train station. There was a sign above the door: DING HO KITCHEN.

"Ah ha!" I cried. "Fortune smile down on him who persist."

We were the only patrons. Everyone for miles around was gathered around the dining room table tucking into their roast goose—Mum and Dad, the grandparents, the children home from school. The fireplace was festooned with holly, a fire crackled in the hearth.

"Ready to awduh?" A waiter stood over us.

"Uh, one moo shu pork, one chicken with garlic sauce, one fried dumplings." Our Christmas dinner. "And could I see your wine list?"

The waiter shook his head. "No have," he said. "Bring own."

I hurried out in search of a liquor store, but the streets for blocks around were dark. Soaked to the skin—it was raining hard now—I threaded my way through the empty tables and slumped down across from Eleanor. "Merry Christmas," I said. "Everything's closed."

"Oh, puppy." She put her hand on mine. "It's not so bad. We'll go to the Trout when the holidays are over. At least we're in England. Let's be happy."

I stared morosely into my tea. The other tables weren't even set. The rain beat against the windows. The red-shaded lamp between us gave off a feeble glow.

"I don't want to be in England. I don't know anyone here, I don't have a tutor, I'm not getting anything done. It's just one more place I don't belong."

Eleanor sighed and lit a cigarette. "Forgive me, but I don't get this idea. You think you'd be any happier in Evanston? I mean, you could have gone to Northwestern if you wanted to stay home . . ."

"Maybe I should have gone to live in a college. It would have been cheaper."

Eleanor looked at me reproachfully. "We have enough money."

What do you mean, *We?* We weren't living off the dollar bills Eleanor's father stapled to his invoices. Every month my parents sent a check to supplement my stipend. But that was "very tawchy subject," as my Grandma Sophie used to say. Writers didn't talk about money.

Eleanor blinked her eyes rapidly. She looked as if she was about to cry. "Don't start that again," she pleaded. "This was your idea. You wanted to come." She was right. It *had been* my idea. But there was something humiliating about the whole arrangement, the two of us living off my parents while we wrote our books. We were supposed to be starving in some garret, like Mimi and Rodolfo. *Thy tiny hand is frozen.*

The waiter appeared out of the gloom with our food. Eleanor helped herself to some dumplings and handed me the plate. "Why do you have to see everything as so cosmic?" she said. "So we're in a Chinese restaurant. It's not the end of the world. We have each other, we live in a beautiful house, we're working on our novels. Why make such a big deal out of it?"

"I'm not making a big deal out of it." I'm making something else: *In the Ding Ho Kitchen on Christmas night,/I dine on fried rice in the fading light . . .*

The Chinese lamp overhead flicked off and on. The waiter hovered in the corner, smoking a cigarette. "I think they want us to leave," Eleanor said. HURRY UP PLEASE ITS TIME Goonight Bill. Goonight Lou. Goonight May. Goonight.

Whenever I got tired of Oxford, I took the train to London and spent the afternoon in the used bookshops on Charing Cross Road. I bought up the most obscure, decrepit volumes I could find: a rain-spotted copy of Edmund Gosse's biography of Coventry Patmore, Southey's *Poems*, Arnold Bennett's *The Truth About an Author.* My attraction for the recondite knew no limits. Books by marginal men, the neglected, the forgotten:

they vindicated my own oblivion—and came in handy when I wrote my father. ("You really ought to look up Léon Bloy's *Pilgrim of the Absolute*.")

Browsing in the basement of Collett's, I was sorry to leave when the lights blinked off at closing time. Out on Charing Cross Road, I swung aboard a double-decker bus and climbed the circular staircase to the top, where I could look out over the traffic, the crowds emerging from the tube, the floodlit Regency facades of the government buildings on Piccadilly. The headlights of oncoming cars glimmered in the wet night like a moonlit river.

I got off at the entrance to the Kensington tube. Two doors away was the café-curtained window of Daqui's, a Russian restaurant full of white-haired émigrés who sat along the mirrored wall drinking tea out of tall glasses. I came here often to remind myself of home. Most of my grandparents' generation was dead by now, or down in Florida, but there were always new generations of old people, promoted to senescence against their will. No sooner had one died off than another appeared in its place—the formerly middle-aged. I never said a word to any of these frail émigrés, but listening to them talk in Russian comforted me; it brought back a vanished world.

I sat in the back and watched the evening deepen through the steamed-up window. At the next table, an old man in a raincoat sat reading a Russian-language newspaper. Seated on a stool behind the cash register, the proprietress, a sturdy woman in a cardigan, was talking intently with a man whose broad face and cheap blue suit gave him an *apparatchik* look. In the library silence of the half-empty room, I sipped my tea and spread open the latest issue of the *TLS*. In the letters column, a Mr. Lucian Treeves, from the Priory, Compton Wynyates, near Bromyard, was challenging a reviewer's interpretation of a line from *The Waste Land*: "And on the king my father's death before him." I thought of Mr. Treeves in his study, the leaded windows overlooking a lawn where pheasants scurried in the twilight. He put another log on the fire, snapped open the *TLS* and, noticing his letter, glanced over it to make sure none of those London editors had tampered with his prose. The wind beat against the windows, but Mr. Treeves was snug in his country home, a lap rug tucked about his knees and a pot of tea by his side.

I felt in my pocket for the letter I'd gotten from Herbert Lowy that morning. He had gone to study with a twelve-tone composer in Munich, and wrote me several times a week:

> Read Barthes's *Writing Degree Zero*. Everything is in this book. Read nothing else until you've gone through it—carefully! It's important that we talk. I would gladly come to England if summoned, but I have no money. Is your stipend sufficient to furnish the fare? Consider it an expenditure for the cause.

Herbert sounded like he was having as hard a time as I was. He was full of projects—*Three Variations on an Unwritten Theme by Kafka* ("Though I might as well call it *Three Unwritten Variations* for all I've gotten done"); an essay entitled "The Economy of Shame: The Genesis of the New Fetish in Contemporary Music" ("You think *The New Yorker* might be interested?"); a "reply" to Adorno's book on Wagner ("*Someone* has to put a stop to his reactionary bullshit"). But he was lonely, living in a student dorm and eating dinner by himself:

> Can this be some unhappy modern formula—that the closer we are to the truth, the more we are spit upon, neglected, and maddened? If so, I doubt I'll make it. My only source of comfort is the inspiration of three useful things: hatred, doubt, and thought. It's not the past but the future that must be made obsolete!

I skipped ahead to the end. "I embrace you!" he'd scrawled at the bottom. "P.S. I am thinking about getting a guitar and trying to make a lot of money playing the blues. A stupid idea, I know, but have no fear: I'll never do it." I had a sudden memory of a night on Sheffield when Herbert, loosened up by a bottle of chablis, sat down at the piano and started to play "Blueberry Hill," singing along in a perfect imitation of Fats Domino. "I found mah thri-ill . . ." In the middle of a chord, he'd broken off and walked out of the room. "We must put away the old toys," he used to say when he found me dancing in the parlor by myself to Motown's Greatest Hits. "Listen to Webern. It's good for you."

That winter I enrolled in beginning Czech at the Oxford Extension School. The language had an exotic aura that appealed to me—all those Roman letters transfigured by diacritic marks. And I admired the Czech poets. They had been through war and revolution; they'd fought in the streets. When I read in Miroslav Holub's preface to a collection of his poems that he'd thought up a famous line while he was crouched in a doorway being fired on by snipers, I was full of contempt for my own experience. I had thought up my best lines on our patio in Evanston, stretched out on the chaise longue.

Czech was an impossible language. "The only thing I've learned how to say is *Mama síla, otec pil pivo* (Mother sews, Father drinks beer)," I reported to Bob—"which ought to come in handy if I ever happen to be in Prague and someone asks me what my parents do. 'Oh,' I'll say offhandedly, 'Mother sews, and Father drinks beer.' " But I worked away at the grammar with insane doggedness, memorizing cases and declensions. How many people could say they'd read Vitězslav Nezval in the original?

"The fascination of what's difficult"—I knew what Yeats was talking about. Hunched over the table in our front room late at night, I struggled through Lévi-Strauss, Roman Jakobson, Foucault. I had discovered structuralism. Dan Robbins, a Harvard classmate who had gone to Paris to study with the famous French psychoanalyst Jacques Lacan, supplied me with reading lists. "Something is definitely happening here," he wrote me. "Lacan is our Vico. Structuralism is the New Science of our time."

A week later, we were on our way to Paris.

Dan had a room on the Right Bank, a walk-up with a skylight and a clutter of Empire furniture: a mahogany bureau, a roll-top desk, a ceiling-high armoire. By his bedside was a stack of paperbacks—Seuil, Gallimard, Éditions de Minuit—the pages still uncut. A gangly Southerner with mild gray eyes and flaxen hair, Dan had a scholarship to the Sorbonne and dutifully sat in his unheated room all winter deciphering Lacan's *Écrits*. But he didn't have his heart in it. He had arrived at Harvard straight from a military academy, and he'd never quite recovered. I think he secretly longed to go back to his hometown in Mississippi; he could talk for hours about the girls he'd dated in high school, the cars he drove, the summer nights when the air was filled with the scent of azaleas. Dan was a philosopher like I was a Marxist; his accounts of what he was reading had a hesitant, improvised quality that made me suspect he didn't always know what he was talking about. "It's kind of hard to explain," he said when I questioned him about Lacan. He handed me a copy of *Tel Quel*. "There's an article in here that sums the whole thing up."

Paris was cold and wintry. The sky was a cloudy oyster-gray. Leaves tumbled over the gravel walks in the Tuileries and swirled about our shoes. While Eleanor toured the museums, I sat writing in a café on the Rue de Buci, a Gitane smoldering in a yellow ashtray with the inscription "Pschitt!"—the name of a popular soft drink, but I read it as a subliminal verdict on my work.

On our last day, I decided to call in at the offices of *Paris Review*. For years I had noted its Paris address on the masthead: 6, rue de Tournon, the proper address for a literary magazine (unlike the New York address: 45–39 171st Place in Flushing). It was a damp, overcast afternoon. The bare branches of the plane trees flailed in the wind. The rue de Tournon was silent and empty, the courtyards sealed off behind old wooden doors. Paris was like a vast museum closed to visitors. I buried my fists deep in the pocket of my raincoat and hurried on, eager to spend the afternoon in what I supposed was a hectic office with writers' photographs and framed magazine covers on the wall, a cast-iron stove in the corner, a table littered with correspondence. Maybe the editors had read some of my work in *Poetry*. Maybe they'd let me do the *Paris Review* interview with Beckett.

The white numbers on the blue tin squares were getting smaller; I was almost there. It was starting to snow, wet flakes that stained the cobblestones. I turned in at a low arched doorway and ducked through a small door in the wooden gate. Green shuttered windows rose five stories up the desert-colored walls. There were no names or doorbells in the entry. I was wandering around in the courtyard when an old woman in a blue smock came up. *"Qu'est-ce que vous cherchez, Monsieur?"* She squinted at me through tired eyes, leaning on her broom as if it were a gondolier's oar.

"Uh, le magasin Revue de Paris?"

She scowled. *"Il n'y a pas de magasin ici."*

"Journal!" That was the word. *"C'est un journal américain."*

"Ah! Revue de Paris, Revue de Paris," she said rapidly. *"Mais ils sont jamais là. Je n'ai vu personne depuis deux mois."*

"Oh. Merci, Madame."

On the way out I noticed a café with a sign above the bottle-green facade: CAFE DE TOURNON. Hadn't I read somewhere that *Paris Review* editors gathered here? I had seen a photograph in the Gotham Book Mart of William Styron and George Plimpton in the '50s, fedoras at a gangster angle on their heads, surrounded by a gang of cronies: the founders of *Paris Review*. I pushed open the gauze-curtained door and stepped up to the bar. Two men in blue smocks sat playing dominos at a table in the back. I leaned an elbow against the bar, lit a Gitane, and ordered a kir. Through the window, I watched the snow swirl down, dropping through the winter dusk. Go back to jail.

Eleanor haunted me in my solitude. When she sat on the bed at Shireton Hall, cross-legged like a teenager, a baggy sweater pulled around her knees, and gave me one of those imploring looks—love me!—I was seized with an urge to get in the car and head for London. What Eleanor wanted was so simple: to be happy, get married, maybe start a family of our own. We were students on a year abroad. Why couldn't we just go look at old churches, tour the Cotswolds, do the things that students did? Sorry. We're creative.

Driving back to Oxford one morning after a weekend in London—Eleanor had stayed in the city to shop—I was ecstatic at the prospect of a day to myself. All weekend I'd dreamed of drifting through the afternoon alone, walking in the muddy field across the road where cows huddled against the barbed-wire fence. I raced through the small towns in my Wolseley Hornet, admiring the low stone walls and tidy hedges, the sheep-cluttered hills, the whitewashed buildings that hugged the road. England was beautiful.

I stopped off in Henley-on-Thames, ordered a half of bitter in a pub, and sat down on a bench outside. Ducks bobbed up and down on the river, cleaning their backs. A sparrow scampered beneath my feet scavenging for crumbs. Suddenly I remembered: it was my birthday. Maybe we could have dinner at the Trout if Eleanor got home in time.

When I drove up to Shireton Hall, Mrs. Keithley was out front pruning her rosebushes. "Your Eleanor's just rung up," she called. "You're to meet her at the noon train."

Fuck! I jumped in the car and sped off to the station, hurtling past slow drivers, my thumb on the horn. Eleanor was there when I pulled up to the curb. She hurried over and leaned in the open window, draping her arms around my neck. "Oh, puppy, I'm so sorry I forgot." She held up a split of champagne with a ribbon around its neck. "Happy birthday."

I flinched away from her. "Get in."

She bit her lip and looked down at the ground. "I thought you'd be hurt that I forgot," she said as she got in the car.

"I *want* to be alone," I shouted. "I *like* to be alone." *To wander in a mud-churned field at dusk . . .*

Her mouth twisted in a sob. "I should never have come," she wept, leaning her head on the dashboard. "You don't want me here."

I stared through the windshield. "Well, it wasn't my idea."

"I'll go if that's what you want." The words seemed torn from her throat.

It was and it wasn't. How could I live without her? I wondered that night as we sat on the terrace of the Trout. It was a warm night for March, and the tables beside the stream were crowded with undergraduates drinking their pints. Peacocks strutted up and down on the lawn, piercing the twilight with their angry screams. Holding hands across a picnic table, we drank champagne and reminisced about the night we met. "I thought you'd never call," Eleanor said.

"I didn't. You called me."

"You're right. I did. I couldn't help it. I'd been thinking about you ever since that *Advocate* party."

"Well, I'm glad you did." I gazed at her in the purple dusk. Eleanor had gotten dressed up for the occasion. She had on a cashmere sweater, a frilly blouse, and pearls—an heirloom from one of her grandmothers. It gave me pleasure to gaze at that pale throat of hers, with its graceful swanlike curve.

She gave me a doleful look. "That wasn't the impression I had this morning."

"I'm sorry, Eleanor, I really am. Forgive me." Not that she had any choice. There was a tradition behind these arguments. You didn't see D. H. Lawrence and Frieda what's-her-name walking around hand in hand. Edmund Wilson and Mary McCarthy quarreled like mad; she chased him around the kitchen table. It was all part of the literary life.

One morning I heard the mail drop through the slot and raced downstairs to find a pink envelope on the floor addressed in a familiar looping hand. Lizzie! I tucked it in a magazine and hurried upstairs with a pounding heart. I could hardly wait for Eleanor to finish breakfast and settle down in the bedroom with her novel. The instant I heard her start to type I tore open the envelope, scanning hungrily down the tissue-thin page:

> Mexico has blown my mind. My head's never felt so liberated. I smoke a lot of dope, dance like a savage, and hang around with some far-out people. I'm starting to make a little money on my batiks . . .

What am I doing here? I thought bitterly, staring out the blurred and streaming window. It had been raining for a week; the lawn looked like a swamp. These ecstatic dispatches were hard on me. Only the day before Bob had reported that he was on a "crest of euphoria." "When Archie Bell & the Drells came on the radio this morning I nearly vaulted out of my seat at a red light and climbed on the hood to do the tighten-up." Now Lizzie was off in Mexico on a self-discovery trip. And me? I sat around this Charles Addams house wearing so many sweaters I could hardly move my arms.

I heard Eleanor moving around across the hall and skipped quickly to the end.

> I'd love to give to you, love to love you. What happened in Hyde Park wasn't the end. It's just that when *I* want you you're off with someone else, and when *you* want me my head is somewhere else. But it doesn't have to be that way. Maybe some day we'll love each other and we'll love *us*—and no more bullshit games.

Enclosed was a photograph of Lizzie in a high-backed wicker chair, a maroon caftan accentuating her ruby lipstick and belly dancer's skin. I wandered around the parlor in a haze, rehearsing our nefarious deeds. "Eat me out," she would command, sprawling on Sam Wieghart's bed. She liked to kiss me afterwards. The taste of her own cunt . . .

"What are you reading?" Eleanor stood in the doorway.

"Nothing. I mean, just a letter from, uh . . ."

"One of your little Evanston friends?" She gave a click of disgust and walked out of the room.

Why couldn't I be satisfied? "Oh, Bob!" I cried out to my faithful correspondent when I filed my report on Lizzie's letter. "I'm so obsessed. Just reading her letters gives me a boner."

"Forget Lizzie," he admonished me. "What's important is what you have with Eleanor. You've got to disengage yourself from these hopeless fantasies of girls ministering to your every need." But why? Bellow's Henderson had the right idea: *I want! I want! I want!* Lying in bed with Eleanor, I'd be conjuring up images of Lizzie five minutes after we made love. Those steamy nights at Herbert's apartment on North Sheffield when I stood naked in front of the cold refrigerator drinking a can of Bud in the dark while Lizzie lit up another joint and the Puerto Ricans drag-raced up and down the street, their busted mufflers popping like cherry bombs: gone.

Bob had the opposite problem. One night when he was home watching the Red Sox whip the Yankees ("a heartening spectacle"), a girl he'd met in a bar called up and informed him that she wanted to have an affair; she was looking for "sexual experience," she explained. "Needless to say, this wasn't for me. My head's in enough trouble as it is. I feel like I'm on a magical mystery tour of the psychosoma." Needless to say: why didn't he give her *my* number? But Bob was more intent on self-therapy than on getting laid:

> I'm really beginning to understand the nature of my narcissistic neurosis: the long-buried fear of being left, which has disguised itself in me as the continual rejection of women close to me. I'm still trying to work out the crush I had on my mom when I was four.

So even a Red Sox fan, a guy whose idea of a good time was heading over to Burger King for a Whopper with everything on it, could have an identity crisis. Welcome to the club.

Bob had been talking about coming over for months, and early in April I got a telegram. He was arriving the next day.

I picked him up at Heathrow. "God, what a flight!" he exclaimed as he folded himself into the low passenger's seat and held out an open palm for me to slap. "I had to beg the stewardess for a tranquilizer. Talk about 'turbulence'—I broke into a sweat the minute we took off, and could hardly breathe until the plane was at the gate."

I stared at him in astonishment. "But you've flown a million times."

"I know, but I'm in a transitional state these days. My whole psyche's on display. I ought to charge admission. 'Step right up, ladies and gentlemen: see the madman decathect.' "

Could this be the same guy who had written me all those pious exhortations to straighten out my head? Driving through the quaint thatched villages and sun-dappled fields, I could feel his weakness giving me strength.

"Hey, look!" he cried out happily, ecstatic to be released from the plane's cramped fuselage. "Cows! Are those real?"

"No, they're plastic, like the ones at Frank Giuffrida's Hilltop Steak House on Route 1 in Saugus."

"Or the farm exhibit at the Museum of Science and Industry."

"Remember that farmer you said looked like Mr. Wibbley?"

"That was thirteen years ago," Bob marveled. "I wonder what happened to old Wibbley?"

"Still teaching shop, no doubt. We never change. Why should he?" I turned in at the driveway of Shireton Hall. "I suppose you brought your mitt?"

"I did," he confessed with a shy smile. "You said you had a yard."

Eleanor was sitting on the stoop in jodhpurs and riding boots when we drove up. She ran over and hugged Bob as if he had just saved her from a shipwreck. "You look like you fit right in," he said, appraising her outfit.

"I've been taking lessons," Eleanor said proudly. "I can even canter now." She pushed a lock of damp auburn hair away from her flushed face. "It's incredible to gallop through the fields scattering cows in every direction." Who did she think she was? Lady Brett? I was never prepared for the breezy schoolgirl manner Eleanor trotted out in company. Bob should read her journals. I did, slipping into the bedroom when she wasn't home: "There are times when I wonder if I have any talent at all . . ." "If only *someone* would encourage me . . ." "Last night I finished *Daniel Deronda* with a feeling of utter hopelessness. I'll never be that good." *Daniel Deronda!* I sat around waiting to hear from the *Kansas Review*.

That night we walked up the road to the Lamb & Flag for dinner. "Ah! The Americans!" cried the publican, a brawny fellow with muttonchops and a bushy moustache that gave him an Edwardian look.

"Ian, my friend Bob," I said, making the introductions in a casual, I'm-a-regular-here voice.

"A pleasure," said Ian. "A pint of bitter, a whisky and . . . ?" Hear that, Bob? He knows our drink.

"What's bitter?" Bob asked.

Bitter: I'd never thought about it. All I knew was that you couldn't get it in Harvard Square. "It's, uh, your standard English beer. Quite good, actually."

We claimed a table by the hearth and glanced over the menu. "What's gammon?" Bob said.

"Ham."

"Pasties? Isn't that what strippers wear on their nipples?"

"It's a meat pie, Bob." What a rube. I gazed around the room with satisfaction, admiring the rough-hewn beams, the sporting prints on the wall, the fire spitting and popping in the grate. A far cry from Big Herm's.

"What do you do around here for entertainment?" Bob said after we'd ordered.

"It's pretty quiet," Eleanor admitted. "We read or play bar billiards. And we go for a lot of walks."

"Unbelievable. No TV, no phone. I couldn't last a week."

"You develop inner resources," I said. And dream of getting on the next plane home. It was one thing to show off England to Bob, another to face the empty days of struggling through *Czech for English-Speaking Students* and going to the pub. But Eleanor liked it here. She went horseback-riding, worked on her book, wrote perky letters to her friends. Life punished her enough; she didn't see the need for getting in extra licks. "I've gotten a lot done on my novel," she said. Her novel: Shireton Hall was a regular Yaddo.

"How's it going?" Bob said amiably. Only a person with a contract from Harper & Row could be so amiable.

"It's hard, but I'm getting somewhere."

"What's it about?"

"Well, it's about this girl . . ."

What do you think it's about? The Crimean War? I got up and went to the bar for another round.

"So she's having an affair with this person in her class and her husband reads her journal and finds out," Eleanor was saying when I sat down. "But her mother's from the old school, even though she's divorced herself, and they have this big confrontation when she goes home for Christmas." She had that bright, eager-hearted look in her eye she got around people she wanted to please. The need for love: is there any other? Gazing around at the pewter wall sconces, the wood-paneled walls and mahogany bar, I thought of all those times we had walked out in the fields, clambering over stiles in a light drizzle, or driven up to Woodstock for cream tea. Or that afternoon we'd idled away in the National Gallery. On the way home we stopped in Hyde Park to feed the ducks. Rush-hour traffic swept through the Serpentine, headlights wavering in the dusk like votive candles in a cathedral. Eleanor huddled beside me in a long burgundy coat, scattering crumbs on the graveled walk. Would I have been any happier with Lizzie Sherman?

"So she finally leaves her husband and gets an apartment off-campus by herself," Eleanor was explaining to Bob.

"Sounds good," he said. "Have you shown it to anyone?"

"Just Lionel Trilling here," she said, patting my arm. "He says it's too autobiographical."

"I did not!" I protested. "I just thought it needed work. You're too close to the main character."

"Unlike you," Eleanor retorted. She turned to Bob. "Did he tell you what *his* novel's about?"

chive of our indissoluble past. What did we talk about?
olodny Report, our sociological study of the twins who
ext door to Bob in Glencoe and were "typical suburban
ents" (we'd done extensive fieldwork in the Kolodnys'
om"); whether "The Butterball," our favorite DJ on
, Chicago's Station with a Soul, was still on the air (he
what Bob's mother had said when she heard us, one
r afternoon in our eleventh year, discussing *Animal*
"Are you boys philosophizing again?"); how far Bob
tten with Vicki Molofsky the night in seventh grade
sat in her basement playing records while they
d on the couch ("second base"); and a thousand other
nt episodes in our mutual history. Embellished, ex-
ed, refined, made myth, they constituted a unique and
b and me—valuable lore, the oral literature of North
fe.

ember the night that girl was in our room in Paris and
e me wait out in the hall?" I said as we walked up the
ard Shireton Hall. We had gone to Europe one sum-
a student charter flight and stayed in a hotel on the
ffetard for a month. Bob managed to pick up a Vassar
e lobby of American Express and brought her back
om. I had the flu, but I gathered up my blankets and
down in the hall, curled up like a *clochard* on a
dewalk grate.

ie Broder," Bob said. "I got a letter from her a couple
go. She's living on a commune in New Mexico . . .
me a mantra from her yoga class. 'OM TRAY UM BAH
e chanted. " 'YEA JAH MA HEY SUH KUM PUSH . . .' "
u ever feel that we missed the boat?' I said. "Maybe
be living on a commune." Somehow the '60s had
by. I had driven around in Bob's VW bus, been tear-
the streets of Chicago, hung around when the cops
arvard Square; I had smoked a lot of dope, heard

"I have a notion," Bob said equably.

"It's an old-fashioned novel of ideas," I put in. "Leon Stein is a contemporary prototype of the superfluous man you find in Russian literature, a figure at odds with society. His very grasp of reality alienates him from the practical, money-making world."

"But why shouldn't a grasp of reality enable him to negotiate the world more shrewdly?" Bob said, sawing away at his gammon. "I mean, don't you think David Rockefeller has a pretty firm grasp on reality? Or Casey Stengel, for that matter."

"Knock it off, Bob." I drained my second pint of bitter. "You know what I mean. The *kind* of knowledge he possesses is special, obsolete. It's a different reality that he knows. It's deeper and more complex, informed by certain historical laws that determine, like, how history . . ." Where's that soup can? ". . . how history dictates what we become." Or something like that.

"But it's not history in the sense you mean," Bob objected. "It's what your mother did when you were three."

"I know you happen to believe that," I said patiently. "But if you'd read Walter Ben-yah-mean . . ."

"Who?"

"Benjamin. He's one of the Frankfurt School theorists." Eleanor lit a cigarette. She'd heard it all before.

"You're always dragging in these names to explain why you feel powerless," Bob said. "Look at your situation. You're frustrated because writing hasn't provided you the love and attention you crave. Isn't that what it's all about?"

Not in front of Eleanor, Bob. "Who wants another round?"

"Not me." Bob cupped his hand over his pint. "I've already got a buzz on." Clean-living Bob.

Eleanor, though, would have another gin-and-tonic. "I'm going to the ladies'," she said, rising unsteadily to her feet. She'd already had three.

"So how's it going?" Bob said when she was gone.

"Okay," I said without conviction. "We're thinking of getting married."

Bob studied me intently. "Are you sure that's what you want to do?"

"Of course I'm sure," I said heatedly. "Why shouldn't I be?"

"I don't know. It's just so sudden."

"We've been together for a year."

"I know, but marriage is a big thing. You're only twenty-two."

"What's that got to do with it?" I stared at the charred logs in the hearth. Across the room, Ian was calling out orders in his cheery voice. "Think how many bars we've been in together in our lives."

"Let's see," Bob said happily. The past: our favorite topic. "The Harvard Gardens, the Casablanca, Jack's . . ."

"Charlie's, the University Restaurant," I added. "And that's just Harvard Square."

"Durgin Park and that truck stop near Fanueil Hall."

"And remember that time in Newport?" A warm spring night our senior year. We'd driven over the bridge from the mainland at twilight, freighters gliding beneath the grid that spanned the briny water. "Hey, Jude" was on the radio. "What was the name of that bar down by the docks?"

Eleanor dropped down beside me. "So where's my drink?"

Not her again. "I'll get it," I said.

"I'll go," Bob volunteered. He leapt up and headed for the bar.

"What were you talking about?" Eleanor said.

"Nothing much. Just bars we used to go to."

"The good old days," Eleanor said. "Before I came on the scene." Her eyes filled with tears.

"Oh, come on, Eleanor. Now what?" When I wave my magic wand you will disappear.

She rubbed a knuckle in the
want to be alone with Bob."

"I do not!" I lied. "Where'd

"I just know." She stared do
get that annoyed look in your e

"Oh, puppy." I leaned acros
her wrist. "That's just not true

"Well, you make me feel lef
going back after this drink. I

"I wish you wouldn't." Not
She might change her mind. "I

"Who's arguing? I'm just g

"A gin-and-tonic and a
waiter's unctuous voice as he
who's up for a game of darts

"No, Bob. No games here.
I wanted to hear about Caml
Crescent Street house after
cultural reporter for one of
Greedily I pumped him for
out with his roommate, a che
play hockey? "Yeah, but he
what about his job? What
much whatever I want: cov
street fairs. It's fun."

It's fun? What did tha
Flaubert ever report to Lo
No, it was "torture," "naus
describe his work to Max
for the frozen sea within u

The thing is, though, o
that night was . . . I can'
walked out the door that
voking the names and pla

Jimi Hendrix at the Boston Garden, gotten drunk at Max's Kansas City. But whenever I thought back on those years, I invariably saw myself bent monkishly over a table in Widener, reading Spinoza while the new Dylan album blasted from a dorm in the Yard. Something is happening, but you don't know what it is, do you, Mr. Jones?

"I couldn't live on a commune," Bob said. "I'd starve. Granola, rice, tofu—freak food."

Bob was lucky. He knew what he wanted: to be sane. To live a normal life. I wanted to belong in the world. I dreamed of a job in New York—riding up and down in the elevator, going out to lunch, answering the phone. A nameplate on my desk.

"I'm so homesick I can hardly stand it!" I cried as a lorry hurtled by, its tires sizzling wetly on the road. "Maybe I should just go home."

"What about Eleanor?"

"Forget Eleanor! I'll go live with Lizzie Sherman."

"Nah," Bob said, fluttering a dismissive hand. "That's just a fantasy."

"You should see the letter she wrote me. She really thinks it could work."

"Look," Bob said, suddenly intent. "You know that Zen koan that goes, 'Before Enlightenment, I chopped wood and carried water. After Enlightenment, I chopped wood and carried water'? You keep thinking the right girl, the right place, the right kind of recognition, will make you happy, but it won't—not until you're happy with who you are." How did he know so much?

"I'm glad you're here," I said as we came up the steps.

"Me, too." He patted me on the shoulder. "Remember what Meher Baba says: 'Don't worry. Be happy.' "

I closed the door behind me with dread. Eleanor was asleep, huddled beneath a quilt. I stared out the window. The moon shone through the scudding clouds. A small wet animal scurried across the lawn. A stoat? A ferret? Even the animals were foreign.

Bob stayed a week. We showed him the Oxford colleges and Blenheim Palace, drove up to London, hung around the Lamb & Flag. "How long is Bob staying?" Eleanor said one night as we were getting ready for bed. She stood by the mirror combing her hair with energetic strokes.

"I don't know. He's supposed to go visit an old girl friend in Copenhagen."

"Well, he doesn't look as if he's in much of a hurry." She pulled back the puffy quilt and got into bed.

"He's going, he's going," I said impatiently. "Besides, I like having Bob around."

She turned away from me. "Maybe he should just move in and *I'll* go to Copenhagen."

"Come on, Eleanor. What's the difference? It's nice to have some company for once." I could feel the anger beginning to flow, stifling my chest. "He's my closest friend."

She sat up indignantly. "What about me? You leave me out of everything. Why should I sit around this big old house by myself while you go off to the pub with Bob?" She tugged her nightgown over her knees: You're not getting in here tonight. I perched on the edge of the bed and laid a hand on her forehead. Her eyes were bright with tears. God, girls cried easily. I just got more stony-hearted. What you can't deal with, ignore.

Beyond the heavy curtains, rain spattered against the window.

"I get lonely," I said.

"But what about me?" Eleanor repeated in a miserable voice. "I'm here."

"I know, but it's different. There's a certain kind of friendship people have when they've grown up together. Like a lot of things are just understood."

"Well, I'm tired of hearing about Grandpa Hymie and your fourth-grade teacher and that talk show . . ."

"*Roundtable.*"

"Why are you so hung up on the past, anyway?"

Why? I could just hear Princess Bibesco or someone asking Proust why he was hung up on the past. Because the past is what can never be recovered, the million things that happened, what we've lived, the incredible history of each person's whole experience. Why do you think I lie awake at night remembering my life in such obsessive detail? It's a kind of mourning for the irretrievable: the summer nights in Evanston, the Sundays at Grandma Sophie's, the girls I'll never see again . . .

"I'm not hung up on the past." I headed for the door.

"Where're you going?" Eleanor said.

"To talk to Bob."

Life was more desolate than ever once Bob left. I still got manic letters from Warren, but I hardly ever saw him. Edmund and Beatrice had gone off to Wales. The only other person we knew was Benny Rosen, a Fulbright Scholar from Rutgers who had tried to pick up Eleanor in the King's Arms one night while I was at the bar.

Oxford meant nothing to Benny; he sat around his rooms in Merton as if he were back in his college dorm, reading *Rolling Stone* and chain-smoking Camels, Joni Mitchell going full blast on the stereo. "There's no pussy in this town," he complained in the hopped-up, incredulous cadence of a nightclub comic. "Have you ever tried to *date* one of these chicks? I mean, you send them postcards inviting them to tea, and then you have to go out and buy a lot of little cakes and get your scout to build a fire. And you *still* don't get laid!" He

reached in his pocket for a smoke and tapped it against his
thumbnail. "You're lucky, man. You had the sense to bring a
girl over with you. I'm so horny beating off doesn't do any
good. It's like Chinese food. An hour later, you're horny
again." He rose up off the couch like an invalid struggling out
of bed. "Hey, let's get stoned and go see *The Poseidon
Adventure*."

Night after night we sat around the King's Arms downing
pints of lukewarm lager while Benny flirted with the barmaids.
"Hey, sweetheart," he would address the sallow blonde who
tended bar. "Come on over. Lemme buy you a drink." When
she brushed him off, he came back with another round and
slumped down on the banquette. "What are you supposed to
say to these chicks?" He imitated a BBC accent: "Would you
care to join me for a spot of tea at the Randolph Tuesday
next?" He drained his glass. "Shit, I'll never last out the year
at this rate. I wanna boogie!"

Benny was lonely, too. He'd show up on Sunday afternoons
with a bottle of sherry and sort of hang around the parlor until
it started to get dark and we invited him to stay for dinner.
He was a good cook; he and Eleanor would walk down to the
little grocery at the foot of Boars Hill and come back with all
manner of delicacies: pâté, cheese, fresh dill and mushrooms
for the salad, Marsala and heavy cream for a sauce to go with
the roast loin of pork. They stood over the table next to the
hot plate chopping up vegetables while I lounged in a high-
backed chair by the window reading the *TLS*.

Growing up in New York was a very good source of lore.
This I knew from reading books. Benny's childhood had supplied him with many stories: stickball games on the streets of
the Bronx; loudmouth uncles who fought over the family fur
business; guys who were on their way to lives of petty crime.
The family was very close. His parents' siblings all lived in
the same neighborhood; he had a million nieces and nephews

and cousins. In the summer they shared a compound in the Catskills. In the winter they went to Miami.

Benny's mother couldn't stand it that he didn't have a phone in his room at Balliol. "I need a number, Benny, some kind of a number. Explain to me, please, what I'm supposed to do if your father, god forbid, should drop over dead from a heart attack. Write a letter?"

"Students don't have phones in England, Ma. You can send a telegram."

"What kind of a country is that, they don't have phones? Very quaint. So tell me, Benny: do they have electricity? Hot water?"

"No, Ma, I study by candlelight. I douse myself with perfume, like they did in the old days."

"Benny! You'll go blind. Tell me the truth. Do you have a good light? You need a good strong light. A weak light, it's bad for your eyes."

Benny poured the last of a bottle of Dry Sack into the jam jar that was our glass for guests and fired up a Camel. It was late on a Sunday night, and he didn't look like he was going anywhere soon. Eleanor was in one of her excitable moods; she perched on the edge of her chair, her eyes wide, her forehead damp, her pale ivory skin flushed pink. "Oh, Benny, that's hilarious. So what did you say?"

What difference did it make what he said? The story was over. Eleanor didn't recognize punch lines. "Oh, you know mothers," he sighed, making a vague gesture with his cigarette. "So listen, did I tell you about how she used to put Wash 'n Dris in my lunch box?"

Benny didn't look much like a Balliol student. His preferred uniform was a wrinkled sweatshirt and blue jeans. His wiry black hair blossomed around his head. But he was a serious historian, and spent his days in the Balliol library hunched over books on the seventeenth-century Puritans. At lunch he went down to the buttery for a few pints, and at teatime he broke for a stroll around the grounds, puffing away at a Camel. He was caught up in the Puritans' spiritual austerity—a world away from his childhood in the Bronx. "These old divines were something else," he marveled. "They really had it both ways: worldly power and an eye on heaven. You don't see that combination now." He was fascinated by Donne's sermons; Benny was a great brooder on the tragic brevity of our lives. "You wonder how these guys got through the day, peering down the way they did into their graves all the time. You feel like saying, 'Lighten up, man. Life's not *that* short.' Though I guess maybe it was in those days. Think what it must have been like to wonder if you were gonna come down with some horrible disease every time you got laid. No wonder they called it 'the little death.' "

One evening I ducked into the pub next door to Blackwell's—the one where I used to go to observe the fat girl. In the back, hunched over a table, were Eleanor and Benny. They were deep in conversation, and didn't see me until I was right in front of them. A blush darkened Benny's city pallor. "Where you been, boy?" he cried in his jive accent. He put out an open palm for me to slap, grinning like a plantation darky through nicotine-stained teeth. "Let me get you some of this cat-piss lager. I think they warm it up for Americans." He hurried off to the bar.

"What were you talking about?" I said.

"I don't know," Eleanor said, glancing down at her feet. "Christopher Hill."

Benny was in a very hopped-up state, and kept going on about some girl he'd seen in the King's Arms the night before. "I knew I could fuck her the minute she walked in. She had that available look: tight pants, a knapsack, one of those peasant blouses with puffy sleeves. A lost soul wandering through

Europe. I don't know what it is about that type: they just *advertise* pussy." He tapped a Camel on his wrist. "Only I couldn't think of an opening line—which is so stupid, 'cause with girls like that who even *needs* an opening line? You could just go up and say, 'Wanna fuck?' Instead I sit in the corner getting pissed as a newt while I figure out how to make my move."

Back in Benny's room after closing, we opened a bottle of Jameson's and settled down to our weekly ritual. "Time for the Golden Oldies!" I cried.

" 'Hold ah-ahn, I'm comin', du-du-du-du!' " Benny howled. He put on "Shotgun," by Junior Walker and the All-Stars, and grabbed Eleanor by the hand. "Let's dance." She got up eagerly. They clasped hands, stepped toward each other and spun away, ducking under each other's arms. I watched uneasily: those two could dance.

The next cut was "You've Lost That Lovin' Feeling." The Righteous Brothers. A great slow-dance number. Eleanor draped a hand on Benny's shoulder and they shuffled around the room in the dark, their shadows huge against the wall:

> *Baby, baby, I'll get down on my knees for you,*
> *If you will only love me like you used to do . . .*

Suddenly I remembered a time that summer in Chicago with Maureen, one of those humid jungle nights that made the city feel as primitive and depopulated as the tropics. Sitting on the front steps, I could have been in some remote Amazon outpost if it weren't for the El train rumbling by. A bunch of kids were sitting in a car parked out front, and that song was on the radio. I was drinking a can of Budweiser and watching Melody play in the yard when I saw Maureen coming toward me down the sidewalk in her white uniform. I raised my can in a toast as she opened the gate in the cyclone fence and came up the walk. "Maureen! Next to Melody here, I can't think of a girl I'd rather see."

She sat down beside me and reached for the can. I could see her bra through the open neck of her starched dress, and that soft swelling where the bra's elastic held her breasts. Girls, girls, girls. "How was work?"

"Not bad. I got so much change here I can hardly walk." She reached down and laid a nail-bitten hand on her stomach to see if Raymond or Deirdre was okay. "What are ya doin'?"

"Waiting for you."

"Awww, isn't that nice?" She leaned over and kissed me on the neck. "You're a real gentulman, you know that. I like those courtly kinda guys." Her breath smelled of coffee and Sen-Sen. "How come you're not writin' a poem?"

"Got nothing to say."

"That's a new one." She tousled my hair. "Can I use your phone? I gotta call my mom."

"If you'll stay and play awhile. Herbert's gone to a concert at Northwestern."

In the parlor, she kicked off her canvas shoes and put her feet up on the windowsill while she dialed the number. "My mom's in a bad mood. My brother just got busted."

Busted: that wouldn't look too good on a transcript. "What'd he do?"

"Oh, he was ridin' around in someone's car that didn't belong to him. Hello, Ma?"

Listening, she had a bored look in her eyes. "Yeah . . . yeah . . . yeah," she said at intervals, tipping back her chair and closing her eyes. "He's not a bad kid. It's just a phase." The house was dark, except for the pale city light that shone in through the dusty windows and the blue flicker of a TV set in the apartment building next door. Across the way, my hillbilly neighbors were playing a Johnny Cash album on their stereo. "You worry too much," Maureen was saying. "He's not gonna end up in the pen. He wants to be a carpenter." She held up a hand for me to wait. In the shadows, I could see the swell of her belly. The kid was getting bigger.

I drained my Bud and headed to the kitchen for another. When I got back, Maureen motioned me over and pointed to the floor. She spread her legs and indicated her lap. While she was talking to her mother on the phone? I shook my head. "After," I mouthed, but she kept pointing to her crotch until I knelt before her and reached in. With trembling hands I worked her panties down over her thighs and ankles. She let them dangle on her toes, then kicked them off, still talking. "At a friend's . . . No, someone else." She listened for a while. "I don't know where he is. I don't care if he *is* the father, Ma, and neither does he. It don't make no fuckin' difference . . . Sorry. It doesn't make any difference."

I was kissing Maureen's ankle, then her thighs, then I was lapping between her legs. I pushed her skirt up and burrowed in the sticky folds, inhaling her rank swampy scent. Maureen was panting now. She clutched my hair and braced her legs. "Nothing, Ma," she gasped. "I'm fine. I just came in and I'm out of breath." She clamped her hand over the phone and gave a quick shuddering cry. Then she was still. "Maybe Saturday," I heard her say. "I love you, Ma. G'bye."

She hung up the phone and laid her hands on my head. We stayed that way for a long time.

"What's the matter?" Eleanor was leaning against the wall sobbing, her head on her arm.

"I don't know." She cupped her face in her hands, pressing her fingers to her forehead. "Sometimes I feel so bleak," she whispered. Benny stood uncertainly beside her.

"You want to go?" I said. She shook her head briskly, like a child.

Suddenly I had to get away. Let Benny deal with it. "I'm going out for cigarettes," I said, closing the door behind me just as "Heard It Through the Grapevine" came on. If only I could talk to Maureen . . . I was just drunk enough to consider calling her up. But she'd moved, and there must be a million Duffys in the Chicago phone book.

The night air brought me to my senses. Maureen was a mother now. I decided to go over to the porter's lodge and see if there was any mail.

At the gate, I heard a burst of noise from within. The windows of the dining hall shone brightly and shouts of laughter rang out in the cloisters. In the lodge a porter was sitting with his feet up on the desk, reading *The Daily Mail*. I asked him what was going on.

"Why, it's a Bump Supper," he said kindly. "After the Boat Races, you know."

A dance orchestra had started up in the Great Hall, and I could hear the clink of glasses through windows open to the warm spring night. In the passage, I passed a couple embracing, the girl in a floor-length gown, the boy in a dinner jacket shiny as a seam of coal. Just then a crowd of revelers swept past, trailing a scent of carnations and perfume.

I walked out the gate and down a narrow lane. The ancient walls exuded a mossy damp. On the Broad, a solitary student bicycled past, his scholar's robe flapping in the wind. Climbing the stairs of Benny's entry, I listened for a Golden Oldie, but the only sound I heard was the lone reverberation of the Magdalen Tower bell.

One afternoon we went out for a drive. It was raining, and the fields were green and wet. Soaked-looking sheep huddled beneath the dripping trees. Electrical pylons rose on the horizon, connected by a dense network of wires. Nestled in a remote valley was a trailer camp: laundry lines, weedy patches of garden, rusted cars on cinder blocks. A band of gypsy children loitered in a muddy lane beside the road.

"Boy, is this the middle of nowhere," I said as we passed a shuttered pub. I glanced over at Eleanor. "What's up? You're quiet today."

She lit a cigarette, dipping her head down to the flame. "Nothing's *up*. I just don't feel like talking, that's all."

The car jounced and bounded down the muddy road. "Ba-a-a-h!" I cried out the window as we whipped past a nervous, trotting sheep. Eleanor said nothing.

"What's the matter with you?" I persisted. "Are you mad at me, or what?'

"It's nothing, I said. I'm not mad at you."

It's nothing, it's nothing, I repeated to myself. But when we got back to our flat, she threw herself down on the bed and started to cry. I sat beside her and looked out the window; a pheasant was strutting across the lawn. The sky was tarnished and bruised-looking, and the room was growing dark. I laid my hand on Eleanor's back. When she cried, it came from deep within, a wracking sob that convulsed her like a chill. "What is it?" I said tentatively, stroking her russet curls. But that just made her cry harder, so I sat and listened to the rain.

It wasn't so bad here, really. The shrill whistle of the white enamel kettle as it boiled on the hot plate; the electric fire with its buzzing coil; the long afternoons when we sat in the parlor with our books . . . We had a cozy life.

Eleanor was still crying, her fists clenched on the pillow, her face buried in the crook of her arm. I leaned down and said, "What is it, puppy?"

"It's just not the same," she wept. "You've ruined everything."

Panic swept over me, a clutching fear that seized my chest until I couldn't breathe. "What do you mean, it's not the same?"

"I don't love you anymore." Her voice was clear, emphatic.

"What are you saying?" I jumped to my feet. We'd been through scenes like this a million times. They always ended the same way: I made Eleanor cry and then apologized. She forgave me, reassured me; and everything was okay again. Besides, our quarrels were vivifying. The sobbing recriminations, the tearful pleas: they exercised our spirits in that cold, doleful house. We fed each other's need. "What are you talking about?" I said.

She turned to the wall. "Everything. A million things. The way you talked about going away, the way you talked about my work—the way you hated me." The memory of these injustices stirred and strengthened her. "You can't imagine the look you used to get in your eyes—like you just didn't want me around. But that's over now," she said, a determined look in her eye. "You can't hurt me anymore." There was gladness in her voice, a crisp self-confidence I'd never heard before. "Don't blame me for this. You did it to yourself." No one else was as good at it.

"You hurt me, too," I said feebly.

"Bullshit!" she cried. "I wanted this so much. You're the one who spoiled it."

I cradled her face in my hands. The room was nearly dark by now. "Please, Eleanor. Forgive me. I'll never hurt you again. Never." I spoke the words with a grim intensity meant to convey resolve. But it was too late for that now. I could sense it. She had gotten free. She looked at me with implacable eyes. My cringing request annoyed her: the hatred of the formerly oppressed for their toppled masters. A spray of rain gusted against the window. So this was the suffering I'd heard so much about.

I hurried out to the car and drove into town. I had to find Benny. He was lying on his bed reading *Time*. "Hey, man, what's up?" I dropped to the floor, pounding it with clenched fists, and burst into tears.

"Women are cunts," he declared when I'd sobbed out my tale. "Let's go get wrecked."

For the next few days, we stayed out of each other's way. Eleanor kept to the bedroom (no doubt writing up the whole thing in her journal), while I sat in the parlor working on a poem about Kafka's dog. I didn't think about Eleanor much; we'd weathered these arguments before. It couldn't happen. We were getting married.

One afternoon, I happened to be reading that scene in *Remembrance of Things Past* where Swann, convinced that Odette is in bed with the vulgar Forcheville, stands beneath her window and, seized with jealous desperation, begins to cry aloud her name. I leaped up and hurried across the hall. Eleanor was writing at her desk. "Are you in love with Benny?" I demanded.

She didn't answer right away. When she looked up, her face was calm. "I don't know," she said.

VII

DRIVING through a canyon in the hills above La Jolla, I could see the glittering town below and, just beyond, a dark plateau of ocean. The sky was black. All down the valley were the lights of houses, as if the stars had settled to earth. When my parents had moved here during my last semester of college, their patio overlooked a desert; far off in the distance, trucks throbbed on the highway. Now, two years later, new housing developments stretched toward the horizon; the rumble of cement mixers, the machine-gun bursts of jackhammers, the grinding whine of drills hung in the air. Blots of smog floated over the mountains; it was said to be drifting down from Los Angeles, a hundred miles to the north.

After a year abroad, I didn't recognize the new songs on the radio, but when the Stones' "Can't You Hear Me Knockin' " came on, I had a sickening vision of Eleanor dancing with her sister in the house on Crescent Street. It had been a month since we split up in Oxford, dividing up our books and shipping home our trunks. The day after I confronted her about Benny, I sold the Wolseley Hornet, gave Mrs. Keithley notice, and resigned my scholarship. Solemn in his Gothic-windowed study, the Warden of Balliol showed no surprise or curiosity when I told him I was leaving, and made no effort to dissuade me; his only concern, he said, was that I had paid my parking tickets.

"We've had chaps decamp and I end up before the magistrate," he said mildly, scraping the bowl of his pipe.

After a few wrong turns, I found my parents' street. Their house, stucco-walled and surrounded by fruit trees, stood on a vine-covered knoll. I pulled into the driveway and flicked off the lights. The engine turned over once, shuddered, and was still. A deep silence surrounded me. I had arrived home late so many nights and stood in the driveway breathing the odor of damp sand and rotting fish that came in off Lake Michigan; only here, less than a mile from the ocean, the air was bland, as cool and neutral as the draft from an air conditioner. No insects swarmed around the yellow light above the door the way they did in Evanston, no crickets chirped in the dark.

It was strange to think how young my parents had been then—Father, tanned and trim in his tennis whites, going off for his Saturday game of doubles while Mother, in a cotton summer dress, waved from the patio. Now my father was retired. He played his oboe in the garage and tended his bonsai trees. He was trying to learn Spanish. Driving downtown on an errand, he would listen to language tapes on a cassette, repeating after the cheerful voice, "*la carta*, the menu; *hacer*, to do."

My Grandma Rose, now in her eighties, had come out here to spend her remaining years. She lived in Château La Jolla, a nursing home that wasn't even finished when she moved in. Landscape gardeners crawled beneath her window planting shrubs; electricians wandered up and down the corridors with power drills in their hands.

She had managed to cram all her possessions into two small rooms: Chagall lithographs, paintings by Chicago artists, family photographs in easel frames. On the living room floor was a frayed Persian carpet I remembered from the house in Wilmette. The glass case was crammed with miniatures: ivory

seals, wood-carved Russian dolls, jade figurines, clay replicas
of Mexican peasants, tiny porcelain vases, Cossack soldiers—
a lifetime's worth of *tsotskes*. I had spent thousands of hours
as a child examining the contents of this cabinet. It was as if
whole nations had been compressed and classified into a realm
of tiny, precious objects. A boy-sized world.

Cluttered as it was with relics, my grandmother's apartment
was oddly modern. The furniture was out of the 1950s: teakwood chairs, ceramic lamps, a couch in beige upholstery. She
had always thought of herself as progressive: she and her
friends smoked cigarettes, wore embroidered blouses, listened
to folk music. She had known Mayakovsky in Moscow. "And
Akim Tamiroff," she reminded me. "The actor. You met him
when you were a little boy, at the Remisovs in Palm Springs"
—Remisov, whose portraits of my mother and grandmother
hung on the wall in our garage.

Nearly blind, scarcely able to walk, Grandma Rose was still
bohemian; she shuffled around in a gold-brocaded caftan and
enough jewelry to fit out those replicas of ancient queens on
the first floor of the Metropolitan Museum: bracelets, necklaces,
rings inlaid with amber stones. All day she sat behind drawn
curtains in this tasteful shrine to her past, the end tables
crowded with family photographs of cousins, nieces and
nephews, her seven sisters—and me, her beloved grandchild,
sheynuh punim. On the coffee table were copies of magazines
I'd published in, with a braid of yarn to mark the page.

I had brought her a Russian-language edition of Pushkin
from Blackwell's. She reached for her magnifying glass, opened
to a random page, and began to recite in a guttural sibilant
whisper, staring sightlessly at the dark lens of the television
set. Her voice was powerful, resonant, harsh. Then she forgot
the words and sat very still, hands folded in her lap.

"That was beautiful, Grandma."

"It was all so long ago," she murmured. Her wrinkled, rouge-stained cheek was like a rotting nectarine. I rose to leave, and bent down to kiss her, inhaling her musky perfume. Soon she would be "going to Chicago"—her phrase for the final destination.

Mother and Father had a lot of time on their hands. Every morning after breakfast we would suit up and jump in the car for the four-hundred-yard drive to the YMCA courts. My mother, after decades of sitting beside the court knitting and watching the men play, had started tennis lessons at sixty. She had a whole wardrobe of fashionable tennis outfits: pleated skirts, velour warm-up jackets, powder-blue terrycloth jump suits. She had embroidered her shoes with a gaudy pattern from a book on needlepoint.

At the Y, rows of women lay on their backs doing exercises. "Now, right leg up as far as it will, then *left* leg up," the instructor chanted through a megaphone. Father signed us in while I unloaded the metal basket of old tennis balls we used when we were playing with mother. "Now go easy," she said, tightening the laces on her gaudy shoes. "Remember I'm an old woman."

I stood close to the net and started hitting lightly to her forehand. She rushed over and swung as hard as she could, hurling herself into every shot. The first few sailed out of court, but soon the ball was skimming over the net; her lessons had paid off.

Five minutes later, she was exhausted. Father hurried over and grabbed her wrist. They stood in bashful silence, like the bride and groom in Van Eyck's *Arnolfini Wedding*, while he felt her pulse. "That's enough, Mother," he announced. "I can feel palpitations." And he led her away, as if from the scene of an accident.

The next day she appeared on the tennis court with a heart-monitoring apparatus strapped around her neck, wires and electrodes visible beneath her tennis blouse. We rallied for a

while, Mother bounding with great energy after the forehands
I fed her while Father hovered anxiously by the net. Every
few minutes he would trot over and adjust the device. She was
tiring visibly in the sun, but returning everything. "Nice
shot, Mom," I called, lunging after a crisp drive.

What was I doing here? I sat on the patio all afternoon,
reading *The Los Angeles Times* until a bluish dusk crept over
the new subdivisions. Once I called Eleanor at her mother's
house in Shaker Heights. "I don't want to talk about it," she
said over the static hum of the long-distance wire. "There's
nothing more to say. It's over." A few days later, when she
thought I was ready for it, she wrote me that she was going
back to England with Benny in the fall.

That night I drove up and down the coast, speeding like a
maniac. The air was heavy with the fragrant scent of eucalyp-
tus trees. Rage squeezed my chest in a suffocating grip. I
would go to New York and look for Benny, drag him out on
the sidewalk and fight. I would buy a gun and hunt down
Eleanor in Shaker Heights. I sobbed and shouted as I drove,
biting my knuckles, pounding the wheel. Oh god oh god oh god
oh god. The ocean beat against the shore, whitecaps foaming
in the moonlight. She'd be sorry if I swam out and drowned.

But not that sorry.

My father nosed out onto route 5, six lanes of traffic streaming by in both directions, and headed for the airport. I had
gotten a job as a staff writer for *Time* magazine, and was
going to New York. Feinstein, now a graduate student at
Columbia, had offered me a room in his apartment on Morn-
ingside Drive.

A park with tennis courts and weeping willow trees ran
alongside the highway. Beyond it was a marina filled with
boats. Tidy new housing developments jutted out in the azure
bay. It was nice here. I could live at home, in the guest bed-

room. Like my grandma's brother Igor, who'd slept on a cot above the garage in the house on Laurel Avenue. Igor made clocks. I could make model airplanes. Get stoned on glue.

"So what are you working on?" my father said.

A history of the Western world, Dad. In Latin. "Not much. A few poems."

He nodded. What else?

"I've got a book review coming out in *Shenandoah* and, uh, Derek Holmes at *Poetry* asked to see some new work."

"You mean he just wrote you out of the blue?"

No, he turned down a batch of poems I submitted, and said he'd like to see more.

"Yeah."

As we neared the airport, a jet descended over the bay, its fuselage glinting in the sun. "Time Inc.," my father mused. "I can't quite see you fitting in there."

What would you like me to do? Poets haven't made a living since the Troubadours, and that was about six centuries ago. "It might be fun," I said. "James Agee worked there, you know."

"He did?" My father sounded dubious.

"He reviewed movies."

"Oh." Movies didn't count.

"And so did Irving Howe," I blurted. "And Alfred Kazin. And Dwight Macdonald." Card-carrying members of the Happy Few. "There's a whole tradition of writers working at *Time*."

My father drove. He didn't believe me. "You'll do fine," he said without conviction. In other words: no matter what you do, it will never be enough. How could it be? The son he was looking for didn't exist. Only God had such a Son. God and George Steiner's father. How could I get him to love me for what I was? Maybe if I died, like Bazarov in *Fathers and Sons* . . .

"I mean, what exactly is it that bothers you about the magazine?"

My father thought a minute. "It's that damned style of theirs," he said. *"Vowed Ike. Said he.* Who do they think they think they are? The Bible?" He veered across two lanes, provoking a burst of angry horns. "We got a note from Janice Glabman the other day," he continued, oblivious of the truck driver glowering down from the cab of a Mayflower van as he roared by. "She said she had Wally Pinsker in one of her classes, and he's going on to graduate school at Yale."

"That's nice," I said stonily. The only good thing about leaving Evanston had been the prospect of never again having to look out my window and see Wally Pinsker taking out the garbage three times a day—without being asked!

"He's thinking of doing his Ph.D. on Joyce."

Too bad Joyce is dead. I could write him up in Milestones.

"Good for Wally Pinsker, Dad."

He glanced at me as he turned off at the airport exit. "You think I expect you to be like Wally Pinsker?" he said. "You should do whatever is best for you. Whatever you enjoy." He paused. "Anyway, at least they don't have by-lines."

He pulled up in front of the terminal. "You'll call us when you get there?" He laid a hand on my neck. Tears glistened in his eyes. I might be a staff writer for *Time*, but I was still his flesh and blood.

"I will, Dad. I promise."

I grabbed my suitcase and headed for the terminal. When I looked back, he was still at the curb, staring through the windshield.

I flew East by way of San Francisco so that I could spend a few days in Berkeley with Winston Walker. He had gone out there to teach for a semester and decided to stay. Trudging up a steep hill past turreted Victorian houses with big wide porches and lemon trees in the yard, I could see why; Berkeley was Cambridge without the ice and snow.

I climbed the steps of Winston's house and rang the bell. No one came to the door, but I peered in through the screen and saw Winston sitting cross-legged on the floor, a pair of earphones on his head. He didn't look up until I was right in front of him. "This song will be over in a minute," he yelled.

I scarcely recognized him. He had traded in the three-piece linen suit he'd worn around Cambridge for bell-bottoms, an embroidered silk shirt, and rope-soled sandals. His hair was Jesus-length. Beside him on the floor was a ceramic ashtray with a roach on the lip. Winston pulled the earphones off his head. "Good to see you," he said in his languid Tennessee drawl. A girl in a terrycloth bathrobe wandered in and sat down on the floor. "This is Suki," Winston said.

Suki glanced at me and asked if there was any more dope. Winston handed her a plastic bag of grass and a packet of rolling papers. "Put on the Stones," she said.

Winston put on "Sympathy for the Devil" and walked around watering the hanging plants while Suki and I passed the joint back and forth. The room was simply furnished: a country French table of light wood with a bowl of fruit on it; a low couch covered with an Indian shawl; a fan-backed wicker rocking chair; a rush mat on the floor. Suki and Winston padded around in bare feet; I had on penny loafers.

"Are you writing much?" I said. They may have transcended such earthly matters; I still dwelled in the here and now.

"I'm writing songs," Winston said, squatting down and leafing through his records. "I wrote some lyrics for the Sufi Choir." He pulled out an album and handed it to me. The cover photograph, a grainy sepia made to look as if it dated from the 1890s, showed a group of men and women standing in an open boat—among them Winston in a crinkled turban. A lot of the men had scraggly beards and wore their hair in ponytails. The women had on robes. The title of the album was "Cryin' for Joy."

A girl's clear airy voice floated through the speaker, backed up by an electric guitar:

> *Thank you for giving me hands,*
> *Thank you for giving me feet,*
> *Thank you for the pavement*
> *And for the city street.*

I studied the names of the Sufi Choir printed on the jacket: Fatima Jablonski, Vashista Davenport, Sita Mulligan. Winston sat cross-legged on a pillow with his eyes closed and listened to the music ("Like a dog I need love/Like a tree I need the sky . . .") while Suki brought in supper: a bowl of rice and a plate of bean curd doused in soy sauce. "Wow, I'm hungry," Winston said, opening his eyes and digging in with chopsticks. We ate in silence. Winston wasn't "into talking," Suki explained.

After dinner, we got in their beat-up VW and drove over the Bay Bridge into San Francisco. The hills of Marin County were purple in the twilight and the lights of the Golden Gate Bridge shone faintly in the dusk. The air had a briny, sea-rinsed feel. "God, it's beautiful here," I exulted as Janis Joplin's grainy voice came over the radio, singing "Take Another Little Piece of My Heart." Winston nodded. Why discuss it?

The old loneliness came over me. If only I could be like them! They piled in someone's funky psychedelic van on weekends and headed up to Mendocino, slept in a cabin beside a stream, got stoned and made love outdoors in broad daylight. Their friends were carpenters and jewelry makers who lived in big old houses where children ran around in the nude. They had dinner in health food restaurants on Telegraph Avenue where they knew the owners; they played flutes and banjos in Golden Gate Park . . . This was it. I would drop out, get a job in Cody's Bookstore, hang around the student bars where they had poetry readings on Saturday afternoons. Maybe I'd even be invited to read.

Winston parked the car in front of a leather store on Market Street. "They have neat things here," he said. "I wonder how I'd look in a sombrero." I browsed through the racks of leather jackets, eager to shed my J. Press duds. What about this leather vest? I tried it on, frowning in the mirror. I never looked the way I thought I did. It didn't quite go with my blue blazer, but I bought it anyway. Winston thought it looked "really good" on me. In the car, he lifted up his shirt and showed us a leather belt. "I ripped it off," he said. Winston really *had* been through a lot of changes.

We had come into the city to attend The Class, a talk given once a week by a man named Steve. By the time we got there, the auditorium was nearly full. Steve sat cross-legged before a microphone in white bell-bottoms and a white caftan. "So the thing is," he was saying when we came in, "that enlightenment doesn't just come to you. You have to come to it. But you can't think about it. You have to just be natural, like you're waiting for a sign."

"Steve?" someone called out. "What happens if there just *isn't* any sign? If, like, nothing happens?"

"Maybe you missed it," Steve said with a shrug. The crowd laughed. A dog trotted in front of the stage. "Or maybe that dog is the sign."

"Steve?" A lanky, nervous boy in a coonskin cap stood up. "Have you ever, you know, felt like you didn't know what you wanted, but you just kept feeling this sort of sensation of wanting *something* and didn't know what it was?" Every day of my life.

"Sure," Steve said equably. "Lots of times. But wanting is a good thing. God or Buddha or whoever you believe in doesn't ask you to give up things, only to know that you don't need them. Besides . . ." He paused, considering. "Things can be spiritual, just like people. I mean, you can love your car if you invest it with your own energy."

Winston nodded. The crowd was calm and quiet, like kinder-gartners absorbed in a story. *How could I learn this simplicity of heart?* Winston had purified his life of worldly ambition. I still carried around a tattered copy of *A Portrait of the Artist as a Young Man. . . . to forge in the smithy of my soul the uncreated conscience of my race.* Gimme that anvil! *I was like one of those crazed soldiers who stumble out of the jungle twenty years after the war. No one had told me literature was dead.*

After The Class we drove to Chinatown for dinner. Walking the steep narrow streets past windows hung with tea-smoked ducks, the gutters filled with clumps of rotting vegetables, I was happy. It was a mild June evening, and through an open basement window I glimpsed four men in shirtsleeves playing cards. We turned in at Sam Wo's and climbed up to the third-floor dining room. It was close to midnight, and we had it to ourselves. Through a door that opened out on a balcony the sound of cars and voices floated up from the street.

I sat across from Suki and Winston—the most pathetic seating arrangement in the world. "Have you read *Black Elk Speaks?*" Winston said. "Steve's a lot like him. They both have a way of thinking that's intuitive but rational."

Black Elk Speaks. Somehow I'd never gotten around to it. "He's interesting," I conceded. "He knows a lot."

"That's not what matters," Winston said. *Wrong again.* "It's not what *you* know, but what your unconscious knows." His gold-rimmed glasses glinted. Suki stroked his arm. *Where was Eleanor? In New York, with Benny. Like a dog I need love . . .* "I'm writing this poem and I thought of the words *simple/*

ample/apple and just put them in because they sounded good."
I nodded. I did a lot of nodding these days.

The waiter brought our food. "I'm trying to do that more now," Winston said, seizing a shrimp with his chopsticks. "You feel so many poets are still ruled by what they've been taught about poetry. They're into all these hierarchies: the best Augustan poet, the best Romantic—Old Brain stuff. They haven't gotten to the prerational, the Mammal Brain."

You feel: Morgan Ames's idiom. A vestige—the only one—of Winston's linen-suited Harvard days. "You've really changed," I murmured.

"Life out here has been good for my work," Winston admitted. "It's made me loosen up. I'm writing out of a deeper place in my head. This new collection I'm working on feels right. Sometimes, when things are going well, I really believe my poems will last."

It was my last afternoon in San Francisco. I was in the Caffè Trieste—Ginsberg's old haunt. I'd read somewhere that he still stopped off there when he was in town. It was raining, a cool summer rain that reminded me of Oxford. I sat at a table by the window and watched the droplets stream against the glass. At the next table a man with a beard was writing on a napkin. I wondered if he was someone I'd heard of.

I read over the postcard from Lizzie that had been forwarded from Balliol to my parents' house.

> Mexico got heavy. Too many stoned nights. I'm on my way home. Will you come see me? Elaine loaned me her apartment. She's in Taos for the summer. Let's have fun. I love you. Lizzie.

I was booked on a flight to Chicago that night, but I hadn't talked to her yet. No one ever answered Elaine's phone. I went

over to the pay phone and tried again. A man answered. I
hung up.

Back at my table, I leafed through *The Berkeley Barb*, an
account of a Union Square Be-In. Druggies and folkies,
jugglers and mimes. Be in. I'm trying, man.

Who had answered? Maybe it was just a friend, someone
crashing for a night. I turned Lizzie's postcard over and
studied the photograph: it showed the Floating Gardens of
Xochimilco, tourists in a flower-bedecked boat. I wondered if
Maureen was in Chicago. I went back to the phone and called
information. There was an M. Duffy on Armitage. That
must be her. My heart leaped as I dialed the number.

"Hello?" The voice was cracked and querulous. A ninety-
year-old at least. "Hello? Hello?" I held the phone away from
my ear and stared out the window at the traffic going by on
Vallejo. The score Herbert had been working on that summer
in Chicago was based on a poem by Vallejo. Herbert was in
New York now, working in a record shop on Bleecker Street.
"Pushing records is a bitch," he'd written me, "but it's easy
bread." He was into Muktananda. Marx was wrong. The only
revolution was in your head. He'd sold his books and joined
an ashram.

And I was still wandering the earth with my Harvard bookbag slung over my shoulder. *Homo literarius*. They could put
me in a glass case next to Cro-Magnon Man.

"Who is this?" demanded the crone. I put the phone back
on its cradle and called United Airlines. Chicago was a bad
idea.

The man with the beard was gone. He'd left his napkin behind. I went over and looked at it. "Call Norman," it said.
"Pick up laundry. Dentist."

I caught the red-eye flight, departing for New York at ten
o'clock. I liked flying through the night on a half-empty plane,

smoking in the dim cabin while everyone slept.
of the late flight out of Boston that I used to
came home from school.

I turned on the overhead spotlight and o[
Free. Soul free and fancy free. Let the dead
This Dedalus was onto something. I stared ou
the darkness below, listening to the engines ch[
For a long time I saw nothing; we were flying
Canyon. Then a scattering of lights on the plai[
of black emptiness, a town—maybe one of th
we used to stop in at three in the morning on
when I was a child, on our way to California. I
berth, I would push up the shade and peer th
that billowed from the tracks, haunted by the
scene: the vacant platform, the empty waiting
across the street with a neon sign above the
in those godforsaken towns? No one I woul[

On our left, the pilot told the drowsing pass
see the lights of Chicago. I cupped my han[
and looked down. A cluster of lights shone ou
cold and distant as a galaxy. Then it was gone

JAMES ATLAS was born in Chicago in 1949. His first book, *Delmore Schwartz: The Life of an American Poet*, was published in 1977. He has been a staff writer for *Time*, an assistant editor of *The New York Times Book Review*, and an associate editor of *The Atlantic*. He is now a contributing editor to *Vanity Fair*. He lives in New York with his wife, a physician, and their daughter, Molly.